WALKING HOME FROM ROCK ISLAND

A NOVEL

BY

WALTER ADKINS

To John & JoAnn
With warm regards
Walter [illegible]
May '02

This book is a work of fiction. Places, events, and situations in this story are purely fictional. Any resemblance to actual persons, living or dead, is coincidental.

ISBN: 1-4033-8793-1 (e-book)
ISBN: 1-4033-8794-X (Paperback)

This book is printed on acid free paper.

1stBooks - rev. 11/16/02

TO

MY WIFE

JACKIE BOYETTE ADKINS

CHAPTER SUMMARIES

CHAPTER I—WALKING AWAY FROM ROCK ISLAND

John Wesley Logan, Captain, CSA, imprisoned at Rock Island, released 28 May '65; he meets Hugh McLemore; they start south toward home in Alabama; with three Georgians they raid Yankee barracks to steal shoes; the five men walk south to Dixon Farm, where they stay six days; they fight with and kill two bandits.

CHAPTER II—ACROSS TENNESSEE

The group walks to Clarksville, meets judge, moves to Nashville; McLemore wins money in poker game; men move to Moore place near Franklin; McLemore arrested; lawyer gets McLemore released and signs him up as a security man on ride south moving blacks to Mexico; Logan stays in Franklin because one man is very sick.

CHAPTER III—SOUTH TOWARD THE RIO GRANDE

McLemore joins group moving ex-slaves to Mexico; Johnnie South is hired as security helper; blacks fight among themselves; evangelists visit bivouac area; McLemore rides into Vicksburg, gets involved in fight in tavern and is arrested; South gets McLemore out of jail.

CHAPTER IV—INTO NORTH ALABAMA

In north Alabama the group visits cotton place in Tennessee River bottom and picks up new man named Slaughter; they visit people living in cave near Sipsy River, pass through Winston County and its guerrilla warfare area, move to Luxapillilia Creek area and stop at Captain Burleson's store.

CHAPTER V—THROUGH THE SWAMPS

Group moves through swamps toward Cahaba River with very little food; they encounter big tornado; Slaughter struck by lightening but lives; they find swamp man who guides them to Cahaba; at Cahaba River they encounter fish and fur trader, whose people attack the group.

CHAPTER VI—MONTEVALLO AND SOUTH TOWARD HOME

Logan visits with small planter and visits small town at edge of up-country; McLemore rejoins the group; they start walking along railroad tracks toward Selma, have contacts with white-trash people and move on south to Ebenezer Church battlefield; they are attacked by outlaws; McLemore kills one of the outlaws.

CHAPTER VII—BACK INTO DALLAS COUNTY

Logan visits US Cav unit; group walks on to Summerfield but cannot find news of their families; they continue into Selma; Hood almost dies; Logan moves group on toward town of Cahaba; Logan and Sergeant Jackson visit abandoned prisoner of war cage at Cahaba.

CHAPTER VIII—HOME AT LAST

Logan leads starving men to parents' house; parents and farm hands overjoyed; mother takes charge of Hood, cleans him up and puts him to bed; Cook serves meal to men; Logan's father talks in detail about how things were at war's break-up; Logan and father visit McLemore plantation and hear about war and aftermath from perspective of big time planters.

CHAPTER IX—THE TEAM BREAKS UP

Hood's condition improves; elder Logan prepares to establish sharecropping as new labor system on farm; Ole Sharp recognized as overseer on Logan place; Li'l Georgia saved from drowning by Cora the Cook's son; Cora is to be first sharecropper; Ole Sharp and laborers give barbecue and entertain with singing; after three weeks rest, others start for home.

CHAPTER I

WALKING AWAY FROM ROCK ISLAND

John Wesley Logan walked away from the main gate of Rock Island Prison about 1030 on the morning of 28 May 1865. He was much too weak to actually hurry, but he stumbled along with as much speed as he could muster. He walked across the road, found a shade tree and sat down on a log to rest. He looked around for some sign of the twenty prisoners he had seen the guards releasing early that morning, but they had all disappeared. He had been brought over from the officers' barracks around 0830, but he had been held by the Yankee corporal until the Sergeant of the Guard had led him out to the guardhouse. There he had been released into the bright shinning world with several curses and a few promises about what would happen to him if he was ever seen again.

General Lee had surrendered over a month before, but many of the Confederate prisoners—some had been held since back in '63—remained locked behind the fence. Logan supposed that the Yankees still considered them dangerous. He looked down at his pencil-thin legs and his arms with their bleeding sores and chuckled bitterly. It was hard for him to believe that he had weighed over 150 pounds when they brought him in six months ago. Now he must be down to around 100 pounds; but, at least, he was still alive and was outside those walls.

Looking back across the road, he could see a shabby sign over the main gate proclaiming that this was the Rock Island Military Prison and marking the sally-port that was the only entrance to the prison on the Illinois side of the island. This entrance was controlled by a guardhouse built outside the compound fence. On the roof of the guardhouse he could see a howitzer positioned so that it could sweep the inside of the prison. He knew that there was a barge carrying two other cannons anchored in the south branch of the Mississippi.

He was over a hundred yards outside the perimeter fence; but the stench of the place was still almost overpowering, so he forced himself to his feet and began walking toward the bridge to the Illinois side of the river.

He remembered that they had marched across this same bridge when they brought him into this sickening place. That was ten or twelve days after he had been knocked off his horse and left for dead during that scrimmage near Brandy Station in Virginia. A low tree limb had finally gotten him and left him on the ground, only partially conscious. In fact, he could hardly remember the Yankee troopers picking him up and sending him to the rear in an ammunition wagon. His recovery from the fall had been fast enough—no broken bones—but he had passed through two or three prisoner collection stations and into a small POW camp before his head cleared. After a three-day ride in a freezing boxcar, the Yankees had marched him across this same bridge and into confinement.

Undoubtedly, the following five months had been the low point of his life. So he'd just better start walking and get away from that damnable place before someone, probably that miserable Sergeant Stevens, changed his mind and dragged him back inside. Undoubtedly, old Stevens would like to get him back and kick him around some more.

Maybe that creep might even drag him down into the quarry and try to have him cut one last block of limestone.

It was hot for late May, especially considering that this was way up in Illinois, and his old slouch hat had too many holes and rips to turn the sun very well. About a half mile south of the town, near where the road ran along a few yards from the railroad tracks, he found a little stream and a clump of oaks. He took off his shoes and then his old gingham shirt, which he washed in the stream—maybe that would get rid of some of the lice—and lay it out on the grass to dry. Finally, he waded out into the little creek, trousers and all, and splashed around until both his body and the clothing began to feel somewhat cleaner. Later he sat in a sunny spot back in the trees and waited for his rags to dry. He was virtually naked, so the sun quickly dried his skin and drove him to the shade of the oaks. There he fell asleep.

After the sun had fallen somewhat lower, Logan awoke as a man and a woman came along in a wagon and pulled off the road to let their horse drink from the stream. He rolled over into the thick brush and lay still. The man, in a voice that the captain could barely hear, said, "Look, somewhere down there's one of them damn Rebels they've been letting out of the stockade. Or, maybe, the one down there just escaped. I ought to shoot the rascal, just to be sure." Logan lay very still in the dark shadows. He could see the man pick up a rifle from the floor of the wagon.

The woman said in a voice full of scorn, "Let him be, he's not hurting anybody. He'll be gone on south tomorrow. And besides, if you shoot at him and miss, he and all them others that are most likely down there will get up and kill—" evidently she almost said "you," but she ended up by saying "us."

The man grumbled a bit but let the rifle slip back down on the floorboards. The horse had finished drinking; the man straightened his blue forage cap, picked up the reins and drove on. Logan could see that the woman had turned away from the man and was smiling a little mocking smile. He went back to sleep.

Just before sundown Logan awoke, put on his ragged clothing and began to walk down the railroad tracks. Keeping the setting sun off to his right, he moved off in the direction he took to be south. He walked until it became quite dark, perhaps for a couple of hours, and finally came upon four boxcars sitting on a siding. He noted thunder and lightning off to the west, and it had begun to smell a little like rain, so he pulled himself up into one of the open cars. It was a taxing effort for someone just one day out of Rock Island, but the car was dry and smelled clean. Blind luck, it could have been a cattle car with manure six inches deep or one full of fresh hides. The exertions of the day had left him weak and listless, so he lay down on the floor and immediately went to sleep.

He awoke to a continuous banging against the floor of the car. Through his crusted, unfocused eyes he made out a man standing on the ground, slapping the floor of the car with the flat of his hand. The intruder wore a torn blue forage cap and a dirty, ragged gray jacket.

"Don't jump around so, I know you're Wes Logan," said the man with a dry laugh. "Did you think that I was old Sergeant Stevens, that guard over in the officers' barracks who was such a bad actor? Better wake up so's we can go forage up some grub."

When he had rubbed some of the sleep out of his eyes, Logan recognized the man. "Well, Hugh McLemore, alive and kicking. I thought that you were still inside—and down in the hole at that."

"Nah, they let me out of the damn hole last Saturday, and I jumped the ditch and got away yesterday."

"I heard the shooting around nine o'clock. Guess they missed you." Just like a damn McLemore, running across the dead line when he knew that he had only a day or so to go anyway. Logan rolled over on his stomach and slid out the door to the ground.

McLemore looked at Logan when he had straightened up. "Damn, man, you don't look so good." His eyes took in the scar on the side of the older man's head and then went over to his left ear, where the top half had been ripped away. "What the hell happened to you?"

Logan put his hand up to his ear. "This happened at Yellow Tavern, but it soon cured up. What got me looking so thin was all that work on the inside, cutting and loading that stone. Of course, the kicking around they gave me, along with the starvation rations, sho didn't help. Where were you? Someone told me you were at Rock Island, but I never saw you, not once."

"Well, Wes." But four years in uniform tend to make a man do things the military way. He corrected himself, "Cap'n," a bit of irony crept through, but still, "Cap'n, I heard you got picked up near Brandy Station, but I got to work out in the cookhouse, and the people that I got to know in there took pretty good care of me. Even with my time in the hole, I don't think I lost over five or six pounds. Course, I never got shot up much before I got captured neither. But right now, I'm awful hungry. Let's see if we can rustle up some vittles of some sort."

Down the tracks they could make out the top of a farmhouse set back in a grove of big oaks. They made for it with as much speed as they could muster, stumbling along in shoes out at the toes and with soles so thin the men could feel each gravel they stepped on. McLemore found an ear of corn in the grass and attempted to eat it, dry and hard as it was. However, he gave up and put it in his pocket for, as he said, when he could boil it some.

They approached the house under cover of the trees and finally found an unwary chicken in a fence row. A few grains of McLemore's corn lured it into his reach. Logan had to go very near one of the barns to find a bucket. But his luck held, and he got away with his prize without disturbing the dogs he saw playing around the back door of the neat Illinois farmhouse.

With the bucket and the recently deceased chicken, they walked back into the woods until they found a stream. There they skinned the chicken, not taking time to scald and pick it, and soon had it boiling away in the bucket. While the chicken cooked, they lay down in the shade to listen to the roiling water. McLemore soon fell asleep.

Captain Logan, CSA, age 26 years, had been wounded three times and had been a prisoner at Rock Island for six long months. Most of the people he had started out with in '61 were either dead or short arms or legs. He could think of no good reason for his own luck—and, really, luck had never seemed much of an explanation for one man's survival while his mess mates all found their fatal minie ball or saber. However, he had no better explanation as to why his minie ball just took off two left fingers while the man three feet to his right got his through the head. And if that saber at the Crater had been over a couple of inches, it would have sliced his head like a cantaloupe, rather than just leaving him with half an ear and a scar on his cheek.

Now that it was all over, he really didn't know why he'd stayed around for the entire war. There had been plenty of chances to slip away into the mountains. It was obvious from the beginning that he had little, if anything, to gain from secession and nothing at all from war. As for people such as McLemore, well, that was a bit different. The McLemores were real cotton capitalists with over 5,000 acres of land and some 80 slaves. He had to think that they had plenty to gain from a successful war. Of course, that was the problem. Who on earth decided that the southern states could fight a successful war? Looking back, it was hopeless from the beginning. Maybe it could have been done in 1845, but by 1861 there was no way. In 1845, however, it really hadn't seemed necessary.

McLemore awoke, got up, stirred the fire and poked at the chicken with a stick. "I'm thinking that this damn Yankee chicken is about ready to eat. What you say we let it cool for a few minutes, and I'll cut it up with this sorry pocket knife—likewise stolen from one of our masters and betters."

Even without salt, the chicken turned out to be good. It was probably the best meal that Logan had eaten in several months, but McLemore informed him that he had eaten much better plenty of times when he was working in the cookhouse at Rock Island. In spite of this pessimistic view of the cuisine, McLemore volunteered to look for more chickens, and at dusk he moved out to hunt some more. He returned in a couple of hours with two chickens and even some salt—which he claimed someone had given him, but which Logan figured he had gotten out of some cattle trough. With all this food, Logan began to feel a bit better. In hopes that they could find more in this good farming country than they could farther south, they decided to stay in place for another day.

By the end of their third day of freedom, they were feeling much stronger, so they decided to move on farther south. Over McLemore's objection, Logan took the stolen bucket back to the farmyard where it had come from. The Yankee farm family didn't look all that prosperous and, who knows, they'd probably lost plenty in the damn war, like everyone else. He'd never thought much of reasonless destruction and had never practiced it. Although, God knows, such action had been common enough.

As soon as dusk fell, they started walking south along the railroad and after an hour or so came upon a siding with four or five empty cars. They selected one and crawled in. Three Confederates, released from Rock Island on the previous day, according to the oldest looking of the trio, were already in the car. These men, dressed in the rags that all released prisoners wore, immediately volunteered that they were trying to get back to south Georgia. Two of the three Georgians appeared to be quite young while the other man was older with hard, rough features, the most outstanding being his flaming red hair and beard. Logan saw the man as an NCO if he'd ever seen one, and the first question asked established that he was indeed Sergeant Jackson of the Thirteenth Georgia Infantry. There was plenty of room—the Georgians had nothing except their clothing and a small burlap bag, which contained a dozen or so turnips—so Logan and McLemore moved to the other end of the car and lay down on the bare floor and went to sleep. One thing that hard soldiering teaches a man is to eat and sleep anytime because he very well may be dead before he gets another chance.

Sometime during the night a locomotive picked up the cars from the siding and moved off toward the south. Logan was much relieved at the direction taken, so he was able to go back to sleep immediately. There was a lot of switching and car coupling during the night, but the five men slept through most of it and finally awoke to find that it was day. Eventually the train stopped at a small station where an idler leaning against the station platform informed them that they were in Terre Haute, Indiana. The man's total lack of interest at seeing five men in what passed for Confederate uniforms in an empty freight car told Logan that they were not the first such group that had come this way. As the day wore on, they saw quite a few people, some working in the corn fields, some repairing track, and at each station a large number just standing around. None of these Yankees seemed very interested in the five Rebels. After all, Lee had surrendered over a month before, and if there was any guerrilla warfare going on down south, these people obviously hadn't heard about it. Disinterested or not, no one offered them anything to eat, so they got by on the sack of raw turnips that the Georgians had brought along.

At the end of the second day, they arrived at the Ohio River across from Louisville, hungry as a cave full of bears in springtime. The raw turnips were long gone, as was the cheese and loaf of bread that the youngest-looking Georgian had managed to steal from a peddler's cart at one of the stops in central Indiana. From inside the freight car Logan had seen that the peddler was missing a leg at the knee and that he didn't seem too disturbed when the skinny little Georgian grabbed the bread and cheese and ran into the crowd.

When they reached the Louisville rail yard, they found it a busy place overrun with company security men, who immediately ran them out of the freight car and the yard with a lot of talk about Rebel scum. Logan led his companions out away from the town until they found a gravel road, which they followed for three or four miles to a rather substantial covered bridge.

They crawled down the creek bank and took shelter under the bridge. Logan saw all sorts of signs indicating that their spot had been used before. There were several dead campfires—one very recent—several worn out boots, a canteen with a bullet hole through the top and a torn and dirty jacket that was barely recognizable as an item of Confederate uniform. Several names and addresses, some unit numbers and a long scribbled message warning that the creek rose almost to the floor of the bridge during rainstorms had all been written in charcoal by previous occupants.

Logan, who some two days back had been accepted by the Georgians as the group leader, was now being referred to as Cap'n. This, of course, had been picked up from McLemore, who always used that title in any stranger's presence. Accepting this status, Logan sent the three Georgians out to gather pine boughs for bedding. McLemore claimed that he knew someone in Louisville who had sold some horses to his father before the war, so he was sent back to the city to beg some information and supplies. Thanks to the Rock Island cookhouse, McLemore was by far the strongest of the five refugees, so he moved off toward town with what could have passed, maybe in a leper colony, for a jaunty air. Logan built a fire and went out to look for something to use as a cook pot. For this purpose, he eventually had to settle for a battered lard bucket that had been abandoned in a trash pile.

Late in the afternoon, the smallest and youngest looking of the Georgians came walking back to the bivouac with a half dozen eggs and a sack of new red potatoes. Sometime later, just before dark, McLemore returned from his walk into the city. "Cap'n, that Louisville's a damn busy place. There's people everywhere. I found the horse trader's office, and at first he wasn't too eager to help a bunch of dirty Rebels. However, he finally came through with a sack of cornmeal and a jug of molasses. I guess the bastard thinks we'll be buying more horses in a year or two."

"Don't look too likely, McLemore. During the next year or two, we'll be damn lucky if we're able to keep from starving to death. Where did you get that new shirt?"

"Found it on a clothesline. Hope it belonged to some Union bastard. How you like it?" All this with his usual little lopsided grin.

"Well, keep in mind that when you're running 'round stealing everything that ain't got a steamboat setting on it, that not everybody in Kentucky was Yankee." Wes Logan had to grin inwardly at the sheer audacity of McLemore; but if he wanted to maintain enough control, and control he felt to be absolutely necessary to bring this group safely home to Alabama, he must show no partiality to anyone. And certainly not to someone who had been his lifelong friend and neighbor.

McLemore brought back all sorts of information, most of it unwelcome. No railroads were operating in the states of the old Confederacy, and only a few in Kentucky other than the one between Louisville and Lexington. Conditions were evidently not too bad, and the people were not unfriendly in most places in Kentucky. But the word was that once they reached Tennessee to expect no help. The countryside in all the Confederacy had been stripped bare, and the population in most areas was almost starving. Shoes were particularly hard to come by, and this was bad news indeed for men who would evidently be walking for several hundred miles.

The next day Li'l Georgia McCalab—Li'l because of his size and a face that suggested an age of twelve—returned from his foraging with two dozen Irish potatoes and four or five pounds of bacon all tied up in an old apron. He insisted that a kind lady in the next village had given him all this, and after close study of the boy's most innocent face, Logan came to believe him. Within minutes the potatoes and bacon were boiling in the lard can, and McLemore's cornmeal was turning into some crude hoecakes on a piece of flat metal liberated from a rail construction site.

Later, when all had eaten their fill, Logan got them seated on their piles of pine brush, and there in the flickering light of the fire he began to talk about how they were to get home. The faces, even Li'l Georgia's, told him that they knew it was going to be a hard go. He started out by saying that they must be prepared to walk the whole way and that the entire walk would have to be made on short rations because there just wasn't much food in most of the country through which they were to go.

With his most solemn face, Logan continued by pointing out that they should get some better clothing or at least try to boil the lice out of their old rags. For this job they needed lye soap, which just now they did not have. So as a start, no later than the next night everyone should use the lard can to boil the clothing he was then wearing. Logan would show the way by putting his entire wardrobe of one gingham shirt, a pair of pants that were more holes than pants, one pair of underdrawers and his torn forage hat—every stitch of clothing that he had—into the can as soon as they finished breakfast the next morning.

He continued by telling the group that good footwear was absolutely critical to their further travel. Without five pairs of fairly new shoes, he could almost guarantee that they would never make it home. Jackson, the oldest and strongest of the Georgians, had the best shoes in the group—he had worked in the supply building in Rock Island—but even his footgear must be repaired. Because of their sorry physical shape and the condition of their clothing and shoes, Logan told them that he thought it best that they remain right where they were—after all, they were not likely to find a drier camp area or one that had access to so much food—at least until they could gain some strength and hustle up some clothing. He reminded them that they could expect to find little food, and certainly no clothing, in any area south of the Tennessee line.

"So, I think we should stay right here until we feel some stronger and until we can manage to get, at the least, some better footwear." It was stated as his thoughts, but he knew it would be accepted as a command. "One thing more. We're all in this together, and we're all going to get home together. No one is to be left behind so long as he's alive. And you know that there will be times of sickness. All of us will band together to care for those unlucky ones who are sick. All go or nobody goes, I promise you that. Tomorrow we'll start working this plan." And so they crept into their pine brush beds and went to sleep on the sixth night out of Rock Island prison.

The following morning everyone seemed prepared to receive and carry out missions as assigned by Captain Logan. Li'l Georgia was sent out to look for food, and Jackson was sent back to Louisville with McLemore to look for a shoe repairman. Thad Hood, the third Georgian, remained with Logan at the campsite, where they took turns boiling out their clothing in the lard can.

Li'l Georgia turned out to be a brilliant forager, and by noon he was back with a tow sack full of vegetables—mostly turnips and sweet potatoes—and another chunk of side meat. The skinny Georgian swore that some kind lady had given him the food just because he had asked for it. Logan took charge of the food and would not allow any cooking until all of the Georgian's clothing had been boiled out in the can.

When McLemore and Jackson returned in the late afternoon, the team was informed that they now had one good pair of shoes within the group, thanks to a black shoemaker who had been persuaded to repair Jackson's shoes in return for getting a pile of hides moved from a storage shed to his shop. Needless to say, McLemore had not helped Jackson move the hides. Also, Jackson was a bit disturbed at having to do hard labor for a black; however, everyone was happy to see one pair of shoes that now looked almost new. After the shoes had been appropriately admired, McLemore's and Jackson's clothing went into the boiling can. Jackson protested a bit; it's amazing how the human can come to tolerate lice to the point that he will not go to any great amount of trouble to get rid of them.

And so they stayed on for a week, resting, eating the things that Li'l Georgia brought in and stealing or begging a couple of items of clothing each day. Slowly they began to regain some of their strength. Hood's case of dysentery began to improve, and everyone's lice disappeared. McLemore had completely outfitted himself with new clothing, except for shoes. Thad Hood, the weakest man in the group, was of course the first to start complaining that they were wasting time that should be used in walking south. This in spite of the fact that no one except Jackson had footwear that would hold together for more than the first twenty miles of such a walk. However, Logan knew that he must soon face up to explaining why they must still delay their departure for home. So on their eighth day under the bridge, he got them together for another meeting.

"Surely, we would all agree that we can't start out for home until we all have shoes. And right now there is only one pair of shoes among us that is good enough for any kind of long walk." He would always be grateful that Jackson, the only one with shoes, did not start talking about setting off on his own. His silence paid down on gaining the status of a real sergeant. "We're in pretty good shape for other clothing, even if Hood and I have to wear women's blouses for shirts. Lieutenant McLemore, of course, looks downright snappy. But in order to get going toward home, we simply must get four pairs of shoes from somewhere. Has anybody got any ideas?"

No one had any brilliant ideas as to how they could come up with four pairs of shoes, but Logan let them talk on for a while. This sort of aimless discussion seemed to make them feel better and, who knows, maybe some good information might surface.

Finally Logan began to talk again. "I figure that the only place we might find shoes to fit the likes of us would be in that Yankee barracks down near the railroad yard. I hear that there's a whole company of the Second Wisconsin Infantry in that building. There should be sixty or seventy pairs of shoes in there just for the taking—so it ought to be easy picking. I hear that a lot of those infantrymen have extra pairs of shoes under their cots. Besides all that, I wouldn't mind stealing from a bunch of Union blue bellies. While we're at it, maybe I could find a horse to steal. Us cavalrymen think a lot more of riding than walking."

"I think we ought to know a lot more about that building before we try to steal any shoes," said McLemore, completely ignoring the remark about stealing horses as he thumped dust from his almost new slouch hat. "And why can't we grab the shoes from that cavalry detachment quartered between here and Louisville? That's a whole lot closer."

"Yeah, that's the whole trouble, we're too close. If we go all the way up to the Louisville railroad yards, maybe they wouldn't come all the way down here looking for four pairs of shoes. Those cavalrymen are only a couple of miles away, and if we steal their shoes, they'll come down here for sure. Particularly if there's any shooting or anything like that during our little raid."

"Any shooting? There'll be shooting. I've been on operations with you before," said McLemore.

"Yeah, I suspect there'll be some shooting, of course, only from the Yanks." After a short pause Logan continued, "And I guess we really ought to know more about that barracks area before we try to break in." So the next morning Logan, McLemore and Li'l Georgia walked into Louisville to scout out the barracks of B Company of the Second Wisconsin.

The scouting party did not return until late the following day, but they came back with a rather complete picture of their objective. A large part of this information came from a very cooperative barmaid in a tavern located only a couple of blocks from the Yankee compound. Logan had gone in to talk to her at the insistence of McLemore, who obviously had made her acquaintance on one of his previous visits to Louisville. She was known as Black Eyed Susan because she wore a black patch over her right eye. However, in appearance she was far from a pirate. In fact, she was a most striking looking young woman who, except for the eye patch, could have passed for a sixteen-year-old girl. She was clearly taken with McLemore, and as they sat at a table in the corner, she passed on all sorts of detailed information about the Federal compound. She, of course, made no claims about how she got these details.

According to Black Eyed Susan, there were three buildings inside the compound fence. Most of the company was quartered in the two-story house sitting immediately behind the entrance gate, but one of the smaller buildings was the quarters for the third rifle platoon of the company, which could not be fitted into the main quarters building. Every third night this platoon went out to pull sentry duty in the rail yard, leaving two or three men behind to guard the gear. These men usually stayed in the small room in the front of the building, which was the sleeping quarters and office of the platoon sergeant. A big, mean dog roamed inside the compound and walked in and out of the buildings at will. A fire was always burning in front of the cookhouse. McLemore had been told that this fire heated the water that was used to scald mess gear after each meal.

According to Black Eyed Susan, the men from the Second Wisconsin complained continually about being stuck guarding the Louisville rail yards some two months after the end of the war. Of course, they talked a lot about going home and spent much of their energy passing on rumors about when they might be moving back to Wisconsin. Logan marked them down as being poorly led and with low morale. But low morale or not, and even if their officers were usually away at one of the nearby taverns, they would undoubtedly put up a big howl and become most dangerous if they were to catch anyone breaking into their compound.

McLemore's friend, the barmaid, assured them that the Yankee soldiers went around armed during the day, but at night the weapons were stacked in racks. However, no weapons were ever left completely unattended. As for the men themselves, Black Eyed Susan had heard enough to know that almost all were veterans of the fighting in Virginia. After listening to all these details and having asked scores of questions, Logan took Li'l Georgia to a position in a pine thicket across the railroad track, where they spend the remainder of their time observing the coming and going of the soldiers of the Second Wisconsin. Of course, McLemore insisted that he be left to finish his visit with the cooperative barmaid before he joined the others for the walk back to their camp.

Two days later, after the other men had been thoroughly briefed on information picked up on the reconnaissance, all five men moved back into Louisville and into a covered position about two hundred yards from the front gate of the Wisconsin unit's quarters. From that position, they spend the rest of the day watching their quarry's activities and studying the buildings and their environs.

As the sun began to set, Logan realized that his mouth was full of cotton, just as it always had been before all those operations during the war, but he knew that the feeling would disappear as soon as they climbed the fence and the thing actually got underway. He and McLemore lay in the deep shadows that covered the little rise just behind the railroad and watched the activity inside the campsite. The Federal soldiers had finished eating their evening meal and were drifting back by twos and threes to their sleeping quarters. Four of the Yankees were cleaning their weapons at a table behind the main building. Logan could see two horses tied to a railing just in front of what he took to be the cookhouse—undoubtedly officers' mounts. Now and then a man would come out of the cookhouse and drop kitchen utensils into a big pot hanging above the fire in the middle of the open space between the buildings.

Suddenly there was a commotion in front of the smaller of the two main buildings, and men came rushing out amid much adjustment of equipment. A platoon formed up, after the usual amount of milling around, and marched out the front gate and off down the road toward the rail yards.

After it became quite dark Logan moved his people to a ditch only a few yards from the rear fence. There they waited again, for what seemed like hours, until the dim light in the front windows of the small building went out. After another twenty minutes Li'l Georgia, McLemore and Logan climbed the fence—which turned out to be surprisingly easy—and dropped over into the open space between the fence and the back door of the small barracks. Hood and Jackson remained in the ditch outside the fence to gather up the shoes that were thrown over the fence and carry them away.

Logan crept up to the back door, tried it and found it locked. He then climbed up on McLemore's shoulders and pushed up a window; everything inside was very quiet and very dark. He dropped back to the ground and helped the other two men up and into the window then moved around the building toward the fire and the horses. A heavy, cast-iron pot was sitting near the fire; and with some vague notion of carrying it away for a cooking pot, he picked it up and hung it on his heavy leather belt.

Logan spoke to the horses in an attempt to calm them. Almost immediately he heard several soft thumps, which almost certainly were made by shoes being dropped from the barracks window. In a few more moments Logan saw a dim figure crawl out the window and drop to the ground. He knew the shoes were now being thrown over the back fence to Jackson and Hood. All was going well—then, as usual, it all came apart in a moment. A dog somewhere in the front of the barracks began barking furiously, and in a moment an explosion of activity erupted within the building. Yankee voices were yelling, and men were running across the floor, cursing and screaming as they ran into beds and lockers in the dark.

To create a diversion Logan ran to the fire and jerked up a burning knot, throwing it toward the pile of hay the two horses were eating. Trailing a shower of sparks, it fell into the hay, which immediately ignited. In thirty seconds true pandemonium reigned. Men were running out of the main barracks into the open court, and the frightened horses were screaming and rearing up against their tie lines. A half dozen shots were fired at nothing in particular. Logan ran over to help with the shoes and immediately stumbled into Li'l Georgia, who blurted out something about being hit. In the next moment he was on top of the fence with a pair of shoes—laces firmly tied together—in one hand and Li'l Georgia's arm in the other. They ran across the field toward the railroad embankment, dragging shoes and each other. Just as their lungs would surely burst, they rolled over to the back side of the embankment, and it was over. For the first time Logan realized that the heavy cast iron pot was still tied to his belt.

All five of them moved along the back side of the embankment for a ways and then climbed up a little rise to enjoy the chaos in the barracks area. The open space inside the compound and the street in front of the gate were filled with half-dressed Federal soldiers. The firing, which had been brisk for two or three minutes, had died out. Logan noticed with satisfaction that the two horses were being led away, evidently not injured. He would have certainly felt bad indeed if those poor creatures had injured themselves because of the hay fire or had gotten shot in the melee.

Sitting there in the dark, they sorted out the shoes and found they had ten pairs and one unmatched shoe. During the ten minutes they had been inside the Yankee barracks, Li'l Georgia had managed to fit himself with a pair of shoes. But when the firing started he had abandoned his Confederate shoes and had fled with the laces of his new shoes still untied. They remained untied and flapped up and down on his feet during the run across the open field to the railroad.

Finally, Logan pulled up Li'l Georgia's sleeve and looked at the shallow, two-inch trench that a minie ball had cut across his lower arm. His sleeve was wet with blood, but the wound was obviously superficial. Of course, for the next sixty-five years he would show it to one and all as "where the Yankees shot me."

When all were rested, Logan moved them back to a ridge line a few hundred yards beyond the railroad. Then, with ten pairs of shoes securely tied to their belts, they dropped down just below the skyline and moved off to the south. Ten pairs of shoes in exchange for one flesh wound. Not a bad night's work.

By daybreak they were back under their bridge, and with a single sentry posted, four of them slept and rotated the watch. Just in case a Yankee patrol should come by, the liberated shoes were hidden in heavy underbrush downstream from their campsite, and Li'l Georgia's minie ball cut, now bandaged with a strip torn from McLemore's new shirt, was hidden under the only long sleeve shirt that the team had managed to steal.

In the late afternoon, to a chorus of gaiety directed at his wound, Li'l Georgia had gone out to find food. His quest was successful, and the confidence of the others in his foraging ability was borne out by the water steaming away in the new iron pot upon his return. Some eight eggs and five big Irish potatoes were not bad for an hour's mission. The pot received them with quite a hiss of approval.

"And I suppose some nice lady gave you all this," growled McLemore as he washed his knife and spoon.

"Yes, sir, she sure did. It was that nice Rebel lady—three houses down, on the right." Li'l Georgia picked up the look of disbelief on Logan's face and changed the subject. "They told me that a Yankee cavalry patrol was out looking for whoever broke in to that infantry barracks last night. I told them that—"

"I don't doubt that, you little bastard. I suppose you showed all of 'em your big wound," this from Jackson.

"Sergeant, you'll be sorry about talking to me like that if my mother ever meets you." The young man laughed a bit to show that he understood that it was all in fun. "But, Cap'n, the Yankee lieutenant was saying that the Wisconsin boys had hit a couple of us. What if they start looking for wounds and find mine?"

Thad Hood, who clearly was a believer in the Bill of Rights, his recent participation in the Great Rebellion not withstanding, advised, "They can't do that, Li'l Georgia. They can't just start searching people without a reason."

"You'd be surprised what six or eight big Yankee cavalrymen might do if they feel like it," said Logan. "Hood, I guess you and McCalab had better get all your stuff together and go downstream about a half mile and hide out. I'll send for you tomorrow."

The two men, really still boys and not at all happy with leaving the group, grumbled a lot, but they gathered up all the evidence of their existence, took their part of the food and moved off down into the deep thickets along the creek. Thus, when the cavalry patrol came riding up two hours later, there were only three ragged men under the bridge. All were wearing shoes that looked like they had walked through Jackson's Valley Campaign.

The Federal lieutenant made them strip to their drawers to satisfy himself that none of them had fresh wounds. The exposed scars on Logan and the sergeant seemed to gain the grudging respect of the Yankee officer, and his inspection became considerably less pointed. After a few more blustering questions, he finally gathered up his patrol and rode off with a parting comment to the effect that they were probably the culprits he was looking for, but they just hadn't been hit. "I don't believe that the Norwegian Infantry can shoot straight, anyway."

And so, in the late afternoon of the following day, the five Confederates, all decked out in rather substantial footwear, gathered up the iron pot and moved south into the interior of Kentucky. They left the extra shoes, which didn't fit any of them anyway, hanging from one of the bridge beams. Maybe another bunch of ex-prisoners would find them. As darkness began to fall, they were walking briskly along the dirt road that they had been told led to Bowling Green and, eventually, to Hopkinsville down near the Tennessee line. They had only the clothes on their backs and the iron cooking pot, which was traded back and forth among them as they walked. Jackson did not want Logan to take a turn, but the captain insisted.

By daybreak they had moved some twenty miles farther south and had found another bridge to hide under. Forty or so miles should put them out of danger from the Second Wisconsin, but none of them wanted to risk the rage of that outfit at any nearer range. For the next three or four days, they moved at night and hid out during the day. Gathering and preparing food while following such a schedule would clearly be a big problem. Logan drove them hard to cover twenty miles each night, which meant they must walk about ten hours. They were moving through good farm country that had not seen much of the war, so vegetables at least were rather easy to come by. But it took time to beg or steal any sort of food, even vegetables, and it took more time to cook it. The iron pot turned out to be invaluable, so they continued to lug it along on their twenty-mile forced marches. When he was first captured, Hood had spent a couple of months being dragged around by a Federal company in northern Missouri and had been put in charge of such a pot. He told the group that the Yankees called this kind of pot with legs a dutch oven, and he showed them some of the tricks that he had learned in its use.

Everyone was most happy when, after four days of this schedule, Logan announced that he thought it was now safe to start moving during daylight. Further, they would hide themselves at night and discontinue posting a security man, sleeping during the night and having a little more time to find and cook their meals.

Li'l Georgia and Hood were busy rounding up squash and potatoes, both of which were to be had on just about any farm but often had to be stolen when their begging failed to produce any results. After a couple of days of this begging and stealing, they managed to catch a chicken. And two days later, a southern sympathizer gave them a piece of side meat. Really, they were eating rather well, and although they grew very tired from the walking, all five had grown visibly stronger.

The first two weeks of June had been dry and walking had been easy; but about noontime of the sixth day since leaving the bridge, the sky suddenly became quite dark and a tremendous storm blew in from the southwest. Just as the storm broke, the five men took refuge in an old tobacco barn. The driving rain blew through and wet them all; but the lightning, which was striking all around the barn like an artillery barrage from the heavens, spared them. In half an hour the squall had passed, and Logan got them back on the road, which had turned into a river of mud. To save footwear and tempers he led them out into the fields and moved along parallel to the road. Their clothing and shoes were wet and uncomfortable, but these slowly dried out as they moved along. Off to the southwest dark clouds threatened more rain; so when they came upon a substantial looking old cattle barn, McLemore suggested that they stop for the night. All the weather delays would probably cost them some five miles of their day's assigned walk, but Logan decided to agree with McLemore, who almost never suggested anything. They moved into the barn and up into the hayloft, half full of newly cured hay. Blind luck again. Within three minutes all the wet gear was off, and everyone was once more asleep.

The rain began again during the night, and when morning came it was still coming down hard. With water everywhere Logan decided to hold up and wait for the downpour to stop. They hadn't eaten for some twenty hours, but there wasn't going to be much chance to look for food until there was a break in the weather. Further, it appeared totally impractical to start walking in the face of the storm. They waited and slept.

Finally, there was some rustling around down below, and Li'l Georgia shook Logan awake. "Cap'n, there's a cow in the barn, and I think she's got a lot of milk. Maybe we can catch her and get our breakfast."

Logan didn't like the odds that anything worthwhile would come of this adventure, but he mumbled his approval and Li'l Georgia immediately woke Hood. With the iron pot in hand, they dropped from the hayloft to the barn floor. In a couple of minutes they had driven the cow into one of the stalls and attempted to bribe her into standing still by offering her a handful of hay. They had no rope, and it became quite clear that the cow did not intend to cooperate. The two milk thieves soon found that both ends of the cow were dangerous. Li'l Georgia got kicked, and Thad Hood was thrown against the side of the barn, barely missing getting hooked in the process. In a moment both men came flying out of the stall like a couple of drunks leaving a tavern on Saturday night. As a final insult the cow butted the iron pot out the door after them.

At this point Logan ordered them back up to the hayloft. He certainly couldn't afford to have a couple of cripples on his hands for the remainder of the trip. Both men came away grumbling that they could get a pot of milk if only they could be given a second chance. They came crawling back in the hayloft to the accompaniment of laughter from McLemore and Jackson.

A few minutes later a bright-faced girl, certainly not over fifteen, came whistling down the path that lay alongside the main road. She poured a can of grain into a trough in the hallway of the barn and without further preparation began to milk the cow into a tin bucket. For the cow's part, she stood perfectly still, mouthing the grain and appearing to be most content with the procedure.

"Now, that's the way you're supposed to milk a cow, Georgia," whispered McLemore, as he shook with silent laughter. As the girl finished her task, Logan motioned to Li'l Georgia to go down and talk to her. After a few seconds of panic on her part brought on by the sudden appearance of a ragged stranger, they began a conversation punctuated by a lot of arm waving by both participants. Li'l Georgia then called out for Hood to come down and join them. The older men looked down in fascination as the new arrival was dispatched to the well at the edge of the barnyard to bring back a gourd dipper. The girl then poured it full of hot milk and passed it to Li'l Georgia. She then refilled the gourd and gave it to Hood. Up in the loft Logan wondered to McLemore how these two, who must have looked to the country teenager like Blackbeard the Pirate backed up by Colonel Quantrill, could end up being presented with milk from the family cow. They could see her smiling away, so they had to assume that she was not motivated by fear. Li'l Georgia turned his head toward the hayloft and gave a big wink. The girl picked up her bucket and moved off in the direction from which she had come. Li'l Georgia and Thad, covered with smiles, crawled back up the ladder.

"Sir, the girl is going to get her daddy and see if he can help us."

"Oh, great," from McLemore. "He'll probably circle around back and start shooting into the barn."

Yeah, maybe." said Logan. "Let's spread out up here so we can watch all sides. Just in case."

They had hardly gotten into position when a big gruff-looking man came down the path followed by the girl. He was walking along at a sharp clip and did not appear to be armed. When he reached the fence surrounding the barn, he stopped and called out, "Hey, up there, you Rebels. Come on down, and let's talk."

A few moments later Logan swung from a low rafter and dropped into a standing position on the barn floor. "We're just resting in the hay. We're certainly not out to cause anyone any trouble. If it's not all right, I'll get my men down and move on," this last to make sure the big red-haired man understood that he had more men hidden above.

However, the man just laughed, "It's all right. We've seen you people coming through before. We had two last week. If you'll come up to the house, we'll see if we can find you something to eat." So they all crawled down and followed the man and the girl up the path toward what turned out to be a dogtrot house set back in a grove of trees. As they came into full view of the house, Logan could make out a rather large woman standing on the front porch. She was wearing a green and white homemaker type apron, but homemaker or not, she did not appear overjoyed that she was gaining five more mouths to feed.

"Margaret, we got to find these men something to eat. They've walked all the way from Louisville and are near starved. The Good Lord would not be pleased if we sent them away from our house still hungry, Rebels or not." Without a word the woman turned and went into the house.

The captain watched his dirty men climb up on the porch and seat themselves on the floor, leaning back against the wall. Two cane-bottom chairs were back in the dogtrot, but no one was presumptuous enough to sit in those. It suddenly occurred to Logan that this was probably the first time in at least a year that any of these men had been in a real house. Their host seated himself at the front edge of the porch and leaned against one of the posts holding up the roof. Logan sat down on the edge of the porch and leaned against a similar post.

After a moment, their host began to speak, "Well, I'm Bud Dixon, and I might as well tell you that I'm a good Union man myself. But I don't cotton to having nothing around me hungry, neither man or beast, so we're going to rustle up some sort of vittles. It won't be much, but I bet that my Margaret can fill you up."

And, sure enough, she could. When she finally called them back to the kitchen, she had a big bowl of milk gravy, a plate of fried middling meat, about thirty biscuits, a pound or so of butter, and a quart jar of ribbon cane molasses set out on a big pine kitchen table that shone from scrubbing.

As they pulled the two benches up to the table, the farmer's wife finally spoke. "If it was up to me, I'd probably let you go hungry, but it ain't up to me. Mr. Dixon wants to feed everybody who comes along the road, and we've done it so far. Now that it's ready, I want it all et up."

"M'am, I guarantee you, on my word as a Soldier of the South, that it'll all be gone in about twenty minutes. Hood, say the blessing." Logan's time estimate was a bit off; it was all gone in fifteen minutes.

They finished eating and returned to the front porch. Dixon had lighted a pipe and looked the picture of contentment. "You know, we've had so much rain that we won't be able to do anything in the field for a day or two. You men ought to think about staying here and resting for a few days. You could help me around the farm; there's more to do here than one man can handle. I've got a boy, but he went for a soldier in the Federal Army and got caught by you folks outside of Atlanta. He got took to Andersonville, made it through, but he's still in the Federal Hospital in Indianapolis. I need all the help I can get, and you people need to get in better shape before you start out through Tennessee. I hear it's just a desert down there. No food nor no help of any kind, and it's even worse down in Alabama." All this as he drew away on his old pipe.

Logan thought about it awhile, then decided that the offer was too good to turn down. By early afternoon the five men found themselves shucking and shelling corn in the crib down behind the house. Obviously they would have to turn out quite a bit of work to earn the food that they would consume. Although they weren't be able to do too much in their weakened condition, the men seemed to sense the sacrifice the Dixon family was making and fell to with a will. There was no sign of complaint or any obvious dissatisfaction with his decision to delay their progress toward home. At least not yet.

One day lengthened into three, and they were still sleeping in the hayloft—not much in the way of discomfort for soldiers—and working on the farm during the day. Logan pushed them as hard as he dared. All the wheat had been cut, tied in bundles and stacked. Nine acres of corn had been thinned and hoed out.

On the fourth day they were in the creek bottom cutting hay. Jackson had borrowed a shotgun from Mr. Dixon and used it to kill two wild turkeys from a flock he had sighted the day before. They had begun to slip into the farm's daily routine. Dixon's wife continued to come up with plenty to feed the five extra people, but she looked no happier about it than she had the first day. Surely Jackson's turkeys helped, but there was no overt sign.

After the first couple of days the farmer began to talk rather freely to Logan. It seemed that the farm had done well during the war, perhaps better than ever before. After all, there had been very little fighting in this area and no real destruction. Prices had been good, and the Dixon's had been able to sell their products rather than have them seized by marauding armies. Despite all this Logan could tell that the landowner was not really enthusiastic about either the operations of the war or its overall purpose. He had not owned slaves nor had he wanted to. However, many of his neighbors had, and he saw very little wrong with the slavery system other than he felt that it was, as he expressed it, a poor business proposition. According to Dixon, the blacks in his area were the world's worst workers and a constant source of trouble for their owners. If they weren't stealing, they were running away, sick or playing sick. True, he'd have done the same if he had been a slave. But he really didn't see how farmers who had owned a gang of these people had escaped bankruptcy. At the end of this discussion, Logan decided not to tell Dixon that McLemore's family had owned eighty blacks or that his own people had eight.

However soft Dixon appeared to be on the slavery issues, he was clearly a true Union man. To his mind this was the basic reason that the war had to be fought. He surely agreed with old President Jackson—the Union must be preserved. He really could not see how anyone could put the Union itself in jeopardy just to win out on any of the issues involved. He thought that the fire-eating States' Rights people were no worse than those damn abolitionists. As far as he was concerned, the Good Lord could just put a plague on both their houses.

As Logan listened to this explanation of Dixon's position, he was a bit shocked to realize that it was not so far from his own. About the only basic difference was the farmer's complete worship of the Union. Now that was going a little too far. But he supposed that point of difference had really brought on the war and caused those thousands of deaths. And now the South was ruined for his time and his children's, if he should ever have any children.

Dixon did not appear to be very curious about Logan's or the other men's backgrounds or even about what had happened to them during the war. The captain's missing ear and mangled hand usually brought on indirect questions as to how all this had happened, as did the bayonet scar across Jackson's cheek. But not from Dixon. If he wondered, he kept it all to himself. His wife, who said very little about anything, certainly asked nothing about her battered visitors. She always seemed to be at her pots and pans in the kitchen or walking in her long striding way up and down the hill to the spring, carrying water in a big wooden bucket or sometimes the milk and butter that were stored in a tiny stone building in the spring branch.

The food continued to be very plain but very good. Milk and butter made up a large part of the Dixon's diet. It turned out that they had two cows in addition to the monster that had defeated Li'l Georgia and Hood. Some form of hominy, cornbread, side meat, potatoes and dried beans always seemed to back up the milk and butter at each meal. Other than Jackson's wild turkeys and the side meat, there was no meat, and Dixon kept explaining that it was too early to get much green produce out of the garden.

Only the girl of the family, whom Logan had determined was only thirteen years old, seemed curious about the hungry visitors, and she appeared to be interested primarily in Li'l Georgia. After the second or third day these two began to talk and giggle a lot, and Logan was sure she, at least, was getting a full report of all their backgrounds. He knew for sure when she suddenly started calling him Cap'n.

At noon of the sixth day of their stay, Logan was a bit surprised when Dixon suddenly asked that he go with him down to the spring. It was obvious from the farmer's silence and deep frown that something was wrong; so Logan was prepared for the worst and was a bit relieved when he found the three milk jugs lying in the water with some of their contents floating away downstream. Farther downstream the empty butter bucket had drifted up against some brush.

"One of your people did this, Logan. I know it and you know it." The deep growling voice sounded less than encouraging for whoever got caught.

"Well, maybe. Maybe not. I don't think that any of my people would have done this, but I realize that you can never know for sure."

"Sure, but your men are the only ones around. And before you start talking about bears from the woods, just remember that we haven't seen one around here in over twenty years."

"Mr. Dixon, I know it was a man. Just look at the tracks in the mud. However, I would like you to notice that whoever stole your milk and butter was wearing very worn shoes. I don't think any of my people have shoes that are that worn down."

Dixon, who was busy pulling the jugs and bucket out of the tiny stream, was obviously skeptical. He was still grumbling when Clara Pearl came running down the hill, breathless and white-faced. "Papa, Papa, there's two men that just come out of the woods and went in the house! I was out in the garden and I saw 'em!"

Logan was surprised at how fast the big farmer moved. Before he could be stopped, he was gone up the hill and out of range of the caution warning that Logan was giving. There was no way to know whether Dixon thought the intruders were from Logan's group. Long before the captain could reach the top of the hill, Dixon had disappeared into the house. Logan hesitated only long enough to demand that Clara Pearl go back to the spring and wait until the intrusion could be investigated.

A soldiering background wouldn't allow him to burst into the house without any idea of what was going on inside. He moved around through the kitchen garden, running along behind a couple of rows of tall corn, until he could sprint over behind the kitchen house. Pulling himself up to a back window, he attempted to look through the front of the room and through another set of windows into the main house. He wished he didn't have to get involved in all this, but he knew he must. He knew it just couldn't be any of his people inside the house, but still—

After a moment Logan began to pick up figures in the dark front room. A big burly man with a dirty beard was standing over Dixon, lying sprawled on the floor. The burly man, dressed in a Confederate jacket and butternut trousers, was busy tying up Dixon with a plow line. Margaret Dixon was seated limply on a chair by the fireplace, looking straight ahead with a blank look on her face. Logan had seen many men in shock, but this was a woman. He could see her sewing basket lying on the floor with its contents strewn about. Just then he saw a pillow come sailing into the middle of the floor from some place over to his right, and he realized that there was someone else in the room who was evidently tearing apart a bed out of sight in the corner. Suddenly the big man in the middle of the room jerked the rope tight around Dixon's wrists and turned back to the woman.

"Look here, you Yankee bitch. Tell us where the money's at or I'll beat your brains out with this rope. I know you Yankees bastards have the first dollar you ever made. Show it to me or, by God, you and old Pop here are sure goners." With that, Dirty Beard brought the end of the rope down with tremendous force on the arm of the chair in which Margaret Dixon was sitting. If she followed any of this, she made no sign. Logan finished pushing up the back window, slid through onto the floor of the kitchen room, then moved to the wall and toward the door to the front room. Out of the corner of his eye he could see someone picking up a stick of firewood off the pile stacked on the front porch.

Suddenly there was a tremendous shattering of glass and wood and Sergeant Jackson leaped across the front room and onto the burly man holding the rope over Margaret Dixon. Even without surprise it would not have been an even match. Jackson brought the heavy stick down on the back of the neck of the intruder with sickening force. Logan rushed through the door and into the front room just in time to meet the second man, also wearing parts of a Confederate uniform, who sprang from the back of the room. As his eyes took it all in, Logan realized that the man had a pistol. He grabbed the weapon and tried to push it aside, knowing instantly that this was going to be very, very difficult. Logan hung on and pushed desperately against his opponent's arm. Every moment he expected to lose the contest and feel the slug go through his body. The man's free hand was around his throat, and Logan realized that his arm and shoulder had him trembling on the edge of eternity. But just as hope was slipping away, he felt the intruder's arm weaken, and in an instant the pistol was turned back toward the Confederate jacket and Logan somehow got his finger on the trigger. The explosion was deafening inside the house. For an instant the hand on his throat retained its strength and Logan's mind told him that he had somehow missed. But then the weakening came, and the man staggered back and fell. The little hole in the gray jacket was a small red spot in a big black burned area. Logan fell to his knees from weakness just as Jackson came rushing up beside him. He noticed a curious whiteishness around Jackson's bayonet scar, which he had never noticed before. The incident was over.

When the excitement had died down a bit and the bodies were out on the porch under a sheet, Logan asked Jackson how he had decided to jump through a closed window. Jackson wiped blood from a couple of cuts on his face and replied, "Ah, Cap'n, that dirty fellow was going to hurt Miss Margaret." It sounded like a good enough reason.

In the late afternoon, the county sheriff and a deputy came driving up in a buckboard wagon. They listened to the story of the incident as told by Bud Dixon and then walked around inspecting the scene. The sheriff's reaction would have probably been much different if the two dead men had been Federal veterans, and it certainly would have been much different if the Dixon family had been Confederate sympathizers. The sheriff was none too happy to find two dead men in his county, no matter how they had died or by whose hand. After a bit of bluster, however, he decided the killings were justifiable. Despite the story told by the Dixons—even Margaret Dixon talked at some length about what heroes Logan and his men had been—the sheriff appeared to think that if the truth could be known, the whole business was a falling out among thieving Confederates. But then, what's a couple of dead Rebels, more or less? In any event the sheriff ended up saying that no arrests would be made but that Logan and his men had better be across the state line and into Tennessee by the next afternoon. He then threw the two bodies on the back of his wagon and drove away.

Logan decided to stay one more night in the friendly barn and start out fresh the following morning. Each man had only the battered clothing that he had on his back, a knife and a spoon—the common item was the iron pot that was still being carried—so not much time had to be set aside for packing. The Dixons were clearly sorry to see them go. The wife cooked them a last breakfast with ham suddenly appearing on the table to back up the two eggs she expended on each man. Everyone seemed quite happy, with the exception of Li'l Georgia and Clara Pearl Dixon. At the breakfast table the girl's eyes were red and rimmed, and Li'l Georgia had told Logan during the previous night that he wanted to stay behind when the group moved out for Tennessee. This idea had been squashed rather ruthlessly.

He had expected it and was prepared, letting the youngsters have it from both barrels. In the end Li'l Georgia seemed to accept that he owed it to his family to return to Muscogee County; and if such loyalty wasn't enough, he owed it to his comrades to help hold the group together until they all could get safely home. His skills at foraging would be desperately needed after they got into the old Confederacy, and certainly Thad Hood, whom all recognized as physically the weakest member of the team, needed his close friend's help. And finally, Logan simply could not allow the youngster to remain behind. So in the end the boy sharpened his pocketknife, cleaned his spoon and took first turn at carrying the cooking pot.

When they had all gathered in front of the house for their final departure, Dixon came over and led Logan down the road out of earshot of the others. There they exchanged their final words and the farmer wished them good luck and reminded the captain that he was now coming upon the hardest part of his journey. Suddenly Dixon turned and walked quickly back to the house and went inside. Logan moved his people down the trail and into the main road. Li'l Georgia was left behind to say goodbye to Clara Pearl, out of sight of his comrades and her parents. In three or four minutes the boy came running to catch up with the iron pot banging against his leg. All five then moved off at a brisk pace for the Tennessee line.

CHAPTER II

ACROSS TENNESSEE

The men walked along briskly for the four or five miles from the Dixon farm to the state line. It was quite cool for the end of June, and Logan knew that they were making better time than usual. He also knew that they probably would never be able to move at this rate again. They were coming off a six-day rest simply stuffed with good food, with shoes that were still in good shape and clothing passable. He realized that the hard part lay ahead and he could not expect it to get easier as they pushed on through the old Confederacy. All warnings indicated there would be little to eat in the countryside of Tennessee and certainly no way to replace clothing or shoes. Logan had seen enough of war's aftermath to know this had to be true. Nor was he looking forward to the philosophical blow to his people of sights of burned houses, destroyed fences and uncultivated fields with briars and bushes taking over on farms that had not lain fallow since the War of 1812.

All these thoughts were hastily pushed aside when Logan saw a detachment of Federal troops blocking the road ahead. Obviously the Yankees had not seen them yet, so Jackson immediately suggested, "Cap'n, let's slide over into the woods and by-pass them blue bellies."

"No, I don't think that we can start running from these people. We're legal, and we'll just have to start acting like it. They're going to be everywhere from here on."

"Yes, sir, but you got to remember that we killed a couple of men yesterday."

"Yeah, Jackson, but everyone seems to agree that those two bushwackers got what they should have expected, if maybe not what they deserved."

By this time the Federals had seen them, and it was too late to take to the woods. Three of the men had picked up their arms and moved up to block the road. From a tent at the edge of the woods, an officer came trotting up to the roadblock. Logan thought they were probably lucky that they had no identification; at least there would be no long string of questions about their documents.

"You people have any sort of papers?" The officer, a roly-poly lieutenant whose collar was unbuttoned, looked like he had never heard a shot fired in anger.

"No, we were all released from Rock Island back last month, and we're just trying to get home." Logan thought it best to ask for something under these circumstances, which always seemed to get the interrogator's mind off track. "Sir, one of our men has dysentery pretty bad, and we'd sure like to get some of that good medicine that you people are issued for that stuff. And we sure could use a better pair of trousers for one of our soldiers."

"Look here, fellow. You're not soldiers anymore, if you ever was. The damn war's over. Ain't you heard?" All this free advice came from Lieutenant Roly-Poly before he got around to telling them that he wouldn't give anything to any stinking Rebel, and besides he didn't have anything extra anyway.

An officious-acting sergeant had them turn their pockets out and take off their headgear. Marching slowly by each man, he looked into their hats and pulled down on their wrong-side-out pockets. Turning to the lieutenant, he said,

"Sir, each one of 'em has a spoon and a knife of some sort, and other than that they seem to have one iron pot."

"That's probably all they're going to need, and I bet damn little of it's going to get worn out shoveling up grub down in Tennessee." The lieutenant buttoned his collar and launched into a long harangue on the Union having been preserved despite the best effort of old Lee and Davis and all the rest of the Rebels. He seemed particularly put out at Stonewall Jackson, giving over some three or four minutes to his special vilification. He finally wound up—after reminding the Southerners that they were really still prisoners and that they would still be in Rock Island cutting stone if he had his way about it—by telling them to be on their way and to get the hell out of his district.

Logan moved his people off immediately. He noted the unit guidon hanging lazily from its staff near the path leading into the detachment's camp. Their encounter had been with B Company of the Third Massachusetts Infantry. They moved quickly on.

At the next break Jackson said, "Cap'n, Li'l Georgia got the company guidon from that checkpoint back there. I think that the whole business is pretty funny, but that fat lieutenant may come after us about it anyhow."

Logan exploded, "Funny—funny hell! Georgia, you trying to get us all shot? That stupid-looking lieutenant will probably chase us all the way 'cross Tennessee to get that rag back. Now we'll have to get off the main road and cut through the country. Throw that thing out here, and let's look at it."

The crestfallen youngster pulled the guidon out of his shirt and threw it on the ground. It lay there in all its infantry blue glory with the unit designation printed in white. Everyone except Logan seemed to be trying hard to keep from breaking out in open laughter.

Finally Logan motion to Li'l Georgia to pick up the emblem. "Now, put that thing back in your shirt. I guess that just comes naturally to a born forager. So we'll take it with us, and when we get far enough away, we'll patch your breeches with the damn thing. And every time we pass a Yankee checkpoint, you'd better be walking backwards."

They left the main road and began walking cross-country. After a few miles of stumbling through brush and climbing in and out of ditches, the entire group began to express displeasure with Li'l Georgia's impetuous act. Hungry and much the worse for wear they stumbled on for a day and a half before Logan pulled them back onto the main road. Li'l Georgia was so relieved to be back on the road and on somewhat better terms with the team that he sang through all the verses of "Onward, Christian Soldiers" three times.

Four days after leaving the Dixon farm, the group walked through a sparsely inhabited area and approached Clarksville. There the destruction of warfare was vividly apparent. Virtually every house along the main road had been burned or pulled down. Fencing had all but disappeared. Barns and stables had evidently been down for two or three years, with weeds and brush already starting to take over. They passed an area that must have been used as a campsite by a small unit of one of the armies, no way to tell if by blue or by gray. Deep ruts had been cut throughout the adjoining fields, and old cooking fire locations were scattered about in what once had been a pasture. Grass had almost disappeared from several acres around the central campsite. Logan's farming background told him that nothing worthwhile could be grown there for three or four years. The first job would have to be the removal of the piles of junk still spread throughout the area. Only then could farmers turn their attention to the horrendous job of breaking up land that had been packed by hundreds of horses and wagons. It was going to be a long, hard task even if people were available to do the work; and judging from the complete absence of all forms of humanity, few workers would likely be available.

As they walked, they occasionally noted graves beside the road. Sometimes there would be a single grave, but more often three or four together. None of these were marked. Later as they neared the edge of the town, they passed a neatly organized cemetery containing at least fifty graves, all having wooden markers. Logan knew that the scattered graves were dead Confederates and the organized cemetery probably contained Federal bodies. He guessed that Jackson and McLemore knew this also, but he thought it unwise to discuss the matter with Li'l Georgia or Thad Hood. Luckily Jackson and McLemore must have felt the same.

As they neared the town, they began to see a few people. Some were working in the fields, but the majority appeared to be just standing by the road or on the porches of the few houses still upright; the people along the road looked out listlessly at the five men walking by. A few dogs barked, but only occasionally did anyone speak. Logan had seen similar scenes before; he recognized it as part of a picture of complete defeat.

Shortly after reaching the town itself, they were in the center of the downtown area. They walked past a livery stable and a couple of stores before reaching some backless benches in front of a tavern. There they sat down. The tavern was open for business, but it seemed only the blue uniforms of the occupying force were going in. Occasionally a well-dressed civilian was seen among the customers, but most of the people went past the building without acknowledging its existence. After a few minutes a poorly dressed, older gentleman rode up on a bony mare and dismounted at the watering trough. He tended to his animal and walked over to stand in the shade of the trees behind the benches.

"Where you men coming from and where are you trying to get to?" he asked in an assured manner. After receiving no immediate answer, he continued, "Oh, pardon me. I'm Judge Smith of the County Court here in Clarksville, and sometimes the Yankees even let me actually hold court."

"Judge, we're just five Confederates out of Rock Island Prison trying to get back to Alabama and Georgia," answered Logan, looking at the elderly man, who had removed his hat and displayed a head of thick white hair matching his beard.

The old man ran his hand over his hair and said, "You're going to find everything pretty scarce from here on south, I'm afraid. This country has been just about stripped. Both armies have been everywhere in this area. At least a half dozen times big outfits have rolled across Clarksville, and it really didn't make much difference which side they were on because when they left there wasn't much of anything worthwhile still around. Of course, towards the end of the war the Yankees were burning most everything by intention, and our people at least didn't do that. But it didn't matter much if the Confederates pulled your house down and burned it for firewood or if they confiscated your mules and paid you in Confederate money, you were just as bad off as if the enemy had burned you out and grabbed your livestock by design."

Logan answered, "Yes, sir, war is just about the most wasteful thing that was ever invented. It's going to take us fifty years to get over this one. That is if we get right to work on it and don't spend ten years grieving over the loss. I'm not saying that I can get right to work on it myself. Reckon I'll probably do plenty of grieving, but—"

"Yeah, I hope you young men live to see us get out of the fix we're in. The Yankees are going to hold us down for a long, long time, of course. Particularly after that damn fool shot old Lincoln. We have simply hundreds of blue bellies around here, so there's no hope for people of my age living to see the end of the occupation. We just have to do the best we can as we live out our time." Then after a pause pregnant with sadness, "Let's stop the grieving and try to keep looking ahead. We've been trying to feed the ex-prisoners who come through here, so if you'll bring your men down to the Methodist Church, I think I can come up with some sort of vittles. I will say that your people look a little better than most of those we've seen come through recently."

The five got up and followed the judge although McLemore grumbled that he would have liked to go in the tavern, it being there and all. However, he trailed along behind the group making their way down to the Methodist Church. The judge led them to a small building in the rear of the sanctuary where they found an ancient white woman busily stirring up cornbread batter in a big yellow bowl. Logan had expected to see a black at this task but remembered this was not Alabama or Mississippi but Tennessee.

"Miss Emma, here's some of our boys who've walked all the way from Rock Island Prison, and they're plenty hungry. See what you can do for 'em." After they had listened to Miss Emma's story of her own family and their losses in the war, it turned out that she could do quite a bit for them. She pulled two big pones of cornbread out of a pie safe and produced a bowl of butter and a pitcher of buttermilk from somewhere in the back. So once more, hunger was held at bay.

The temperature was still too hot to start off for Nashville; so while the others dozed on the floor, Logan, McLemore and the sergeant continued to talk with the judge, who seemed eager enough to continue his conversation with these veterans of the fighting in Virginia. The old man apologized for spending so much time telling about the problems of his own people and went on to say that he realized that soldiers who had followed the

Confederate banner for four years had seen things that he could not even imagine. However, after this introduction he brought out the common complaint that President Davis and General Lee had spent too much time and effort defending Richmond and had tended to forget there was a war going on in the West. In particular they had forgotten the fighting that had smashed his beloved middle Tennessee. The judge ended by asking if any of his listeners had seen Davis or Lee during the time they were fighting in Virginia and across the Potomac.

Logan had heard this question before and was ready to reply. "Yep, at Second Bull Run I got sent back to the main headquarters to pick up some maps for our colonel, and I saw President Davis riding off to the south. He was all surrounded by his escort, of course."

"But you did see him, even if he was quite a way off. And that's a lot closer than anybody here in Tennessee ever got."

"And that very same day when I had ridden all the way into the headquarters, there out in front of the house they were using was both General Lee and General Jackson sitting on a log right alongside of the road. I had found out sometimes back that it's usually a mistake to talk to these kind of people, so I tried to slip by without getting noticed. But sure enough, General Lee called out to me, got up from his log and walked over and took a real close look at my horse and asked some question about the animal. But I tell you I was so disturbed by being in the presence of the two greatest men in the Confederate army that I really can't remember what he asked. I must have managed to say something because he turned and went back to his log. Later I found out that the general was always very interested in horses, so I suppose he was satisfied with my answer, whatever it was. As for Jackson, all I remember about him was that he was sucking a lemon, and I've always wondered how he got such a thing in the middle of a battlefield.

When the two generals turned back to continue their talk, I scurried away. That was my total contact with the real heroes of the Confederacy."

The judge smiled and nodded in appreciation. "Well, you know, of course, that getting that close to these two will eventually make you a sort of hero in your own right."

"Yes, I suppose when I'm about seventy-five, I'll tell everyone who will listen about that incident. Before I leave the subject, though, I should say that we people assigned to the cavalry saw quite a lot of our own generals. That included seeing and even talking to General Stuart three or four times. One time, he had his banjo player with him and he had this fellow play for us. I suppose I'll have to say I remember the banjo man about as well as the general."

The judge chuckled again and continued, "Did any of the rest of you men actually see or talk to any of these people?"

The sergeant simply shook his head, but McLemore said that he had seen General Lee once—but since he was reviewing the troops at a parade and was so far away, his features were indistinct. McLemore supposed this would excuse him from being some sort of hero by reflected glory.

After this light moment the judge sank back into his seemingly natural gloomy state. He talked on at length about the problems the town faced, being particularly worried about what was going to happen to "his people" when winter came. In midsummer most of the population was getting along fairly well as far as food was concerned, but very little was being stored for winter. So come November, there simply would not be enough to eat. And, of course, most people's clothing would be in rags. Any shelter that had survived the war was in bad repair. Here in the upper part of Tennessee the weather got quite cold for some four months, so the judge expected a lot of suffering. Then he dropped his voice as though passing on secrets and almost whispered that the thing worrying him most was that the bulk of the population did not seem capable of attacking the problem. They were drifting through the summer of '65 as if they were in shock and doing very little to prepare for the winter ahead.

The judge talked on for hours about the horrors of war as it had impacted middle Tennessee—the robberies, rapes and burnings. He thought the Confederates were almost as bad as the Federals. There had been a dozen rapes and four murders in the Clarksville area, and no one had ever been tried. The judge confided that he was sure no one ever would be.

His own farmhouse had been burned out in '63 and all his livestock had been confiscated. His wife of fifty years died within a month of the burning, her death coming directly from the shock of losing their home.

An incident in which the Federals had piled up fifty or sixty Confederate bodies and burned them seemed to weigh heavily on the old gentleman's mind. Logan and McLemore, following the thinking of most hardened campaigners, found it hard to accept the judge's expressions of horror concerning this act. Like most soldiers they could accept that this was likely necessary. In addition, they followed the usual thinking of men of their background that a dead body couldn't be hurt. An early lesson learned by professional soldiers was that only a fool risked his people trying to bring out dead bodies. Logan knew, of course, that the judge would never understand such a position.

Displaying his background as a lawyer and judge, the old man complained at length of the collapse of the system of justice. The conqueror's military court was by far the ranking court operating in the area. Any case that could be pushed under that tent was sure to be tried there. His court got only the insignificant cases—and not too many of those.

The judge continued with this deeply disturbing discourse until Logan finally gathered up his men and got them ready to move toward Nashville. Miss Emma came springing out of the back room and gave each man a pone of cornbread and her prayers for God's guidance on the long trip home. Judge Smith walked along with them to the edge of town, continuing to tell stories about the innumerable tragic events in Clarksville during the war. Past the last standing building, the judge pointed them down the road to Nashville, shoot hands with each man and wished them luck.

The judge pulled Logan aside and spoke in his solemn voice. "You know, of course, that now you've got to walk through the Valley of the Shadow. It'll get much worse from here on. I hope that you can force these men to keep putting one foot in front of the other until they get home. The South needs every man they can muster, so get these five back alive." With one final handshake they were gone off toward Nashville.

Despite the warning of dangers ahead the four days it took to reach Nashville went by smoothly. They ate the Clarksville Methodist's cornpone for one day and got by the second day on some green corn growing near the road. On the third day Li'l Georgia got a peck of meal from a grist mill he found by foraging some three miles to the west of the main road. As they approached Nashville on the fourth day, a well-dressed, middle-aged man—whom Logan suspected was a scalawag but because of the circumstances he thought it best to keep his opinion to himself—bought them all the brunswick stew they could eat from a stand by the road. They had eaten nothing at all that day, so the act was much appreciated. When the man paid the black woman for the concoction, Logan knew his opinion was right because the man talked Southern but paid Yankee.

At the Cumberland River they were ferried across by a peg-legged ferryman who made no comment on how he had lost his limb; however, he did not demand a fee for his services. From the river landing they found the center of town by following the majority of the horse-drawn vehicles and the foot traffic. It was midmorning, and the city appeared to have been awake and hard at business for some time with drays unloading into warehouses, messengers scurrying between offices and street peddlers screaming out the value of their wares. Some carpenters were framing a new building on a vacant lot that still bore the marks of the burning of its previous building. Nashville appeared to be recovering from the shock of defeat rather quickly.

The group attracted little attention as they walked along; apparently the people of the city had become accustomed to seeing half-clothed men slumping through toward the south. Thad Hood and Li'l Georgia gazed with open mouths at all the sights. A rather officious-looking man, whom Logan took to be a policeman in spite of having neither uniform nor weapon, directed them to a building that he said furnished shelter for returning soldiers.

The building turned out to be an almost empty warehouse near the railroad station. The inside was not as hot as they had expected for midday in July. The ceiling was about thirty feet high and several large doors stood open to catch any breeze that dared draft through the warehouse section of Nashville. Twenty or thirty bales of cotton were scattered along one side of the huge open room. Logan and his men crawled up on the cotton and went to sleep.

A couple of hours later McLemore came to Logan's bale and said in a conspiratorial whisper, "Cap'n, I'm going out for a while to look around and see if I can come up with some better clothes. One of the darkies out in the street gave me some leads."

"Hey, wait a minute, McLemore. You know we can't run around in Nashville stealing stuff off of good southern clotheslines. What the hell is the matter with you?"

"Ah, you know I wouldn't do that. Looks to me like there's plenty of Yankees around to steal from. I saw platoons of the blue-bellied bastards marching along the street—I suppose that's what they thought they were doing. All those sons-of-bitches have to live somewhere and hang out their clothes someplace. Besides, all those duds will look a lot better on me than on some slob from New Hampshire, right?"

"You know the city's going to give us something to eat after a while."

"To hell with that, I may eat in that hotel I saw uptown," this with McLemore's famous grin.

"Sure, you'll probably eat grits without gravy in the Yankee stockade. If you've just got to steal something, what about getting some pants for Hood? His are just about gone."

Logan went back to sleep until two blacks showed up with a big bucket of soup thick with black beans, rice, okra and a little white pork. It wasn't at all bad, and his people and the five or six others who had wandered in ate it hungrily. He was beginning to think that perhaps the towns were doing better than the countryside in starting to move away from the total disaster of April of '65. Perhaps it was because the foodstuffs and other material coming in was off-loaded at the towns and never made it beyond the city limits. It probably helped also to have a lot of people in close to give each other moral support. Whatever the reason, spirits did not seem as low in Nashville as they did in the ruined farms along the road. However, he supposed that a few citizens or at least a few Yankee occupiers would soon have lower spirits after falling afoul of McLemore.

* * * *

McLemore headed immediately for what he guessed to be the residential district. He walked quickly past several blocks of modest houses and then slowed down to give careful attention to several imposing residences. He made a selection of three fine looking Greek Revival houses for closer study. These took up an entire block and were side by side. The center house was a three-story mansion displaying four massive Corinthian columns across the front. The three looked like a good bet, so he went to the end of the block and turned down the alley behind them.

No clothes hung in the service yards of the two end houses, but a long drying line behind the center mansion loaded with sunning garments delighted McLemore. He walked along the alley as slowly as he dared, trying to pick out from thirty feet away a pair of trousers and a shirt that might fit him. This would have been impossible to do if he had been anything other than near-average size. But at five-foot ten and 150 pounds he could choose from several items that would come close to a fit. He walked to the end of the block and down a side street, where he picked out a wooded area that fell off down to the Cumberland to use as a fallback position in case he got chased.

Back at his mark he simply jumped the fence and grabbed the selected trousers and shirt. As he was stuffing the items inside his own shirt, a side door of a small building in the back yard burst open and a huge black woman in starched apron and bandanna came flying out, yelling first something about thieving Yankees and then changing to Secess as he cleared the fence and landed at a dead run down the alley. He turned down the side street, slowed to a walk, moved down the street and crossed over into the wooded area.

He half expected someone to come after him raising a huge hurrah, but evidently no one attempted to follow him. He reflected on how strange it was that in a society ripped apart there was little cooperative action of any sort—even between members of the conquering host. Walking into the woods to roll up the stolen shirt and trousers, he heard no voices from the residential area only a few yards away. A few dogs barked, but otherwise all was silent. All those big houses had to be occupied by Yankees or turncoats and someone must have seen him, but evidently these people were not into helping each other.

He waited until dusk. Then with his newly stolen garments in a tight roll under his arm, he walked boldly back out on the street and made his way downtown. He found Mrs. Wiggins's boardinghouse right where his colored friends back at the warehouse had said it would be and immediately made his way back to the kitchen to talk to the cook. She was very big and very black and at first was disinclined to help this white boy who must have smelled planter class to her. She eventually agreed to iron his newly stolen clothing in exchange for a promised U.S. dollar to be paid as soon as he could get it. She finally smiled when she saw him dressed up in his new outfit, going so far as to direct him to the Maxwell House Hotel, which she had heard ran the biggest poker game in Nashville. This intelligence backed up what he had picked up at the warehouse, so he left for the Maxwell with full confidence that he had located the right place to begin his operation.

McLemore strolled around the hotel lobby certain that he looked as well dressed as a third of those present—which he figured was good enough. He looked around for some free food, something he remembered from pre-war visits made with his parents to hotels in the North. But he soon found that Nashville either wasn't far enough north or hadn't moved that far from April of '65. He struck up a conversation with a flashily dressed man standing outside the barroom. In five minutes McLemore had the room number of the big poker game. Mr. Flashy Dresser even threw in some free information, perhaps some of it true, about how the game was run and who was involved. McLemore found the room, gained admission and then stood against the wall with several other watchers. There he stood, the pride of Dixie, all dressed up in stolen clothing and without a cent in his pocket, waiting to get into a poker game.

No one said anything to him for a while, but eventually an ancient old fellow who looked to be at least eighty began a conversation. The old man knew several people who had lived in Selma; after a little prodding McLemore learned that the old man, Mr. Moore, had had dealings with McLemore's father several years before the war. From that point the conversation became friendlier, and the elderly man finally asked if McLemore would like to get in the game.

"Well, sir, I sure would, but in that Jefferson Davis ain't paying his army too well these days, I guess I'll just have to watch."

"Just stay around for a while longer, and I'll try to figure how you might overcome that problem," said the old fellow.

Eventually this representative of the generation of the War of 1812 led McLemore out into the hallway. "Listen, son, I played all afternoon, and I've just got to go home. You look like you could play this game. I'll stake you forty dollars for half of what you win. If you're Hugh McLemore's boy, I reckon I'll get my money back. Someday, at least."

Mr. Moore then came on with a long explanation of the peculiarities of the men who were in the game now and of those who would probably come in later. The middle-aged guy in the green vest was running the game for the hotel, and the little baldheaded man was a shill. Both were clearly professionals. The swarthy fellow with the mustache was a scalawag who ran a clothing store in town and who in Mr. Moore's opinion deserved to be cheated. But even Mr. Swarthy probably did not deserve to lose at the rate he had been doing for some time. The other two men sitting in were strangers and would soon lose all they could afford and be gone. A couple of the watchers, according to Mr. Moore, often played but were evidently short of money now. Everyone was waiting for the major from the Yankee headquarters who played almost every night. This Yankee major won often and evidently had plenty of money from somewhere. A carpetbagger who worked at the Freedman's Bureau came in some nights. This Bureau man was not as good a player as the Union officer, but he won more than he lost.

At the end of this discussion the old gentleman went back into the room and whispered a few words to the man in the green vest. He returned to McLemore and told him to expect an invitation to play when the next man dropped out. Also, the Yankee major was expected within the hour, and Mr. Moore would consider it some form of treason if a cavalry officer from Alabama couldn't beat the bastard.

The old fellow wandered off into a long tirade about the horrors of Reconstruction, pouring out all the old stories of rape, murder, confiscation of property and outrageous acts by the freed slaves. Undoubtedly it was all true, but McLemore had heard it all before. Further conversation revealed that the only one of these infamous acts that Mr. Moore had personally encountered was the confiscation of two cribs of corn by the occupying force. No ex-slave had been disrespectful to Moore, nor had any of the rapes or murders been perpetrated on any of his close acquaintances, but just losing his property had been bad enough and he knew all the other incidents were true. Finally he seemed to run down a bit, handed McLemore forty dollars in greenbacks and stumbled off down the stairs.

McLemore went in to watch the card game. After a few minutes a stir in the room signaled the entrance of the Federal officer, attended by two men in civilian clothes. The major looked unkempt in a uniform that was a bit too tight over his belly, and his fleshy face was glistening after he had climbed the two flights of stairs. The two civilians folded themselves into the corps of watchers while the officer went to stand behind the man running the game. The major was clearly disturbed when McLemore was invited to join the game and was only partially mollified when almost immediately another man cashed in and he was then invited to take that place.

The Yankee officer looked closely at McLemore as he said, "Reb, how did you people play this game? Did you bet goobers or maybe strings of catfish?"

"Right, major, and sometimes we bet fat possums," without a sign of a smile.

"Yeah, well, somebody told me that you cotton pickers cheat like hell. It won't do you any good here, though. Old Blevins here, that's supposed to run this game, had already introduced all the cheating that this little old game can stand."

McLemore took a quick look at the other players and at the major and decided that the remark was supposed to be taken as a joke. However, old Blevins did not appear to be amused.

"Oh, we were plenty straight at cards down in Alabama and, for that matter, in the First South Carolina Cavalry. We didn't cheat a bit more than that General McClellan of yours retreated."

Everyone, including the major, laughed a bit as old Blevins began to deal the cards.

Around midnight McLemore realized that he had been playing for a couple of hours but had won only two small pots. His stake had gone down to eight dollars, and it began to look like he might have to leave the game soon. Then he drew a full house and pressing his luck a bit won a fifty-dollar pot, giving him a little breathing room.

McLemore got some decent cards and made some bold decisions. By two o'clock he had pulled ahead by almost a hundred dollars and felt a bit more secure. The Yankee major was beginning to feel the pressure, so it was no surprise when he began to bait McLemore in earnest. Mopping his face with a big checkered handkerchief, he growled out, "You Johnnie Rebs always had plenty of luck,

I'll sure say that. But where were you when we were running all the butternuts down after Gettysburg?"

"Well, just like our infantry always said, we cavalrymen just saddled up and ran away. And after Gettysburg that was pretty much just what we done. Didn't see many blue bellies during the ride. And I understand that the infantrymen didn't see a whole lot of 'em either."

"You must of had a good horse. We caught lots of you traitorous bastards, and I saw plenty of dead ones, too. Plus, I know you must have been a prisoner or you wouldn't be coming through here this late. When did we catch you?"

"Major, if it's any of your business, I got knocked off a horse near Port Royal, Virginia, this past February and ended up in Rock Island. That's a real sweet place to spend four or five months of your life, let me tell you."

"Port Royal in February. You must have been with that murdering rascal Mosby."

"That's for sure. When my time ran out with the First South Carolina in '64, I went with Mosby, and I got to get in on the killing of a lot of you Union patriots," McLemore said, looking the major straight in the eye. Although the Federal returned the look with heat, McLemore knew from his expression that he had scored points with the mention of being with Mosby.

"You're lucky we didn't shoot you out of hand, if we picked you up out of Mosby's gang. You know they weren't a damn thing but a bunch of thieving, murdering guerrillas. If I had been in charge, it would have been a no quarter deal when we caught any of Mosby's people."

"Yeah, just a little of that and you would a had another Quantrill on your hands. Of course, in the long run, that probably would have been good for the Confederacy."

"Quantrill!" The fleshy Yankee's face was red and his eyes dark. "Anyone connected to that assassin is eventually going to be tried and hung. It's not over yet. Quantrill was—"

Suddenly Blevins spoke up sharply, saying that this was a card game not the first battle in the Second Great Rebellion. Avarice defeated patriotic fervor in both men, so the card game continued in sullen silence.

By this time of the players from the early evening only McLemore and the major were left. Several others had drifted in, played a number of hands, cashed out and gone home. The early watchers had long since departed, and three strangers filled the otherwise empty seats. McLemore pocketed the forty dollars he owed Mr. Moore and continued to play with about eighty.

Near three-thirty in the morning McLemore drew a straight flush and finally put the major out of the game. The Yankee departed with some black curses and threats to come back the next night and put a licking on anyone—particularly any rider for Mosby—who dared to play. With the departure of the major, McLemore lost his concentration and immediately dropped twenty dollars to a couple of the strangers. They seemed satisfied with this and suggested that Blevins close out the game. The game ended as the clock downstairs was striking four.

Blevins gathered up the chips and the cards and began sweeping the room. On taking count McLemore found that in addition to Mr. Moore's forty dollars safely hidden in his pocket he had seventy-two dollars in winnings. That would leave him with thirty-six dollars after paying Moore his half. Not a bad night's work, remembering that he hadn't even touched a dollar bill in many months. He was busy securing the greenbacks inside his shoe when Blevins came over and said, "Young man, I was some proud of you tonight. If ever a man needed cleaning, that damn Yankee major did, and you sho did it up right."

"You got to get the cards. That's what you have to do. Without the cards it jes can't be done. What's that major do around here, anyway?"

"He runs some office that's supposed to help the ex-slaves git started as free men. God knows, I don't envy him his job, if he's really trying. But I don't know how he could be trying very much, in that he plays poker here every night. Sometimes 'til dawn. I reckon he gits money out of the darkies someway. He seems to have plenty."

"Well, Mr. Blevins, he must have some special advantage, 'cause the army's pretty good at making you work—even the Yankee army. It's awful hard to stay out all night and get by the next day."

"Well, this guy lords it over half the people in Nashville and gets away with it, so I suppose he does have some special advantage. Anyhow, I was glad to see him get his comeuppance tonight. You saw he didn't take kindly to getting beat, so if I was you, I'd get out of Nashville as soon as I could. And I'd try to be extra careful moving about."

"Thanks, sir. I'll try to be careful."

"Well, start being careful by not going out and wandering around the city at four o'clock in the morning." Blevins dropped his eyes and continued, "I'll let you stay here in this room for a half dollar. Nobody will bother you until late in the afternoon. I've got to go home, so you'll have it all to yourself." Blevins, looking down at his shoes and shuffling around in shame, continued, "We've all got to make a living, you know. I'm sorry I have to charge you, but it'll be worth it."

So ten minutes later McLemore propped a chair under the doorknob and lay down on the floor to sleep. Blevins might be leading men up the stairs to rob and perhaps murder him, but his alternative was to go into the street and attempt to outwit whoever was enforcing curfew. He had to take the chance and stay. He went to sleep.

McLemore awoke to loud pounding on the door. Opening it, he found Mr. Moore, still dressed in an old black suit clearly a little worse for wear. The old fellow walked in without being asked and immediately spoke up.

"I've already heard that you licked the britches off of that Yankee bastard, and I've come to tell you how much we all appreciate it. It would be further appreciated if you could stay over tonight and give it to him again."

"Oh, I just can't do that, sir. I'm here with my old company commander, and I just know that I've got to go back to our group tonight. Cap'n Logan is just not the sort you go off and leave without telling him."

As McLemore handed over the money he owed, Mr. Moore changed the subject, rattling on about how bad things had been in Nashville since the surrender. The old fellow was clearly glad to pick up a little extra cash, but he did not seem to want to admit it, quickly folding the money and pushing it down into his snap-top purse without counting it.

However, he never skipped a beat in his stories about the improprieties of the freed slaves and their Yankee protectors. The burning of a plantation house on the Franklin Pike during the war was the current subject of his rage. His face reddened as he told McLemore that the family had been his neighbors. After the disaster the owner had taken his wife and daughter to his wife's folks down near Huntsville in Alabama. The planter then joined his son in the Confederate army, and they both had been killed in far-off Virginia.

McLemore tried to look attentive as the ancient fellow began a rambling attack on the Virginians for running everything in the Confederacy to their advantage and letting the rest of the states, particularly the border states like Tennessee, go hang. Lee, Jackson, Davis and that crowd had robbed Tennessee of the troops that were rightfully hers and then squandered them trying to protect Richmond—and so on and on.

Mercifully a maid finally came in and broke into Mr. Moore's tirade. Having calmed himself, Moore advised, "It sounds like you ought to get out of Nashville before the

Yankees pick you up. I have a pretty good place for you people to hide, out on the Franklin Pike. Why don't you go gather up your group and move them out for my place as soon as it's dark? I'll guide you out."

"It sounds like a pretty good idea, but you know that I can't speak for the cap'n. I'll pass this on to him as soon as I get back. I'm sure that between us we can find our way to Franklin."

Ten minutes later McLemore was sliding out the door and down the street toward Mrs. Wiggins's boardinghouse. He went to the kitchen, where he found the cook busily preparing cornbread for the noon meal. She almost dropped her mixing bowl when he handed her two dollars. Her eyes rolled around in her head as she looked at the money; and finally realizing that the money was indeed for her, she broke into a big generous smile and reverted to her slave self.

"Li'l Massa, I knowed you was coming back! I reckon you must have done big. Roses on you. Yes, sir!" The eyes were flashing with total approval.

"Cookie, I won a little, all right, so you get what I promised and a little extra. If I had lost, you'd never have seen me again. And I need to pick up that roll of old clothes that I left yesterday."

"Maybe you wouldn't of come back, but we don't haf to think about all dat. You won, and now we both done good. Is you gwinn to change yo clothes again?"

"No. I thought about it, but it's a long way over to the house where I stole this stuff I'm wearing, and I'm in a big hurry, so I'll just keep 'em on."

"You mighty right. All them rich carpetbaggers over on that side of town got plenty of money. They don't need nothing back from the likes of me and you." The greenbacks disappeared into the bosom of her dress.

McLemore felt much better after he finished eating the cornpone and the big hunk of butter that the cook left within his reach. His having thought to stop at the boardinghouse kitchen made him think well of himself, too. As he slipped through the back door and prepared to move toward the Cumberland and the cotton warehouse, the cook called after him, "Good luck, Li'l Massa."

But he never felt good about going back to face Logan after one of his little fun episodes. However, McLemore had known for a long time that the severe look he got from the captain under such circumstances masked a certain mount of toleration of his juvenile antics. Just after he took command of the company, Logan went to a great deal of trouble to get McLemore and a sergeant out of a Richmond jail. That must have been at some cost because the major running the guardhouse was clearly in favor of court martial, at least for Lieutenant McLemore, First South Carolina Cavalry, who had been drunk and disorderly when he was dragged in. He knew that Logan's tolerance must have always cost him points with the men and maybe even with the regimental commander. The men surely read this as a favor granted to officers only, while the regimental commander—and the commander was certain to have heard about it—marked it down as a breakdown in discipline. So even if Logan chose only to swear and shake his head, McLemore always felt badly about what he'd cost his captain and the group—and it didn't make much difference if the group was a cavalry company or a little bunch of starving ex-prisoners.

When he reached the warehouse, McLemore found Logan sitting on the floor with his back against a bale of cotton, busily sewing a patch over a hole in his shirt. The captain glared at the lieutenant and immediately launched into the grumbling tirade that he reserved for such culprits. In a low, level voice he demanded, "McLemore, where the hell have you been? We should have been on the road early this morning, and here it is nearly sundown. I reckon you don't ever want to get back to Dallas County." The vein in his neck was swelling a bit, but McLemore had seen it jump much higher. "A Yankee sergeant and two civilians have been here looking for you a couple of times. What sort of trouble have you got in now?"

McLemore had to tell the story of the poker game and the Yankee major—but only the barest essentials. He tried to give the impression that there wasn't much to the whole thing and that surely the sergeant wanted to see him about some other matter. Then he played his big card; he had thirty-one dollars concealed in his shoe top. Of course Logan's glare fell away as he calculated how many things that money might buy. Hood would get his pants, after all, and maybe everyone would get some extra foodstuff. That was, if he could get the money away from that juvenile, and immediately.

Within fifteen minutes the five had gathered up their iron pot and were slipping down an alley behind the warehouse, pushing on rapidly until they found the Franklin Pike and then slowing down to their traveling speed. There were no patrols, either military or civilian, to delay their progress as they walked toward Franklin. It was a beautiful evening, and everyone except McLemore was rested and happy to be again moving south toward home. Li'l Georgia sang for an hour.

They passed a couple of burned-out houses as they walked, but surprisingly enough the area appeared to be in fairly good shape. Just before dawn they came up on a two-story, frame house set well back from the road. In the semidarkness it matched the description that McLemore remembered from Mr. Moore's conversation. Wanting broad daylight before approaching the house, Logan moved the men into a clump of trees situated between the road and the fence in front of the house. Like any group of soldiers who had just walked fifteen miles, Logan's men immediately went to sleep.

Logan crawled on the stone fence to watch the sun come up over the house and its outbuildings. A cock was crowing somewhere behind the barns, and a milch cow soon became visible grazing between the house and the front gate. A thin, bony horse walked out of the darkness behind the barns and joined the cow in the grass. As daylight grew brighter, Logan could see that the paint on the house was peeling badly and several shutters were lying on the ground. One of the square columns that had supported the roof was also down and lay propped up against the house. The trees and shrubbery were still in place and the house was still standing, but it would be a long time before this place was brought back to its former splendor. Surely thousands of similar cases were scattered throughout the South. The question was would there be enough energy left after Appomattox to attack these problems. As usual Logan thought of Dallas County and what he might find there. He knew nothing of what had happened in that part of Alabama, but facing reality he must assume that it was as bad—most likely much worse—there as it was in middle Tennessee.

It was full day by then, so he woke the men and sent McLemore up to the house. About half way up the drive McLemore met a decrepit old black man with a broken-handled hoe slung over his shoulder coming slowly down the drive. McLemore stopped to talk and they both turned and walked back up the hill to the house. A couple of dogs began barking furiously as they went around to the back.

The sun had begun to show above the horizon when McLemore came striding back with Mr. Moore, a short, red-faced old fellow. The old man welcomed the group to his home and began to apologize for its appearance, assuring them that all he needed was a few weeks to have it back to its rightful position as a showplace of the county. As he talked, he insisted on shaking hands with everyone. Thad and Li'l Georgia hung back, but he sought them out and presented each with his bone-crushing handshake.

"Captain, I'm sorry to say this, but I've got to hide you people in my barn until the Yankee patrols cut back some on their prancing about. I barely got off my poor old mare last night when up they came looking for McLemore here. You know they're accusing him of theft, assault and all sorts of crimes against the state, just as if our poor country was anything other than a prison," Mr. Moore said as he flung his hands about and looked nervously down the road toward the south.

Within five minutes the group was in the Moore hayloft, and with the exception of the captain who remained in the barnyard talking to their host all were again asleep. Mr. Moore continued to apologize for hiding the men in his barn while still appearing nervous about possible Yankee patrols. He explained that he had been getting along fairly well with the local occupying forces but that cavalrymen from Nashville had come by a couple of times during the night. No one had searched any of his buildings, but this could happen at any time and McLemore would certainly be arrested. However, there were too many people around who could not be trusted to risk moving anyone to a better hiding place during daylight. They would just have to stay put until nightfall.

Moore asked Captain Logan into his kitchen where the cook immediately put down two cups of steaming black coffee on the battered worktable, following with a plate of scrambled eggs and bacon. While they ate the old man talked about the desperate poverty after four years of war capped by a complete defeat. Logan looked out the window and saw four or five blacks moving around in the back yard. Finishing the last of his breakfast, he asked how the Moore place could feed all the people who seemed to be around.

"Well, it sure ain't easy. But up to now, we've been getting by. I hang around the Maxwell Hotel and manage to win a little money at their game table, almost all from our conquerors and betters, I might add. And for a price you can still buy food in the town of Franklin. However, it takes everything I can earn, anyways I can earn it, to keep us all eating."

"How many of our black friends do you have around?"

"There's only eight here now. They keep coming and going. Been that way since Federal units came in here. The bad thing is the ones that stay around are too old or too sick to do anything much," said Mr. Moore with a sigh. "Of the ones who are here now, only two of the women and one man are able to do a day's work. The rest eat and piddle around. But I guess we owe 'em."

Over Moore's shoulder Logan could see the cook nodding in agreement with the planter's last statement. This continuous discussion of the shortcomings and problems of the black people while they were standing by had always seemed discourteous and almost foolhardy to Logan. He had thought this during slavery days, and it certainly was even less sensible now that they were free. Logan offered a quick prayer that if the cook decided to poison some whites it would be after he and his people had left. The bacon and eggs with grits were awfully good, arsenic or not.

Moore mumbled at great length about how bad things were now and how so many of their problems could be traced directly to the new freedmen. It was going to be hard to make it, black or white, when winter came. Those who did not starve would probably freeze, and little if any work would get done until spring. He would hold everything together, but that would require a lot of card playing at the Maxwell. Logan wondered if the old fellow was about to ask that McLemore be left behind to help in this noble effort—but McLemore wouldn't be much help from a jail cell.

After half an hour of conversation the older man motioned to the captain to follow him. Draining the last swallow from his coffee cup, Logan walked after him into the bright sunshine. As they leaned over the back yard fence, Mr. Moore explained his plan to move McLemore to a shack a mile or so up a nearby creek as soon as it was dark. Before the war the shack had been used as a deer hunting base, but it would still turn away the rain. The old man said that in the meantime a man from Franklin had sent word he would like to come to see these recently released prisoners.

Around three o'clock a well-dressed man riding a flashy gelding arrived and hitched his mount in front of the house. Logan was talking with Mr. Moore in the shade of the oaks at the edge of the side yard and wondered what such a prosperous-looking individual could want with anyone on this run-down place. The visitor came over, all smiles, to greet Mr. Moore. Without waiting for a reaction from the old planter, he put out his hand to Logan and said, "Cap'n, I'm Sidney P. Ochs. I practice law in Franklin, sell a little property and that sort of thing. Just call me Sid."

Mr. Moore looked a bit annoyed at Ochs's enthusiastic entrance into their conversation, but he turned to Logan and said, "Yeah, Cap'n, Sid here wants to talk to you and your people about a plan he's working on."

"Yes, sir. I've got a real proposition for you people. I've got me a contact in that warehouse you stayed in up in Nashville, and he let me know when you came in. I came right on out because I know you're going to be interested." Ochs fixed Logan with a pair of piercing eyes and kept moving about as he talked.

Moving away from the eyes Logan said, "Mr. Ochs, me and my men are at the point that we have to consider anything that's legal and that doesn't keep us from getting to Selma, Alabama, by Christmas. However, I can't imagine what we'd be worth to anyone in our present shape."

The lawyer moved over to the shade and sat down without waiting for an invitation. Mr. Moore scowled at this presumption but motioned to Logan that they should join him on the bench.

Ochs continued, "Cap'n, I've heard of you and McLemore, and I'm ready to make you a proposition that you'll just have to grab up. I'm ready to take your other three men along as well, if they'd like to join us."

Logan made no reply. He simply looked back at Ochs and waited for him to continue. Moore shifted about nervously as though he knew full well what was coming and was not particularly looking forward to the experience.

Ochs pushed on, "I'll come right to the point. I'm helping organize a group from Nashville that will be going down into Mexico to help stabilize the dangerous situation down there. Some of our important businessmen think they can find land down there that will support some form of plantation agriculture. We've contacted Maximilian's government, and his people go along with our plan. However, there's rebel groups all over the place in Mexico, so there will be some fighting to be done, and that's where people like you come in. Both you and McLemore have excellent reputations as fighting men. We know that we need you, and we hope that you will see that you need us."

Disbelief probably best described Logan's reaction to this harangue. He sat there with half his hand shot away and most of an ear sliced off, and this fool lawyer was trying to sign him up for some kind of contract war. With difficulty he refrained from outright laughter and managed to maintain a poker face.

"Well, sir, I can't speak for McLemore, and he just might consider such a thing—but as for me, I must push on for home as fast as I can. I wouldn't recommend two of the enlisted men for such an affair. One is sick and the other is quite young and immature. The sergeant in my group would undoubtedly do you a good job, but I think he's got his heart set on getting home to Georgia before

Christmastime. But I'll pass on your proposition to them and let them decide."

Like any true salesman Ochs did not give up easily. He continued to argue his proposition. As he talked, it became clear that he had no plan personally to go south of the Rio Grande. He droned on about organizing black labor gangs for shipment to Mexico to work on ranches, which sounded a whole lot like plantations, to be set up there. The Mexican laboring class would not be overjoyed about this competition, so force would probably have to be used. Ochs talked vividly of the obscene amount of profits they expected to make, not giving many details about how this would be done but generalizing about how easily money could be made in primitive countries. He ended by asking Logan to come to Franklin and meet some of the other men he described as shareholders in the project.

After Ochs had ridden off toward town, Logan turned to his host. "Is this sharpie for real? This whole business sounds a bit like an opium dream. How's he going to get a bunch of ex-slaves to follow someone down into Mexico and voluntarily return to slavery on some white man's plantation? No wonder he's looking around for some unemployed professional soldiers to sign up. There ought to be plenty for them to do in their field."

"Yeah, Sid Ochs is a sharp trader, but I'll have to say this, he's plenty clever and gets things done. I'd say that there's a good chance that he'll have a bunch of field darkies, along with some white killers, down below the Rio Grande by late winter. As for himself he'll be in San Antonio in that hotel across from the old Alamo."

"Well, I'm sure the Mexicans leave a little bit to be desired in the organized fighting area, but there's plenty of 'em. So old Sid had better get together a whole bunch of recently released Rebels, and maybe a Yankee or two mixed in, if he hopes to do anything worthwhile down there."

"Cap'n Logan, he's already got a half dozen or so signed up. They're hanging around Franklin waiting for the starting signal. I'd really guess that your Lieutenant McLemore is a prime candidate to get mixed up in such a project. Of course, before he signs anything, he should know that the men who're waiting around town haven't seen a dime yet, and they're nearly about to starve. Another thing, I don't think Sid's got any idea where he's going to get his field hands, either. You know, there's not too many of these people here in Tennessee—thank God—so he's talking about going down into Alabama and Mississippi to do some recruiting."

Logan shook his head in disbelief that anyone would take such a scheme seriously. "I'll tell McLemore, of course. He's pretty wild, but even he'll be a little skittish of this. I guess I'd better go into Franklin to see Ochs and look a little deeper into this thing just to try to protect my lieutenant. He won't be able to go in himself without risking arrest, and besides I've got to go into town to get a pair of pants for one of our men."

Later Mr. Moore took Logan to see the place where he planned to hide McLemore. When they had walked down the pike about a half mile, they came to a mill on a creek. The dam and millpond seemed to be in good repair, but the building had several boards missing, leaving a hole through which some of the machinery was visible. Logan could see the mill wheels, several belts and some of the gear system connected to a large water wheel seen through a second hole on the opposite side of the building. The mill was badly in need of repair, which evidently had been started already judging from the sawhorses and carpentry tools scattered about.

As they walked by, Mr. Moore explained that the mill had been the most profitable enterprise on the place before the war but that marauding military units had left it in its present state. His son had been working on the project ever since his return from the army but still had a long way to go. At least it had not been burned, and the dam and millraces were still in place. Not much grain would be available for grinding this year anyway, and he hoped to have it going in time to handle the next year's crop. It would help if a couple of the blacks who had worked in the mill during slavery days would come back.

The edge of the millpond was a tranquil scene that seemed far removed from war and the destruction so evident along the pike. Here it was just a summer day in middle Tennessee with dragonflies darting about over a millpond where a bass jumped out now and then in an attempt to catch an insect venturing too near the surface. Moore led Logan away from the millpond and up the creek for several hundred yards, walking briskly until they had to slow down for the swampy area that followed the stream back into the thick woods.

After pushing through heavy cover for half an hour, they broke out into a clearing containing a small log hut. They walked up the slight mound to the building and pulled open the door, which was hanging by one hinge, and went inside. It was dark and smelled of decaying wood, but it appeared to be dry enough. A broken-down bed without a mattress in one corner and a battered table and two chairs with flat boards for seats took up most of the room.

Once more Moore began apologizing for the poor accommodations. "I'm sorry, but this is the best we can do. It don't look like anyone's been around for some time, so I suppose it's pretty safe. Most of our people do know about this place, and I would feel a lot better about it if they didn't, but that can't be helped. We'll bring McLemore up here after dark and hope they don't see us. I don't think that over two or three of our people saw your group come in this morning. When we move McLemore, we'll bring along some foodstuffs and make sure that any other contact with him is made during darkness."

"This is fine, Mr. Moore. McLemore is an old soldier and a tough one; he'll get along just fine. He'll know he can't build a fire, chop wood, or anything like that. This is a whole lot better than a jail cell in Nashville. I'll probably send Li'l Georgia to stay with him. That's to give the lieutenant a lot of good church singing to keep up his morale."

When they went back outside, two white tail does that were grazing in a clearing no more than fifty feet away spun around and bounded into the heavy cover. The two men walked back toward the mill, accompanied only by the chattering of squirrels in the timber. They walked in silence while Logan thought about how much trouble McLemore could be. All of this difficulty simply because he had insisted on taking money from a Yankee officer in a poker game. Logan had to admit, though, that without the poker game there would have been no money for those new pants he hoped to buy in Franklin the next day. Then his mind pulled up the picture of what a wild man McLemore had been at Brandy Station, and he suddenly felt less troubled about the whole thing.

When black darkness came, Moore led Logan with McLemore and Li'l Georgia back to the shack. There they left McLemore and his companion with five corn hoecakes, a piece of cooked middling meat, six baked sweet potatoes and a promise to return the following night.

As they prepared to move off into the darkness, McLemore said, "Cap'n, why don't you all just leave me here? After all, I'm to blame for all this. And you know that I'll get home sometime. The rest of you need to get going toward Dallas County."

"Now, lieutenant, you know damn well that we're not going off and leave anybody. Not even you. However, we don't feel a damn bit sorry for you, 'cause your setting out here in the woods is all of your own doing. So just calm down and lay around until we come back and tell you it's all right to come back to the house." This said, Logan followed Moore into the darkness and was gone.

A couple of days went by with Logan, Jackson and Hood eating in the family kitchen; they even met Moore's wife and ten-year-old grandson. However, the son who was supposedly working on repairs to the mill did not appear. The wife did not enter into the conversations about the war and the horrors of life after defeat, subjects that dominated all talk at the Moore table. She seemed to Logan to be withdrawn. Certainly that attitude applied to domestic life; she appeared totally disinterested in the activities of the cook although Mr. Moore seemed to monitor the muttering black woman's every move. The other blacks, who were constantly hovering about the kitchen door, were ignored by the mistress of the place. She did not seem to know or care about the welfare of any of those people. Only once did she display much interest in anything—when one of the ex-slaves announced that the planter's ancient mare had gone off her feed. At that point Mrs. Moore immediately left her chair in the corner and went to the stables to investigate.

"That's typical of Martha," announced Moore. "She's not much interested in what takes place around here unless it happens down at the stables. And all we got down there now is my old mare, three broken-down mules and a milch cow. Just barely enough to keep her interest up. I'll have to say, though, she's damn good with 'em."

The next day Logan walked into Franklin and searched out Ochs's office. The lawyer was installed in rooms over a dry goods store directly opposite the courthouse. Logan climbed the stairs and went into a reception room. The office door in the back wall was closed at the moment. Two men were already seated at a bare pine table in the middle of the room. One was a slight, nervous fellow, perhaps fifty years old. The other, a huge man with a short-cropped beard and a long, livid scar across his face, was somewhat younger. He glared at Logan, who noted that three of the man's lower front teeth were missing. Logan exchanged nods with the men and sat down in a chair placed against the wall.

About twenty minutes later, the office door opened and Sid Ochs came out to greet them. He introduced the big man as John Paul Slaughter, one of the shareholders in the Mexican project, and the other man as Jeff Jones, Slaughter's assistant. After a few moments of talk about the heat of the July day, he gave a large envelope to Slaughter, who began to go through its contents, handling over some of the papers to his assistant. Ochs motioned Logan to follow him into the office.

The office contained a big table piled high with papers and books, several wooden chairs, two bookcases and a closed cabinet. On the walls were pictures of Lee, Napoleon, Sir Walter Scott, and, of course, Washington. A short barreled carbine was hanging over the fireplace. Logan wondered why the Federal authorities had not picked up that little souvenir when they swept through Franklin. He sat down across the table from Ochs and waited for the sales talk.

Ochs straightened his tie and began. "Well, I'm very glad that you could come in, Captain Logan. I know you're going to like what I've got to show you." With that preamble he launched into an unbroken speech, listing the many good things that awaited the true, southern entrepreneur in the land south of the Rio Grande. After several minutes of this assault Logan concluded that he would be offered no more concrete facts about the Mexican scheme than he had already been given. His mind had begun wandering when suddenly the lawyer stated that Slaughter was a trusted underling who was to go to Alabama and Mississippi to recruit field hands. Logan immediately felt sorry for any black who fell into that individual's hands.

"Just what do you expect the military people that you're recruiting to do?" Logan slipped in his question when Ochs paused to catch his breath.

"Oh, there'll be plenty to do. However, I suppose security will be the biggest job. We're moving out of Nashville in a few days with a couple of wagons and a dozen or so blacks who'll be used to locate campsites along the Natchez Trace. We hope that we'll be following this route when we start moving the main labor force down towards Mexico. We'll go from Natchez to New Orleans by foot and wait there for a boat to carry us across to the mouth of the Rio Grande. Naturally, we'll need some security people to keep control of the column."

"Naturally," said Logan. "And you'd better have a bunch of good horses for the security people to ride if you expect to maintain control."

"Of course. That's why we're looking for cavalrymen. We've got most of the horses already and they will go with us on the boat over to Mexico. You'll want to come out to our farm and look at 'em."

"Your farm?" asked Logan.

"Yes, sir. We've rented a place west of town where we're gathering up a lot of the things we think we'll need for the trip. Wagons, gear, tools and things like that."

"And what do the military people do once the expedition gets to Mexico?"

"Well, first off, we think that it will be necessary to drive most of the natives away from the area we're going to operate in. Then, almost certainly, we'll have to maintain watch on the labor force so that it stays in place." Ochs shifted around nervously and straightened his new suit. The lawyer's burning eyes shifted rapidly back and forth between the captain and a pile of papers that he continued shuffling as he talked.

"Yeah, seeing that these people don't wander off should be quite a job. But probably not as tough as seeing that they stay bunched up and walking tor'd Mexico. Now, that's going to be bad." Logan meant to sound sarcastic, but Ochs did not react to his effort.

After a bit more conversation, none of which seemed to be leading anywhere, Logan reminded Ochs that he was not interested in the proposition but would pass the information on to Lieutenant McLemore. Logan was ready to leave when Ochs suddenly asked if he could send Slaughter along with Logan and his group on their way to Alabama. Slaughter had not traveled in that area before and might need some guidance. Logan left without making any promises and began walking back to the Moore farm. He wished he could refuse to accept Slaughter as a member of the group, but he feared that such a position might queer the whole deal.

When Logan reached the Moore house, the blacks who were normally puttering about the yard were nowhere to be seen. Opening the kitchen door, he saw Moore and his wife sitting at the table with worried looks on long faces. Neither spoke as he walked to the table and sat down.

"Well, what's the bad news? What's happened?"

"The Yankees have arrested McLemore," said Moore with a deep sigh. "One of our people told the patrol leader about the shack up in the woods, and they went and picked him up. They let your boy, that one from Georgia, go."

"Damn it, that's all from gambling with those people. I guess he got what was coming to him. Where did they take him?"

"There's good news there, at least. They took him to Franklin, not back to Nashville. Here, I'm trying to determine which one of our people turned him in. I've sent them all to their quarters without anything to eat, and I'll start questioning them after we have our supper."

Breaking her customary silence, Martha said, "J. D., you'd better go get that sorry cook out of her cabin and get her in here rustling up some supper; that is, if she and the rest of those almighty freedmen want anything to eat today. I think we've been too soft with these creatures, and that's what brings on things like tattling to the Yankees. And it don't help any getting tangled up in their card games in the first place." No suggestion of just who might be the indicated gambler, but the old planter's glare told that the comment had struck home. He got up and went out to find the cook.

Much later they sat eating grits and side meat dished up from the cook stove by Martha Moore herself. The planter had told them that the cook and one of the men had left without good-byes and were the prime suspects as McLemore's betrayers. Mrs. Moore was clearly outraged because she would now have to do the cooking. She argued that the six remaining blacks should not be fed until they came up with the whereabouts of the cook, which she held that they knew. Mr. Moore denied this plea without comment as to its wisdom. He did, however, go to work assisting her in preparing the food for the labor force. Martha Moore looked thunderbolts at the blacks as they shuffled by the back door to pick up their portion of the grits and side meat. Despite the looks they got from Mrs. Moore, Logan noticed that they appeared to get about as much food as the whites got.

The following morning Logan, this time with Moore, walked back into Franklin and again climbed the stairs to the office of Sidney Ochs, Esquire. This time they had come to plead for help in getting McLemore released from the Federal guardhouse. Of course, the lawyer knew they had no money, but he listened to their story as he smoked his cigar and rested one foot in one of the desk drawers. A couple of horseflies had flown in the open window, and the lawyer appeared to be giving his undivided attention to their travels about the room as Logan completed his story and waited.

Finally Ochs spoke. "Yeah, I heard this morning that the Feds had McLemore in their guardhouse. I understand that they're holding him on suspicion of grand theft, assault and maybe attempted murder. If I'd a known that he was such a bad actor, I don't suppose I would have been looking for him as a stockholder in our project."

Stockholder indeed, thought Logan, but he said, "Let me tell you, he's done none of those things. McLemore's a bit wild, but he's no criminal and certainly not given to random violence of that sort. However, he's a very fine soldier and violent enough in that sense—and that's for sure."

"So I understand," said Ochs with a little wry smile. He continued, "That's why we still want him for our project. I'll look into getting him released." Ochs straightened his cravat and ended, "Understanding, of course, that he'll sign on as a security man for our little trip into Mexico."

"You know that I can't commit McLemore to that. But if you'll get him out, I promise not to advise him against going. That's as far as I can go."

One of the horseflies continued around the room and finally came to rest atop Napoleon's picture. The lawyer stared at the fly and drawled, "Well, if I can get two axe murderers and half the thieves in Williamson County out of jail, surely I can figure out a way to get your certified Confederate hero out of the calaboose. And just in time to make his fortune down south of the border."

"You won't regret doing something for this boy, Sid," said Moore. "I feel sorta responsible for his predicament because I got him into that card game up in Nashville. That damn Yankee major should have taken his losses like a man instead of whining around trying to get money back that he had lost fair and square."

"Well, I said I'd see what I can do for this prize lieutenant. I think the thing to do is to get in to see the lieutenant colonel who's the area commandant here in

Franklin. Once we get in, we'll expend all our capital—using the term very loosely, of course—in trying to get McLemore released before any formal charges are brought. These occupation officials have tremendous power to make decisions as to who gets held for trial, and maybe we can touch this one's heart."

Twenty minutes later Ochs, Logan and Moore were in the waiting room outside the force commander's office. The room was full of people hoping to see this august official. Logan and Moore sat on a bench in the corner while Ochs circulated, making himself familiar with everyone's business. When he returned to his companions, he had a rather complete sketch of everyone's mission. The two seedy men near the door to the inner office were to present a plea for a 500-pound sugar allotment to be used to make a batch of corn liquor, which according to them was badly needed by the population. They even went so far as to hold that their little project would stimulate the local economy. An old woman and her daughter, both in near-rags, were there to plead for the release of the daughter's husband, who was being held in the guardhouse on suspicion of assault with a deadly weapon. Since this assault had been on a member of the occupying force, the women had a difficult task when and if they got in to see the commandant. The pimply-faced youth wanted to join the Federal army, and the pregnant girl in the gingham dress was there to accuse one of the Yankee enlisted men of being the father of her onrushing child. That mature man was waiting to see the commandant because he had been in his old company back in 1862. And a flashy man smoking a cigar was offering to sell the Federal officer a bay saddle mare.

Two hours later Ochs and his companions were ushered into the inner office by a sergeant who said he was the commandant's secretary. As they entered, the Yankee officer got up and walked around his desk to shake hands with Ochs, who then introduced Logan and Moore.

Lieutenant Colonel Barker was tall and rangy and looked much younger than Logan had expected. In fact, he was almost sure that the Federal officer was younger than he was. Since there were no obvious scars or missing body parts, Logan assumed that the commandant had been some sort of headquarters soldier.

As the lieutenant colonel sat back down, he looked at Logan and said, "Well, I can see that you were a soldier in the Rebellion. What was your rank and outfit?"

"Sir, I was a captain and, at least at the end, I commanded A Company of the First South Carolina Cavalry."

"Wade Hampton's own, eh?" I was an infantryman myself. Had C Company of the Third Indiana during the early days of the war. I saw something of you people at Gettysburg and again—a couple of times really—around Petersburg. Can't say as I enjoyed the experience."

"No, neither of those places was all that amusing," said Logan, questioning his original assumption that the commandant was a headquarters type.

Ochs and Moore presented their case for the release of McLemore, Ochs coming right to the point by saying that he needed McLemore for his Mexican venture. The commandant obviously had some previous knowledge of this scheme. The discussion included generalities about what McLemore would be able to do on the trip south and once they reached Mexico. Still no details about the plan, such as routes or final destination, were given. If such details had been worked out, they were certainly being held close to the vest. Logan began to get the impression that they did not exist.

Ochs was clearly trying to convince the commandant of the value of his plan for the Franklin area, mentioning the money that would come back to Franklin and Williamson County and dwelling at length on the number of local people to be employed. Eventually he got around to saying that every black who went to Mexico would be one less left in the Franklin area to be taken care of by Federal funds. Barker's reactions gave no indication of an opinion of the merits of Ochs's arguments. It came as a bit of a shock to Logan that this commander of the occupying force might even be interested in the well-being of his assigned area.

Ochs was back to why McLemore should be released. "This guy really didn't do a damn thing, Colonel. You know that. Just gambled with people that he should have left alone. Too bad that he won; if he had lost, the commandant of the Franklin area would have never heard that he was alive."

"Maybe so," said Barker, "but I've got a signed complaint here that tells another story. Captain Logan, just what kind of man is this McLemore?"

"Colonel, he's no Sunday school boy, that's for sure. If there's liquor to be drunk, women to be chased or gambling to be done, he's right there in the front row. But he's honest, and I'd bet my life that he never assaulted nobody 'cept in self-defense. I know for sure that he was a very fine soldier who had his part of a lot of campaigns. He was in my company in the First Carolina Cav until the last year of the war, when he went off to ride with Mosby. Around January of '65 he was captured. Ended up in Rock Island with me."

At this point Moore broke in. "Sir, I knew the lieutenant's father back before the war. He's from a very fine family who are big time planters down close to Selma."

Logan cringed at this statement. No points would likely be made by reminding this Yankee professional soldier that he was deciding the fate of a member of the southern planter class. But the damage, if indeed there was any, had been done. Barker's poker face betrayed no reaction to the statement.

"Ochs," said the commandant, "I think your venture should be good for Franklin and the whole Nashville area, for that matter. We must get some business efforts going and quickly. I'm ready to support such plans in any way that's legal and within my authority. However, I'll have to look further into Lieutenant McLemore's case and try to decide what's just and fair for all concerned."

"Thank you, sir. That's all we ask," replied Ochs.

As they were moving toward the door, the commandant suddenly spoke to Logan. "Captain, thanks for your comments on McLemore. I'll keep them in mind at decision time."

Leaving the commandant's office, they walked the two blocks over to the guardhouse to visit with McLemore. Ochs must have greased some palms for the prisoner was brought from the stockade to the visiting room within five minutes of their arrival. The lieutenant was his usual cynical self and showed no signs of being disturbed by his latest confinement, his only complaint being that the food was evidently meant for pigs and had ended up at the stockade by mistake. The sheds under which the prisoners slept were hot, and he expected a lot of roof leaks if it should rain; but as a Southerner he did not find this so bad. At least it wasn't cold.

The possibility of a trip to Mexico in exchange for his release was introduced by Moore. McLemore asked for details, of course, but did not appear shocked by the outline of the plan as explained by Ochs.

McLemore was still smiling his little crooked smile as he said, "So, we're going to keep 'em in slavery somehow. I'd guess you could get a couple of hundred to sign up. That is, if you throw a little money around as bait. But after you get them all grouped up here in Franklin and ready to start south, that's when the fun begins."

Ochs smiled a bit tightly and continued, "We'll start 'em off easy, walking about fifteen miles a day and work up to around twenty-five a day by the time we get down into south Mississippi. Only the sick get to ride in the wagons."

"I assume you're taking men only—no women or children."

"Of course, we don't want any hangers-on when we get down into Mexico. Just workers. And once they're down there, we've got to control 'em so we can keep 'em there. We can't handle a lot of moving back and forth between here and the production site."

"Well, I'd sure try to keep that a secret as long as I could," again with the twisted smile, "because once they find out they're going a thousand miles away to work some kind of Mexican plantation, with the women back in Alabama and Mississippi, they're going to be awful hard to hold in one bunch."

"Yeah, I'm sure you're right," said Ochs. "That's why we need people like you to help maintain control."

"As I understand it, there's also a lot of revolutionary activity going on down there. I don't see how we can operate very well in an area that's got guerrilla operations going on. Just where in Mexico are we going?"

"That hasn't been decided yet. We're in contact with the people in Emperor Maximilian's government about the best place to set up our farming operation."

By this time Logan felt that McLemore had decided this whole scheme was a farce—which Logan had decided for himself long ago—and that agreeing to assist Ochs would be a relatively easy way out of the Federal stockade. McLemore's aims became quite clear when he began questioning Ochs about contracts on specific terms of service—such things, of course, would not be determined until later. The only ongoing activities were recruiting and planning for the great march south. Logan guessed that the lieutenant would agree to almost anything so long as no papers were signed. This proved to be the case, and twenty minutes later they had departed with Ochs completely satisfied with his new recruit.

Ochs went back to the commandant's headquarters to make final arrangements for McLemore's release, and Logan and Moore started the long walk back to the plantation. The midsummer day was beautiful, with mockingbirds, squirrels and cardinals chattering in the trees along the road. Logan marched along thinking about how everything was falling into place; it looked like McLemore would be released in a day or two and would probably go off to Mexico with Ochs's people, leaving Logan free to gather up his other three soldiers and move out for Dallas County. With any luck they should be home within a month. Maybe things weren't so bad after all.

When they reached the gate to the Moore place, Jackson was sitting on a stump waiting for them. He got up and crushed Logan's vision of Dallas County within a month by announcing, "Cap'n, Thad Hood's sick again. Pretty bad sick."

CHAPTER III

McLEMORE RIDES TO NATCHEZ

McLemore turned in the saddle and looked back at the blacks toiling slowly up the hill. Although they numbered only twenty-three, scattered out over two hundred yards they appeared to be a much larger group. Looking over them and to the rear, he could still see the church steeples in Franklin. Not a whole lot of distance covered in four hours.

The clothes he wore were those he had stolen in Nashville. Nothing had been added, not even boots. He had the same low-quarter shoes that he had worn since the raid on the Yankee barracks in Louisville. At least he was on a horse, boots or not.

Strangely enough, he had a pistol, obviously a weapon in violation of some regulation of the occupation. Without an explanation of any sort and in view of the Yankee commandant, Ochs had handed him the weapon just as they moved off from the courthouse. A former Confederate officer wandering around the countryside three months after Appomattox certainly couldn't have a pistol, at least not legally—and a .44 caliber LeMat at that. During the war he had once seen a brigadier with one although he wasn't close enough as a mere lieutenant to get a good look at such a prize. To be issued the magnificent pistol three months after the end of the war was about like being handed a life preserver after safely landing on the beach, having ridden out a hurricane in a rowboat.

The whole adventure didn't look promising to McLemore, but, after all, he was out of jail. That was saying quite a bit, considering that he had been asked for neither a written nor a verbal promise. Ochs had paid a twenty-dollar fine to secure his release and undoubtedly there were other considerations unknown to him. He had overheard Wes Logan promising Ochs to take someone named Slaughter along on the walk into Alabama; Cap'n Logan didn't look at all happy about this, but Ochs had insisted. Additionally, Logan would keep that thirty dollars of poker winnings that must be hidden at the Moore house.

Whatever the pressure used to arrange for his release, it had been applied before he had been brought out of the stockade. The Yankee commandant had simply released him to the custody of Ochs without any explanation other than saying that the only charge that was backed by a convincing story was disorderly conduct. Therefore, the twenty-dollar fine paid by Ochs had closed his account with the Federal government. He got the impression that the commandant wasn't too happy with Major Cleary's gambling habits, which seemed to be well known, nor with his devotion to duty.

In addition to himself and Ochs, five other whites were along to herd the party south. All the white men were mounted on fairly good-looking horses. The black laborers were all walking, and the two supply wagons had black drivers. The driver of the kitchen equipment wagon was also the cook. The other wagon was loaded with bedrolls, tent flies and tools.

Their targeted two miles per hour—which would be increased to two and a half miles per hour after a couple of days—were rolling by without incident on a nice, bright day. The road was reasonably smooth, and they had encountered only two small creeks, which were forded without difficulty. Some of the steeper hills in this part of Tennessee made for hard climbing, but the roads were graveled and most mud holes had dried up in the summer sun.

McLemore felt good to be riding again. The little mare that he had been issued proved to be sure-footed and gave every indication that she could carry the old McClellan saddle and the 150-pound man for ten or twelve hours without any danger of stumbling. Such a mount made a man feel like riding off after Mosby again, turning east out of the Shenandoah and riding in search of the headwaters of the Potomac. It had been seven or eight months since he had done anything such as that, and this was probably the first time since then that such a picture had crossed his mind. He sure wished he had some better clothing, at least some boots, but otherwise things were coming along rather well.

As he rode along, McLemore thought about Wes Logan—still Captain Logan to him, of course—and the people back in Franklin. Hood was sick again and that meant it would be at least two or three weeks before the group could get moving for Alabama. Maybe he could get back off this wild safari before they moved out. The only thing he knew about this trip was that they were to reconnoiter a route down to New Orleans for a larger group who would be coming along in a month or two and cross over by ship to the Rio Grande before heading down into Mexico to operate some sort of plantation. He supposed that he was armed so that he could furnish the necessary encouragement to the blacks when they found out that they were going to walk at least a thousand miles and would have to work on a cotton plantation when they arrived. He wondered if Ochs knew just where they were trying to go in Mexico. As though she were the one who knew, the little mare trotted along on the level stretches and took her time on the slopes, reacting happily to the loose rein he gave her.

At the three o'clock break, Ochs told McLemore to go on ahead with Trab Scott, who evidently was second in command, to find a place to bivouac for the night. Following a short conference with him, Ochs handed Scott a map; McLemore followed Scott out to the road and off toward the southwest. Scott held the map upside down, squinting, rolling his head from side to side and looking uncomfortable.

The two horsemen soon left the walking group far behind and an hour later located a grove of trees on the far side of a wide creek. The ground was firm and partially protected from the elements by the trees, and it was certainly shady. Several burned out campfires and some downed trees told them that the spot had been used as a campsite before. While Scott sat in the shade of a big oak and puzzled over the map, McLemore rode over to a farmhouse visible at the edge of a clearing across the road. The farm family had evidently seen plenty of armed men since they came out reluctantly and were visibly relieved to learn that their visitor seemed to want nothing more than a chance to pass the time of day. The farmer's wife even offered him a gourd of water from the well in the corner of the small fenced yard. He drank and refilled his canteen.

The farmer loosened up enough to volunteer that during the war the big oak grove had been used at least a dozen times as a bivouac area for large parties—some Blue, some Gray—but no big group had been through during the past year. He was clearly relieved when McLemore told him that the Ochs party was not military and would be moving on after staying overnight. The farmer was not interested in what these new visitors were doing, as long as they moved on the next day. He seemed pleased when McLemore told him that the blacks would be tightly controlled by the seven whites riding with the operation.

After twenty minutes of conversation, the farmer relaxed enough to tell McLemore that one of his sons had joined a Federal cavalry unit late in the war while his two older boys had gone off much earlier with the Confederates. One of these had been killed at Shiloh, and the other had been captured and not yet released. This son had sent a letter some time ago telling them that he would soon be coming home. The wife explained that the son could not write and someone from his barracks had helped him out by doing the actual writing. Then they confessed that the actual reading had been done by the village storekeeper since the parents themselves had some trouble with this baffling science. The boy who had joined the Federals had gotten through the war in good shape and had already returned.

Preparing to leave, McLemore invited the farmer and his wife to share their evening meal, to be cooked as soon as the main party closed on the bivouac area. The farmer accepted with enough enthusiasm to tell him that food was scarce in this part of Tennessee.

When he returned to the bivouac site, McLemore helped Scott in the laying out of their encampment. They selected and laid out a trench latrine, which he naturally thought of as the sinks, and picked out a spot for the blacks to use for sleeping. They hoped that merely a spot on the ground would be all that was needed for a summer night in the South. A canvas tent fly would be stretched between the two supply wagons, which would be satisfactory for the seven white men since two would always be on watch. McLemore suggested that two of the blacks be placed on each watch to assist the whites. Four people up and awake at all times should be satisfactory for this size encampment. Scott was clearly not enthused by McLemore's scheme—it probably smelled a bit too much like the old army—but he went along without falling into overt opposition. After all, any guy who looked like this fellow just might know what he was talking about.

"When we start bringing the next bunch of these people through, we've got to get a couple of pieces of canvas for 'em to sleep under. They're not campaigning soldiers, and if we don't arrange for some sort of shelter for 'em, we're going to have somebody sick with pneumonia." Scott looked rather skeptical about the whole approach, but he let McLemore continue. "They can fix up a fairly good shelter out of a strip of canvas and some rope."

"Okay. We'll ask for it on the next trip. I guess Ochs can come up with that much, and it'll probably be worthwhile." Scott looked away and almost sighed. "That is if there is a next trip, and if you and I live through this one."

"We will, we will. Think about how good it's going to be when we get to Natchez," said McLemore with his little cynical smile. "And just think about that Natchez Under the Hill spot."

Turning their attention to gathering wood for the cooking fire, they walked into the woods and found a dead tree felled by a recent storm and with a little work soon had enough piled up for their needs. They moved part of the wood to the campsite in order to have a fire going when the cook arrived. Of course the cook would keep the fire going all night so that he could prepare the morning meal. The blacks would be sent to get the remainder of the wood later. McLemore organized most of these preparations, clearly impressing Scott and putting him on guard against losing his position to this new man. They finished their preparations twenty minutes before the main body arrived.

Within another twenty minutes, the cook was busy cooking potatoes and salt pork for their evening meal. Some corn pone and three big pots of hot coffee were available to all hands. Scott stood with McLemore and watched the blacks file through for food dished out into their metal plates and cups. The whites got their food served family-style on a small folding table, but all got the same fare. Scott seemed to accept this procedure without question and waited with McLemore until all the other had picked up their food.

About the time the main group had completed their meal, the farmer appeared, accompanied by a younger man, dark and swarthy and with a strong resemblance to the older man. Seeing them together in the half-light, McLemore suddenly realized that they were probably part American Indian. Scott, who had been told about McLemore's invitation, took the initiative and asked the visitors to sit at the folding table and eat with him and McLemore. The older man asked if he could send his wife a plate. It was immediately dispatched through the younger man, a slender youngster who had been introduced as the farmer's son without mention that the boy had been in the Yankee army. The young man returned after a quarter of an hour and, seating himself on a log, began to eat with a will. McLemore noticed that the farmer and his son ate more hungrily than did the blacks, despite the fact that the ex-slaves had been walking all day.

As they finished eating, the farmer began to talk about the difficulty of making a living during these stressful times. For at least a year it had been almost impossible to do more than just put skimpy meals on the table. Of course, there had been no repairs on buildings and equipment and no new clothing or shoes. The farm was operated with two old oxen since there hadn't been a mule on the place since 1862. Finally, after all this, which evidently had been used to prepare his listeners, the farmer ended up with a bold request. "Can you take my boy along to help out on your trip? He won't expect any pay or equipment, just his grub. The three of us are just too many people to get by here right now. He's a hard worker and surely can earn his keep. Think about it tonight and let me know in the morning."

Ochs broke into the conversation. "Well, I can tell you now that we can use him, if he is prepared to walk and if he can pull his load. He looks like he could."

"Yes sir. He's ready to go. He only got the clothes on his back. You won't be sorry."

The young man said nothing. He simply smiled and nodded in agreement.

"Okay. Be here and ready to go about an hour 'fore day. As for coming home, which I know you're interest in, we should be through here on the return trip in about three or four weeks. You should know by then if you want to stay with this project."

McLemore decided to let the young man's association with the Federal army slip by for the time being. There would be plenty of time to face that after someone else found out about it. After all, they were really doing this whole thing at the sufferance of the Yankee army anyway. So he went over and lay down under the tent fly.

The farmer's son, who had been introduced as Johnnie South, joined them the following morning just as the formation started to move out. They fell immediately into their routine of two miles of walking per hour with a ten-minute break at the end of each period. This routine was followed throughout the day with an hour break around noon. When they bivouacked at the end of the day, Ochs announced they had covered twenty-five miles during twelve hours of walking. Studying the map, McLemore figured they had come almost thirty miles. But Ochs's little misrepresentation was no big thing; when the going got rough because of storms and bad roads, they would be lucky to make fifteen miles a day.

Johnnie South, walking straight and tall behind the supply wagons, appeared to be doing as well as the blacks. The laborers each had a bundle on the wagon, but McLemore know that South had nothing other than the clothing he was wearing. The new man was slight in stature, almost gaunt, but he appeared to be as tough as most of the ex-slaves as he moved along after the supply vehicles. To this point, nobody had expressed any curiosity about the new man's background, and there was no indication that the man had volunteered any. Riding in the rear, McLemore came to the decision that bringing along another white had been a good move. The cheap hustlers running this operation were getting another man for the cost of his food. As far as McLemore knew, that might be all that he was getting himself; but, after all, Ochs had gotten him out of jail. Additionally, he was confident that if anything was made out of this long march then he would somehow get his part.

After three or four days, the group settled down to a routine. They were walking about ten hours a day with one hour out at mid-day. Ochs was still announcing that they were making twenty-five miles per day, but McLemore's map kept telling him that it was more like thirty. The exception was the day they were delayed for almost two hours by thunderstorms. Picking up the old Natchez Trace, they crossed a corner of Alabama and were moving into Mississippi toward Jackson.

Just after they crossed into Mississippi, Johnnie South pointed out a rough trail that he said led back into Alabama and to the village of Waterloo. The steamboat landing on the Tennessee River near Waterloo had been used by President Jackson to load out many of the Cherokees from Alabama and Georgia for the trip to Oklahoma. One of South's grandmothers had escaped from the compound where she and her child were awaiting loading and had hidden in the vicinity for two years. She had eventually located the South family and resumed her life as the wife of South's grandfather. McLemore thought this story explained both South's physical appearance and his unusual stamina.

McLemore was finding the whole trip not totally unpleasant. Certainly the unpleasantness was not much compared to that of the war. These days on the trip and the days during the war were similar in their monotony, but the severity of the war days made any other comparisons inappropriate since the whole experience of the trip was several notches ahead of anything he remembered about 1862-1864. The really bad time spent at Rock Island in 1865 was not even in the running.

In this operation a kind of sameness extended from day to day. One of the blacks slipped down a steep bank and ended up with a broken arm and a badly twisted knee, so he was now riding in the supply wagon. A white had accidentally fired a pistol round through the fleshy part of his leg and had to be left behind in a tavern near the Mississippi line. Johnnie South was now riding that man's mule. Otherwise, everything seemed to be moving along fairly well. The weather was not bad, and the food, although the same each day, was plentiful.

As soon as McLemore made it clear that he was not interested in taking over as second-in-command, Trab Scott began to soften toward this assistant who could relate the terrain to the paper picture of the map. McLemore overheard Scott telling Ochs that they could depend on the lieutenant to find his way cross country if they found the road closed. Ochs had even asked advice on two stream crossings and appeared satisfied with McLemore's answers. At lest no one was drowned when his advice had been taken.

Of the whites, McLemore sensed that he could trust the two O'Leary brothers to do almost anything they were assigned. Both of these short, talkative men appeared aggressive enough to attack almost any problem within reason—and even this limitation seemed to be flexible in their case. Johnnie South was riding his mule like a true cavalryman and had managed to conceal his past association with the Federal army. The last white was the big, rawboned Manesco—no one had ever heard his first name—who rode his tall awkward gelding rather badly, somewhat like an infantryman. A little conversation revealed that he was indeed a veteran of the Twenty-third Alabama Infantry. He had the impression of a big pocketknife in his pants pocket, and he wasn't much for smiling. McLemore felt that Manesco would be his man when it came to disciplining the blacks.

Trouble among the blacks was not slow in developing. A small yellow man with the straight features of an East African was evidently the instigator of the first incident. McLemore guessed that he was at least a quarter white. The other blacks, who shared the common West African features, called him Toby Bee. He complained to Scott that the leader of his gang was not dividing the tasks assignments during the evening break evenly. Although there were not many duties, nor were they stressful, after a few days on the road it seemed that they were just looking to quarrel about something. This accusation was well on the way toward a fistfight when McLemore broke them up. Both of the men seemed happy that someone forced them to be peaceful, but undoubtedly the blood still boiled beneath the surface.

Manesco volunteered that he would have just let them fight, but McLemore ignored this input. The O'Leary brothers might have been happy to see the fun, but they seemed to recognize that such entertainment often came at too high a price. Johnnie South, as usual, gave no indication of his feelings in the matter. The only reaction among the blacks was their moving in for a closer look when it appeared that a fight among their own people was about to start. McLemore was glad that Ochs and Scott were away on other business.

A break in the hostilities between the two blacks came after this incident as the group toiled slowly through two days of rain and slick roads. Stumbling through ankle-deep mud and the continuous pushing and pulling to keep the wagons moving kept all tempers cool. Another black ended up riding in the supply wagon, and everyone was constantly wet and covered with mud. On the second day of rain, they had to cross a swollen creek, which almost cost them the kitchen wagon. But thanks to the driver and the O'Leary brothers, a line was finally fastened to a tree on the far bank, allowing the frightened animals to pull the load through without loss. On the third day the rains stopped, and the road began to return to normal—still bad, but passable.

At the evening stop the next day, Toby Bee and his gang leader renewed their quarrel. Almost immediately a blow was struck and they went at it with a will, rolling about on the ground. Toby Bee seemed to hold his own against the bigger man until fatigue began to take its toll. The yellow man finally got a mouthful of the gang leader's shoulder and tore out enough flesh to assure a bloody mess. McLemore emptied one of the water buckets over the thrashing men, and the black spectators pulled them apart. Enough of the overseer psychology remained in McLemore to be sure that the fighters were separated in time to save valuable manpower. Toby Bee clearly got the bad end of the incident, but he emerged alive and able to walk. However, the fight ensured that there would not be much more complaining from the smaller man.

"Why didn't you let 'em go?" complained Manesco. "We'd probably be better off to have let the big black one kill the yellow."

"Well, it probably wouldn't have come to that. The gang leader would have banged him up quite a bit but probably wouldn't have killed him. Most of these people aren't really all that violent. Now, we might have had a problem if the half-white had been winning."

"I sure haven't seen it that way. I wouldn't have layed round and cried if they had both ended up dead. I know that a lot of the planters think that the yellow bastards are the worst kind, but they tend to think that all of 'em, troublemakers or not, are worth their weight in gold. Believe me, that's not my thinking. No, sir, not at all," Manesco explained without a suggestion of a smile. McLemore noted that the man hadn't actually called him a planter, but he got close to it. He wondered how the man could think of him as a planter since he even rode without boots.

"Yeah, I know these people have their problems, but we're going to have to rely on 'em for a long time. Maybe forever. We can't let 'em kill each other off over nothing." McLemore added, "That's the way it looks to me, anyhow."

Manesco looked somewhat disgruntled but decided to let the conversation drop rather than disturb a man he clearly thought might be dangerous.

McLemore did not discipline either black but allowed things to drift along, letting tempers cool and things slowly return to normal. When he talked to Scott about the incident, McLemore found that the older man tended to agree with his handling of the matter and hoped that the disagreement would be forgotten.

A day later Ochs came to McLemore about the incident. He hadn't see any part of the fighting but immediately assumed that no good could come from this sort of disturbance. He transferred Toby Bee to another gang, giving him plenty of instructions about how he was to avoid such disagreements in the future and the consequences if he got into another fracas. Ochs let McLemore know that he was displeased at having to lower himself to get involved in such matters and that he did not expect to have to do so again.

The big gang leader came out with only a sore upper arm where the yellow had bitten him.

Eventually Manesco came to McLemore to explain his position. He felt that the blacks must be tightly controlled—evidently accepting brutal handling as part of control—in order to get them safely to Mexico. "I tell ye, we got to keep right on 'em. Otherwise, they're going to get out of hand, and we'll really be in a hell of a shape. If they start fighting among theirselves, we'll have to kill a couple of 'em to get in charge again. These blacks just don't understand nothing but the gun and the lash."

"Well," said McLemore, "I worked with a good many of these people back before the war, and I think that we've still got fairly good control. Now that they think freedom has come, they're awful eager to figure out just what it means. And I know they don't have much idea what it does mean other than that now there's no more 'Ol' Massa' and somehow they won't have to work quite as hard as they once did. Of course, we don't know what it means ourselves.

"I guess that these particular men have figured out that they've got to do some work, free or not, or they wouldn't have agreed to come aboard for this operation. I know they don't know much of anything about what they've gotten tangled up in, but we've got to keep 'em organized and moving along toward Mexico. Maybe before we get to the Rio Grande, we whites will learn a little more about what to expect when we get south of the border, and then we can start trying to prepare 'em."

"I sure hope so," Manesco replied, hopelessly shaking his head. "I don't think that these people can do much toward taking care of theirselves, let alone do any real work."

"Well, I agree that it's pretty discouraging, but we got to do the best we can at pushing them along. I realize that changing four million blacks to true free men will take longer than we have years to live, but I suppose the people coming after us—maybe even a hundred years after us—and I include the black folks in that group—will reap the harvest. Of course, it's hard for these dear friends of Mr.

Lincoln to look at this with such a long-range view. However, I'm sure that a few such blacks do exist and that some of these people aren't really looking for much in their lifetime. I'm afraid that we all, blacks and whites, are in for a long spell of hard problems, maybe a couple of hundred years or so."

Manesco retorted, "I can't worry much about what's going to happen in a hundred years or so. I don't even have much hope for what's ahead in the next couple of years. That's as far as I can think."

Ochs came up and ended all their speculation by introducing a couple of immediate problems. McLemore was sent forward to check out the next stream crossing while Manesco on his gangling mount was sent back along the trail to help get the kitchen wagon out of a mud hole.

A couple of days before reaching the Vicksburg turn-off, the group stopped in a pine thicket next to a stand, or roadside inn, that had been welcoming travelers on the Trace since the early days of the road. This particular stand consisted of three buildings—a large frame house and two smaller log cabins—that had somehow managed to come through the war more or less intact.

McLemore walked to the frame building and sat on the edge of its sagging porch. A dirty-looking man who was sprawled on the porch with his head on a saddle informed him that there was nothing to eat in this so-called tavern. The bearded face came up from the saddle and looked incredulous when McLemore informed him that he had already eaten. The man raised up on one elbow, scratched himself and growled that there wasn't anything to do around there either, unless you counted listening to the preaching going on over in the brush arbor. He pointed to a ramshackle shelter in the copse of trees just across the road. Having passed on this information, he put his hand over the neck of the jug beside him, dropped his head back on the saddle and closed his eyes.

McLemore walked over to the brush arbor and stood looking at the dozen people who were sitting on the logs lined up in front of a rough platform, an elevated area made of undressed boards. Two boys, probably ten or twelve years old, were seated on a crude bench at the back of the platform. They were slumped over propped against their knees and looked out sleepily at the audience. A slender, middle-aged woman was leaning over a piece of sawed-off log that served as a pulpit and talking—or rather shouting and whispering by turn—to the people seated in front. One of the boys was suddenly seized with a series of violent jerks. Neither the speaker nor the audience appeared to be disturbed by the jerking or the rocking and groaning of the boy. The woman continued her almost unintelligible harangue while flailing away with both arms above her head. McLemore noticed that the jerking boy appeared to be a mulatto. The other boy, who evidently was white, seemed to ignore both the speaker's harangue and his cohort's jerking.

Suddenly the white boy leaped to his feet and yelled, "Praise the Lo'd! Praise the Lo'd! Jesus, have mercy on us all. Guide us to the light and keep us right. Yes, keep us right!" He repeated his original chant, gradually lowering his voice until he ended in a hoarse whisper, "Praise the Lo'd. Praise the Lo'd. Praise the Lo'd," and dropped back on the bench, slumping forward as though he had completely spent himself.

While this was happening, the lieutenant slipped forward and took a seat on the rearmost log. The woman did not appear to notice his entrance and continued her delivery at the same frantic pace. Finally she appeared to be winding down, speaking at a much slower pace. She leaned against her pulpit for about two minutes in complete silence then suddenly began to dance around on the platform. In her wild gyrations, she pulled the mulatto boy to his feet.

"This here is Soloman. Now, he's a sho nuff young gift from the Lord. Yes sirree. Now, he can moreover preach God's word. He's only twelve, but he can bring you down on yo knees with his pleading and his singing. He knows the word and he can sho put it out. Come on up here, Soloman." With this, she pushed the boy against the makeshift pulpit. The coffee-colored youth grabbed the top of the stand with both hands and suddenly began to jerk and roll his eyes as though having some sort of spasm, frothing a bit from his mouth. The audience moved slightly on their logs, but otherwise showed no reaction to the show. Finally, the boy appeared to calm himself, leaned forward over the pulpit, looked up into the brush of the ceiling and began to sing.

The tune of "Onward, Christian Soldiers" came rolling out of the boy's mouth. McLemore was surprised to hear the audience beginning to pick up the song also, but the mulatto's voice was so clear and sweet that it dominated the singing. The preacher, the white boy and the audience all began to sway with the melody. McLemore couldn't really sing, but he began to hum along with the group.

As soon as the singing drifted away, the white youth stepped forward and raising both arms up toward the ceiling began praying in a singsong voice, with the audience occasionally approving with a loud "amen." As the boy prayed, he stomped his foot for emphasis. At each stomp, the mulatto threw his own arms up and yelled out an "amen." After ten or twelve minutes, the praying boy began to sweat profusely. Shortly afterwards, he ended the prayer and sat down.

One of the men sitting in the front row began to shout in a heavy, impassioned voice, "Amen! Amen!" After a half dozen shouts, he hitched up his patched pants and moved to the pulpit.

"Yes sir, I tell ye that this here Nanoma the Prophet can really tell it to ye. Yes sir. She's a real hoss and there here two little folks are some kind of big colts their ownselves."

"Why, thank you, sir. These two fellows are really young gifts from the Lo'd," she responded. Now that she wasn't preaching, McLemore suddenly realized that he could understand what the woman said. She began a long request for some type of assistance, as she put it, in support of the Lord's work. Obviously she knew there was little chance that her listeners had a single coin among them, so her appeal was in reality for food for her group. This approach appeared to work as three of her audience stepped forward and volunteered to take a visitor home to share whatever vittles they had. Everyone appeared to be pleased with this arrangement and soon all three of the evangelists were chatting happily with their hosts. The mulatto and the white man with whom he had been coupled were smiling as though their visiting together was nothing uncommon.

Before leaving the arbor, the woman went over to the people standing around outside the makeshift shelter, going through the group shaking hands and talking to each person. As the little group began to drift off toward the dusty road, the evangelist came over with a bright smile and stretched out her hand to McLemore.

"How are you, sir?" The greeting was in a clear, well-modulated voice. It was not quite the southern-lady voice, but it was still far removed from the voice she had used with her backwoods audience.

"Well, I'm just fine, and I must say I enjoyed your preaching. And that of your boys, too."

"Now, young man, you don't have to go quite that far. I'm sure you didn't understand over half of the things that I said, but I suppose you did get most of the praying and singing from the boys." The words from of the woman's mouth were clear and smooth as silk.

McLemore threw back his head and laughed with considerable vigor. "Ma'am, I sure did get your boys' drift, but I admit I had a little difficulty with your part. Maybe," with his smile, "because I'm just not very familiar with your subject—I guess, I just haf to own up to that."

"Nobody else is either, I'm afraid. The boys are great, though. Just about everybody gets them. Why, one's a Baptist and the other one—at least he thinks—is a Methodist. Now, that just about covers everybody but the Presbyterians, and I used to be one of them. So—" Obviously the woman wanted to talk, so McLemore followed her into the arbor and sat down across from her on the edge of the platform. Her feet stuck out from under a patched skirt and were in a pair of sandals that had been cut out of heavy boots. These soles without tops were tied on with leather thongs extending up to her lower legs.

She followed his eyes as he looked at her feet and gave a tiny laugh as she hopped up and clicked her heels together. "Yeah, I call these my Saint Paul shoes. That kind of talk lets me tie them to my profession just a bit. That term, Jesus shoes, had to go, in that I decided that I really couldn't walk on the water with 'em. And then, Saint Paul's my favorite disciple, so calling 'em my Saint Paul shoes fits the bill. I cut the soles off a pair of burned out boots that one of my boys rescued from a trash fire outside the Union compound at Vicksburg. I will say that they work pretty good and they could even look worse. You know we can't be very picky if we plan to stay in this business we're in. We eat good enough, so I suppose we shouldn't worry too much about how we look."

"Yeah, I guess you got to look the part of the poor and humble if you hope to be a leader of the poor and humble. That's surely true these days, I reckon."

"You got that right, for sure. It's going to be a long time before we can start thinking again about black robes, organs and choirs. Yes sir, a long, long time, and I don't fit into that world too well, anyway. So I suppose I'm lucky enough just having things bumping along like they're going. I truly think that we're doing a little bit of the Lord's work, but I suppose the two boys are nearer the throne than I am. Maybe by the time they're as old as I am, they might have problems keeping to the high road theirself. I do know that I'm plenty lucky to have 'em. Soloman—he's the mulatto—sho has a lot of religion, not that Abadiah is really wanting in that area. However, I'm sorry to say, Soloman is smarter than the white boy. That darkie's sho going to be preaching and doing the work for years to come. You ought to see a bunch of field hands react to that boy. He's going to be something else."

Seizing on a pause in the woman's speech, McLemore informed her that he was helping lead—he admitted that it could probably be better described as guiding—a group of ex-slaves south toward Mexico. The preacher took in this information without a sign of surprise.

"Yeah, I guessed that you were with those people. We've heard a good deal about y'all, and I think that I can do a little bit to help you out. I'd like to bring my boys over tonight, or y'all could come over here to the brush arbor after your people close in this afternoon. I know that those people are getting pretty hard to handle, and maybe a little old time religion could help control 'em."

McLemore was a bit shocked that she knew about their operation and that her observation on controlling the group was near to his own feelings on the subject. Maybe they could use a little religion. It certainly couldn't hurt; so he found himself inviting the Prophet and her assistants to camp for supper. After she met Ochs, she could ask him if she could talk to the crew and their black charges.

He told Ochs that a crew of evangelists would like to visit and talk to their party. Ochs was not overjoyed, as he showed by rolling his sharp brown eyes, but he told McLemore that he would accept their visit, adding, "You will be responsible for getting these preachers out of here by half after ten and seeing that none of our people follow them off."

McLemore half expected them to fail to show up, but as darkness began to fall Nanoma the Prophet and her two young helpers walked into the camp, showing considerable enthusiasm and immediately mingling with the crew and the blacks. They introduced themselves as servants of the Lord. Ochs, who was watching the entrance of these strange people with considerable interest, pointed out to McLemore that the woman and the boys were careful to shake the hand of each member of the crew and each of the ex-slaves. Clearly, the blacks were not used to such familiarity with whites or with black preachers and were obviously impressed by these strange religious figures. They were most impressed by the mulatto boy and immediately crowded around him.

The evangelists and the white boy left Soloman to the rest of the mingling while they retreated to the camp table to eat the chicken and rice with great gusto. The mulatto remained with the blacks to eat his share of the food. McLemore and Ochs sat with the evangelist and watched the boy Soloman in action. Johnnie South moved over near the group of blacks so that he could get a close look at their reaction.

Gathering the group around him in a loose circle, the mulatto began singing in his clear, vibrant voice. In a couple of minutes, Toby Bee began to sing along with the boy, albeit without much skill. The ex-slaves tightened the circle around the singers and joined in the singing. Much to McLemore's surprise, many were displaying good voices. Suddenly they began to throw their arms into the air in time to the music and their voices filled the clearing. After several minutes of this, Soloman held up his arms and stopped the demonstration. He began to pray to the accompaniment of loud amens from Toby Bee.

In the middle of this demonstration, Nanoma the Prophet turned to McLemore and commented in a low voice, "That's what we call warming 'em up. In a minute, I will start the sermon and start moving 'em forward toward them Pearly Gates." McLemore could not detect any cynicism in her voice.

When Soloman's prayer had ended and Toby Bee's shouts had subsided, the woman got up, moved over to the group and began to preach. All the whites moved over to listen. She started her presentation in a low voice, causing the blacks immediately to become quiet and still. Toby Bee fell on his knees with his arms in a prayerful posture and became absolutely quiet and still. The whites stood in respectful silence.

As the evangelist raised the volume of her presentation, the blacks began to form a circle around her, leaving an open space between themselves and the stump upon which she was standing. As she spoke, she turned around slowly so that she could establish eye contact with everyone in her audience at some point. McLemore could understand her better than he had that afternoon, perhaps because he was becoming familiar with her speech patterns and style. After speaking for about fifteen minutes, she paused and the mulatto began to shot and throw up his arms. Toby Bee immediately jumped to his feet and began to follow the boy's example. The blacks in the audience picked up the cadence and soon joined in with shouts of apparent joy. Nanoma the Prophet turned slowly around on the stump with a look of approval. The demonstration continued for several minutes.

As the audience began to show signs of calming down, the woman motioned to the white boy. "Now, here's Abadiah to lead us in prayer. Let's all get with him now and start talking to the Lord, just like he's going to do. Yes sirree, let's talk to the Lord."

The blacks pushed a bit closer to hear the white boy pray. The usual singsong delivery came pouring out, and the audience began to move in rhythm with the sound.

As soon as Abadiah finished praying, Soloman began singing. McLemore could not recognize either the words or the tune, but evidently many of the ex-slaves did because a majority of them began to sing immediately. The blacks injected periodic handclaps as the hymn progressed and at intervals would suddenly jump into the air and yell with obvious joy.

As this latest demonstration began to lose some of its vigor, the Prophet moved back to the stump and began preaching again. This sequence—five minutes of singing, five minutes of praying and fifteen minutes of preaching—was followed for over two hours. After the first half-hour, the whites began to drift away, but not a single black showed any sign of flagging interest.

Eventually McLemore went over to the cooking fire and began to move about restlessly. Picking up on the restless movement, Nanoma stopped and came back to the fire, but the two youngsters remained talking to the half-dozen blacks gathered around the preaching stump. Johnnie South was the only white remaining near their listeners. At a signal from Ochs, South sent the blacks back to their brush shelter and the young evangelists back to the cooking fire.

Nanoma the Prophet, who appeared spent from her exertions, leaned forward with her elbows on the table to talk with Ochs and McLemore. "I really think that the services we had will calm your people down some, even though right now they look very excited. The laborers really seemed to enjoy the whole night, and everything we did was designed to get their attention and to prepare 'em for what's ahead. 'Course, I know that you know, and I suppose that even they know, it's going to be a hard row to hoe. But, I guess they think that it can't be as bad as slaving—at least for most of 'em. I have always found that most of these people, when they are in the middle of these religious frenzies, are not really open to much guidance from us. Or from their own people for that matter. I'm afraid a lot of the frenzy is really a form of entertainment for many of 'em. I'm worried about our part in promoting some of this. May the Good Lord forgive us and set us straight if he doesn't agree with what we're doing."

Nanoma continued drinking the coffee and nibbling the piece of cheese that the cook had set before her. "That one that they were calling Toby Bee probably could become one of their preachers, or maybe he's already one. Certainly he shows most of the signs, and I'm betting he gets himself set up in this trade before you get down to Mexico. He could be very useful to you on this march and maybe be even more use after you get set up in the deep, deep South. Of course, you people know that you'll haf to watch him very closely." She laughed her deep throaty laugh and paused to allow for her hosts' reactions.

Ochs leaned across the table, propping his head on one hand, and spoke slowly. "Well, as a religious woman, I suppose that you would just naturally think that this Toby Bee is the most important darkie in the bunch. After watching tonight, I guess I'll have to agree. At the most, he's only some year or so away from the influence of Ol' Massa, whoever that might have been. So I'll guess a little bit of extra watching will do the trick for this trip, but in five or ten years—who knows? I'm a good one for looking on the bright side, so I think that the preachers are the only ones that can lead 'em just now. Lord knows, leadership's what they got to have to get through these dark woods between what I think was the almost childlike condition of slavery over into some form of true freedom. My guess is it will take two or three generations, maybe more. This means there's going to be an awful lot for all the Toby Bees to do."

During this conversation, Manesco got up from the table and moved over to poke up the fire. He left the fire shortly and moved back into the shadows toward his blanket. McLemore and Scott, who was almost as quiet as Manesco, were then the only two left with Ochs and the Prophet. McLemore had been familiar with black preachers from back on the plantation, but he had to admit that he had considered their antics to be a form of entertainment was somewhat surprised by the drift of the conversation between Ochs and the Prophet. The silence of Manesco and Scott almost surely indicated that they did not agree with the significance those two had assigned to the ex-slave preachers.

McLemore was relieved when the Prophet seemed to tire of the subject and turned the conversation to her experiences during the Vicksburg campaign. Ochs acknowledged that he had been in Vicksburg during this period too, so the talk easily moved to the spring of 1863.

The two held a long discussion on the hardships of the siege, with neither seeming greatly disturbed by the use of dogs and rats for food. Then the Prophet talked of the facet of the campaign that appeared to interest her most deeply. "I had never done much nursing of the sick before Vicksburg, but, believe me, I caught up with all that in a mighty big hurry. I guess I thought that people would be satisfied with us churchy types just praying and singing, sorter like tonight, but I found that was a long way from the truth.

"I did start out that way in that cotton warehouse where they sent me to work, but almost right away I was doing two hours of religious work and twelve hours of nursing. And that was each and every day. All in all, this thing lasted nearly three months; and you know, after about a month I came to agree that this was the right division of my time.

"I know y'all know that these hospitals are pretty discouraging places, and I thought at first that I wouldn't be able to stand it. However, I got over most of that in a couple of weeks, and in spite of all the cutting and sawing and dying—and God know that's horrible—you came to accept all this. I really think that the army should have grabbed all us people long before they did and put us to work doing all the nursing we were capable of doing.

"I did do all of this kind of thing that I could do for the rest of the war, and I'm still ready to do plenty of it if I could figure out just how I could make such an effort worthwhile. Maybe a little less preaching—and I know that saving people for the Lord is important, but I never could figure out how to save 'em unless they was alive when you started on 'em. A lot more nursing. Yeah, about eighty to twenty, that ought to be about the right division of effort. And I think this division of effort ought to work in peacetime and, surely, during wars."

McLemore laughed gleefully at the Prophet's statement, and even the solemn Ochs allowed himself a controlled chuckle. Ochs talked about what the South's preachers—his term for the religious professionals—could expect out of the collapse of Southern society, clearly expecting this collapse to continue in the coming years. He explained his opinion that organized religions would surely lose their hold on the population of the South in the next few years as the stunned population became aware of the scope of the disaster. He was deeply discouraged about what could happen to the people of his region. McLemore had not seen this side of Ochs and suddenly found himself looking intently at the man's face in the flickering fire light.

Getting up from the table, the woman called to her two young companions and thanked the men for their hospitality, preparing to leave. "Sir, before I go, I must say that I disagree, and I fully expect us preachers to become more important in the operation of our society during the next few years. That's about all that our people will have to fall back on. Please don't misunderstand me; I know that I'm all bound up in this effort, but I really expect us religious types to take over a lot of things we have no business getting ourselves into. I think we'll become even more important in the control of society than we are now. However, in my opinion, this is not too healthy for our people who, God knows, are barely keeping their noses above the muddy waters right now. Let alone worrying about what a bunch of us preachers have to say about life."

"Oh, I don't know. You people of the church, and in your case the church may really have to be a brush arbor for some years to come, will surely find it more and more difficult to hold your flocks together and to keep them pointed in the direction you want them to go. Our people will probably fight hard to escape your guidance." Ochs shook his head, sighed and batted his penetrating eyes, then began to rock back and forth as he gazed off into the black night.

Both of them looked sincere, so McLemore said, "Well, I can't say that I can visualize what's going to happen to our religious life here in our time of disaster, but I believe that you two have laid out the possible routes. I guess I lean toward the Prophet's approach, but who knows? Guess we'll just have to wait around for twenty or so years."

Ochs got up from the table and shook hands with the Prophet. "Well, we enjoyed your visit, and I do feel that your services did quite a bit for our people, both black and white. And I'll keep close watch on our friend, Toby Bee. Hopefully, we'll be able to run things so this fellow can help us out during this march and even when we get down to, as you put it, the deep, deep South."

The Prophet motioned to her young assistants to move out and followed after them with one final comment. "Good luck to ye all, and everybody's going to need luck on this pilgrimage. That's with the possible exception of Toby Bee, who looks like he just found his calling. Bye, now."

* * *

Two days later they were near Vicksburg when Ochs stopped them for what he promised would be two days of rest. McLemore asked that Johnnie South go along to keep him company for the twenty-mile ride into town. He explained to Ochs that he just wanted to look at a place that he had never seen before. So on a beautiful summer morning they rode off to see what they might find in a town that everyone in the South had heard of but which few had actually visited.

Although McLemore knew that it had been over two years since the fighting had rolled over the town, it appeared that warfare had been a more recent visitor. Houses and streets were still in a state of gross disrepair. Most of the buildings in the business district were in shambles. There were few people about, and those who were around looked as if they had barely enough to eat. A couple of men, one with a wooden leg, sat on the edge of a watering trough, looking aimlessly down the empty street toward the river. As they passed, McLemore noticed that there was no water in the trough. When they reached the riverfront, they turned upstream for a couple of blocks until they found a tavern. They tied their animals to the outside rail and went in.

The building was dark inside and it was a minute or so before their eyes adjusted to the darkness and they could see that only ten or twelve people were in the main room. Most of them seemed to be sitting around talking, occasionally glancing enviously at three Yankee soldiers drinking at a table near the bar. Only two civilians in the crowd looked like they could afford to drink; they, of course, were leaning on the bar with whiskey glasses in hand. McLemore dismissed them immediately as carpetbaggers or, at best, scalawags.

It really hurt to sit in a tavern without a cent and with no prospect for bettering the situation. However, it appeared that this was the usual for all ex-Confederates, so they might as well start getting used to it. Johnnie South seemed perfectly content to sit looking at the people. He made no attempt to talk to the Federal soldiers although McLemore knew that he could read their insignia well enough to establish their unit. It seemed that South was content to forget his previous association with the Federal forces. It did seem a bit strange that this recently discharged soldier of the victorious army was just as broke as any of the ex-Confederates. If anything was to be gained in victory, it must have gone to someone other than recently discharged enlisted men of either army or former officers of the Confederacy.

The front door opened and Trab Scott, accompanied by Manesco, strolled in. They nodded to McLemore and South and took their places among the non-spenders at the edge of the room and began talking with their fellow unfortunates. A few minutes later Manesco walked over to the table occupied by the Yankee soldiers.

McLemore tightened his stomach muscles, waiting for the explosion, but Manesco was talking with the Federals without any sign of aggressive behavior. Apparently the uniformed men even asked the ex-Confederate to sit down with them. Manesco sat and continued the conversation. Although he evidently was not asked to share the pitcher of beer on the table, the conversation seemed calm enough. McLemore was beginning to relax when suddenly he heard a loud curse and saw Manesco standing with his hands on the table. The big lanky fellow kicked his chair back, turning it over on the floor. McLemore remained seated but grabbed South's arm and forced him back hard into his seat. A quick look around the room established that everyone was outwardly calm and remaining seated, although they all were looking intently at the developing quarrel.

Suddenly Manesco struck one of the Union soldiers with his fist, which brought an immediate outburst of violent pushing and shoving between him and the three

Yankees. The big Southerner held his own for a moment and even managed to bloody a Yankee nose, but he began to flag when the smallest of his opponents ran behind him and jumped on his back. This rear attack pushed Manesco off balance, allowing the two other opponents to land some telling blows. Finally one of the uniformed soldiers got his arm around the Southerner's neck and jerked him completely around and down to the floor. The biggest Yankee landed a blow to Manesco's head as the ex-Confederate went down and kicked him as he fell to the floor. Then all three Federals continued the kicking.

At the sight of the kicking, McLemore finally jumped up and entered the fracas. Kicking a downed man was just a step too far, so he threw his body against two of the Yankees, knocking them away from the pair who were now rolling about on the floor. A big, black-bearded fellow came running up to assist. McLemore had not noticed this fellow before but was most appreciative of his assistance. Blackbeard made no attempt to strike his opponent but simply lifted him on his tiptoes, pushed him backwards into the bar and held him there. McLemore's opponent attempted a clumsy bear hug and got a knee to his groin and an elbow under his chin for his trouble. As the uniformed soldier stumbled back, McLemore pushed him to the rear and finally backward over a vacant table, lying on top of him in a most undignified position. Out of the corner of his eye he could see that Johnnie South had taken to heart the advice about not entering the fight. He was standing by their table with a bottle in his hand but was making no further move to enter into this little brawl.

Suddenly three big Federal soldiers came running through the front door, carrying three-foot clubs and armed with pistols, which McLemore was relieved to see were still in their holsters. They immediately pulled Manesco and his opponent to their feet and then turned their attention to McLemore and his man. Within thirty seconds it was all over, and all four were under arrest. The black-bearded man and his Yankee were standing alongside the bar with peaceful looks on their faces.

No real injuries had been received in the melee; however, the men who had been rolling on the floor had two or three sharp blows from the clubs landing with fleshy thuds on shoulders and backs. Apparently they had been aimed so that no skulls were cracked. The four men got themselves cursed at in an almost disinterested fashion by the detachment leader. Finally he herded them out the door and into a waiting army wagon. As though it had been designed to hide the shame of its occupants, the vehicle had a white canvas cover over all the bed except the driver's seat. Two of the arresting soldiers crawled into the wagon with the prisoners, and the big sergeant stood on a small step at the back, completely filling the rear opening of the cover. When all were in their places, the driver yelled out a command to the horses, and they were off at a slow trot.

After bouncing along for about twenty minutes, the wagon came to a halt in a neighborhood of big houses that looked like they had been elegant dwellings some years ago. Here the occupants were ordered out. McLemore and Manesco crawled down after their fellow prisoners. They were all herded into a wide hall and to the foot of a stairway that was beginning to look shabby from too many months of hard use. Several Federal soldiers were standing around relaxing, most of them apparently only waiting for the end of the duty day. These onlookers glanced at the prisoners and their escorts disinterestedly as they walked past and began to climb the stairs.

On the second floor the guards pushed the group into a big room that evidently was being used as a courtroom. It has surely been a bedroom in some far away time, but now little evidence was left of any such private use. The wallpaper hung loose in several places, and a raised platform with a battered desk gave the only clue to its present use. A dozen or so people, mostly in Federal uniform, milled around aimlessly. They stood waiting for over a quarter of an hour before a disheveled major came in and sat at the raised desk.

There was some stirring among the spectators when the major indicated by picking up some papers that he was about to hold some sort of hearing. He banged on the desk with an empty water glass until the people in the room finally settled into some semblance of order. Except for the major, everyone in the room was still standing.

The first case, which ran on for several minutes, involved a fight that had taken place in the local stockade. McLemore was relieved when that prisoner got confined for only sixty days for his transgression. The sentences in the remaining cases was about the same, so some of the pressure was off even before the case of the barroom fight came up.

Almost two hours later their case was called. The major simply glared at them for a few seconds and then addressed the two Federal prisoners. "Well, why did you two soldiers, in uniform no less, enter into a barroom brawl in one of the most infamous places in Vicksburg? What you got to say for yourselves?" When there was no immediate response, the major turned his glare toward the men in civilian clothing. "I suppose you two are Rebels? That's just about always the case in these brawls. None of you got enough during the last four years, so you just have to continue the fighting in the local tavern. It doesn't look like either the Blue or the Gray got any clear-cut decision in this one. So, what was it all about?"

McLemore finally spoke up. "Major, I got into this when I went to help my friend here who was about to get all busted up by these big Yankees. I don't know what the argument was about; something about the war, I suppose."

"Well, I'd guess so, but never mind. I don't want to know all the bloody details. Anyhow, the stories always sound just alike; the story I remember from yesterday would fit this one, I suppose."

"Sir, we were just minding our own business," said the older looking of the Yankees. "And all of a sudden this man came up and started cursing General Sherman."

"Naturally, you had to defend a sweet old gentleman like General Sherman, right? I'm sure that if he were around, he would want to thank you personally. However, in the absence of any real evidence to support anyone's story, I find you all guilty of disorderly conduct. You two Federals will be locked up in our compound until your company commanders can come down and take you back to your quarters where he will decide what punishment you'll get. As for you Rebels, it's thirty days hard labor. Any questions? No? Next case."

As the major turned to the next case, one of the uniformed soldiers motioned McLemore and Manesco over to a corner. McLemore felt low indeed as he waited to be moved to some stockade to work out a thirty-day sentence for a barroom fight, one that he had only the vaguest idea of how it started or what it was about. His most prominent memory of the whole mess was that the idiot Manesco had started it all. If he entered into all fights started by all ex-Confederates, he would never get home to Dallas County. Looking at Manesco leaning against the wall, he was almost overcome by an urge to kick the bony old fellow in the behind. However, he controlled himself and waited for the next development.

Still feeling low about how this lark to Vicksburg had turned out, he was surprised to see Johnnie South come into the room and walk up to the major's desk. McLemore had no idea how South could have found his way to this building, let alone why he would have come. As he was mulling this over, a Union soldier appeared and motioned for them to follow him. Looking back as he left, McLemore saw South leaning over the desk talking to the major.

Forgetting South, he followed the corporal back down the stairs to join a group being formed on the ground floor. The corporal told them with a little sneer that the next stop was to be the Federal stockade.

The stockade was not quite as bad as McLemore had anticipated. The Federals had seized an old school building within a tumbled down brick wall and had turned it into a confinement facility. A ramshackle tower had been built at the rear of the old school yard, and two riflemen were posted there to control the rear and sides of the building. A small guardhouse stood in the street in front of the courtyard entrance, and the sentry posted there clearly was to control the front area of this makeshift jail. McLemore could see that the building was crowded and filthy but evidently dry. The half dozen new prisoners who had come in with him went into one of the old classrooms and lay down on the dirty straw scattered over the floor. McLemore passed up the straw and lay down on the bare floor of the hallway; within moments he was as sound asleep as the others.

They slept through the night and did not stir until a guard came in the next morning yelling for them to get up. The man kicked those who were too slow or too sleepy to react properly to this peculiar type of reveille. Half-cold, almost non-edible grits were passed out for breakfast, but McLemore did get a tin cup of coffee that he was sure was as good as any he had ever tasted. When the food had been eaten—and most of the prisoners ate their allocation whether it was bad or not—work details were formed and marched off to their day of hard labor. McLemore and his group were held back for a few minutes to be processed and assigned to a job.

A new group was formed and sent off shortly to dig a ditch through a cotton field. The ditch was designed to drain a mud hole threatening to close one of the town's side streets. It was hot, heavy work but not very well supervised. The guard in charge had a lash, which he used rather liberally, but those men such as McLemore and Manesco who had spent several months in a Federal prison escaped his ire with ease. Manesco got one blow from the lash, but it was far from solid, and McLemore escaped altogether. Of course, for these men with previous prison time, it was a matter of pride that they could survive without doing any real work. Neither did any worthwhile labor.

At noon the prisoners were given a twenty-minute rest period and fed a piece of stale bread. But the water issued with the bread was fresh and the group was allowed to lie in the shade for their rest period. McLemore thought that if this was all there was to Yankee hard labor, then he could make thirty days without breaking much of a sweat. Just as they were going back to work, a sergeant came up and took McLemore and Manesco back to the stockade.

"You two bastards are as lucky as people get," growled the duty NCO. "Some guy from the Second Ohio Cavalry has vouched for both of you pimps and has somehow got your sentences commuted." The Yankee sergeant did not look any happier with this turn of events than did the usual prison guard.

"Who got us out?" asked McLemore. "And why?"

"Don't know and don't care. Just get the hell out of here before somebody changes their mind."

"That we will. That we will. The outside could be a whole lot better than it is, but I guess it's got this damn place beat all to hell."

"Yeah, yeah. Jest git going. The man that got you out is out in the street in front of the guardhouse." The sergeant's face plainly said "good riddance" as he scowled and said no more.

When they reached the street, there was Johnnie South sitting in the shade of a big oak. Behind him were his old mule and two saddled horses tied to an overhanging limb.

"So you was in the damn Yankee Army. I might have knowed it," said Manesco, speaking for the first time since they got back to the stockade.

"Well—yep—I was, and if I hadn't a been, you two fellows would still be out there digging in that ditch." South allowed himself a very tiny smile.

"That's awful good. For one, I thank you a lot." McLemore thought for a moment and then continued, "Where do we have to go from here?"

While they talked, Manesco untied his awkward gelding and McLemore mounted his little mare and reined out into the street. Only yesterday he had ridden into Vicksburg, but all the action of the intervening time seemed to have stretched the hours into days. He could remember very little of the details of the time interval; things must have been moving fast.

McLemore asked, "How did you get us out of that damn Yankee calaboose?"

"It wasn't all that easy," said South. "But I found a sergeant from my old brigade who happened to be working in the provost marshal's office, and he fixed it so I could see the major who was running that kangaroo court. I talked him into letting me ride out to see Mr. Ochs before your sentence got made final. So Ochs came in to see the major this morning and the decision was made that you could go on to Mexico with our team."

"The old army game, eh? You just got to know somebody," McLemore snickered.

"That's about it, Lieutenant. I learned that sometime back but in another army."

"Well, I'm sure glad it worked this time. Spending another thirty days breaking rock wouldn't have been a whole lot of fun. I reckon that I take the lockup about as well as most, but I assure you, even I don't like it."

As they rode along, South mumbled to McLemore, "Mr. Ochs says that you are to come on down to Natchez and help us load out a steamboat for New Orleans. When we get everybody loaded, he wants you to ride back north to take messages to his agents in Jackson and Meridian and then over into Alabama to see the one in Tuscaloosa. He said you could take a little leave time to visit home as long as you're so close, but he wants you back in Nashville by early December. By the way, these agents are all lawyers. So good luck."

"So good old Mr. Ochs thinks that I'm not ready for New Orleans just yet. However, it's fine for me to ride around Alabama and Mississippi and then back to Nashville. Great!"

The horses picked up a slow trot and the party moved out for Ochs's camp. The countryside was as beautiful as the Mississippi Delta could be in midsummer. Mockingbirds flew up as they rode along. Now and then a covey of quail that had somehow escaped the large number of new shotgunners that had developed among the occupying forces flew up and disappeared into heavy cover. McLemore began to whistle.

CHAPTER IV

INTO NORTH ALABAMA

Crossing the Duck River seemed to establish that they were at last on their way to Alabama. They still had a long way to go in Tennessee, but the rolling countryside was like that of North Alabama, and each mile traveled put them that much closer to the valley of the Tennessee and their home state.

The two-week stay in Williamson County had ended without any sign of McLemore returning. As far as Logan knew, the lieutenant could be headed south into Mexico by now. Thad Hood was still not very strong, but Logan felt that they simply must begin moving south again or he ran the risk of losing the group by having it break up by individuals setting out on their own. So on a hot, humid day in late July, they forded the Duck and began walking south.

The time spend at old Mr. Moore's place outside of Franklin had allowed them all to gather a bit of strength. Even Thad Hood, still far from well, had improved over the past ten days to the point that Logan felt he could risk a start. The new pair of pants, enticed from the backroom of a general store by some of McLemore's poker winnings, seemed to improve Hood's morale enough to let him keep up with the others until about two in the afternoon. By four o'clock Logan had to double the usual ten-minute hourly break. Afterwards, Logan was happy to see that Hood could stay up with the team until sundown ended the day's march. He was staggering badly near the end, but he made it. Logan had him lie down and rest while Sergeant Jackson and Li'l Georgia McCalab boiled their grits and salt pork. Hood ate his portion, and part of Logan's, with right good will, so the captain began to feel more encouraged about their situation. Maybe they could all get home alive after all.

Sergeant Jackson was detailed to take Li'l Georgia and search the countryside for food. Logan was fully aware that the younger man was the much better forager, but the sergeant was older and wiser and should add some stability to the operation. However, two hours later they came back with only five turnips and a skinny squirrel that they had stolen from a trap in the woods. Paltry or not, the men's take was soon boiling in the iron pot for the next day's breakfast. Logan did not think it was the right time to ask, but he hoped that the foragers had reset their benefactor's trap.

From the position of the moon the captain judged that it was around ten o'clock when he finally lay down on his pile of brush and began thinking about what to expect in the coming days. His three companions were already still and breathing deeply. This, at least, was encouraging. His immediate problem was how to keep Thad Hood moving with the group. The youth, although still quite ill, had made it through this first day without any real problem; but what about those days out there a week or two in the future? Everyone's footwear was in fairly good shape. All except Hood were healthy, at least for the moment. However, with a few days on half rations, sick days were surely on their way. All sorts of problems were bound to crop up. In any event, he was eternally thankful for the shoes stolen from the Second Wisconsin Infantry. They were magnificent shoes and still holding together like champions. Yankees were clearly useful for something.

It was already clear that food was going to be their biggest problem. They were going into the last third of their trip strong and well fed, thanks to Mr. Moore and the folks at his Williamson County place. Obviously it had been a severe sacrifice, but the old fellow seemed to think that it was his duty to help any ex-Confederate who crossed his path. As for Logan's own position, he simply could not afford to turn down food and shelter offered on almost any terms. Their route would now take them through a sparsely populated area already cleaned out by the Yankee occupying forces. He knew he could expect very little assistance of any sort. In fact, he was unprepared to talk frankly with his people about the desert they now had to cross. He felt that Jackson was aware of the problems they would have to face and in his dour way had accepted it as part of the soldier's life. The two younger men were probably barely aware of the desperate circumstances they must face.

The chaotic conditions of the Tennessee-Alabama border area for the last two years had resulted in a countryside stripped clean of foodstuffs. Few crops had even been planted since the spring of 1863. All of the farm animals had been butchered and eaten by the moving military units, both Blue and Gray. Most barns had either been burned or pulled apart for their lumber or logs. As a final blow, the population seemed to have fled, probably to some lucky area that had escaped most of the fighting and the continuous movement of military units.

As they walked south from Franklin, the countryside seemed to become more deserted by the mile. Within six months or so the bulk of the population would surely return, but his little group had to make their passage through this wilderness within the next few weeks. At least half of the farmhouses they passed seemed to have been deserted for a couple of years. There was little evidence that a crop had been planned for or planted during this summer, so the coming winter should be one to be remembered.

Logan finally drifted off to sleep with few reassuring thoughts to sustain him.

The next two days were without incident. Thad Hood seemed to be as well as when they left Franklin. Late on the fourth day they came upon a small general store still open. Logan went in and in the semidarkness located the storekeeper, an unkempt man, leaning back in a broken chair with his feet, clad in ragged shoes, propped up on the counter. A quick look around established that the shelves were almost empty. In one corner was a small separate room with a barred window.

"Hope you're not looking for your mail," said the man without shifting his position. "There ain't been no mail since February, and I ain't really expecting none, no time soon. The Yankee government man in Athens told us to expect some in a few days, but that was a month ago, and I ain't seed a single letter yet."

"No, we're just some old soldiers released from Rock Island back a month or so ago, and we're trying to go down to Selma. I'm just trying to find out if we're back in the state of Alabama yet."

"Well, I can help you out with that. The state line is back north about three miles, and Athens is only a few miles farther to the south." The man finally pulled his feet back down to the floor. "I don't reckon you need any of our pitiful stock. And I reckon if you do, you don't have a cent more than I had when I got here from Atlanta last month."

"Mister, you got that right. I do thank you, though, and my men outside will feel better knowing they're back in Alabama."

By now Logan could see the man rather well and noted his scraggly beard and pale, washed-out complexion. "Well, I don't know about that. I'd think you might have been better off to have stayed up around Nashville. I hear it's not too bad up there. I sure can't say that about this damn place." He interrupted himself to cough several times and then continued. "As you see, this here thing that they call a store don't have one mouthful of eating stuff in the whole damn place." He hesitated for a moment and added, "I guess that's not quite right. Old Man Groves, who owns this place, brought in something yesterday that I bet you ain't seen in a long spell. I guess I can give you a little taste of hit."

Logan waited until the man went to the back and returned with a small paper packet that he placed on the counter with a smile of satisfaction. Logan looked in the paper and recognized the substance as refined sugar. He picked it up, expressed his thanks and went back outside. The sallow man was coughing again as Logan left, but he did manage a smile that he probably meant to be encouraging. Logan crossed the road to the trees where his people were resting. The four men divided the sugar and gobbled it up with considerable satisfaction.

Realizing that they were finally back in Alabama gave everyone a little boost as they started down the road toward Athens. However, their optimistic mood was short lived as they saw that the countryside along the rutted road was still in bad shape. Houses and barns were either burned or partially wrecked. Windows and doors in most of the surviving houses had disappeared. Few fences were still standing and there was little sign that the land was being cultivated. Logan pushed the group as fast as he could past each deserted homestead, hoping to keep their minds off their surroundings. Yet, as far as he could tell, they moved along without being affected much by the desolate scenery.

They skirted the town of Athens and began walking past cotton plantations in the bottoms along the Tennessee River. Most of these seemed little better off than the smaller farms they had been passing for the last two or three days.

However, just as they approached the north bank of the river, they came upon a big, two-story white house with the usual dozen or so outbuildings that connoted plantation headquarters. Most of the outbuilding were either in fairly good shape or were now under repair. With all the confidence they could muster, the group walked through the front gate, which was still intact, and between the two rows of cedars lining the approach road to the house. As they neared the main building, they could see that it was badly in need of paint but still mostly intact.

Logan could see the plantation commissary and office off to the right of the big house, so he led his people to the store porch and let them sit on a rickety bench leaning against the front wall. He went inside, where he immediately saw that this store was better operated than the one back at the state line. It had few goods on the shelves; but a young man in patched clothes, which seemed to be the uniform of the day, immediately came forward and asked what he could do for the visitor.

"I think that I need to see the owner of this operation. Might that be you?"

"Oh, no. I wish it was, but unfortunately I'm just the clerk. If you want to see Mr. Meroney, he's back in the office." The clerk pointed over his shoulder to a room in the back. Logan walked to the open door and knocked on the door facing. He went in upon the invitation of the big, red-faced man, probably in his late fifties, who was sitting behind a wooden table on the opposite side of the room. The man waved at a rickety chair, which Logan immediately took. Surprisingly enough, it held him up.

They exchanged names as he sat down. "Captain, or Major—I'd say by your looks that you're one or the other—what can I do for you? I have to add that, just now, I can't do much of anything for anybody. But I'll be happy to listen."

"Sir, I'm a captain; or at least I was until Appomattox, and I'm on my way back to Dallas County from Rock Island prison. I'm supposed to pick up a man who's to go down to Selma with me. He's a great big fellow by the name of Slaughter. I'm afraid I know little about him other than his name, but I'm hoping he might be here."

"Well, you're in luck, or I guess you're in luck. At least he's here. Beat you here by three or four days. He's been sleeping over at my overseer's house."

"That's great. Obviously, I can't pay his board bill or anything else that he might owe you, but I'll take him off your hands if that'll help."

"Yeah, that'll help, all right. Seems like we got a lot of people around here that has to eat. Besides me, we've got the overseer and the clerk and a grand total of five blacks who've seen enough of freedom and have come back to be fed. We've all been eating peas and cornbread for a month now, and even that's starting to run low.

"In addition, this man that you're asking about has already caused some trouble. He started a couple of fusses with my overseer, so I'm going to be glad to see him on his way to Selma or 'most any other place. He claims that some fellow up in Nashville named Ochs will send me his board money. Don't know how he's going to manage that in that there's been no mail in here for at least six months, but I sho hope it's true."

"I met this man Ochs when we were up in Nashville, and I know that he's connected to this fellow Slaughter. But I can't say whether he'll stand good for any of Slaughter's debts or not."

"Good riddance, anyhow. Bring your men over to the cookhouse and I'll let 'em have some of our peas and cornbread. We're all going to get by somehow, and we sure can divide what we have with any ex-Confederate. We've done it plenty of times before."

The planter took Logan into the barnyard to meet Slaughter. The captain shook the man's hand and informed him that the group would be moving out in about an hour so he should get his gear together. Slaughter appeared to be happy to hear this, moving off immediately to gather up his gear, which consisted of an extra shirt and a razor.

Mr. Meroney led Logan to the back porch of the main house and into a small dining room off the central hallway. The room contained a scarred table and four or five unmatched chairs, and nothing else—not even tableware of any sort. Logan could see that the hallway and a partly visible bedroom were as sparsely furnished as the dining room. None of the rooms had curtain or window dressings of any sort. Evidently, the exterior of the building had fared somewhat better than the interior. However, he noticed that things were clean, indicating that someone had been doing some daily housekeeping.

As they seated themselves at the table, Meroney said, "As I guess you figured out as you walked in, we don't have a stalk of cotton growing, so picking's not going to be a big job this year. However, I did manage to get a pretty big crop of peas planted back in late May, and the five blacks here now came back early enough to work 'em out. I was able to get enough corn up in Athens to keep us in bread until around February. I don't know what we'll do then, but I suppose that the good Lord will provide. He always has."

"What about the river and all the woods that you have around here? Do you have hope for much fish and game?" Logan meant this to be an encouraging word, fully anticipating the answer he got.

"Not much, I'm afraid. Nobody's supposed to have any sort of firearms or any powder or shot to use in 'em, even if you had some sort of gun. I'll have to own up to having one old shotgun hidden away, and if we can get any sort of powder, maybe we can get us a deer or two come fall. One of the field hands is a pretty good trapper, and we had two or three 'possums and one big 'coon during the past month. Now, I'd never eaten either of these critters before, but I'll have to admit that they tasted pretty good."

At this point one of the blacks came in with a wooden box from which he produced two plates and a couple of earthenware mugs. Next he pulled out a cracked dish full of steaming field peas and a pone of cornbread, backed up by a water pitcher, which Logan was pleased to see had no cracks. Both men took the bread and, following the usual custom of the country, crumbled it into their plates of hot peas. As he ate, Logan thought that if the peas had been seasoned with a little salt pork then this would have been a feast indeed.

While they ate, Meroney talked about how plantation life had deteriorated during the past year. The comments were discouraging, even to a man just six weeks out of Rock Island who had seen his share of discouraging things during the past four years. Meroney's account of the manipulation of the local tax system was probably the most distressing part of his talk. If the carpetbaggers really could do most of the things that the planter was accusing them of, then there seemed to be little hope for his people during the next several years. He couldn't imagine how many Southerners could have lived through to July 1865 with enough property to attract the attention of the tax collectors. However, it seemed that Mr. Meroney had managed to do this. At the moment, the planter was busy explaining that land was practically worthless and that most of the farming equipment had been destroyed in the early days of the war. Nearly all of the livestock had been taken by the summer of 1863. Just by chance four mules, so thin that you could read a newspaper through them, according to Meroney, were still around so that land preparation for next year's crop could be started.

When the man serving the table came in to clear away the dishes, Logan noticed that Meroney's complaints stopped immediately. They went outside to watch the final preparation for the departure of the visiting group, now totaling five men. Just before they left, Meroney volunteered one of his hands as a guide to the river. This man was supposed to know a local farm hand with a boat who could be persuaded to ferry them across.

They gathered their gear—all extremely light except for the cook pot—and moved back down the avenue of cedars, turning south on the main road. Slaughter walked along at the established pace, keeping up with the group with no sign of distress. He took his turn carrying the pot and even assisted in pulling Hood through a swift creek they encountered late in the afternoon. Watching the big fellow in action, Logan thought that, unpleasant as he might be, he seemed willing enough to do his share of the duties. Maybe the big clown wouldn't be as big a drag as he had originally thought.

Their guide found the black with the boat. After a little threatening by the sergeant, they were pulled across to the south bank of the Tennessee. Within a half-hour they were back to the main road and moving south.

For two days they moved along at their usual rate of two and a half miles an hour. By the third day the terrain became a steeper roll, and Logan knew they were approaching the hill country. The hills and hollows of the area were new to him. They came across no villages and only scattered farms. Now and then they passed a dwelling that appeared to be occupied, but for almost two days they had not seen another human being. Finally they saw a ragged boy sitting on the porch of a dilapidated dogtrot house that seemed to be almost swallowed by the chestnut trees surrounding it. They turned into the yard, which appeared to have been spared the usual daily brushbrooming for months, and walked up to the boy seated in a chair on the tumbled down porch.

"Good morning. Are any of the grown folks around this morning?" asked Logan.

"Nobody lives here 'cept me and Pa, and he left to see the people that are staying in that old cave down by the Sipsey River, and then he was going to check his trot lines." The boy got up from the battered chair—the only thing resembling furniture on the porch or in the hallway leading back into the house—and began to rock back and forth from heels to toes while he stared at the visitors. "We ain't got nothing to eat for ourselves, so could you please leave us alone?"

"Don't worry, son. Just you tell me where this cave full of people can be found and we'll be on our way." As Logan was sorting out the boy's answer, Sergeant Jackson stepped up on the porch, walked into the house and looked into the two rooms on either side of the dogtrot.

"Yeah, Cap'n," said Jackson as he looked into the open rooms. "The boy's right. They ain't no people and damn little of anything else in here. They must be sleeping on a big pallet that's on the floor. Guess it's safe to take the trail he's talking about."

Taking the boy's recommendation, they followed the trail until they found the cave. Two small boys playing in the dirt at its mouth seemed to pay little attention to the arrival of five strangers. Logan guessed from their actions that such visits occurred frequently, and his guess was reinforced by the nonchalant attitude of the three men who came stumbling out of the cave.

"Hello, we're old Confederates looking for anything that we might be able to eat," said Logan to one of the men. "We'd also like to get across the Sipsey so we can get on towards the south."

The men from the cave just stared at the new arrivals for a couple of minutes. Finally the older looking man said, "I'm sho sorry feller, but we ain't got nothing at all to eat." Then after a moment of hesitation, "You're welcome to come and look around if you'd want to. There's what's left of four families in this damn hole in the ground. Seven grown folks and three young 'uns. And we'll all about to starve. We had a few dry beans and some okra this morning, and I don't know what's going to be et from now on."

By this time more of the cave's dwellers had come out and were standing in a group at the mouth of their home. The youngest looking man was wearing the remnants of a Confederate uniform.

"Hey, fellow, we're not a gang of robbers. We'll take your word for it." Logan continued, "But I guess we will rest a spell before we attack the Sipsey."

Following the guidance of the young man in the Confederate uniform, Logan and his men moved to an open area under a large oak some fifty yards from the cave. Li'l Georgia hung the cook pot and started a fire. When the water began to boil, the boy dropped in the nine irish potatoes and the small scrap of middling meat they had liberated from an old farmhouse outside Athens.

As soon as the meat and potatoes began to boil, a couple of cave people came over and volunteered some cornmeal that had mysteriously appeared from somewhere. Some hoecake was stirred up and set aside to await the appropriate time to be poured on a piece of flat metal that had also appeared with the cornmeal. Next, a pot of cured pork and field peas was brought down from the cave and hung over the fire. Finally, one of the women brought down a couple of onions and dropped them into the pot of peas.

As everyone waited for the food to cook, the two older squatters began talking about their desperate situation. Logan and Jackson always got the brunt of this type of conversation because they looked older and more tolerant of such stories of disaster than did the other men. Logan had noticed that Slaughter was openly unsympathetic to the hardship stories and that this time he simply shook his head and turned away.

The conversation established that the three families were close kin. The two older men were brothers, and the young man in the uniform was their brother-in-law. The women of the group were the wives of these men; and a fourth woman, who supposedly lived in the cave also but who made no appearance, was a cousin who had lost her husband at Antietam. As they rambled on, the visitors learned that the families had been living in the cave since General Wilson's raiders had burned their homes back in early March.

They had all been residents of a community known as Bobo's Hollow, a neighborhood that had been unfortunate to have had one of its residents shoot at the raiding party. Wilson's people, of course, immediately shot and killed the old fellow and then set off on a carnival of destruction. This havoc included all building, barns as well as houses, and then they carried off all the chickens and cows that they could find. Of course all horses and mules had been gone for two years. However, by consuming all that had been overlooked by the raiders, these people had managed to survive. Using the cave for shelter and rags for clothing, the people of Bobo's Hollow presented a discouraging picture of Southerners in the summer of 1865.

"You know, all these damn Yankees kept calling us slave masters and labor beaters, and this was right during the time they was burning up our things. The last one that rode out had three of our chickens tied to his saddle, and he hit me across the back with the flat of his saber as he went out the front gate. He even tried to ride down my old dog, but he was too smart for the bastard and got away." The old fellow with the gray beard seemed obsessed with the slavery issue. "You know about this slavery thing, you know we never even seen any of these damn black people unless we go up to the Tennessee Valley. I bet there ain't fifteen of them people in this county. But we're going to pay for them being in Alabama for the rest of our lives. That is, if our lives last long enough for it to matter. Right now, it don't look like we'll be around very long."

"Ah, I guess we'll get by somehow," put in the young man in the uniform. "There's still quite a few fish in the Sipsey, and we ain't done much about trapping anything in the woods. I saw two big doe deer last week, and we'll be in pretty good shape if we could catch one of them rascals. There's more food out there than we're guessing. Me, I'm expecting to catch some. Not jus' set around here and starve."

"Yeah, let's hope so," said graybeard. "But just remember that we ain't got nothing to shoot these things with. The damn Yankee patrols will hang us all if they catch us with any shot or powder. You remember what happened to Old Man Strong May and his wife?"

"Sho do, somehow they ended up dead. But you know damn well we got to eat. Even the blue bellies know that, and we'll just have to take the chance and grab whatever we can. I'm thinking about trying to break into that Yankee warehouse up in Decatur. I bet there's enough flour, meat and hominy in there to feed the whole county for all winter."

"Yeah, I'm sure you're right. But if you try to break in there, at least we're going to be a little better off than we are now. That's 'cause you'll have a bullet through your head and we'll have one less mouth to feed. Why don't you start out on that job tonight? Those damn Confederate officers done got you thinking that you can do anything. But let me tell you, my thinking is that there was plenty you Confederates didn't know how to do too well."

"Evidently. I'm afraid you're plenty right about that," put in Logan as he stirred the iron pot. "A big bunch of the Gray's don't have to worry about things like that, because they're dead."

Graybeard looked a bit shamefaced. "Yes sir, I know how bad it must have been on y'all, and we supported you as good as we could until right near the end. Finally had to give it up after '64. Not that it done us a damn bit of good after that devil Wilson came around. His folks took everything they could carry and then burned us out jus' like we was rich planters from the Delta."

"Yeah, that's the way wars are—all wars, I'm afraid," said Logan. Whoever loses gets the short end of everything for the next twenty or so years. But I suppose it will all pass—everything always has."

This somber conversation ended when one of the women called everyone to get their portion of the food. The group fell to eating with a will, and despite the small servings soon there were numerous statements being made that the food was the best they'd had since the Yankees visit back in March.

When all the food had been consumed, Li'l Georgia and Thad Hood cleaned the iron pot as Logan prepared the group to move out. The man in the tattered Confederate uniform volunteered to lead them to a ford to cross the Sipsey. Moving downstream, Logan looked back at the people at the mouth of the cave and wondered how many would make it through the coming winter.

After walking for about a half-hour, the ex-soldier located a shallow ford and stood talking with Logan as the other men began wading across. There was only one deep hole, and everyone managed to miss it except Slaughter, who went in over his head. Spewing and cursing, he was pulled to the other side by the sergeant.

When the others were safely across, Logan thanked his guide and prepared to wade across. The guide offered a departing bit of advice. "Captain, I guess you know that for the next forty miles or so you'll be going through what they're calling the Free State of Winston. That's 'cause there's so many Lincoln lovers in that county. Most of the time they won't be too helpful to any old Confederates. But maybe you'll mainly hit the good ones. And there are some good people down there."

"Yeah, I heard up in Tennessee that they were running a little Civil War of their own in this area, but I'm hoping that all that's died down by now."

"No, they're still running around killing each other and burning down houses. But I ain't heard of any real bad stuff in the last two or three weeks, so maybe they're beginning to calm down some."

"I sure hope so. We can sure do without that kind of stuff. For the next year or so, everybody's going to have plenty of trouble just staying alive without any fighting among ourselves. You people ought to work hard to keep away from all that. Good luck, in any event." With one final touch on the guide's shoulder, Logan stepped into the water and was gone toward the opposite bank.

* * *

Winston County seemed about like the rest of the area south of the Tennessee Valley that they had passed through. The county appeared sparsely populated, and few signs were seen to indicate that its few inhabitants were doing anything to prepare for the coming winter. There was no food to be either begged or stolen, so the little group wandered on southward—Logan figured they were making ten to twelve miles a day—with almost nothing to eat. Li'l Georgia had managed to snare a rabbit and they found a few ears of green corn. They were all too thin for their rags, but Hood was beginning to appear dangerously emaciated. During the afternoon of the third day after crossing the Sipsey, Hood began to stumble badly and the group had to stop early. No shelter could be found, so they made do by crawling under an oak blown down in a spring storm.

They made a crude lean-to for Hood and then sheltered themselves as best they could with limbs from the fallen tree. Since there was no other food, they boiled and ate a few leaves from a tough poke salat plant. It was as near nothing as they had experienced since leaving Rock Island.

Logan waited for two days, hoping that Hood would regain some strength. They begged a little buttermilk and a corn pone from a farmhouse they had passed to give to Hood, but the others ate almost nothing for the entire two days. Logan felt that he had to start moving on the third day; so Hood, who seemed to have strengthened a bit, was paired with Sergeant Jackson and pulled along as fast as the big man could manage. They were reduced to eating berries and a few hickory nuts that had escaped consumption by the local population.

The country road they had followed for the last three days of walking was threatening to disappear completely. Logan suspected they had not covered over five miles during the entire day. He was beginning to stumble himself when he realized that they must stop and try to regain the strength needed for the next day's walk. They came to an old log cabin with partially wrecked roof, but which seemed to offer some shelter for the coming night. They went in and lay down on the dirt floor.

Logan awoke to the sound of human voices and peeped out to see six or eight Federal cavalrymen riding by, walking their horses, who did not appear to have been ridden hard for some time. The patrol gave the old house the briefest of inspections, making no attempt to determine if anyone was inside. They rode past and pulled up to rest their horses at a spring some two hundred yards away. Logan noticed that the horses were carrying a bit too much flesh but that the equipment appeared to be in first-class shape. Strange that after all these miserable weeks he could still pay attention to blacking on boots and shine on sabers.

When he lay down again, he noticed that none of the other men appeared to have been aroused by the passing patrol.

Sleep did not come again immediately, so Logan began going over their situation. As always, his mind turned to thoughts about how to keep his people eating for the coming week. Time beyond the next few days did not seem to be of importance. Their situation was becoming critical because they had eaten almost nothing for three days and there was little prospect for tomorrow. Hood was getting weaker each day, and even if he would consider such an action, there was no place around to leave a man who could barely walk. He cringed at having such thoughts, but still the time might come soon when Hood simply could not go on. Logan stiffened at the prospect and suddenly sat bolt upright. He almost spoke aloud for emphasis as he again took oaths that this would not happen. If he allowed it, then the whole expedition would probably fall apart and the lot of them would end up dead along some country trail. His act of rededication to the struggle seemed to make him feel better as he drifted off into an uneasy sleep.

Hood appeared to be no better when morning came, so Logan decided that they had to stay in place for at least another day. That stretched into a three-day delay, which was discouraging to everyone except Hood, who seemed only barely aware of what was going on. Logan was thankful that the sick man slept a lot; he appeared only partially conscious when awake. Clearly the sufferer needed more food, but the foragers were bringing back almost nothing. On the second day they brought back a duck egg that evidently was strong in taste since it resulted in a long bout of vomiting by Hood.

On the evening of the third day, they gathered their gear and moved slowly away into the deep hills. Sergeant Jackson and Slaughter traded off supporting Hood. The indistinct trail they had to follow through a heavily wooded area caused them to stumble and fall often. By the time the moon rose shortly after midnight, it had become cooler and they were making decent progress when they came across a small log house sitting in a tiny clearing to the side of the trail. A small fire burning in the front yard was evidence that someone was living in the cabin, if such a hovel could be so labeled. Logan pulled his people off the road and had them bed down in the tall grass growing at the edge of the clearing.

As the sun came up over the trees, Logan walked over to the house and slapped the floor of the little porch with the palm of his hand. Finally a small, emaciated woman in a ragged but spotless dress came to the door and stood looking out like a frightened animal.

Logan spoke as gently as possible. "We're not going to bother you, that's for sure. I'd just like to tell you that we're a little party of ex-soldiers who are sleeping over by the road, and I hope we'll be moving out some time after noon. We've got one man who's pretty sick and we're in need of some food for him if there's any around."

"Mister," came the reply in a whiny voice, "we are starving ourselves. But I'll look real good."

Logan looked around the yard and decided there was little help there in their battle to sustain life. There was no sign of farm animals or chickens. He could see some half-burned timbers at the edge of the clearing that must have once been a barn or a smokehouse. A small potato patch, now overgrown with weeds, was near the tree line.

The woman returned after a few minutes with two sweet potatoes. She handed them to Logan and with her whine explained, "Sir, this is the last thing I can spare. I swear it on my mother's grave that we don't have anything else. Please go on and leave us alone."

At that point an older man came walking up with a rabbit hanging from an ancient shotgun slung across his shoulder. The man stood trembling where he had stopped as Slaughter came stalking up and spoke in his usual aggressive manner, "Hey, give us that damn rabbit. We need it a whole lot worse than you damn people do."

Logan held up his hand in Slaughter's face and said, "No, we're not ready to rob anybody yet. Take these two sweet potatoes and go back to the others, get a fire going and start boiling 'em." The big man made a few grumbling noises, but he took the potatoes and moved back toward their campsite.

"Take that rabbit and go on in the house. I don't want our people looking at that thing. They're pretty hungry, and I just don't want to tempt them."

The old man started talking with an Irish brogue that was almost unintelligible, apparently explaining that he was a Union sympathizer and therefore protected from all roving Confederates.

The woman came trotting up, keeping her eyes down while she slowly rubbed her hands together, and started her whine. "Yes, that's right, Daddy, but you take the rabbit and go on in the house." Turning back to Logan, she continued, "Yes, we're Union, which you'll find out soon enough, anyway. My brother was killed in the Federal infantry and my husband got killed by the Confederate guerrillas about three weeks ago. There's nothing real unusual about those kinds of things around here. Every house lost someone and most of 'em were killed right here in the county. For some of 'em, we don't even know which side done the killing."

"Yes, I know that a lot of that kind of thing was going on in this part of the state, particularly here in Winston County. I will tell you from the start that I don't agree with that kind of thing—not at all. Me and all my people were Confederates and Southerners all the way. However, I guess I understand that you people had your reasons."

"Mister, we had reasons, and if you came here to kill us, just go on and do it. I've had my fill of thinking about killing, so just do what you think you got to do and get it over with." As she delivered this speech, she lifted her head and for the first time looked him straight in the eye.

"Look, lady, we're real soldiers and there ain't going to be no killing of civilians while we're around. But I need to move my sick man up here and put him on your porch. That's just in case it starts to rain, and it sure looks like it might." With no further comment he turned and went back up the trail where his men were sleeping.

Early in the afternoon he awakened the men and put them to work cutting and moving pine brush up to the porch of the cabin. They made a brush pallet for Hood and another for Li'l Georgia, who was to stay with the sick man during the night. When the brush beds were completed, they moved Hood to the porch. Everyone else moved back into the woods to construct a lean-to for their own shelter. Because of their weakened condition, these preparations went so slowly that darkness was approaching by the time they were completed. They saw nothing of the woman and her father during the afternoon.

When the sergeant and Slaughter had crawled into the lean-to, Logan went back to the house to check on Hood and Li'l Georgia. The father had put some additional wood on the fire in front of the house and had taken a seat some distance away to escape the heat. Logan went over to talk to the old man. By concentrating he found that he could decipher some of the ancient Irishman's speech. It seemed that he had left Ireland sometime before the potato famine and had been in Winston County for over twenty years. When the Civil War troubles had started, he found himself supporting the Federals without really knowing just why he had come down on that side. Logan sensed that he was trying to blame his daughter and her husband for pulling him into the conflict; however, the Irish brogue was so thick that he could easily have misunderstood the man.

The old fellow rambled on aimlessly but obviously trying hard to tell this Confederate what he wanted to know.

One bit of information spilling out of this conversation was important to Logan. The man's daughter had spent some time working in a Yankee military hospital in Nashville and might, according to the father, be able to help the sick soldier. On hearing this Logan immediately went to the house and knocked on the door.

When the woman answered his knock, she came out on the porch and went over to the pine pallet where Hood lay. "I'll do anything I can for your man; however, I aint' got one thing to work with here."

Logan motioned her over to the edge of the porch and dropped his voice to a whisper. "He's had dysentery for a long time—at least two months—and now he's getting so weak that he's having difficulty walking, going down hill pretty fast during the past couple of weeks. If I wasn't such a bullhead, I'd be thinking about leaving him with some family and going on without him. But I'm just not ready for that yet and, thank God, neither are my people." He continued with as many details of Hood's illness as he could muster. The woman listened attentively and nodded her understanding.

She said, "We'll try to get some of the medicine the Federal army has over at their camp at Double Springs. I'll send my Pa over there tonight. Maybe they'll give him a little of it, knowing that he's a Union man and all that. They did give him a little of it once before. In the meantime I reckon I'd better try to cook up some of the old folk's remedy."

"Well, fine. Would you like me to send one of my people along to keep your father company on his walk? All my people except Hood are in fairly good shape."

"No, I'd just as soon have him walk over by hisself. Don't think it'll do to have any of them Yankee soldiers know that we're asking for medicine for Rebels. I'm not sure my father understands that you're Confederates, and I'd just as soon not have him know. Besides, it's only about eighteen miles over there and back. He knows an Irish lad over there who's a corporal, so he should manage to get a little bit of that stuff. He ought to be back by morning, easy." She seemed to think about all of this for a moment and then continued, "I want you to know that we're Union, all the way, but there's been plenty of dying already, and I'll help all I can. Besides that, I'm almost sure that you're not one of the Home Guard kind of Confederates that did all the killing and burning around here."

Logan nodded and started back to his bivouac area. He saw the old Irishman walking into the deep forest with a loose, swinging gait, which caused Logan to think that maybe he would be back by morning.

Everything was quiet during the night, with Hood sleeping soundly. Logan walked to the cabin twice during the night, and on one of these visits found the woman washing Hood's face with water from the spring. She had a concoction boiling on the fire. She said she had given him some earlier in the evening although she had little faith in these folk remedies but felt it was better than nothing. Logan tended to agree, so he said nothing and merely nodded. Logan finally woke Li'l Georgia and set him to watch the sick man so that the woman would go into the house to rest until morning.

Just as day was breaking, the Irishman came in sight, swinging along at the same rate at which he had left the previous night. He produced a bottle, which he turned over to his daughter. She immediately woke Hood and began to dose him with the Yankee remedy. She then bathed him again with fresh spring water. Watching her, Logan finally decided that the sick man was in the best available hands, so he went back to his bivouac and lay down to rest for a couple of hours.

Sometime during the afternoon, the woman began to talk more freely with Logan. Her conversation was heavily burdened with stories of the horror of the guerrilla warfare in that area. She did not give many details, but it was clear that she knew of burnings, butchery and rape that had befallen her people. A Confederate Home Guard unit had been organized to maintain control of this part of the state; but according to her, this attempt had been largely unsuccessful and had led to an all-out war that ran for virtually the entire four years of the rebellion. Now the war was over for the rest of the country, but people were still being killed in Winston County. The woman clearly thought the situation would continue for years, at least for the rest of her life.

After a half-hour of this desultory talk, the woman broke off her story and climbed up on the porch to look in on Hood. After she had checked him and once again bathed him with spring water, she went into the house without further comment. Logan realized that she had not mentioned the death of her husband. Obviously this last tragedy was still too fresh for discussion with strangers—Confederate strangers, at that.

Logan and his men stayed for three more days. Li'l Georgia and the sergeant went out each morning looking for food, coming in at night to cook what little they had found. Their findings were so skimpy that they had little use for the cooking pot. One day they found an opossum and three sweet potatoes, which produced the biggest meal of their entire stay. Of course they shared whatever they found with the old man and his daughter.

The most encouraging thing during the stay was the steady improvement made by Hood over the three days. Logan decided that Hood had made enough progress to allow for another start south. Late in the afternoon, he got his people together for another attack on the road, first going to the cabin to say good-by to the old man and his daughter. The Irishman simply smiled, shook hands and mumbled something in his thick brogue. Obviously he did not disapprove of his Confederate visitors; of course he may not have even realized that they were Confederates.

Taking leave of the woman was somewhat more complicated. She turned the Union army medicine over to Li'l Georgia with detailed instructions on how to administer it. She then told the captain in no uncertain terms that he must get this man a ride of some sort or they ran the risk of losing him. She added that they must get out of Winston County as soon as they could, but once in a more hospitable area they must leave him in someone's care until he could regain more of his strength.

At the last minute, as the men were assembling at the edge of the clearing, the woman finally talked about her husband. "I guess my Pa told you that the Rebels killed my husband about a month ago. They butchered him, really. They cut off his ears and one of his hands and then they cut his throat. His horse brought him back tied up in the saddle." She began trembling violently, but after a visible effort she gained control of herself. "You know that I can never get over this or forgive the people who done this to him. You know that these kinds of things cannot be forgotten for at least a hundred years by the people here in this county."

Logan simply lowered his head and took the onslaught. Nothing he could say would make sense under these circumstances.

"My Ma was a cousin of Chris Sheets, the leader of us people called Tories. So I think that was the reason they done those things to him. My man might have done some things like that against them. I don't think so, but he could have. And I know that you people was doing things much different up there in Virginia." She paused for a moment then continued, "But it's all so bad. I just can't never get over it. It will be with me to the day I die." She allowed herself a few tears.

There were no words from Logan. He placed his hand on her shoulder and squeezed it momentarily then turned quickly away and led his people off into the deep woods. Yes, war is hell, and guerrilla war is something a bit worse than hell.

* * *

The little band moved, or more accurately stumbled, on for three days before finding an indistinct trail. A local fellow, whose clothing was hanging on his emaciated frame in strips, told them that the trail followed the Luxapallilia Creek. They soon came to a church and a country store and stopped in a grove of chestnuts across from the store to make camp. Making camp had become a simple process of building a fire and hanging the cooking pot. By now they looked for shelter only if rain threatened.

A man dressed in a yellowing but clean white suit came over from the store and introduced himself as Captain Burleson, the storeowner. Burleson invited them to move the sick man into a shed at the rear of the store. Logan accepted this offer and soon had Hood bedded down in the tumbled down building, despite the strong odor that drifted up from the straw on the floor, with the other men outside.

Within minutes Burelson came back and began talking. "Back a couple of months ago, we had four or five goats in this shed. That's why it smells so damn strong. But we ate 'em up sometime back, and the smell is all I can offer you now. Come to think of it, I do have a couple of bags of brown rice, and I should be able to give you four or five pounds of that stuff. Just in memory of old Jeff Davis, who got us in this very fine fix, you know." He ended with a booming laugh that seemed to explode from his little round belly.

At the first break in Captain Burleson's monologue, Logan injected, "I know we're a little south of that Free

State of Winston business, but I understand there was some guerrilla activity down this far south. I hope you were Secesh, like us."

"Oh yeah. Most of us down here were that, all right. I got together a company of infantry myself. That's how I got to be called captain." His booming laugh sounded again. "Now and then we would hear something about a little guerrilla activity. But it was kept pretty quiet until right at the end of the war. By then there was so many deserters around that you couldn't tell nothing about who you was talking to. There was a killing or two right around here, but no big activity like up in Winston County."

"Guerilla activity or not, I know you realize that finding foodstuff is all important to us. You think we'll find a little more as we get farther south?"

"Well, maybe. I'd try to cut down to just north of Fayette and then go to the east, walking cross-country over to around Tannehill. Then I'd just follow the old Tannehill road south toward Montevallo or Centerville. If you can find that old road, it should be pretty easy going down to Montevallo, and that's where the railroad starts. Too, there might be more chances for foodstuff when you get down into that country. You know that things start to flatten out some down there, so they can grow more than we can."

"We try never to forget that, Cap'n Burleson. We've walked out of our way two or three times just to go through some area that was supposed to have more eating stuff." Logan was looking at Burleson as he spoke, thinking there was little chance that this little round fellow could have missed too many meals or spent much time in an infantry company, at least not in recent years.

"The Confederate Army got rid of me after Pittsburgh Landing. You know, that's the place the Feds called Shiloh." Another laugh and then he continued, "I was God damned glad, too. The little hole that I got shot in my leg was probably the luckiest thing that will ever happen to me in this life. While I was home getting cured up, I got old Judge Terrill to put in a word to somebody up in Richmond and I got discharged. That company I recruited kept right on going, though. Made a fine name for theirselves. However, a whole lot of 'em got killed before it was all over."

"Yes, Cap'n Burleson, if you were in an infantry company, you had a real good chance of ending up dead. The smartest thing you'll ever do was escaping that. It's true that men in infantry companies were at the very heart of the war, and they just had to stand and take it. Yeah, even we cavalrymen recognized that."

"Yes, yes, I know. Probably about the smartest thing we ever done with that company towards staying alive was the time we set fire to all them pine thickets on the south side of the Tennessee, just where my regimental commander wanted to cross over with all our people. The Yankees had been firing into that area with their artillery, and they were all set to butcher us when we started to cross; but me and my boys got a good fire going back in the pines and then we moved a whole bunch of hay down close to the water and got it burning. Some of us poured water on the hay and got it smoldering real good. God, it put out a smoke! The wind was blowing just right and that smoke just settled down and hid the crossing place for over an hour. The colonel got us all across and right on the Feds before they ever saw us. We didn't lose hardly anybody during the whole thing. Our people started calling that scrape the smoke screen fight. I heard that General Jackson done something like that later, but we done it first."

The conversation drifted on in this vein until Logan finally got away from the talkative old fellow by going with Li'l Georgia to look for food. Walking away, he looked back and saw Burleson had cornered the sergeant and was busy waving his arms and talking away. The last thing he heard as he walked into the shadows of the deep woods was the booming laugh of the storekeeper.

Logan knew that he would add little to Li'l Georgia's scavenger effort, but he felt that he had to make his presence felt in all activities that were essential to the group's survival. And looking for food was the heart of survival for them all. In this case, he could use the job as an excuse to get away from the talkative captain for a long walk in the North Alabama woods. After about a mile they descended into a creek bottom and found a beaver dam. Eventually they managed to kill one of the little creatures, which Li'l Georgia carried back in triumph. Logan remembered having eaten one of these animals once when he had gone fishing on the Alabama River. As he remembered it, the meat was rather tasty after it had been cooked in a pot with potatoes by the slave who had been taken along on the trip. He supposed that the brown rice that Captain Burleson had given them could substitute satisfactorily for the potatoes.

When they reached their bivouac area, the cooking pot was already boiling, so in a couple of hours they were busy feasting on beaver and brown rice. Logan's memory of beaver had not been faulty as it turned out to be the best meat they had eaten in three weeks. Burleson stayed to share his visitors' bounty. Having eaten his fill, he lingered on entertaining them with stories of life in North Alabama during the last two years of the war.

According to the storekeeper, things had gone rather badly after the summer of 1863. By that time the early enthusiasm for the war had almost drained away. This part of the county had lost several men in the debacles at Vicksburg and Gettysburg, and the people had never recovered their zest of the early days of the conflict. The last year of the war had been a total disaster. Many of their local soldiers had deserted and returned to the valley of the Luxapallilia to hide in the woods and await the end.

The Tory activity up in Winston County became much more popular, with more and more people slipping away to support this rebellion within a rebellion. A few men from the area had even joined the Federal cavalry units. When the war ended, those men who had remained with the Confederacy until the end slowly drifted back, many with missing arms and legs. Of course a good third did not come back at all, most of them killed in Virginia or around Nashville. As far as Burleson knew, just about everyone who had survived the war was home now.

After a half-hour of this discouraging talk, the storekeeper tired of this subject and turned to other topics. Clearly he was optimistic by nature and seemed much more comfortable talking about the steps that could be taken to improve his people's situation. He assumed the Federal government would no nothing at all to assist the ex-Confederates, so he spent his time talking about steps that they could take to help themselves. He saw no way that the native whites could regain control of the political situation for at least twenty years, so they should turn their thoughts to their economic lives. Here, according to Burleson, there was true hope.

Logan listened and nodded now and then as the storekeeper rambled on. Burleson was more astute than Logan originally thought. The sergeant and Slaughter did not speak but sat and listened to their host's discourse. The conversation was spiced with occasional humorous tidbits, accompanied by booming laughter and belly rubbing.

Burleson had obviously given a great deal of thought to his subject. He talked in detail about how the sawmill people and the railroad tie-cutters were trying to work out a system to get a week's work out of the new freedmen in exchange for a weekly issue of food and clothing. He had no hope for a normal hired hand relationship of a week's pay on Friday for six days' worth of labor. That kind of arrangement could not possibly work for another fifty years.

He talked about the possibility of developing contracts with labor bosses who would put together labor gangs assigned to tasks at an agreed-upon scale. The blacks would be fed, clothed and housed in return for their labor.

Logan offered his opinion that he saw little difference in such a system and slavery, sure that the Federal government would never allow such a scheme to survive. Burleson nodded, evidently in agreement, but he continued his explanation as though he had not understood Logan's statement. Expanding upon his labor contract idea as if he were falling in love with its originality, clearly he thought that most ex-slaves would accept the arrangement, particularly after living through the difficult winter coming up. According to him, when cold weather came and food got really short, the black folks would begin to see the light. Burleson leaned back against his tree, patted his belly and issued his laugh with particularly good humor.

Slaughter broke in at this point. "Well, I sure hope that this kind of scheme will work because it's pretty close to what we're trying to work out down in Mexico. I think that our biggest problem will be getting and keeping control of these people. But once we get 'em down into central Mexico, they won't have much of any place to go. Course we know that we'll have to hire a lot of security people to hold them in line."

The storekeeper replied, "Well, I don't really know too much about these people and almost nothing about how to get 'em to work. There's a very few black people around here, and I don't know much about handling 'em—about working 'em or much of anything else about 'em. I had to go down to Eutaw back in March and there's a sho lots of these darkies down there. Everybody down there was figuring that the war was already lost and they'd have to figure out how to get 'em to plant and pick the next cotton crop after they was free." He stopped for a few deep laughs and continued, "I really believe that they were thinking that this year was already hopeless, so they were really talking about the '66 crop. To tell you the truth, the people around this area—and they're just about all white—ain't done nothing worth a killing about a crop for this year. So it's '66 for us, too."

"That's just about the way it is all over," said Slaughter. "I've been all over central and west Tennessee, and it's not quite as bad as it is here, but it's still plenty sorry. A lot of people are going to be starving come next February, and I'm thinking that a whole bunch of 'em are going to be our black friends. If we're going to make it through next year, we just have to figure out a way to take the strap to these people."

"I don't know about that," said Burleson. "I suppose every man and a lot of animals understand a good beating, but I wonder if that will get the job done. I don't reckon I've had a good strapping like you're talking about since I was twelve. Can't say it hurt me too much, neither. However, if we ever get back to that kind of business, it's going to be a lot longer than a year or two. You know the Yankees are going to feed all the new voters, one way or another. Probably by raising taxes on the rest of us. I can't see how the new freedmen will be forced to do much of anything for two or three years. Certainly not until after the next general election."

Slaughter drew up his long legs and looked down at his battered shoes. "You may be right about that. There's plenty of Federal troops all over the place, and it's going to be tough for us Southerners to get control again until the blue bellies leave. I did hear something just before I left Nashville that sounded to me like it might work. You know the darkies are just about all scared to death of haints, so a few boys up in middle Tennessee set out to try to scare 'em into doing right and into staying away from the polls at election. It seemed to work pretty well, but I don't know just exactly how they did the scaring. Played like ghosts, I reckon. Anyway, I think we ought to look a little further into that kind of business."

"Yeah, some soldier who came through here a week or so back was talking about something like that. I guess the people down in the flat country have got to do something, and that might work." Burleson laughed a few times before continuing, "Come to think of it, some of our white people could stand a little of that type stuff. Plenty of 'em are scared enough of haints, and we could stand having fewer of the white trash cast votes. And, you know, that kind of thing sounds like it might be fun, too."

"Yeah, that fun part would be some of the problem," broke in Logan. "That kind of thing is awful hard to control. You'd sure get a bunch of murdering and stealing going on under cover of the scaring. I'll admit, though, that we simply have to do something, and maybe that's all we got left to us. As long as the Yankees are occupying everything, we're not going to make a nickel trying to be legal and aboveboard. We sure can't lead the ex-slaves into anything until their dear friends and supporters are out of here. But maybe they'll get tired of it all and leave in a year or so. Then maybe we can set about reinventing our world."

Slaughter said no more, but his expression indicated that he was not pleased with Logan's comments. The sergeant and McCalab barely followed the drift of the talk. The sick man slept through the entire conversation.

The storekeeper got up, hitched up his baggy pants and, with one more burst of laughter, moved off toward the back door of his store, commenting that he had to shelve a few bolts of cloth that had just arrived from Tuscaloosa. He added that it was too bad that he hadn't received any foodstuff since the surrender and his guess was that it would be at least another month before he could look for any.

As darkness was falling, they all lay down in the grass near the goat shed and prepared for a night of rest. Logan lay awake for a while running over the situation that he must face the next day. Hood's physical condition was improving, but he really should rest another day before beginning the walk east toward the Tannehill-Montevallo trail. Burleson had advised going cross-country until they intersected that old road. That was probably their best route, but the first leg went across several swamps and streams without any road to follow. His last thought before drifting into sleep was that despite the goat smell the shed was not such a bad place to spend a few nights.

The next morning Logan went through the back door of the store and walked up to Burleson, who was busily building shelves. Seeing Logan, he immediately stopped, put down his tools and prepared for a long conversation. By now, of course, Logan knew his man; so he made sure that he controlled the subjects introduced so that he could direct the conversation. Unfortunately he could think of no way to control the laughing and belly rubbing. After Burleson asked after the sick man—thank God, not quite so sick now—he pointed out that the shelves were virtually empty. A barrel of salt and a couple of sacks of brown rice were evidently the entire stock of edibles. Logan was a little ashamed of himself for wondering if there wasn't something more hidden in the attic.

Logan could see a few bolts of cloth on the shelves, a few vegetable seeds in glass jars, some nails and a keg of horseshoes on the floor. Otherwise the building was empty except for the odds and ends of building materials scattered around.

"You see, we had a visit from Wilson's raiders. That's what happened to the glass we used to have in the front window. I can't say that old Wilson's people took a whole lot, 'cause it was all gone before they got here. But a bunch of 'em stayed in here overnight and left the place in an unholy mess. However, they didn't burn down the building when they left, and I'm most thankful for that. Particularly in that they did burn Old Liberty Church. Of course, they did bother to claim that it was an accident."

"Well, Captain Burleson, you remember from your service days that people who are sent out on these kinds of raids are almost impossible to control. If they show up with no officer with 'em, the locals just know they're really in for it; sometimes it's almost as bad even if they do have an officer. There's always somebody in the bunch who's all hot to burn everything in sight, and in a lot of cases, he's the one who'll start killing folks. Of course, the people who are running the operation damn well know all this, and that's why they sent them in the first place.

"I don't think that it's got much to do with which side you're talking about. You can just imagine what would have happened if the old First South Carolina Cav had been sent out in ten-man groups, with no officer, to scour the New York countryside. You can't let that kind of thing happen even in your own country, using your best people. That is, unless you do it intentionally."

Burleson pulled himself up on top of the counter and sat down. He controlled himself so that there was no laughter as he spoke. "Well, whoever is to blame for what, it's all in the past now, and we all have to start over from just where we are today. I still own this shabby old building and that dogtrot house you see across the road. My wife went off to visit her sister in Tupelo back some two months ago, and I haven't heard from her since. There ain't no mail, of course, but I suppose she's all right—'cause I know that she's a pretty tough woman. Our daughter is all grown up now and living in Tuscaloosa, so I guess I have a lot to be thankful for. We'll slowly start to get straightened out, I reckon. Maybe in ten or fifteen years we'll be getting back to where we were in 1860."

Sliding off the counter, Burleson went back to work on his shelving. Logan made no attempt to continue the conversation with the storekeeper, who looked as though the subject was just too discouraging to continue. Obviously Burleson had avoided the issues that had been the source of most of the ill feelings in this part of the state against the Black Belt counties.

This area had very little slavery, and the people here undoubtedly felt that they had little to gain from secession or the war to follow. Probably not a common attitude during the early days of the war when hopes for an independent Confederacy were high, but it must have become more and more prevalent as those hopes faded. This area originally had little open rebellion against the Confederacy such as had become common in Winston County, but it apparently become more common as the end approached. Certainly there was no way the hill counties could have been a hotbed of secession.

As he returned to the goat shed, Wes Logan felt somewhat less sure of the injustice that fate had dealt the South. Clearly he felt less sure of his own position than he had before coming in contact with the people of the hill country. Certainly these citizens were far removed from most of the things that had been so important to his people down in Dallas County.

The next morning Burleson came out to see his visitors off on the next leg of their journey. His usual good humor had replaced the previous day's grumpy attitude as he walked among the men, shaking each one's hand and wishing them well on their trip. He then turned his attention to spreading good cheer among the travelers.

"Sergeant, the Cap'n tells me you're the designated finder of roads and trails and also the group cobbler. I suspect that the cobbler part will turn out to be the bigger of the two jobs. There's damn few trails through the woods and swamps around these part, and besides that, your shoes are going to take an unholy beating from wading through all the water you'll have to cross. If you can keep some kind of footgear on your people, you'll sure be earning your pay. If you can get Slaughter here to do most of the work looking for trails—they just ain't any roads—you can use your time to scout out most of the fords."

"Yeah, I reckon I can take care of the roads and trails, seeing there ain't hardly any," growled Slaughter with almost a smile.

"Mr. Slaughter, you're the strangest looking traveler that's supposed to be half-starved that I've ever laid my eyes on. You must be licking up a little more than your share of the stuff that comes out of that iron pot."

"Oh, I would, but the Cap'n keeps too close a watch for that. Even on the boiled poke salat."

"You mighty right about that," put in Li'l Georgia, who was using a piece of rope to rig a carrying sling for the pot. "Otherwise I reckon me and Hood would have already starved."

"Now, Georgia, Cap'n Logan says you bring in most of the grub, so I'm guessing that some of the stuff might find its way into your mouth on your way back to camp." Burleson put a hand on Li'l Georgia's shoulder and laughed with affection.

"Yeah, I'll admit that I've grabbed up a couple of things on my way back from my begging trips. I remember that a lady up in Tennessee gave me a fried apple pie that never made it back. I ate it 'fore I got back to the main road. Never told nobody 'bout it, neither." Li'l Georgia laughed at the memory.

They all seemed to be in a mellow mood; even the sergeant entered into the spirit of the moment. "Georgia, you little snake, I thought you was putting on more weight than you was authorized." He ran his hand through his red hair and frowned playfully at the group's chief scrounger. "When we get out in the middle of this here swamp, you can eat all the alligators that you find. All by yourself; that is, if you can kill 'em all by yourself."

Even Hood, sitting propped against a tree, smiled a bit in support of his friend and benefactor, who was holding his own in the banter with the awesome sergeant. Cap'n Burleson allowed himself a few deep laughs and several slaps across his belly.

Having finished his jollying of the lower ranks, Burleson turned his attention to Captain Logan with no attempt to continue the jocular mood. He plunged into a serious conversation with the group leader on the problems facing them as they continued walking south.

The most logical route to follow in an attempt to intersect the trail from Tannehill to Montevallo would run to the southeast, crossing both the Warrior and Cahaba rivers and their swamps. Burleson had already discussed the route with Logan in detail, so he simply went over the difficult points. The swamps were going to be rough going, and the shortest route across that obstacle would involve at least thirty miles along low ridges with water and swamp creatures on either side. However, this route was by far the shortest and quickest way to the Tannehill Trail. Assuming little rainfall, which was the norm during late summer, a walking party should get through without too much difficulty.

Logan asked about the people they could expect to encounter. Burleson replied that the population was spotty, those they did find would be mostly ignorant and almost always extremely poor but would usually know plenty about life in the swamps. The storekeeper added that he had heard that several outlaws were supposed to be operating in those wild areas and should be watched for at all times.

Logan once more pointed out the importance of reaching Montevallo and the railroad as quickly as possible. Even though the trains were not yet running, maybe they would be by the time the group could get to the track. He was convinced that somehow he could get Hood on board if the trains were running and thus into Selma. Burleson, the eternal optimist, talked at length about all the food—fish, beaver, deer, snakes and chestnuts—that was available for the taking. Logan smiled and expressed his hope for the best in the area.

Burleson added one final warning about the wild hemp growing in some of the drier places in the swamp. This plant had been introduced as a cash crop back in the fifties, and although it was no longer cultivated plenty of it still grew voluntarily. Logan laughed and assured Burleson that his soldiers had discovered this plant up in Virginia. Since smoking the weed had resulted in several drunken incidents, he realized he would have to watch carefully for this substance and was grateful for the warning.

"Well, I suppose that I've mother-henned enough, and I know that if you've lived through the whole damn war and some hard time in Rock Island that you know what you've got to do to get yourself and your people home in one piece." Burleson reached out and pressed Logan's shoulder in farewell then walked over to a burlap sack and removed five old stockings, bulging out and tied up with a piece of ribbon. "It's cornmeal and it's about all I can spare right now. It ought to come in handy, though. Just think of it as the hills' present to the prairie."

"I appreciate any help, including advice and guidance, that I can get. God knows I need any and all that I can get if I'm ever to see Dallas County again. I know that there's no way to know for sure, but somehow I feel that I can make it with all my people still alive. You helped plenty. Dallas knows she owes you."

"Come by and see us again when you're up this way. In a year or so I'm hoping to be set up as a small-time furnishing merchant. That ought to be a good life, and I'm looking forward to it."

"We're off to Dallas. Thanks a lot." Logan pushed his sack of cornmeal under his belt and stepped away.

CHAPTER V

THROUGH THE SWAMPS

By midmorning after leaving Captain Burleson's store, Logan and his men had forded the Luxapaillia and started cross-country in the direction that Logan judged would eventually intersect the Tannehill trail. Although he had never visited the area himself, Burleson had explained that the road ran from the furnaces to the town of Montevallo. According to him, up until sometime in 1863 ore had been moved by ox wagon from pits near Montevallo to Tannehill and pig iron had been backloaded to the railhead; but the effort had been abandoned in the summer of '63 and the road had grown up since that time.

As Logan moved his men in a southeasterly direction, he found no roads worthy of the name; but they were able to follow a series of indistinct trails that looked like they had been around since Indian days. With the assistance of the sergeant he usually found fords across the numerous streams, and he guessed that they were making reasonable time despite the heavy cover. The few inhabitants they came across—all living in cabins near stream crossings—were eager enough to help them along, if for no other reason than to get rid of the intruders. These forest people usually could pass on some imprecise directions to the next house, even if it turned out to be several miles away. In addition, these settlers usually had some vague ideas about the direction to the Tannehill road although none of them had ever been as far as this famous trail.

The going was not easy. Hood was the only member of the group who appeared to be better off now that he had been when walking the dirt roads back in the settled areas. The paths were too rough to allow the stronger men to walk away from him; he seemed to dodge the underbrush and the rocks about as well as the others. Except for the stream crossings, Hood was doing better than he had for some weeks.

The walk seemed particularly hard on their shoes. By the second day Logan saw that they would have to do something to extend their use until the group could make it back to better roads. He began to question the inhabitants of the cabins they passed about cobbler's tools and leather. On the third day they found a family who had some rather crude tools and a little rawhide. Assuming that they wouldn't be able to do any better, Logan stopped the men for shoe repair.

The sergeant, who knew something about shoe repair, patched each piece of footwear in the party; he was assisted by Slaughter, who admitted to having some knowledge of how footwear should be made. These two worked for six hours on the shoes of all the men. When they got back on the road, everyone claimed to feel some improvement in his footwear.

In an attempt to make up some of the travel time lost during the shoe repair break, Logan pushed his people on for over an hour after the fall of darkness. It quickly became very dark, and the wind began to pick up. Soon the lightning that had been sporadic for some time became continuous, and within a short time thunder rolled in from all sides. It was obvious that a major storm was about to blow through the area, so Logan took his people into a clearing that he found by the light of the electrical strikes.

Suddenly it began to rain, the downpour driven in almost horizontal sheets by the wind. The trees around the edge of the clearing blew wildly with clouds of leaves and small branches sailing off in all directions. The lightning strikes were hitting all around the clearing, so Logan pushed those who were within reach down flat and then yelled to the others to lie down in the grass to avoid becoming a target for the flashing bolts. All got flat on the ground, pushing their faces into the standing vegetation. Logan was a bit unsure of the value of his advice, but at the moment he thought this was the action prescribed in some long-ago training session. He was confused because he had never been in such an intense electrical storm before, at least not while out in the open.

For some minutes the storm continued in full fury; but after what seemed like an eternity, the wind shifted and the lightning began moving away from their clearing. Logan kept them down for three or four more minutes and had just pushed himself up on his hands and knees to tell Slaughter to stay flat when there was one final blinding flash, which knocked the half-standing man flat. Logan's hair seemed to stand straight up, and the entire area was instantly saturated with the odor of ozone. Slaughter was knocked into the standing water and appeared to be lifeless. Logan rolled over to the flattened man and began to pull at his arms in an attempt to pump life back into his inert form. The sergeant almost instantly joined Logan, crouching and pumping Slaughter's arms back and forth, attempting to start the man's breathing cycle. Slaughter started to breathe again, although he appeared to be only partially conscious. The downpour suddenly stopped, and the men were now all up and helped drag Slaughter to higher ground.

The intense darkness was broken only by the slowly receding lightning flashes, but Li'l Georgia found an uprooted tree and pushed back some of the smaller branches to form a rudimental shelter for the injured man. They pulled him under this cover and checked out his condition as well as they could. Their efforts were rewarded when the big man suddenly sat up and tried to talk. The electrical storm was drifting off to the east, so they all stood around the injured man and marveled at his attempt to speak. He was still in such a state of shock, however, that his efforts to communicate were mostly unintelligible grunts and mumbles.

Suddenly Li'l Georgia grabbed the sergeant's arm. "Sir, listen at that train coming up through the woods, and it's coming rat this way. Listen at that thing a'coming!"

The sergeant moved away from the group to hear better but soon came running back yelling, "God damn, that's got to be a cyclone coming. Cap'n, Cap'n, get everybody down! The big blow is coming down on us! Right now!"

Logan heard the rumbling of the moving storm for the first time and suddenly realized what was happening. "Everybody get down! Now! We got a bad cyclone coming right this way. Get everybody down!" He tried to keep his voice steady but realized he wasn't doing a very good job of it.

Suddenly the rain squall was back in all its violence, and the lightning was drilling into the woods on all sides. In the light produced by the electrical strikes, a funnel-shaped cloud was clearly visible on the horizon. Now it was again raining very hard. But their attention was held by the violent wind uprooting trees on all sides. Debris was flying through the air and dropping all around, but by some miracle none fell on the men.

Suddenly the roaring that had sounded like a passing locomotive was past and going off into the timber beyond them. Logan sensed that the center of the storm was gone, and in a moment the wind and rain had gone off into the darkness. Across a small valley to their right he could see where the storm had cut a track through the timber. In that area everything was wrecked, timber was smashed into splinters along a cleared route some two hundred yards wide. He could see that they had escaped the path of the principal violence by two or three hundred yards.

The captain got his people out of the water and back to the uprooted tree where Slaughter was still lying where they had left him. The violence of the storm had evidently missed him completely, but he was still incapable of sensible conversation. Logan had a twinge of conscience when he realized that he had virtually abandoned the man while getting the others down on the ground for the second time in twenty minutes.

It was still raining, although not quite so hard, but the windstorm had passed and evidently had followed the twisting part of the storm into the darkness. Amazingly Logan could clearly still hear the sound of the disturbance receding into the distance. The freight train was roaring on, but now it sounded as though it was a couple of miles away. Despite the great speed at which everything seemed to have happened, by the sound of it the storm seemed to be moving off rather slowly.

Finally all was quiet. The rain had stopped and the winds had dropped to a stiff breeze. Logan spoke as slowly and as deliberately as he could manage. "Damn, that was some show. I think that thing was what I've heard called a tornado. It just tore down everything over there where it went through. You can see that every living thing is just smashed into splinters."

Sergeant Jackson replied, "Sir, I saw a storm sorta like that once down in Louisiana. That thing got down in a cane field and just tore the whole thing up. Didn't leave a damn thing standing. It picked up a pretty good sized house, blew it across the road and sorta threw it down still in one piece. But it grabbed a barn behind the house and just blew it off in the other direction and then smashed it into a million pieces. I know it's hard to believe, but in that thing's path, I saw a pine board driven all the way through a six-inch tree."

"Yeah, I know that these storms do all sorts of strange things. This was as close as I ever want to get to one—that's for sure. Let's find some high place and try to get a little sleep. I don't reckon we can do a thing for Slaughter 'cept hope for the best."

When dawn came, Logan gathered up his people and prepared to move out. The earth was soaking wet and a lot of timber was down. However, the trail was open except for an occasional uprooted tree, so there was a good chance that they could make fairly decent time. The big problem was that they now had two men who were partially disabled. Hood remained about the same as usual for him, but now Slaughter was barely able to speak or to stand. Logan and Jackson got the big man to his feet and passed out his handful of gear—a tin plate and cup, a battered hunting knife and a spoon—to other members of the team.

Slaughter still could not talk intelligently nor walk in a straight line, so it was clear that they would have to take extra breaks to enable the two cripples to keep moving south. Unfortunately the previous night's storm had precluded any search for food, so they had nothing to eat. Hood clearly was in need of food, but Slaughter got ready for the day's walk with no real sign of hunger. As they moved off, the big fellow seemed to grab hold of himself, straightening his back and walking almost normally. Logan suspected, however, that the burly man barely knew what he was doing.

As they pushed on through the downed timber and twisted underbrush, they began to realize the extent of the tremendous force that had blown through the area. They even found some dead crows that had evidently been killed by the storm. Later they saw a couple of blue jays and a large pilot rattler lying dead in a ditch. There was no indication of how such creatures could have lost their lives to a windstorm, but their mangled bodies, already covered with blue flies, simply emphasized the power of nature on a rampage.

Pushing forward they walked over a gentle ridge, and there, as though by magic, all evidence of a storm had disappeared. "Cap'n, this sorta reminds me of something else that happened down there in Louisiana that time. It looks like that this whole thing just sorta blew up into the sky and moved off up high. Down there that time, all of a sudden all that twisting and tearing just sorta bounded up into the clouds and blew over for four or five miles afore it dropped back down and started tearing hell out of things in another place." The sergeant pulled his old forage cap off, ran his fingers through his red hair and shook his head as though the storm was a bit beyond belief.

After half an hour of walking through an area with no signs of storm damage, Logan noticed that Slaughter was moving along with little sign of weakness. Now and then he stumbled and sometimes appeared to stagger, but the big man moved along with the group. The other men took turns attempting to talk to Slaughter, but none of them were successful in getting a response other than grunts and mumbles. His eyes had the far-off stare of heavy shock, but his strength evidently overcame any tendency to allow nature to take its course. Slaughter followed along without breaking pace.

Near mid-day they found a catfish that had been stranded in a shallow puddle alongside the path. Li'l Georgia and Hood caught the fish, and within minutes it was boiling in the iron pot. The group lay in the shade until the sergeant judged that it had cooked long enough to be eaten. Logan had never eaten a boiled catfish, but after consuming his portion he was called upon to tell Li'l Georgia that his efforts as a cook were much appreciated, adding that with a little salt and pepper the fish would have been simply delicious. The young man smiled broadly and accepted the compliment at face value.

The sun was already low on the horizon when they came upon another area virtually destroyed by the storm. Again, timber had been twisted and smashed by the previous night's violent wind. Here the storm had set down in a heavily wooded area and had been satisfied with smashing all the timber unlucky enough to be in its way for about a mile. Then the damage began to lessen, even leaving some of the timber standing. Suddenly all evidence of the storm was again gone, and the group was again walking in woods peaceful enough for a summer afternoon's stroll.

The following day they pushed on into the swamps that Logan understood lay northwest of the Warrior River. These swamps and the river proved to be the most serious obstacle they had encountered for several weeks. They wasted most of a day stumbling up and down the edge of the swamp looking for a solid area for crossing, but they finally had to wade in and splash from one hillock to the next. They stopped to rest at each of these solid islands floating in a sea of brackish water, usually displacing a couple of raccoons, several turtles and once a white-tailed deer. They would gladly have eaten any of these creatures, but they all left their dry havens for the water as the men approached. Of course the clouds of mosquitoes that were everywhere in the swamp were not disturbed, descending on the men like a flock of crows on a newly planted cornfield. In addition, hundreds of black flies joined in the attempt to drain all the blood from the cursing men.

On one of the hillocks, Li'l Georgia killed a black snake, declaring it to be nonpoisonous and immediately cleaning it for the cook pot. Later he admitted to Logan that he really didn't know if the reptile was poisonous but he was sure it made no difference as long as he removed the head before cooking. The snake turned out to be quite edible, as good as any food they'd had since Captain Burleson's brown rice. Everyone else ate his share, but Hood barely held down a little of the water in which the snake had been boiled.

Their first night in the swamp was made truly miserable by the mosquitoes. They kept the fire going all night, burning green leaves to produce smoke that supposedly would drive off the bloodthirsty insects. However, this tactic turned out to be nearly worthless since they were covered in red welts when daylight came. They gathered up their gear and waded off into the swamp again. For hours they waded in knee-deep water, falling into numerous holes deep enough to threaten to swallow them up, before they finally found dry land about noon. Shortly afterwards, they found the main channel of the Warrior River.

After the swamp, the river turned out to be rather easy. The sergeant could not find a ford, but he located a log, which Slaughter, despite his recent brush with electrocution, swam back and forth across a narrow spot until he had everyone and the precious cook pot across the river. After this effort, Logan was forced to let everyone rest for two hours. Then they were up and pushing on toward the Tannehill trail, which Logan knew had to be somewhere opposite the setting sun. That was as precise a guess as he could muster under his present, exhausted condition.

During the night it began to rain again, and they again crawled under a downed tree for shelter. However, when dawn broke everyone was wet and miserable. As Logan looked the party over before starting the day's walk—part of his morning ritual—he noted that Slaughter was almost back to normal but that Hood had changed for the worse. To add to their problems the fire had gone out during the night, and for the first time in several weeks the sergeant could not get it going again. They sloshed off down the trail, sloppy wet and discouraged. Even Li'l Georgia could not muster the courage to sing, and of course the mosquitoes and flies descended upon them again.

The rain continued throughout that day and into the next. On the third day Jackson finally found a small cave that they all crowded into and lay down on the sandy floor. They remained there for two days without food or fire. While they were there, Slaughter returned to normalcy. However, Hood had descended into semi-consciousness and the group fell into a state of black discouragement.

Finally the rain broke off and the sun made a feeble effort to shine. Logan did not have the heart to call for more walking, so Li'l Georgia and Sergeant Jackson were sent out to look for food of some sort. This turned out to be the day they had long dreaded; the scroungers found nothing to eat other than grubs and roots, no vegetable matter of any sort that mankind would recognize as edible. So it was grubs and roots—and not many of these. The heaviest blow was the continued failure to get a fire going. Logan began to wish for lightning strikes, which would at least start a fire.

On the following day they stumbled into a small clearing containing a tumbled down shack. Two half-starved people, a man and a woman, came out of the little cabin and stood staring at the group as though they were the first humans they had seen in weeks. A couple of saucer-eyed children of undetermined sex peered around the door of the shack. Logan hurried his group on past and into the woods beyond. Surely these emaciated people had nothing they could share with strangers; and even so, eating anything from such a place would probably give the entire group cholera or typhoid. Logan left his people seated in a shade and walked back to talk to the couple. Over his shoulder he could see the sergeant was having to apply a little force to keep the group from raiding the shack. Obviously their hunger was reaching a dangerous stage.

The couple at the shack immediately began to plead with the captain to leave them alone. They had no food other than what they were able to catch in the woods or swamps. However, the man seemed eager enough to guide them to the next creek, which he said was only two or three miles away. Dropping his voice to a hoarse whisper, the swamp man told Logan about a couple of men who had been camping out for a week or so at Big Turkey Ford over on the Black Warrior. He whispered that it would be worth the time to locate these two in order to pick up some guidance over to the Cahaba crossing sites.

The thin, dirty little man volunteered to guide them to the Black Warrior. He took his woman and children back into the cabin and soon reappeared, alone, wearing a stout-looking pair of boots and carrying a long, oak stave. He jabbed this up and down in the muddy earth, giggled and then announced that he was ready to go find the Black Warrior.

Logan looked at this volunteer guide and wondered if he was really strong enough to make it to the river. His cheeks were sunken, making his yellowed eyes appear to be pushed out on stems. His shoulders slumped, he was missing half his teeth, and his hands had a slight tremor. But this swamper was the only man around who wanted the job, so Logan took him.

Despite his appearance the guide turned out to be skillful at finding his way through the swamp. The group had walked for only a couple of hours when they found a slow running creek that the guide followed in what Logan estimated to be an easterly direction. Several hours later as the sun was beginning to set, the shaky little man led them away from the creek and into a swampy valley. Within less than half an hour they were standing on a dry section of roadway, evidently abandoned for several months, which led into what their guide informed them was Big Turkey Ford.

It had been a brutal walk, with Slaughter and the sergeant virtually dragging Hood along toward the end and with even Li'l Georgia and Logan stumbling badly. Logan wasn't even feeling hungry any longer, being past that stage, but he realized that the group would have to have food soon or some of them would just lie down and wait for the dark angel. Even Li'l Georgia seemed to have lost interest in looking for food.

At this point the dirty, emaciated guide proved to be an unlikely source of help. He led Sergeant Jackson down into a little cove to look for a set trotline. When they returned, they were carrying a large catfish. Then, miracle of miracles, the guide fumbled around in his clothing and produced a flint and steel and soon had a fire burning.

Logan, who had carried the cook pot for the last several miles, had been tempted to finally give up and throw it down. However, he somehow found the strength to keep on, so now he was looking at a steaming pot. The fire and boiling water seemed to revitalize everyone except Hood, who had collapsed on the ground. Within minutes the catfish was boiling away.

The sergeant came to sit by Logan, who was stretched out on a patch of dry grass. "Cap'n, I couldn't believe that old scarecrow, but he went down in that slough and found a trotline within five minutes and came up with that fish. I sur hope the poor devil that set that line is better off than we are, 'cause we stole that cat sur as shooting."

"I don't see how he could need it quite as bad as we do. I hope that's the way it is, anyhow. "'Cause we just have to have this thing just now. May God send him another fish, and tonight."

"Sir, you're mighty right about that. But, tonight, I think I'd haf stole it from my own mother. And just look at that monster boil away." In spite of the heat the sergeant stretched his feet to the fire and almost instantly began to snore.

Logan sat watching the fish boil for another thirty minutes before he decided it had cooked enough. With Li'l Georgia's help, he pulled the cat out of the pot and cut it into chunks. Even Hood ate a few bites while everyone else gorged down their portions. Within two minutes every sign of the creature had disappeared down their gullets.

Ten minutes later Logan look around the little dry hillock and saw that everyone else except the guide was fast asleep. The tattered swamp man was squatting on his heels with his usual apathetic look. Logan studied him for a few moments before speaking. "It looks like you know this country pretty well. How's the walking going to be from here over to the Cahaba? You can see that we're just about barefooted and that our man Hood is just about past any sort of walking."

"Yes, sir. I can see you'll be needing to move as easy as you can. Howsomeever, I can't help y'all that much beyond this here ford. I did cross the Black Warrior once here at Big Turkey, but I just turned around and came back. So I ain't never really been any further than right cher."

Despite his state of mind, Logan managed a chuckle at the swamper's statement. "You mean you were able to hide here in this swamp during the entire war?"

"Well, I was here in the swamp a long time 'fore the war. All my life, really. But when the war came on, the Confederate patrol caught me and took me away to that town of Huntsville. That's the furtherest I'd ever been away in my life, and I sur didn't like it. They tried to make a soldier outer me up there. But it didn't work out too well. After a couple of weeks they put me out on guard, and I just took my old musket and skedaddled out of there. Didn't stop running 'til I got all the way back here to the swamp. Ain't been out since. Don't figure on ever going out agin."

"Yeah, but don't you find it pretty hard to scrape out a living out here so deep in the sloughs?"

"Naw, me and my old lady have been getting by. We done pretty good until the damn war came along. I was trapping a lot then, so we could get us a little money along. There was always fish to catch and a few beaver and now and then a deer would fall in our pit. When the war came, the fur market dried up, and then the soldiers came thrashing around and drove off a lot of the game when they started setting fires everywhere. We've been having it pretty rough for the last year or so."

"I guess you know that's a lot better than getting shot at—at least getting shot at and sometimes hit."

"You might right. I knows that well enough. I just want to stay away from that kind of thing forever and ever. All my folks on both sides have been swampers as fer back as any of us knows. And not a single one's been no soldier. 'Cept me, of course, during that two weeks up in Huntsville."

Logan smiled a bit. "Yeah, I suppose you can really take credit for never having been a soldier, even if you do have that two-week spot on your record."

The guide either missed the sarcasm or chose to ignore it, continuing to talk about life in the swamps. Logan drifted into sleep listening to the man complimenting his wife—something about how she was a good woman and a good plow hand. The last thing he remembered was something about the swamper's kids having the chills and fever every summer.

The guide was the first one awake the next morning. Logan awoke to find him busy punching up the fire. As Logan walked over to the cook pot, the swamper smiled a snaggletooth grin and drawled, "Cap'n, you'd better get yo people up and get them started pulling the ticks off theirselves. They's all over the place here. I tried to keep the fire smoking to run the mosquitoes off some, but I see them red welts all over you, so I guess it didn't work too good."

A quick look at himself showed that his arms and chest were indeed covered with red spots and that the itching on his legs was caused by a number of crawling ticks. He shook the sergeant awake and sent him to rouse the others.

Within moments everyone was busy picking ticks off his body and cursing their luck for being in such a godforsaken place.

The swamp man watched with obvious amusement and finally chuckled, "Aw, learn to live with them things. They ain't no getting away from 'em. Just brush the worse ones off and live with the rest of 'em. Come on over to the cook pot and get your part of dese here turtles and their eggs. I found enough of 'em last night to get you folks through the day."

Day had come, partially clear and already hot. Li'l Georgia almost forced some of the turtle down Hood as the others gobbled up their portions. The men gathered their simple belongings and followed Sergeant Jackson into the water to move toward the east bank of the river. Li'l Georgia held the cook pot with one hand and pulled Hood along with the other. They would keep upstream from some rock marking the lower edge of the ford. The water was still high from the recent rainfall, but they crossed without incident except when Slaughter fell into a deep hole and had to be pulled out.

Before following the others the captain shook hands with the guide, thanked him and bade him good luck and an easy trip back. As he turned to go, he finally said, "You know, living in that swamp is real hard on your wife and youngsters even if they've never known anything else. There's going to be a lot of changes now that the war is finally over, and it might be good if you hooked on to one of those changes and get your folks up on higher ground. Someone will be building more railroads, bringing in new steamboats and putting in steam sawmills. The people who run these things are going to need people like you. They won't know it at first, and I guess you won't know that you need them, but . . ."

The guide accepted the wink and the slap on the shoulder from Logan. Then for the first time during their acquaintance, he broke into a sly smile. "Yes, sir. Maybe it would be good if we could do that. I knows that there's going to be a lot of changes and maybe we might just grab on to one of 'em. I knows my woman would like that. Thank ye."

* * *

After crossing the river, Logan led his people along the trail toward the morning sun. It appeared that it had been some time since any vehicle had used this pathway, but he did see some indistinct wagon tracks and signs of oxen and horses that seemed to be several weeks old. The day was pleasant, at least as nice as any they'd seen since leaving Burleson's store; so despite the rough trail, they moved along at a good pace. Even Hood pulled himself along with the help of a thick hickory stick that Li'l Georgia had cut and trimmed into a crude crutch. The chief scavenger even whistled a couple of hymns and sang two verses of "Annie Laurie."

Around noon they came upon a creek. As soon as they had managed to wade across, they were startled by a nicker, which turned out to be from a gaunt, almost skeletal, mule tied to a tree alongside the stream. Just beyond the mule was a dead campfire and a crude brush lean-to. Logan halted the group and sent the sergeant and Li'l Georgia in search of the animal's owner. They returned a quarter of an hour later with two men in tow.

The two men, dressed in the patched and torn clothing so typical of the time, came up to the edge of the fire pit and introduced themselves as ex-Confederates. To Logan this was obviously true for the older man, who had an arm off above the elbow. However, the younger man couldn't have been over sixteen or seventeen and could possibly have missed the war entirely. Logan nodded to the men and prepared himself for the usual recitation of battles and units. The younger man was indeed a latecomer to the war and had been, as he put it, just a guard at Selma. The older fellow waved his stump of an arm as he identified himself as a veteran of the Third South Carolina Infantry, adding hastily that he had started off as a trooper in Stuart's cavalry. Of course, that had been before his foot soldiering days.

Putting the story all together, Logan suddenly said, "Why, I remember you. You and I were in Q Company together back right after First Bull Run. Our mounts had been killed in that fracas, and we were there waiting to get ourselves another horse." He turned to the younger man and explained, "That Q Company business is just what us cavalrymen call the holding company a regiment puts people in who've lost their horse and are waiting for a replacement."

"Yeah, you're right. I lost my horse at First Bull Run like a lot of other people. Anyway, it was old Q Company for me. I never could get another horse, so they shipped me off to the infantry. I spent the rest of the war as one of Longstreet's braves. I finally got this bobbed arm at Chicamauga, so I just hung around a while afore they finally let me leave. I came on down here in late '64 and have been right around here ever since."

"Yep, I was lucky about my horse. Had to go all the way down to middle Tennessee, but I finally got me one. I kept that old animal all the way to Petersburg. There he finally fell and had to be put down. That's after missing all those slugs in all those fights."

The ex-infantryman suddenly recognized Logan and said, "Now I remember ye. Ye was a sergeant, weren't ye. Somebody told me that later on ye got to be a officer. Was that right?"

"Yes, I was a sergeant then. Hampton—he was a colonel at that time—asked the company to elect me a lieutenant when he was reorganized in the fall of '61. And they did. Just dumb luck, I guess. I really don't know why."

At this point Sergeant Jackson broke into the conversation. "This here is Cap'n Logan. He commanded A Company of the First South Carolina Cavalry for over three years, and he's still alive. How about that? I guess ole Hamp could see all this, even if nobody else could."

There was a short pause as the two strangers took in this statement. Then the one-armed man said with a touch of awe, "Oh, so you got to be a company commander for General Hampton?"

"Well, yeah. Don't know how I lucked out so well. But I did stay around until I finally got captured in November of '64. I spent the rest of the war in good old Rock Island. The damn Yankees turned us loose in May, and sinçe then we've been walking south as fast as we could manage."

"Yeah, we've seen a few come through here walking back from the North. Hadn't seen any for a while, though. I'd begin to think that everybody was back."

Logan smiled a bitter little smile. "Our friends the Yankees ain't going to make that big of a mistake. They're still using us to clean up those prison hellholes. However, I suppose the bulk of our men are back, but I'm betting you'll see a few coming along for three or four weeks yet."

As Logan and the amputee continued their reminiscences, the younger man went to the fire pit and dug around in the ashes until he uncovered a live coal, which he used to start a small fire. Then he walked into the woods, pulled a small sapling down and removed a greasy tow sack. This improvised larder yielded a few cooking utensils and a small bag of ground coffee. So in this unlikeliest of spots the group was soon passing around a bowl of very hot coffee. Li'l Georgia reminded the men that this was the first real coffee they had tasted since they had left the Dixon place in Tennessee. They had parched corn done up as coffee at the Burleson store, but this was the first real stuff.

One-Arm laughed at the eagerness with which they slurped the coffee. He told them that a few things like coffee, salt and sugar were coming in from Mobile but that it did little good if you had no money. This coffee and a little salt had been picked up over on the Cahaba at a trading post being run by a hustler who had come up river from the town of Cahaba. This fellow made a living buying furs and fish. That's how they had come by the coffee and also how they hoped to get some sugar and a few fishing supplies sometime in the next few days. He warned Logan that he would have to be very careful when he got to the trading post because it had attracted several unsavory characters who were camping in the woods downstream from the store.

Logan decided to question One-Arm rather closely. "Just what are these people doing, and what's their connection with the trader and his family? How are these folks making a living, and just where are they making this living?"

"Well, Cap'n, these people are real drop shots. I know for a fact that the boss of the group and his second knocker was both galvanized Yankees recruited out of Rock Island prison. I guess you know what I mean by galvanized Yankees."

"I'm afraid so. The Federals were doing that recruiting while I was there. I know they got quite a few, but I never knew any of 'em personally. After they got 'em all signed up and sworn in, they dressed them up in blue and hauled 'em out to Fort Leavenworth to join a unit. That must have been a high-class outfit, whole companies made up of nothing but traitors. 'Course, maybe these newly minted blue bellies thought that was the only way open to 'em to get out of that stockade alive. Things were pretty bad in those places, particularly during the late winter of '65. And maybe they were guessing that going galvanized was the only way they could get home again alive."

Wildly waving his stump of an arm, the ex-infantryman began degrading the turncoats with loud threats and promises of instant disfiguration if he ever saw one of them alone. But as he put it, they never were alone—always traveled in bunches. Besides that, he thought the trading post depended on these people to bring in the few trade goods that found their way into the swamps.

After several minutes of this tirade, the one-armed man finally calmed down a bit, so Logan broke in with a request for the services of the decrepit mule staked out by the creek. Negotiations led to an agreement to allow them to use the mule to carry Hood at least part of the way to the trading post. The young man who had been a guard at Selma would lead the mule to the crossings at the Cahaba and maintain control of the animal during the trip. As soon as they reached the river, the young man would immediately return with the precious mule. When Logan was satisfied that he had reached the best bargain possible, he paid the older veteran with two of their precious greenbacks and pushed Hood up into the makeshift saddle. If he had been alone, he wouldn't have dared let the fishermen know that he was carrying money, but in the group he felt safe enough.

After a few more pleasantries, the group was off toward the trading post with the one-armed man's blessing and some final advice about the trail and what to do when they reached their destination. Walking along with the group for a while, he was full of apologies for having to charge for the use of the mule and for it not being a younger and stronger animal. He reminded Logan not to let the people around the trading post know that he had greenbacks or he might end up getting himself killed by some of the campers. Finally, just as he turned to retrace his steps back to the campsite, he reminded the young ex-guard to be back to camp by sunset the next day.

It was a hard day of walking and the sun was dropping behind the trees when Logan stopped the group and they made camp. Just for safety, he turned the mule over to Sergeant Jackson. Although the young fisherman obviously wanted to protest this, he took a close look at Jackson and made no audible objection.

By midmorning of the following day the group had reached Slippery Rock Ford of the Cahaba, where they planned to make their way across to the two or three cabins visible on the other side. Despite the recent rains, here the water flowing over the rocks at the ford was not very deep. So the men waded across with Hood still riding the mule and holding tightly to the rope tied around the animal's neck.

When they were safely across, Logan sent the mule and the Selma guard back across the river to return home. Just to make sure, Logan sent the sergeant along for the first mile or so of the return trip.

Their approach to the cabins was greeted by a couple of big cur dogs putting up a ferocious outcry against this invasion of their territory. A dirty little man suddenly bounded out of the largest cabin and issued the curses that drove the animals back under the cabin. When quiet had returned to the glade, the man came forward.

Without acknowledging the existence of the other men in the group, he walked over to Logan while extended his hand in greeting. The man wiped his hands over the front of his shirt and announced in a whinny voice, "I'm Alexander Hamilton Mays, and I own this here camp. We'uns don't have much to sell, but yo'all come in and see if I can help you somehow." Mays's eyes swept over Logan and hesitated for an instant at the mutilated ear and the scar across the cheek. "I'd guess you folks is walking home from the North, and so I'll tell you right now that I can't do nothing to fix up them shoes of yourn. But come on in and see if there be anything I can do to help you out in any other way."

They passed the two curs looking out from under the porch with great suspicion and went inside. Logan could see that the ramshackle shelves were almost bare, holding only a few bolts of cloth and a dozen or so tow sacks. A low fire was burning in the fireplace on the end wall, and a big coffee pot was making a feeble effort to put out steam. Mays walked to the pot and poured some dark, thick liquid in a couple of tin cups and offered them to the men. "It's shore not real coffee, but we're getting pretty good at roasting up a little burnt corn. I've been drinking it so long I'm starting to like it. Now, I could sell you a little something stronger," he said waving at a big jug prominently displayed on the shelf behind the rough counter. "It's just regular old pop skull, but we got plenty of it. We sell lots of that stuff, by the way."

At that point a woman in a patched, dark dress that was almost as dirty as Mays's clothing came in from the shed room in the back. She withdrew into a dark corner of the barroom and stood peeping out from under the scraggly mop of hair that was falling into her face. Logan noted that she had no front teeth. Suddenly the storekeeper walked across the room and began a grumbling tirade against the woman, but she did not appear to be much influenced by this display of authority. As Mays raised his voice, however, she picked up her ragged skirts and withdrew into the back room.

The group looked over the barroom and then withdrew to the trees shading the front of the store, leaving Logan to talk to the storekeeper. Mays revealed that he was one of the Winston County men who had joined the Federal army and that he now hoped to be able to get on the Federal pension rolls. He said that several other men around the area, who helped him run the place, had been members of the Federal First Alabama Cavalry at the same time that he had served and they were now waiting to board the United States gravy train. Logan thought that the wait might be a long one, but he said nothing. At the very least, the Union veterans from Alabama would be at the end of the line when the Federal free money was passed out. There must be about a million Yankees already standing in that line, and they certainly wouldn't drop their claims in this lifetime.

Mays added several additional bits of information about how he planned to get on the Federal pension rolls. Then rolling his eyes and clearing his throat often, he gave a detailed explanation of just how he was managing to survive here on the Cahaba. Sorting through this torrent of information, Logan determined that the little Tory had moved to the swamp after his discharge with enough money from his last pay to rent this camp, setting himself up in the business of buying fish and furs from the swamp people and selling them needed equipment and supplies.

However, he was still finding it difficult to get the goods he needed from Selma or from Montevallo. A few traps and some fish hooks and lines had come up from Selma; but because the trains were not yet running into Montevallo, he had gotten nothing from that source. As he rambled on, it became clear that his main business was running a distillery. He had managed to get several bushels of corn from one of the local swamp people, and he had immediately turned this into some sort of corn liquor, which he found could be sold about as fast as he could make it. His customers had no money, of course, but he ended up with a lot a fish, which kept him busy cleaning and drying them on racks behind the store. Even though he had been unable to buy much foodstuff, footwear, or shoe leather from his suppliers, he felt he'd be able to get along all right in this business because, as he said—Logan thought a bit too proudly—he had been an impressing corporal in the Alabama Cavalry and understood about this sort of things.

Finally Logan broke into the river of talk to ask if he and his group could bivouac for a day or two somewhere in the vicinity of the fish camp. Mays rolled his eyes back as though he might have a lot more information to impart, but after a moment he gave his permission with a resigned sigh. He stuck two fingers into his mouth and blasted out a shrill whistle. Almost immediately a tiny black boy came running from the back room and led Logan away to pick up the rest of his group. The boy then motioned for them to follow him down the river to a bivouac area that turned out to be a crude lean-to covered with pine brush.

Li'l Georgia took Hood inside and eased him down on a pile of old pine branches that appeared to have been there for several weeks. Sergeant Jackson then went to the river in search of food while Logan and Slaughter began dragging in fresh pine straw for bedding. The black boy immediately scurried away toward the trading post. Li'l Georgia followed him back to beg a couple of live coals from the fireplace.

Within a few minutes the storekeeper's wife showed up at the bivouac area with an axe and an invitation to cut as many pine branches as they needed for bedding. Accepting this invitation, Slaughter took the axe to cut the branches, dragging them into the arbor. By the time Sergeant Jackson returned with a turtle in one hand and a muskrat in the other, a blazing fire had the water in the cook pot at a boil. The trader's wife, who turned out to be much more pleasant than first appearances indicated, went back to the store and returned with two cups of hominy. This followed the turtle and muskrat into the pot. She even gave them a little lump of salt, something they had not seen since leaving the Burleson place. Just as she turned to go back, she whispered to Logan that he should keep a sharp lookout during the coming night. Without further explanation, she trotted off up the path toward the store.

Logan squatted by the fire feeding wood into the flames and giving silent thanks that his small group was usually able to scrounge up a little food a couple of times each day. And at night they could gather enough pine branches to make an acceptable bed. Surely most of these actions would have been nearly impossible if their long walk had taken place in mid-winter. Hood would surely have been dead weeks ago, and most of the rest of them would have been barely alive. Luck again—much better to be lucky than smart. He walked back to the store to beg a little pepper.

Approaching the cabin, Logan heard a sudden eruption of curses from within as Alexander Hamilton Mays busily berated his wife for giving away good grub to a bunch of worthless Secesh. As far as Logan could tell from the uproar, though, no blows were being passed; nor from the reaction of the Mays woman did it sound as though she was frightened or, for that matter, very concerned.

After hearing this domestic disturbance and Mays's loud berating of the Secess, Logan returned to the brush arbor without pushing his luck any further by begging for pepper. Jackson already had the other three men inside the shelter and bedded down in the fresh pine branches. The sergeant was a true believer in axiom of sleep now before the officers come and give you a job to do. Hood, totally exhausted from the day's activity, was already fast asleep. Slaughter was entertaining Li'l Georgia with one of his long stories about Nashville during the war. Logan listened to the tale until he recognized the drift of this particular story, which was now to the part about the women of Nashville during 1864.

Slaughter's stories about women were usually not to their advantage, so Logan laughingly broke up the session by asking Jackson to come with him to set up a guard for the night. Slaughter asked to go along to familiarize himself with the terrain, thus effectively ending his story.

Normally a guard was not set up for their small group, but tonight Logan thought it unwise to sleep without security. Of the several people he had seen around the area, none appeared to be candidates for the priesthood. So taking their heavy hickory sticks, they moved up the slope to a position commanding both the bivouac shelter and the trails that paralleled the river. Jackson clearly was not thrilled by the prospect of a long night of sentry duty in the middle of the Cahaba bottoms with little chance of seeing anyone or anything other than a couple of scroungy Winston County Tories and maybe some lost black kid. However, he had been around for a long time, so he made no objection other than a long sour face. Logan recognized the sergeant's feeling but took no action other than allowing him to take the first sleep time.

Sometime after midnight Jackson shook the captain awake and whispered that he thought he could see some people moving around down by the river. Logan got up and went with Jackson down the hill toward the lean-to in an attempt to put themselves between the shadowy figures and their sleeping people. They moved along as silently as possible, but they soon realized that the intruders were moving too fast to be intercepted before they could reach the arbor. They were still fifty yards away when the intruders suddenly broke from the underbrush and ran into the lean-to. Logan gave up all pretense of silence, signaled to Jackson and began running as fast as he could toward their sleeping shelter. As they got within a few yards of the lean-to, Jackson issued his own version of the rebel yell, came running past Logan and leaped into the middle of the shadowy figures moving about inside. Approaching the shelter, Logan could make out a man dragging Hood along the dirt floor and down the slope toward the campfire. Out of the corner of his eye he saw Slaughter wrestling with another figure. The sergeant had already closed with this intruder and was slashing at him with his hickory stick in an attempt to knock him away from Slaughter.

Hood had been unable to get to his feet, so his opponent was dragging him into the circle of light radiating from the fire. Logan jumped at the man, swinging his heavy hickory stick in a whistling arc. Just at that moment there was a blinding flash and a deafening explosion. After three years in combat, the old soldier knew instantly that he had been shot at but missed. He brought the hickory club down on his opponent's neck and shoulders with all his strength. The man loosened his hold on Hood and staggered back wildly. Logan stumbled over a tree limb in the dark and fell heavily on the ground. As he fell he saw his opponent stagger back and fall into the fire pit. In an instant the man rolled out of the pit and ran down the hill, but by the light of the fire Logan had caught a glimpse of a big, bushy, unkempt beard. As the man staggered away, Logan noted that his beard was a dirty red. Getting to his feet, Logan flung his stick after the running man but missed him by several feet. Slaughter ran by after a second man.

A few seconds later another bullet whistled by his head, but the shot must have been high because there was no indication that anything was hit. As Hood's assailant went careening down the hill toward the river, Logan saw him beating frantically at the fire that was blazing in his hair and clothing. Then the darkness closed about the running men, and the episode was over.

The following morning Logan and Slaughter walked up to the fish camp and jerked the front door open just as Mays was finishing his breakfast. Immediately confronted with the story of the assault, the dirty little man shuffled his feet around as though he were standing in hot ashes. Then a torrent of explanation came flowing out of his broken-tooth mouth, emphasizing that he knew nothing about anyone around his camp who would dream of doing such a thing. The comments, married with a flood of scratching and coughing, finally caused Slaughter to seize the man by the front of his shirt and lift him clear off the floor. Mays continued his explanation, although now in a pleading tone. Logan motioned for Slaughter to release his prey, and Mays instantly found himself crumpled on the floor.

Logan growled, "I'll assume that what you're saying is straight, but let's have no misunderstanding about one thing. If anyone around here shoots at our people again, they'd better make damn sure that they hit at least a couple of us from the first cylinder. You understand that?"

Mays was now on his hands and knees, whimpering like a kicked dog. After a good two minutes of this reaction, Slaughter jerked the groveling storekeeper to his feet. Then Logan admonished him to make sure that things were quiet during the next two or three days because, as Logan put it, his traveling party expected to remain right where they were until their sick man could gather a little more strength.

As Mays regained a bit of his composure, he began making promises that everything was certain to be very quiet for the next few days. "Yes, sir. Yes, sir. That man you're talking 'bout with the red whiskers is a bad 'un. He and his big buddy, who hangs around here some too, are both galvanized Yankees. They're both bad 'uns. Yes, sir."

"All right, jes you keep in mind that we know about those galvanized types. And you might tell those sons-of-bitches the next time you see 'em that shooting in the dark is jus' 'bout useless," Logan said as he poked two fingers into the little man's chest.

The group stayed at their bivouac for the next two days, but nothing more was seen of Alexander Hamilton Mays. All contact was with the wife, who appeared to be enjoying standing in for the proprietor. Even the little black boy seemed to come out of his shell after Mays disappeared. He talked with Li'l Georgia and even brought the cook, as he called him, a nice size lump of salt from somewhere within the store. Finally, he did a little buck dancing for Slaughter, who showed appropriate appreciation with much laughter and applause.

During one of his visits the young fellow even tried to show Li'l Georgia something about the buck dancing routine, but it was obvious that the Georgia boy would have to practice quite a while to approach the skill of the child. At least the effort afforded the group a little laughter. Li'l

Georgia smiled and accepted the men's reaction to his clowning and then called for more applause for the boy.

After this impromptu entertainment Logan called on the boy to tell them all about life in the fish camp, starting the conversation by asking him his age. The little fellow immediately held up nine fingers and flashed a broad smile. A few more questions established that the boy's name was Jessie and that the folks around the store called him Going Jessie because, as he said, he was always going. He hadn't seen his mother since Wilson's raid, and he had almost starved until Massa Mays picked him up down by the river several days later. Since then he had worked here at the fish camp, sometimes as the "pig boy" who drove the sows and their litters in and out of the woods and sometimes as the Missus' helper down at the liquor still.

He ended his story by saying that he wanted to learn to read and write just like the white folks. Missus Mays, who according to the boy could read and write real good, was teaching him.

"That's the way. You work hard and you can learn to read and write. Remember, plenty of white folks can't read and write neither. So soon you'll be able to read the Bible better than a lot of preachers, and that's for both black and white. Then you'll be a sure enough Going Jessie."

The little boy smiled, clapped his hands and danced with delight as he moved off up the trail to the store.

The next day Logan made a thorough search of the area and questioned several people he found camping in the vicinity, but all signs of the two men who had raided the bivouac had of course disappeared. Sergeant Jackson found where three or four horses had crossed to the western side of the river, so Logan assumed that the renegades who had attacked them had decided to move on in search of easier prey.

After two days Logan assembled his people and they walked off toward the southeast in search of the Tannehill trail. For the first day even Hood was able to walk with his back almost straight and his head held high.

CHAPTER VI

MONTEVALLO AND SOUTH TOWARD HOME

According to the estimates of the men fishing near the Cahaba ford, the town of Montevallo should not have been over a two-day walk to the south. The distance in miles appeared to be in question; but when Logan and his group reached the settlement, it was clear that it would not have taken much over a day and a half if they had not been burdened by the struggling Hood. As it was, it took them almost twice that long to complete the trip, but eventually they reached the edge of the town.

The sergeant and Slaughter had borne the brunt of assisting the stumbling Hood through the last two days to Montevallo. During the final hours of the walk they were almost dragging the man along, and Logan was thankful that the clay surface was dry and in reasonable repair. Evidently there had been no chert or gravel put down for the last two or three years, but the dry summer had ensured that most of the road was at least passable. The captain attempted to keep up their spirits by reminding the group several times that they were approaching the biggest railhead in the central part of the state.

Just before they reached the creek north of the town, they came to a large, two-story farmhouse that had evidently come through the war without major damage.

One of the barns behind the house had been burned out, but otherwise everything appeared to be in reasonably good shape. As was so common throughout this part of Alabama, there appeared to be almost nothing growing in the fields surrounding the house. Logan could see only one bony cow grazing between the house and the creek. Everything looked peaceful enough, however, so he pulled his people off the road and let them sit down under a large cedar tree near the edge of the front yard. He opened the gate in the badly damaged paling fence, walked past the well house up to the porch and knocked on the door.

A huge black woman came to the door and looked out quizzically at this stranger on her front porch. She straightened the bandanna covering her head and picked up a worn brush broom as though she was about to sweep the front walkway.

As usual Logan identified himself as an old Confederate soldier recently released from Rock Island prison making his way south toward Selma. The woman appeared to accept this identification as though she had heard many such statements before. Without smiling she went back into the house mumbling something about telling her white folks.

Within a couple of minutes a white woman came to the door and announced that she was Mrs. Jarvis, the lady of the house. After listening to Logan again identify himself and his men, she asked them to come to the side of the house and wait in the shade of some large oaks until she could send for her husband. She walked along with them and stood talking to Logan while they waited.

She first made clear that the town was occupied by a detachment of the Eighth Iowa Cavalry and that nothing went on in the area without the approved of the commander of that unit. No serious incidents had occurred yet, but the townspeople were just holding their collective breath for the first one to take place. Despite the almost peaceful situation she described, she emphatically pointed out that being occupied by the enemy was most unpleasant. As soon as this was established, she went on to say that food was very scarce and that it looked like this would be the situation until at least the next spring. Logan got the impression from her tone that this last comment was just in case he or his people were thinking about begging for food. After this warning, she rattled on about the problems of the conquered for several minutes.

Finally her husband, a wiry little man who appeared to be in his sixties, walked up from the barn area. After she introduced Captain Logan to her husband, the talkative woman immediately became silent and retreated into the house.

"As my wife told you, I'm Charles Jarvis; and I'm very glad to see you and your men." He looked around at the disheveled group who were already sinking back into the shade of the oaks.

"Our Confederates coming down from the Yankee prisons have been drifting by for several weeks now, but the number has been decreasing lately. You're the first ones for some two weeks. What can I do to help you? Not that it can be very much, but I'll sure try." The planter looked the captain straight in the eye and appeared to Logan to be absolutely sincere.

"Well, we've got a man with a bad case of dysentery who's just barely able to walk, so we've got to stop somewhere and let him rest for a day or two before we start off toward Dallas County."

The little man smiled sympathetically, nodded his understanding and continued, "Well, we ought to be able to put the sick man in the storage shed behind the cookhouse, and the rest of you can sleep in the hayloft above the horse barn. I'm afraid that's about all I can do for you. I know it's not much, but I suppose you people are used to lots worse. You're pretty lucky, really, because from here to Selma you can just walk down the railroad tracks. You're only about fifty miles from home, and I think all the trestles are back in, except for the one 'cross that big creek that empties into the Cahaba. That one is way down in Dallas County."

At that point the big black woman came out with a bucket of fresh water, and the men crowded around to drink. When all had had their chance at the drinking gourd, the woman led Hood to the shed behind the cookhouse. Before they reached the shed, Logan noticed the woman was almost dragging the sick man as they moved along. Within minutes the men back under the trees were, as usual, fast asleep.

Mr. Jarvis led Logan to the back porch of the house and asked him to sit in a wooden rocker. The host then sat down across from his guest. Over a pitcher of cool water he settled back ready to take in all sorts of stories from the war years.

Logan intentionally disappointed the man by confining himself to talking about problems and hardships that had arisen during the trip south from Rock Island. He was careful to stay well away from the war itself for he had found that most people he came across were willing enough to spend a lot of time on war stories, so he really felt that his listener needed little encouragement in that field. In addition, he felt that unless the audience had some sort of background in such matters, very few were prepared to understand a detailed discussion of such dreadful affairs.

After half an hour of tales of the hardships of their walk, Logan finally felt free to discuss how things were going in central Alabama now that autumn was approaching in this first year of defeat. He asked a couple of leading questions about the local situation and was pleased to find Mr. Jarvis willing enough to allow the conversation to go in that direction.

"Cap'n, everybody around these parts has a long, hard winter coming up. As you see, we got almost no cotton and very little else growing in the fields, except for grass, and we don't have many animals around to eat the grass. You couldn't buy garden seed this spring for love nor money, but we did have a few things like sweet potatoes that we saved from last year. There's a big patch of okra growing down by the creek, along with a bunch of field peas. I think that these things were left 'cause the damn Yankees didn't know what they were. They took every Irish potato that we had on the place—and naturally all the seed corn except for a couple of bushels that we had hid in the woods. To add to our troubles, it's been mighty dry this summer, and the corn that we already had planted when old Wilson showed up in March didn't make hardly anything." Jarvis ended with a long, drawn-out sigh and some nervous shuffling.

"How you fixed for work stock? Got enough to start cleaning up and breaking for next spring?"

"We're a lot better off than some folks. We got one yoke of oxen and three broken down old mules. The Yankees let one of my boys bring a pretty good horse home from the surrender. That's probably less than half of what we need, but I suppose we'll get by somehow."

"Of course you will, but I'm sure you're worried about how many plowhands you'll need and what kind of shape they're in. Up in the Tennessee Valley just about all the field hands left. How did you come out down here on labor?"

"Better than most. Yeah, a whole lot better than some of our neighboring folks. We were keeping a 400-acre place in the early days of the war with eight field hands, four women and a couple of children. We tried to keep seven or eight plows going." The little man moved his feet around nervously and coughed several times. "Of course, our people all had to go see the elephant after they found out that they was free. We got 'em all back except two, just as soon as they got good and hungry. We lost the very best one only two weeks ago. He was riding one of the mules in from the field and the critter spooked. The boy got tangled in the trace chains and the mule ran for a half mile 'fore we could stop it. Horrible."

"Yes, I saw one of those accidents when I was a boy. They're truly terrible. It happens sometimes even if the hames are untied." Logan shook his head, paused and then went on. "How many people do you have on the place that you've got to get through the winter?"

"Fifteen in all. Eleven of the hands including their families and me and my wife and two sons. My daughter is already married and gone. So, with my sons working in the fields, we'll be able to keep six plows going. Of course, some, or all, of the blacks might leave again at any minute. Even my own two boys might leave, as far as I know. That's what's so bad about this new system. You can't count on a damn thing." He jerked around in his chair and nervously crossed and uncrossed his legs. "But I guess if we can't get cottonseed for planting next spring, we got a whole lot more labor than we can use. That's the trouble, of course, if vittles get scarce, you can just bet we'll have all these people to feed. And if we really need the labor, half of 'em will be gone in the middle of the first week after planting. I don't reckon I can say that I'd blame 'em. Food was about all these people got out of the deal, and that's been getting much more scarce than it used to be."

"Yes, it's going to take a lot of getting used to, that's for sure. I just know we're having these same problems down in Dallas County. Maybe worse."

After quite a bit of feet shuffling and hair smoothing, Jarvis continued, "I'm afraid it's a lot worse down there in the prairie counties. Here, we're close enough to know how bad it must be around Marion and Eutaw. Christ, I just don't know how you people are going to keep those darkies fed until spring of '66. And you people have gotten so that you depend on 'em a lot more than we do. Every time I went down there I thought that everybody depended on 'em to do just about everything. If you wanted the cotton chopped, you'd yell for a hoe darkie. If you got hungry, you'd yell for the house darkies; and, I swear, if the house caught on fire, you'd let it burn down without turning a hand if you couldn't find a fire darkie."

Logan threw back his head and laughed boisterously, suddenly realizing that he hadn't laughed at anything for two or three weeks. "You got us, all right. I know we've got some further to go than you do—and we're only some fifty miles away—but we sure depended on these people much too much. It became a problem when some of our people first went into the army. A few of us even drug a black orderly around for the first several months of the war. I'm not talking about the generals, who kept these orderlies for most of the war, but even down to the captain level. It was a shock for some of our people when we made the lower rankers get rid of 'em in our outfits, I tell you."

"Yeah, and the people in the prairie counties have got to get over this way of doing things. We use plenty of black folks 'round here, but let me tell you, we work right alongside of 'em. My boys have been plowing in the field with our darkies since they was thirteen years old. And if it comes to it, I still know how to twist a mule's tail, and my wife can sure pull a hoe."

"Yeah, I'm afraid that all of us down in Dallas County are going to have to do a lot of things differently. Down in the prairie most of the big planters are just ruined, and I'm afraid that these people are not prepared to do what they're going to have to do in order to survive. I see no hope for a return to anything like we had before the war, for at least two generations and maybe more. I think you're better off here in the edge of the uplands because you never got as big as some of our people did."

"Yes, sir. It's going to be plenty tough for a long time, and that goes for us here just about as well as for you people in the flat lands and river bottoms."

"Well, it's really going to be tough on the black population. They're always been dependent on the plantation people, and now it looks like these big owners are going to lose what little bit they had left when the war ended. The land will go to other people who haven't the foggiest idea how to make one of those places pay. I'm afraid that the blacks will just be left to starve. All this loose talk about the slaves working so that culture could develop was ridiculous from the start, and we all know that the whole damn system grew up here in just over forty years. Cultures just don't develop in that short a time."

Jarvis shook his head as he shifted his feet and legs restlessly. "Yeah, I'm afraid that we're just in for it and that goes for us upland people, too. I don't suppose that it'll be quite as painful for us 'cause we don't have so far to fall. But still, we can't look forward to much for the next twenty or thirty years," the little man said as he shifted his feet around again and twitched a bit, staring off into the gathering twilight without ever looking Logan in the eye. After a couple of minutes of silence, he continued, "Well, the sun is well down and we'd better start getting your people over to the horse barn so they can start getting ready for the night."

The next morning Logan sent Li'l Georgia out on his usual scrounging mission. Upon his specific request, the sergeant was sent along to assist. Walking down the creek for a mile or so, they finally found two rather large mud turtles, which they bore back to the dutch oven in triumph. Seeing the start of their meal preparation, Mrs. Jarvis, accompanied by her cook who was still wearing her starched bandanna, came out to donate a small bag of cornmeal. The farmer's wife chatted with them for a few minutes, inquiring how they felt after their night's rest. Although she never spoke, the cook nodded her understanding of each statement and smiled her agreement with any positive comments from the group. In a few minutes Mrs. Jarvis sent the cook back to the kitchen for a cast iron skillet so that the men could make some hoecake with the cornmeal.

As the food cooked, the housewife rambled on about the state of the community, evidently enjoying her freedom from her husband's stifling presence. She seemed impressed by the fact that everything had been peaceful enough since the Eighth Iowa had moved a detachment into the Academy building. She appeared eager to establish that they really didn't seem to do very much. Every time she walked by on her way to town, the Federal soldiers were doing little other than polishing their horse gear and boots. She mentioned that every day five or six of them got on their horses and rode around the town and then out the country roads radiating from Montevallo. Mrs. Jarvis was surprised that these Yankees seemed to be much better behaved than the soldiers of General Wilson who had come by in March. Logan simply accepted this statement with a nod and made no attempt to explain the difference between soldiers engaged in raids of destruction and those on occupation duty.

Mrs. Jarvis suddenly realized that she was almost praising the enemy, so she quickly threw in some stories about the difficulties of life under Federal occupation, reciting a long list of crimes, or least misdemeanors, which the occupation troops had either committed or allowed the freedmen to commit. Logan could tell, however, that she was primarily disturbed by the seizure of foodstuffs, which the Yankees were presumably using to feed their horses. Not much of this had been taken from the Jarvis place, primarily because they had very little that anyone would want. She did have several believable stories, however, about seizure of corn and hay from some of the bigger places in the local countryside. She finally admitted that as far as she knew, no human foodstuffs other than grain had been seized since the surrender, saying this was probably because there was almost nothing left around worth picking up.

Little Mr. Jarvis walked up from the barns; and, as usual, his wife and her escort, the cook, almost immediately disappeared into the kitchen. The captain had come to expect this pattern of behavior. Evidently the wife did not wish to give her husband further evidence that he had an overly talkative wife, particularly one who talked with people who were almost strangers.

"Mrs. Jarvis tells me that the sick man is some better, but she thinks he should rest at least another day before he's ready to move out." Jarvis delivered this report while looking down at his toes sticking out of his ripped shoes.

"Yes, he does seem to be some better, but I've found out that it's best to take it easy with this fellow. I figure that we've fallen behind about ten days by taking care of him, but we really couldn't do it any other way. We're just too close to Dallas County not to get him home now. We're not even going to think about it. If we go, he goes."

"Well, I can sure understand that," said Jarvis. With a lot of shuffling around, he continued, "You'll probably be here for a day or two; so if I was you, I'd just walk up into the town and see what it's like here in the edge of the upcountry. In most ways it's damn little different than it is in your area, but you might notice a few things that you'd want to remember."

"Mr. Jarvis, I've never been in this area before, so I'd like to look at everything that I can while I'm here at the center of the state. I'd like to walk down to your main street and then go over and see the railroad. Anything else, of course, that you might think would be interesting. I'll probably just have today because if Hood keeps getting stronger, we'll start out moving south sometimes tomorrow."

"In that case, I'd walk by the walnut grove that's down by the creek. It's a real pretty place where we have the town gatherings and, back before the war, some real fine barbecues. I sur had some might fine times there, back in the forties and fifties. It's sad, but I guess it's going to be a bunch of years afore old Montevallo has its next barbecue."

So following their host's advice, as soon as the discussion with Jarvis broke off, Logan and Li'l Georgia walked up to look at the town. It turned out to be very similar to any number of other towns found throughout the South. The business district was a single block long, a scattering of store building clustered on either side of a graveled street. A couple of shops on either end of the street appeared to have been tacked on as an afterthought sometime after the business area had been filled. Logan noticed a couple of dwelling houses still holding their places in the middle of the main business block. There appeared to be virtually no activity on the street other than in the vicinity of three farm wagons, whose teams were tied in front of what he took to be the town's general stores. Two small boys, one black and one white, were eating a watermelon in the shade of a large oak near the wagons. The mules harnessed to the wagons were switching their tails at the attacking flies in the usual fashion. Other than the watermelon eaters, there was no sign of human activity at all. After looking up the street for a few minutes, they moved on in search of the railroad, following the directions given by Mr. Jarvis.

Li'l Georgia walked on ahead and found the ford across the creek and the railroad track just beyond it. With Li'l Georgia leading the way, they walked up the track for several hundred yards until they came on a work crew repairing a short trestle that evidently had been wrecked for several months. The foreman told them that almost none of the track was usable between Montevallo and Selma but the track supervisor hoped to have it repaired all the way to Selma within three or four weeks. Several of the longer trestles still were not completely repaired, but with an optimistic grin the man pointed out that the roadbed itself was just about all back in place. He added that back there at the end of the war, old Wilson and Forrest had sure done a super job of tearing everything up. Logan nodded his agreement about the destruction but then set about determining if he and his group could walk down the railroad into Selma. He was assured that they could but not to expect to do any riding for a month or so.

Afterwards Logan and Li'l Georgia walked back toward town and found the walnut grove easily enough. They gazed for a while at the hundred or so tall walnut trees located around a big spring flowing off into the creek. Several old campfire sites and evidence of horses and mules were scattered around. They walked for some time among the trees and found two brush arbors, evidently built for some sort of meeting. Nearby they found an old barbecue pit, now beginning to fill up with dirt and weeds. The description given by Jarvis had been quite accurate; it was a very pretty place.

Leaving the walnut grove they walked back into the settled area and strolled slowly along looking at the dwelling houses. Some of these buildings were rather substantial with the usual garden patches, wells, stables and chicken houses arranged about in the backyards. There was little evidence of war damages to the buildings, but Logan noticed that during the entire walk he saw only two or three cows and two horses and that these animals appeared to be barely alive. As for chickens, he saw less than half a dozen along the entire route. As usual, very few people were about, and those that he did see were just sitting on their porches looking off into space.

Logan commented to Li'l Georgia that it looked like these people were going to have a hard time living through the coming winter unless they had more things going on inside the houses than was indicated by what showed in the backyards. Li'l Geogia nodded his agreement, but Logan saw by the look on the boy's face that Li'l Georgia had little understanding about what he had said. Evidently the young man thought that things looked rather prosperous.

Walking past the main street, they continued up a gentle slope, following an ungraded, graveled road to a bulky brick building that had the universal look of a public institution. An adolescent boy sitting at the gate that evidently once had closed off the walkway to the building confirmed this suspicion when he told them that the two-story brick structure was once the old Academy. The boy added that a unit of the Yankee cavalry now occupied the old school. Logan could see some barns off to the side of the big building where some Yankee soldiers were busily grooming a number of horses.

The captain and Li'l Georgia moved over to the barns and stood watching the stable activity until a corporal finally walked over and addressed them. "What you Rebs want? I suppose you were cavalry, or you wouldn't be watching so long."

"Yep, I qualify; I was in the First South Carolina Cav—that was one of General Hampton's outfits—but my friend here was an infantryman. We've been walking south since we left Rock Island back in May, and we're getting pretty close now, 'cause we'll be nearly home when we get down to Selma. We really don't want anything more than to pass the time and look at the horses."

"Well, I don't suppose there's much harm in that. The lieutenant might not agree; he's always talking about fraternizing with you Rebels. But he's not here today, so I guess you can look all you want to." With that, the corporal turned back to supervising the grooming.

Logan leaned on the paddock fence and studied the gear and the horses. The horses were carrying a bit too much flesh, but they were fine looking animals as cavalry horses go. The gear appeared to be in great shape, and the soldiers' uniforms were clean and their boots well shined. The unit was undoubtedly a very good one. Suddenly the piles of half-naked dead at the Crater with their clothing hardly recognizable as Confederate gray came rushing to mind. After the first year or so of the war the Southern army had no chance for the morale lift that soldiers get from good gear and good animals. It was at times like this that it was hard to believe that the Confederate Army had held together as long as it had.

After a few minutes, Logan motioned to his companion that they should move on down the dusty road toward the Jarvis place. As they walked along, he could see that there had been little rain for several weeks, the few garden patches alongside the road drying up as a result. The corn was completely brown, and most of the peas and beans had been abandoned as not worth working. Even the okra, which he remembered would grow almost anywhere and under very dry conditions, seemed to be in poor shape.

He supposed that it would be difficult for the occupation folks not to feel a certain amount of sympathy for a people suffering through this first summer of defeat, occupied by the enemy army and with the added hardship of living through a hot, dry summer. Looking at the dry brown fields, he found it difficult to think of much that these people had to be thankful for in this dreadful summer of '65. These people must feel abandoned by the saints and the fates.

Back at the Jarvis house, they found their host eagerly waiting to hear their impressions of the town. Logan thought it wise to gloss over anything that Jarvis might construe as being disrespectful of Montevallo and its people. After all, they were guests—sort of, anyway—in a relatively comfortable place for an occupied area. So Logan was careful to mention the four or five big two-story houses he had seen during his walk. He made special mention of the King House, which he had heard one or two people refer to as the only brick residence in this part of the county. But he did not mention that all these houses looked run-down; he also failed to say that he had seen almost no livestock. After all, the buildings were still standing, and he remembered Jarvis having said that a standing house was all that could be hoped for under the existing circumstances. Logan pretty much agreed with Jarvis's position on this point.

"I suppose you've noticed that almost no cotton is being grown in this area. I've been all around, maybe twenty miles on 'most every side, and I've seen only a half dozen little patches that looked like they were worth picking," Jarvis said, nervously running his hand through his mop of gray hair while crossing and uncrossing his legs. "The real disaster time's going to come when we have to pay our taxes this December. I'm thinking that that's when we're going to start losing our land and our homes. I know that a bunch of people will just have to start moving out of their houses. I think maybe us Jarvises will get by—at least this first year, and maybe we can make it a second—if we have decent weather in '66."

"Yes, I'm sure these carpetbaggers will be pushing to get the tax rates raised so they can foreclose on as many folks as possible. But I suppose this kind of action will be much more common in '66 and '67 than it will be here in '65. After all, they're just getting organized this year. I reckon that the people who can make it through the next five years, say to around '70, will be all right." Logan raised his eyebrows in question before continuing.

"I'm sure that down in Dallas County we're going to lose a lot of our planters and some of our good yeoman farmers. They simply don't have the money to pay the taxes required by today's rate, let alone what's going to happen when the Yankees and their good friends start to raise the rates.

"I'll admit that I don't have any idea how I'd feed all these new freedmen if I were one of the carpetbaggers or scalawags. But as I've said, it's not a matter of just changing ownership of the real estate. These places are very hard to run, and there just ain't no way that an outsider, let alone a recently freed black, can run one of these places and make it pay."

As Logan talked, Jarvis kept shifting about and running his fingers through his hair. When the captain paused, he replied, "Well, of course they can't. I've been involved in the business for my entire life, and I can barely make it. Some of our neighbors think they'll have to go to work running their places as overseers for these Yankees and their scum. I'll tell you, I'd starve first. If they take this place, we're leaving. I don't know where we're going, but we won't be staying around here. No, sir."

Logan smiled a tight smile at this bold statement and then continued the conversation. "The Yankees who are down here working with the ex-slaves keep talking about breaking up the big places and giving each black family forty acres and a mule. I guess nobody has really thought through this flowery statement and tried to figure out just what it means."

"No, Cap'n, I don't suppose they have. There's just nothing these people can do with a farm and a mule. They have no earthly idea what to do with any of this. I suppose their northern friends will be standing by to tell them what to do and to buy up the farms when the blacks have to give them up. It would almost be worth it to stand by and see the fun. I'm betting that not one in ten would have any part of this gift left after two seasons."

Logan shook his head and said with a sigh, "No, of course not. In my opinion, it would take at least two generations of hard work for them to get to the place where they could handle forty acres and a mule—even if someone gave it to 'em. This talk about forty acres and a mule has become so common that I think it's now almost sacred. Of course, it's just because that's the size of the smallest subsection in the federal survey, and we've found that in most of the South a family can cultivate with a mule and live off that part of a forty-acre block that is cleared—usually about half of it. The remainder of it goes to woodland and pasture. However, I think that maybe it's right and proper that the new freedmen get a lot of help from somebody—I guess I'm talking about the Federal government because, God knows, very few Southerners can help themselves, let alone all the ex-slaves."

"That's for sho right," said Jarvis. "I understand, of course, that the national government could do this. I guess that they can do just about anything that occurs to them, but I don't think that such a move will get them one bit closer to a solution to the freed slave problem. Of course, I realize that these people have just got to be better off than they were when they were slaves. At least they're not going to be separated from their people and sold off to Texas. I admit that I always thought that the selling of people off to far places away from their families was a disgrace to humanity. And when I cross the River, that's something that I just can't be accused of."

"And, I suppose," added Logan, "that they really should get started preparing to make it on their own. They've got to start someday, and maybe they need to start by getting a lot of advice from some Federal official. I hate the idea, but I don't see much of any other solution, other than us supporting the black population—and that means support from the Federals, for at least thirty or forty years. The occupation troops are maintaining order now and seeing that the government's policy is carried out. And I'm just afraid that the occupation will have to go on for several years."

As Logan continued talking, Jarvis kept squirming around as though he was fighting hard to stay awake. Seeing the discussion had run aground, the captain excused himself and went off toward the horse barn.

His conversation with the planter triggered thoughts of the predicament that he and his people had gotten themselves into. These thoughts had been coming several times a day now and sometimes lingered on at length. He thought a lot about slavery and usually ended up wondering how anyone could have believed that such a system of labor could have continued for many more years—at least in the form it had reached by 1860. He was sure that the whole system would have fallen of its own weight within twenty or thirty years. After all, the British had abolished slavery back in 1833, and it was hard to imagine that such an organization of society could long endure in the United States.

But now the system had collapsed in such a way that there could be no form of gradualism; the problem of the reorganization of society in the South had to be faced by his people—and now. There could be no delay. Within three or four years the direction that southern people would take, at least for the next fifty years, had to be chosen. Maybe the Federal government would direct the path that would be taken; but this course looked less likely with each passing week. If the society was to be reorganized by Federal direction, it should have been done back in June or July. The time for this approach had almost slipped away as Southerners were beginning to recover from the first shock of Appomattox.

When he reached the horse barn, Logan climbed up into the hayloft and lay down on his pile of straw, but sleep did not come at once. As it seemed to happen more often the nearer he came to home, his thoughts stayed on Alabama and her people.

One thing for certain, the people who had chosen—or who had been forced into—an occupation prior to the war would almost certainly have to follow that same means of livelihood for years after the war. A steamboat man had to find another steamboat; a railroader had to get back on the trains; and in the most common case of all, a farmer or planter had to get back to the soil. Obviously few of these people could get back into their workaday world at the place and level they had left it in 1861 or 1862. But the vast majority had to get back into their occupational group at some level of responsibility. The planter might have to become an overseer, and the overseer might be forced into the laboring ranks, but still the bulk of these people would have to work in the same occupation they had left.

Also, there was no reason to believe that cotton had given up its crown. Logan had moved around the South enough to realize that this was most unfortunate since the lower the significance of cotton in an area, the better off the area seemed to be. He could not see, however, how the cotton-dependent sections could change this relationship short of a couple of lifetimes. But surely there must be some way. After all, the whole situation had grown up in forty to fifty years, so something could replace cotton in a similar length of time. He had trouble visualizing, however, how cotton could be replaced in the prairie counties in his lifetime. And, after all, that was the time span he was primarily interested in. The Southern people just did not have the energy left after the gross expenditure of themselves during the last four years to attack such a problem. He finally drifted off into a troubled sleep.

Logan was awakened by loud voices coming from the cookhouse. Walking outside he could hear the plantation cook yelling at someone who had evidently walked into the kitchen without an invitation. After a moment he recognized the male voice trying to make some sort of an explanation as Slaughter.

He could then make out the cook saying, "Nobody comes in my kitchen lessen either me or the Massa or his wife axes 'em in—and that's nobody! When we had a overseer he didn't come in, and I sho ain't going to let no white trash soldier come in. No, sir!" All this was delivered in a low pitched, angry voice.

"Look here, you yaller coon, I don't have to put up with that kind of talk from the likes of you. You ain't nothing but a darkie belly robber. And we still got charge of you, and that's going to be the way it is from now on. I need some coffee and right now!"

"Git yo hand off my arm, you white rat, fo I mash yo brains out with this iron skillet."

Logan began running as fast as he could on his stiff legs. When he reached the front of the cookhouse, he could see the cook, starched bandanna and all, swinging a heavy iron skillet that was knocking Slaughter back on his heels each time it smashed into his chest.

"Come out of there, you idiot! You trying to get us all shot?" was the explosive outburst from Logan. He then dropped his voice back to command level and continued, "Come on out of there—and now."

"Cap'n, I was just trying to get a cup of coffee. I know that crazy darkie has some 'cause I saw it," offered Slaughter in a subdued whine as he backed out of the cookhouse.

"Yeah, maybe so, but it's not our decision to make, and you know better than to go into a cookhouse on any of these places. Surely, you've always known you can't get away with that. They run it just like we control the army by watching the issue of the vittles. It may be even tighter here than it was in the old First South Carolina Cavalry."

Logan, his face red and sweaty, continued this controlled chewing as he jerked Slaughter out the door and pushed him toward the horse barn. "And one more thing, Slaughter, don't ever put your hands on these people unless you think it's going to be necessary to hurt 'em bad. On a good place they didn't even put their hands on 'em when they had to use the strap. You're lucky that big strong darkie hit you on the chest with that skillet. If she'd slapped you over the head with it, you'd be unconscious right now. Now get back in the barn and stay there until you're told to come out." Logan turned on his heel and moved off to meet Mr. Jarvis, who had come running to the back porch to investigate the commotion.

"Well, I heard part of what you said to that man," said Jarvis. "And let me tell you, I agree a hundred percent. We've never put up with that kind of stuff around here, and we're sure not going to start. We got plenty of these yellow folks now. And we know that's how all that business commences. Course you know better than I do that you can't let your people go in and out of the cookhouse, for several reasons. Even my sons can't do that on this place."

"Yes, sir. And that buck knows a lot better than that. That's just him; he's always trying to run the wagon. You got to watch folk like that one, every minute."

The planter just shook his head and sighed as he walked back into the house. Logan washed his face and hands in the horse trough, stumbled back to the barn and climbed up into the hayloft. Before lying down again, he first had Sergeant Jackson move to the front doorway of the barn and position himself so that he could see anyone attempting to leave the barn during the night. Next he gathered up the dutch oven and his extra pair of socks. He supposed that they had about worn out their welcome here in good old Montevallo and would have to move on the next day.

The captain woke the men just as dawn broke the next morning and prepared to move them out past the town toward the railroad as their best route south toward Dallas County. As they were about to move out, Mrs. Jarvis walked out and handed each man a small corn pone. Bidding them farewell, she made a statement of regret that they had been unable to do more for them. The cook was standing back in the hallway of the house watching the departure. She returned Logan's smile as he walked by.

Just as they were leaving, a horse and rider came trotting out of the near darkness from the north. Everyone stopped to look at this unusual sight of a rider who was not in uniform but mounted on a lively horse. As the unknown rider drew near, Logan saw that he was somewhat better dressed than anyone he had seen in at least a month. Then he recognized the horsemanship—McLemore.

McLemore pulled up, slid to the ground and tossed the reins into the dirt. The little mare stopped and gazed at the group of people as though she had never seen such a sight. McLemore immediately shook hands with everyone, including Mr. Jarvis although he had not yet been introduced to him. He swept off his hat in cavalier fashion to both Mrs. Jarvis and the cook. The cook was fascinated, and Mrs. Jarvis obviously has just met one of the Three Musketeers.

After this flurry, McLemore went over to Logan and said, "Cap'n, Mr. Ochs let me ride back to Alabama on a little home leave, and I thought I had better hook up with y'all if I could. I figured that you would be walking south toward the railhead in Montevallo; and sure enough, I ran into a couple of people up north of here who had seen you last week, so I just rode south until I found you."

Within minutes and without further explanation of his recent whereabouts or why he had returned, McLemore was busy getting Hood into the saddle and showering him with instructions on how to stay in the saddle and control the prancing mare. Hood did not seem to be looking forward to his meeting with the animal, so the captain quickly assigned the disgraced Slaughter as horse leader. Then with a last word of thanks to the Jarvis family and still shaking his head in disbelief at this sudden turn of events, Logan led the group away toward the railroad.

* * *

The railroad tracks were the nearest thing to a graded highway for the walking men. At times the roadbed of ties became difficult to negotiate because they were not spaced to allow an even stride to be established. However, this difficulty, which seemed to cause a bobbing effect in the pace, was overshadowed by the absence of the steep grades, not to mention the ruts and deep mud holes, that were so annoying on all the poorly graded dirt roads. The mare, being led by Slaughter, was able to use the railroad for much of the way; but at times they found a parallel trail that seemed to please the animal so that she tried to pick up a trot when free of the tracks. The three days of rest they had gotten in Montevallo seemed to improve the spirits of all the men, with the exception of Hood, who was clearly no cavalryman and who wished that he could walk or perhaps lie down under a tree.

They pushed on down the tracks past the village of Randolph toward the town of Maplesville. Late in the afternoon they stopped to rest at the edge of a creek where a man and woman were washing clothing and spreading them on the nearby bushes. Logan spoke to the couple and introduced himself and his group as ex-Confederates on their way back to Dallas County. After a moment of hesitation during which his little squinty eyes darted from one to the other of the group, the man held up his left arm, showing that part of his left hand had evidently been amputated. This seemed to establish the necessary closeness between the two groups so that they could then talk about the situation that existed in the surrounding countryside.

The washing couple explained how they lived in the hills back north of the railroad. They then added that they were woodcutters by occupation; and although there was plenty of wood to cut, there was almost no one with the money to buy it. The reopening of the railroad was the topic that appeared to be of overriding importance to the man and his companion. The fellow was quick to point out that repair crews had been working on the track since back in June but that no sign of a train had yet been seen. He ended his complaining by suddenly giving a snorting laugh and saying, "But you guys may be happy that there ain't no trains to dodge while you're walking down the tracks to Selma."

Sergeant Jackson said that they surely would like to see a train even if they couldn't ride. Then Logan worked the conversation around to how the people in the area were going to get by the coming winter. The woman finally entered the conversation by saying they figured the ex-slaves would be getting plenty from the Federals and surely they would be able to get a little it. Looking at the weasel-faced man, Logan silently agreed that they undoubtedly would get enough to escape starvation.

Suddenly the thought occurred to Logan that these people were the kind who would probably spend the rest of their lives surviving in just this same way. Feeling discouraged and disturbed by this chance meeting with some of the South's great corps of white trash, Logan took his leave of the washers, moved his people back to the tracks and pushed off toward the southeast.

As they moved out, the captain continued to think of the couple at the creek. Living from hand to mouth in these difficult days probably meant that the two had not had enough to eat since at least 1862. Their clothing had disintegrated into the rags they were now drying on the bushes; they were probably living in a brush lean-to back in the hills. As the group moved up the embankment to the track, he looked back to check out their footwear and of course could see no sign of any sort of shoes. Maybe it wouldn't snow this winter.

Pushing south they occasionally met a few men walking along the tracks back toward Montevallo. All of them seemed to be moving at a pace that threatened to cease altogether at any moment. Although Logan stopped and talked to each group, none of them had much of anything to pass on. All agreed that no trains were operating yet, that labor crews were hard at work on all the trestles but that for a certainty several of the trestles had at least a couple of weeks of work to go before they could be used. Finally two men came hobbling along with the information that Ebenezer Church was a few miles ahead. They added that General Forrest had fought a battle there back in April but that despite the fighting most of the village was still standing and someone was even running a store down by the railroad.

Early the next afternoon Logan and his men reached Ebenezer Church and the adjacent store. There were two ancient looking horses at the hitching rail; and a two-horse wagon, whose animals looked like they could barely walk, was tied across the road under some oaks. Logan stopped his group to rest and for a chance for them to again communicate with some fellow humans.

He went into the store, introduced himself and asked about the fighting that had taken place in the vicinity of the church. As he had come to expect, no one in the store seemed to know anything about the incident, which, after all, had come off all the way back in April. Finally one old fellow offered to take him down to the creek where he thought the fighting had taken place.

When they had walked down to the stream running parallel to the railroad, the ancient guide suddenly knew quite a bit about the fighting. According to him, the operation was probably brought on by a chance meeting between the two rival forces, but once it started it turned out to be quite a scrap. The local people thought that General Forrest had shot and killed a Yankee captain down by the creek. In any event, when the whole thing was over, there were several dead soldiers from both sides. Despite the violent scrap put up by the Confederates, they evidently got the worse of it because they rode off toward Selma as fast as they could go. The next day a Federal detachment came along, buried the bodies of their soldiers over in the Baptist cemetery and then piled up the Confederate dead and burned them. They didn't do too good of a job of the burning, however, and the local people had to go down the next day and finish this gruesome business. Some Yankee sergeant had come along and grabbed everybody around to do this dreadful job.

As Logan and his guide walked back to the store, they met McLemore, who was riding the mare and pushing her along rather recklessly. Punishing horseflesh was certainly out of character for McLemore, so the captain thought it best to slide back into the trees lining the road. The rider saw Logan, however, pulled up his mount and immediately slid to the ground.

"Cap'n, we got troubles. There's three or four outlaws up at the store and they've already robbed the place. Now they're going through the pockets of all the people. I think they're looking for horses, too."

"Well, I guess we'd better try to ambush 'em. Head your horse up into the woods, and let's see what's going to happen." Logan pulled his ancient guide down into a shallow ditch and then turned his attention to the road leading from the store. He felt almost naked lying there in the ditch—no arms of any sort, not even a pocketknife—looking up the road and waiting for the appearance of four outlaws, undoubtedly armed to the teeth.

The old man suddenly began to talk. "Sir, there's two or three gangs of outlaws operating around here, but old Brantly and his bunch are probably the ones. He's usually down in the swamps along the Cahaba, but he's been up here two or three times already. There just ain't many worthwhile horses left to steal, so he'd sure like to get ahold of that mare."

Logan grabbed the old man by his shirt and demanded, "Just what are these people doing around here, and what the hell are they after?"

"I don't rightly know, sir. There ain't much to steal, that's for shor. Most of the time they are likely just trying to hide from all the Yankee law we got around here now. 'Course, they're always looking for horses, but they'll steal anything they can find. Brantly's the worst of 'em. He's done killed a bunch of folks. They say he burned down a house over in Perry County with a man and his wife still inside. He's a bad one."

Four riders suddenly came around a curve in the road and approached the bridge at a slow trot. As they neared, McLemore's mare suddenly neighed. Alerted by the sound, the horsemen immediately pulled off the road and moved toward the noise, leaving one man sitting on his horse in the water just below the bridge.

Leaving the old man behind, Logan slid across the road and began to work his way through the brush filling the ditch on the other side. When he reached the bridge abutments, he climbed up on the floor of the structure and rolled over to a position just above the man on the horse, who was still in the edge of the stream. Logan could hear the other three horsemen moving through the woods toward the noise that had alerted them.

The man in the creek did not move his horse, but Logan could see him squirming around in the saddle, evidently looking for the horse that could be heard moving around in the brush near the road. Logan knew that McLemore might ride out in the open at any moment, in which case he would be an easy target for the man under the bridge. The fellow drew his pistol and leaned forward in the saddle while looking into the woods along the creek.

Logan pushed to his knees, leaned forward and finally came to his feet. Then with a final push against the edge of the bridge, he launched himself into the air and down upon the unsuspecting gunman. The horse screamed, reared and threw both men into the water.

The two men and the horse floundered around in the creek for a moment, until the horse broke away from the melee and left the two men rolling about in the water. Logan fought desperately to keep his head above water and simultaneously to force the outlaw's gun away from his body. He could feel himself weakening and knew that he was slowly losing control. Suddenly a pistol was discharged close at hand, and the outlaw loosened his grip and fell away. The water was red with blood as Logan pushed away and stood up in the flowing stream. Immediately he found himself being pulled up on the little mare by McLemore, who had a smoking pistol in his hand.

"Hang on, Cap'n!" yelled McLemore. "We got to get over this damn road and find some cover!" The horse reacted magnificently, pulling them over the road and into a deep ditch on the other side. There both men got off the horse and looked frantically for cover. The mare, without a rider, ran into the woods.

Suddenly the three outlaws who had pushed their horses into the woods came splashing back into the creek just below the bridge. They crossed the stream and scrambled up the embankment and onto the road. McLemore fired at the three as they pushed their horses up the embankment, but he evidently missed his target. They rode off at a gallop. McLemore fired again, this time at an extreme range. The rearmost rider slumped in the saddle, but he held on as they disappeared around a curve. Following the retreating outlaws, the dead man's horse came running out of the creek with its stirrups flying back from the empty saddle. The animal was running at full speed in an attempt to catch the other horses.

Logan dropped down against the embankment to catch his breath. Looking over into the woods along the creek, he saw Sergeant Jackson and Slaughter running along the edge of the clearing. Likely the appearance of these two explained the sudden departure of the three bandits. Neither the sergeant nor Slaughter had any sort of weapon, but the outlaws had no way of knowing this. They undoubtedly thought they had used up their daily ration of luck, so they had slipped away to wait for another day.

After a short rest, Logan and McLemore crossed the road and crawled down into the creek to look for the man McLemore had shot. They found him in a pool of bloody water near the bank. They pulled the dead body out of the creek and dropped it in the grass on the bank.

"I don't like killing people at all—never did. But I guess this had to be done." McLemore was busy checking the shiny LeMat revolver as he spoke.

"No, I don't know any balanced man who doesn't hate it, but in this case I guess I'll have to say that I'm very glad you came along with that gun. If you hadn't, I suspect that would be me laying there in the mud." Logan pushed the dead body over on its back with his foot and started to move away. But the outlaw's pistol had been uncovered when the body was moved, so the captain turned back and picked the weapon out of the water and pushed it under his belt.

McLemore looked at the revolver and said, "That's what the Feds called the 'New Model Army.' It was put out by Colt in '60, and the Union Army used thousands of 'em. I carried one of those .44s for a couple of years, courtesy of General Sheridan's cav. It's a good weapon."

"Lieutenant," Jackson gasped for breath after his long run down from the store, "them were the bandits that was robbing the store. Ole Brantly had a sack full of all the stuff they stole, so I guess they got away will all that. You sho was lucky you had that gun, but if I was you, I'd get on away from here with it. Lots of people would try to kill you for that thing."

"Yeah, I know. We'd better get going just as soon as we can. I sho don't want to give this gun up to anybody, and just as soon as Slaughter catches the mare, I'll get this little prize back in the saddlebags where it belongs." As he talked, McLemore continued to wipe the pistol with a rag he had produced from inside his shirt.

"Well, here comes the village people to see what happened, so I guess we'd better start back to the store. McLemore, get on back up there and pick up Hood. You'd better find our friend Li'l Georgia, too. Maybe he's found something that we can eat." The captain was still wringing wet from his fight in the creek, but the hot Alabama sun was already starting to take care of that.

Walking back toward the village, they heard the grizzled old guide telling some villagers, "Well, I don't know who these people are, but ye better stay clear of 'em. That young one leading the horse just shot that bandit down like a dog while that scarred-up one held him. Brantly and his bunch sho saw enough, right quick. They just ran their horses full gallop up the hill and off towards the swamps. Ye better keep well away from all them fellows. And I thought that scar-face there just wanted to see the battlefield. Boy, if I'd seed any of that wild stuff beforehand, I'd done run half way to Selma afore they could've got close enough to talk to me."

CHAPTER VII

BACK INTO DALLAS COUNTY

On a hazy September afternoon the six men shuffled into the village of Plantersville as the sun was dropping below the horizon. Crossing into Dallas County, a milestone which they had discussed hundreds of times during the past three months, gave everyone a bit of a lift. They looked a little more lively than usual, even after Logan reminded them that they still had over forty miles to go before they need start looking for the village of Orrville or the Logan and McLemore places.

McLemore was smiling as usual as he led the mare over to a hitching rail in the normal place before a shabby store building. He tied the horse and held Hood's arm as the sick man slid from the saddle and slumped down on the worn bench in front of the store. Li'l Georgia stayed with Hood as the others walked into the building.

Inside, it was clear that this was the usual southern store of the fall of '65. The building was fairly large, but the shelves were almost bare. A few bolts of rough cloth, a dozen horse collars, six or seven plow points, a coil of plowline, three barrels with no indication if their contents and a keg of horseshoe nails made up the inventory. Half a dozen loafers, all in homespun at the point of total disintegration, were sitting around on some empty goods boxes.

Logan walked over and introduced himself to the storekeeper, who did not appear to be either shocked or even very interested that they were recently released prisoners from Rock Island. Upon being asked if anyone had ever heard of the Logan family of Orrville, one of the loafers answered that he had heard of the town but knew nothing about any of the people who lived around there. It was true that they were back in their home county, but they could have been back in Illinois as far as learning anything about their homes or families was concerned. After getting a few directions about the road to Selma, Logan motioned his group to move outside and on southward. They walked by another store, apparently closed, and on past a big house with the requisite white columns. As they passed, someone lit a lamp in one of the upstairs rooms. Other than this light there was little indication of life in the village of Plantersville.

Finally they came to a small, unpainted church with two pyramid tents in the small clearing behind it. A small American flag and a cavalry guidon were stuck in the ground in front of the building. As Logan entered the church, he noticed this detachment was from the same Iowa unit occupying the town of Montevallo. Inside, he found himself in a room with the usual uniformly spaced windows along each side but with no sign of church furniture. He could see that it was now being used as a combination office and mess hall.

He waited in line behind two men, evidently local farmers, inquiring about payment for two hogs that they claimed had been seized by some federal patrol. The desk sergeant dismissed the men without serious discussion of their claim, and the two stumbled into Logan as they rushed out. They displayed more haste in their withdrawal than seemed necessary. Logan waited silently as the sergeant stacked the papers on his desk. Finally he looked up. "Yeah," he started out in a low growl, "what can I do for you?"

"I'm an ex-Confederate who, along with some other old prisoners, is on his way home to Orrville, down below Selma. We thought you people might go down there now and then and that you might be able to tell us something about that area and maybe about our folks down that way."

"So, now we're a damn post office for a bunch of whining Rebels. Hell, no, we don't know a damn thing about this Orrville or its worthless people. We ain't never been there, and I hope we never go. What else you want?" This was delivered with a building roar.

"Well, Sergeant, I have one man that has dysentery real bad. I'd sure like to beg a little of your medicine if I could." From the first reaction, this request seemed almost hopeless, but it wouldn't cost him anything; and even if he got nothing, it almost surely would annoy His Highness, the Sergeant.

The man behind the desk jumped to his feet and screamed, "You slimy Rebs can die in a ditch for all I care. You can't have a damn thing that belongs to the federal government. Now, what else do you old women want? No wonder you lost the war, none of you can do a damn thing for yo' self."

His loud outburst finally aroused a captain lounging in a chair leaning against the rear wall of the church. He came forward rather deliberately and said quite smoothly, "All right, Sergeant, let's calm down. I'll take care of this." As he spoke, he motioned the man away and moved in behind the desk, planted both hands and leaned forward over the scattered papers. "Now, what's all this?"

"Captain, I was inquiring about my family down in Orrville. I ain't heard anything from them in over a year, and I thought you people might go down there on patrol."

"No, I'm sorry. We don't go that far south, so I can't help you at all. I heard that business about the dysentery medicine, and I suspect you know that it's against regs to give anything like that away to anybody. However, it don't make any real difference; we've not been able to get any of that stuff for over three weeks." The captain's tone was quite civil, and he even smiled.

"All right, Cap'n. Sorry I bothered you." As he backed away, Logan stole a quick glance at the sergeant, who was glowering at him from the rear of the room. Logan gave the sullen man a little smirk as he withdrew from the building.

The Yankee captain followed Logan as he walked out and give him his opinion that the dysentery medicine wasn't worth much anyway, the only luck that he had had with the illness coming from giving the sick party plenty of rest. Logan nodded his thanks and led his people back toward the road. The federal officer then said, "Good luck, Cap'n. That's the right rank, I assume?"

* * *

A couple of days later the group reached the village of Summerfield and again stopped near a church to rest. After about an hour the ringing of the church bell disturbed their sleep. Logan left the men in the shade of the trees and walked over to speak to the man with the bell rope. After the ringing had stopped and the rope secured to its nail, he asked his usual questions about Orrville and the Logan family. He was rewarded by finding someone, finally, who at least had been to Orrville during recent months. According to the bell ringer, there hadn't been much damage to the town. He believed that only one store had been burned out; he remembered that one as the building with the little post office built in one corner. The man was sorry, but he did not know anyone from that area by the name of Logan or McLemore.

The bell ringer then wandered away from the subject of Orrville and began talking about the troubles of his own town. The church, which turned out to be Baptist, had only five or six families left after the war had killed off four of their most faithful members. But since this was a Methodist town with a big church school operating down the road, he couldn't expect a larger congregation, especially now. Logan thanked him for the information and went back to his people.

A few minutes later two groups walked by going toward the church. All were evidently dressed in their Sunday best, the clothing having been washed and the holes at their elbows and knees neatly patched. But their outfits would not last more than a couple more wearings before they fell from their owners' backs. McLemore whispered that neither the women nor the children had shoes; the men had some semblance of footwear, but even theirs appeared ready to disintegrate at any moment.

Logan told Li'l Georgia that these people were not to be asked for anything since they couldn't have much more than the ex-prisoners did. After all, as old Confederates they had not yet starved. The unit scrounger looked a bit disappointed but withdrew into the shadows without approaching these new groups.

Slaughter grumbled audibly that if they would just follow these people home then they would be able to pick up some sweet potatoes, at least. The captain glared at him, and Slaughter also withdrew into the shadows. After ten more minutes Logan gather his group and moved off down the Selma road.

Three medium-sized plantation houses stood around the crossroad that appeared to form the heart of Summerfield. One of these houses was fairly well smashed up with most of the glass missing from the lower floor windows. A side portico was lying in ruins against the end of the house, and two of the outbuildings had been burned. About two hundred yards up the Selma road they passed a two-story house set back some hundred yards from the road. This house appeared to be in good shape except for a lack of paint and the grounds had been literally torn to bits. Thousands of wagon tracks showed where vehicles had moved back and forth over every inch of the yards. Logan recognized immediately that the building had been used as a headquarters for a large unit, probably by both sides at one time or another. When they got immediately in front of the house, however, he saw that the house itself was virtually intact. He saw no broken glass or smashed fences; even a small flower pit in the side yard still had most of its window glass.

The sergeant spoke to McLemore as they moved slowly past the intact house. "There you are, Lieutenant. If you want to save your house, run out and meet the blue bellies and get 'em to stick their big headquarters in it. I've never seen one of them burned down yet. And I guess that would have gone for us too if we ever had a chance to put our command people in a Yankee house."

"Yeah, I think you're right. Hope my folks figured that out before the Federals got out as far as Orrville. Otherwise, I suppose they're living in one of the barns about right now." As he said this, McLemore gave the mare a jerk, causing her to swerve and almost unseat the swaying Hood. McLemore pulled her up short and with a few curses moved on, but at a slower pace.

Li'l Georgia looked over into the rutted yard and whispered softly, "Well, Mr. Slaughter, I s'pect that the rich folks that own that place are awful glad that the Yankees are finally gone."

Slaughter laughed his low, gurgling laugh, pulled up on his wide belt and said, "Young fellar, them people must have got along pretty good with the Feds. I'm sorta surprised that they didn't get burned out by our people after the war ended. I'm guessing that they would have been 'cept for the occupation folks that are still around."

"Oh, I don't know, Mr. Slaughter. A man up in Tennessee told me that the Yanks let some people live up in the attic of their house while the Federal headquarters was using the two bottom floors."

"Goddamn, boy, that was just exactly what I was talking about. You just can't get very friendly with the occupier, if you expect to stay around after the occupation is over."

"Aw, sir, you know that everybody's going to forget all about them things a long time 'fore the occupation is over. I sure hope they do over in Georgia, anyways."

Slaughter looked over at the boy, shook his head and walked on without further comment.

After walking for a couple of hours, the group came to the outskirts of Selma. They had been passing abandoned earthworks for some time, and here and there they saw pieces of web gear and other signs of the recent fighting. Now and then a few chimney stubs marked where houses had been burned. They had to wade across a creek that evidently had lost its bridge in the April fighting. An abandoned cannon, with the end of the tube blown away and with both wheels missing from its carriage, lay covered with rust in an old firing position, now half-filled with water. As usual, few people seemed to be anywhere about. As they neared the built-up area of the town, they did see a few blacks working in the small patches along the road but saw almost no sign of white people doing anything.

They walked through several blocks of dwelling houses that formed the circumference of the town before coming to an area dominated by boarding houses and churches. Finally they came to Water Avenue, which ran parallel to the Alabama River. As Logan remembered, most of the town's business houses were on Water. He had not seen the Selma business district since the first year of the war.

Although he had seen many similar sights since leaving Illinois, still he was shocked at the extremely decrepit conditions of the buildings and the streets of this, the only place in his home county that could lay claim to being any sort of city. Several buildings had been burned out, but the majority were at least still standing although few showed signs of being used for commercial purposes. Many of the surviving store buildings were evidently now being used as temporary shelter for homeless people, both black and white.

In the shade of several big oaks in front of the biggest store, half a dozen black teamsters were busily shooting marbles—pronounced "marvels" by the blacks and by plenty of the whites. The laughter and loud talk rising and falling was punctuated by the click of the colorful glass objects. The players had drawn a large circle in the dirt and were shooting from outside this area at a large number of marbles set up in some sort of pattern in the center, with lots of loud talk and yelling about the hand position taken by each shooter. Most players had a small cloth bag that appeared to contain several handfuls of marbles. Back before the war these playthings had been a favorite Christmas gift from planters and overseers to their laborers. Logan was surprised that so many of these toys were still around since they must have been impossible to buy during the last couple of years. Obviously they were highly prized by the laborers and closely guarded.

Looking through the burned-out buildings on Walter Avenue and on down to the Alabama River, Logan could see three seedy steamboats tied up at the landing. The Alex Stephens, the largest of the three, had taken on a dozen bales of uncommonly filthy cotton held together by tattered bagging. It occurred to Logan that cotton that looked like this must have spent most of the war hidden in a cave or a shack deep in the swamps. He hoped that someone who had something to do with producing the bales could now finally get something out of it. However, he know this outcome would be most unlikely.

Other than a few wooden crates, the two smaller boats were evidently empty. No crew could be seen on any of the three, one of them in such poor repair that it appeared unable to make the trip up the river to Montgomery. Out in the river two skiffs were floating slowly downstream carrying indolent fishermen.

As they turned to walk away, the captain said, "Sergeant, I recognize that old, beat-up boat there at the end of the pier. Back before the war, some joker from Montgomery used it as a showboat. He had a pretty good minstrel show put together, and he took it to every good-sized landing from Mobile up as far as the thing would float on the Coosa and the Cahaba. If you look close, you can see where he had the special torches set up to light the stage at night. I suppose it will be a hell of a time before we ever see a showboat on the Cahaba again. Probably never in my life. From now on, it's just going to be work, work, work to try to hold off starvation."

They walked back down Water Avenue until they found a store building that Logan remembered as being the biggest furnishing merchant before the war. Amazingly the building was still being operated as a store. Again Logan and McLemore left the other men sitting on the benches outside while they went in. Surprisingly enough there were a few goods on the shelves, more than they had seen in any other store they had visited on their trip.

They recognized some of the older employees. and one of the older clerks recognized McLemore. After asking a few questions, he commented that for a McLemore he had lost a lot of weight. Yes, he had seen old Major McLemore sometime after the surrender and he appeared to be doing all right. The clerk knew nothing about anyone else from Orrville. On the way out, Logan looked at the rolls of heavy cotton cloth, the coils of plowline, and the dozens of horse collars that evidently were still the basis of the business's inventory—still a skimpy display compared to the mountain of goods, everything from needles to broad axes, according to his father—that these stores had on hand in the days before the war.

Going through the front door, they met an emaciated old fellow who was shaking with palsy and dressed, of course, in the customary rags. McLemore recognized the gentleman and stopped to talk. Logan waited while McLemore inquired about Orrville and his family. Apparently most of the town was still standing and the McLemore family was still living on their homeplace. Then Logan asked about his own people. After a number of questions, Logan learned that, while the trembling old fellow knew the Logan family, he had heard nothing about them for a couple of years. The news was discouraging to Logan. He had by now asked half a dozen people about his family and had yet to get any solid information about the Logan homeplace or its owners.

Finally one of the bystanders volunteered the advice that he could probably get better information down in Cahaba. A number of people still lived down there, and the Yankees had done very little burning in that area. Yes, there had once been a big prisoner of war camp down there, but it had been pretty much closed up before the end of the war. In any event, most of the town was still standing and he should be able to find someone who knew most of the people down around Orrville. The bystander ended his suggestions by telling Logan that he and his men could find some food over at the Presbyterian Church, where the town had set up a sort of soup kitchen for returning soldiers.

Logan took the man's suggestion and moved his people over to the church. There they found some bread and a pot of boiled cabbage. Two elderly ladies and a teenage boy welcomed them and ladled out the cabbage, which the men devoured hungrily. Afterwards Logan thanked his hosts and was preparing to leave when he found that it had begun to rain. By earnestly pleading they were allowed to remain in the church overnight. They lay down on the back pews; after setting a watch over Hood, everyone else went to sleep.

Early the next morning Logan was awakened by the sergeant vigorously shaking his shoulder. "Cap'n, excuse me, sir, but I think you'd better come take a look at Hood. He's been having a bad night. Throwing up blood and coughing all night."

Li'l Georgia had managed to find a candle somewhere and had located a couple of pillows for the sick man's head. Hood was breathing hard and rolling back and forth on the pew. The captain held his arm to take his pulse. Observing Hood, Logan was assailed by troubling thoughts. After all this time and after all the pain he had forced on Hood, they might still lose him, or at least have to abandon him here only twenty-five miles from home.

"Cap'n, I know where a doctor lives. I saw the house with his sign when we were walking in yesterday. Let me go get him. Hood's got to have a doctor, and he's got to have one now," Li'l Georgia spoke earnestly. Logan could see his face in the flickering candlelight, but he felt sure that this trembling boy had almost no chance of convincing a grossly overworked physician to come through the darkness to see a man who was probably dying. However, the face was too intense to be ignored, so all that Logan could do was ask that the mission be delayed until the break of day, only half an hour or so away. Li'l Georgia accepted this although he obviously did not agree with the delay. As soon as there was the barest break in the darkness, he was off into the misting rain.

Sergeant Jackson helped Logan hold the sick man down against the narrow pew, pressing his hand against Hood's forehead and throat. After a few moments he said, "His temperature is way up, Cap'n. We've just got to get it down somehow. I'm going to take that cloth from up there on the pulpit and soak it in the ditch outside, and we'll see if he can get that heat down some before the doctor gets here."

This improvisation seemed to help the amateur nurses, even though it seemed to have little effect on Hood. Logan found a bucket in a closet and was soon soaking the man's clothing. Although he had little faith in what they were doing, he continued to assist the sergeant in his attempt to get water on the feverish man. As daylight came, the church doors were suddenly flung open and Li'l Georgia rushed in, accompanied by a short little man who looked like he might have been in his late sixties. The stranger was dressed in a worn, dark blue suit and carried a small black bag.

The man introduced himself as Doctor Smitherman and immediately went to examine Hood. He whistled softly to himself as he worked. After ten minutes of prodding, listening and feeling, he turned to Logan and said, "I don't think this fellow is quite as bad off as you seem to think. He's plenty sick, all right, but I think he's got a good chance of making it; just keep trying to get his temperature down. I really don't have a thing to give him, and I doubt plenty that there's anything anywhere that would really help. Just keep bathing him with cool water and get him out of this pest hole of a town as soon as you can. Half the people of Selma are down with something right now."

Li'l Georgia began rubbing the sick man down with the wet altar cloth. Logan replied to the little old man, "Doctor, I'm sure the fellow who brought you here has already told you that we're on our way down to Orrville where I hope to find my folks. They're the Logans who live on a farm that's some ways outside the town. Maybe you know 'em."

"Well, yes I do. I've been to their place two or three times. Last time was about a year and a half ago. But, I'm sorry, I can't tell you anything about what's happened down there since. But if I was you, I'd try to get this fellow down there as soon as I could. He's beginning to come around now, and if I was in charge, I'd rest him up today and get him on the road tonight. That's the best chance he has. Get him down to your folks. I remember those two pretty well, and they know what they're doing."

"Right, Doctor. We got a horse we can pack him out on. If he looks like he can stand it, we'll be on the way tonight. Thanks a lot. I suppose that's the only way we can pay you."

"Yes, I'm sure that's going to be the only payment you'll be able to make for several years. That won't put you in any special class either. Just forget it; we're all still alive anyway." Old Doctor Smitherman began to whistle again as he picked up his black bag. He turned to Li;l Georgia, smiled and said, "Young man, you just keep pulling this man along. You're almost to Orrville—just make sure he gets there. If I was you, I'd fight like hell to get down to James and Earlene Logan's with this fellow still alive. Then, I think he's got a pretty good chance of making it through."

The doctor smiled again and continued whistling as he walked around the group, shaking hands with everyone. Then he picked up his black bag and walked quickly out the door, still whistling, breaking into "Lorena" as he disappeared up the street.

Following the advice of the pleasant little physician, Logan and his party were already two or three miles south of Selma when dusk began to fall. The little mare moved along with a swinging pace that seemed to help Hood stay balanced in the saddle. McLemore was leading the animal while Li'l Georgia walked alongside the half-conscious man, pushing him back into the saddle each time he swayed dangerously away from the vertical. The road was muddy from the showers that had fallen during the previous night. But, except perhaps for Hood, their spirits were higher than usual simply because they were stumbling along toward Orrville and someone who might care about them.

Over all the weeks of their trip, self-pity had not appeared to have influenced the men. Now, however, Logan could feel this condition slipping over the group. He could even admit to himself that something quite like this feeling was beginning to crop up in his own mind. Only McLemore seemed immune from these thoughts. If such feelings were disturbing the lieutenant, there was no visible sign. He whistled softly as he led the horse around the puddles in the road. Logan noticed that he was following the lead of old Doctor Smitherman and repeating the tune of "Lorena" over and over.

Shortly before dawn the group pulled up in a pine thicket and prepared to bed down for the day. Obviously the men would have liked to push on for the goal, now so tantalizingly close. However, Hood had to be rested, no matter how the other felt about a stop so close to their final goal. A bed of pine branches was pulled together for Hood. He moaned without speaking as they lay him down, and they were all thankful that he soon fell asleep. The mare was hobbled and turned loose to graze. A guard was set up, primarily to watch over Hood, and the others collapsed into a troubled sleep.

As he drifted off, Logan remembered that they had eaten nothing since devouring the one corn pone they had divided just before leaving Selma. Only the mare seemed happy as she fed on the surrounding grass, and even this must be turning tough in anticipation of the approaching fall.

In the middle of the afternoon, Logan and the sergeant left the others sleeping and walked the mile or so into the town of Cahaba. McLemore, who was always ready for such an adventure, would have loved to join them, but he was left behind to stay with the men. Just before leaving,

Logan checked Hood and found that even though his temperature was down he still appeared to be very sick.

Reaching the town of Cahaba, Logan and Sergeant Jackson found two stores, along with a cotton gin and a sawmill, still operating. Otherwise the town looked considerably less prosperous than when he had last seen it back in 1861. Very few people around. He saw two or three blacks working in garden plots and half a dozen or so whites loafing around each of the stores that appeared to be in operation. The sergeant walked down to the river and found a couple of decrepit steamboats that evidently hadn't been moved from the landing for weeks and, nearby, the abandoned prisoner of war cage.

Logan followed the sergeant down to look at the old prison site and found that it was already falling into ruins. The original building, obviously an old cotton warehouse, had been partially burned out. Several of the sheds around the central structure were already down and blown into wreckage. Both panels of the front gate were already off their hinges and leaning against the adjoining guard shack. Logan and the sergeant walked through the front gate and examined the stockade fence, which had collapsed in several places.

As they stood looking at the ruins, the sergeant turned to Logan and said, "Cap'n, do you get that damn smell? This place's been empty since sometime in April, and it still smells just like that damn Rock Island did when we were penned up there."

"Yes, I guess we'll always remember that scent. I reckon it comes from crowding hundreds of men together under the conditions that we had at Rock Island and that the Yankees must have been under here."

"Yeah, I guess the odor will be around until most of this stuff rots away. Three or four years, I'd guess."

"Sure, time will take it all. My guess is, however, that ten years from now, when the seasons have taken everything but the stone walls, you and I will be able to smell it if only in our imaginations. It'll never return completely into the earth until all the people who went through this experience are dead and gone." They turned and walked slowly back into what was left of the town.

At the sawmill a group of men were gathered around a stationary steam engine watching one of the crew half-heartedly tightening some of the connections on the rusty, decrepit monster. The work crew clearly expected the repair job to take some time, for they were already wandering away to the shade of the scrubby oaks circling the mill site. The foreman finally became restless at the delays and walked over to Logan and the sergeant.

"Hi, my guess is that you guys were recently the guests of our kind-hearted Yankee friends," he said as his eyes swept quickly across their ragged clothing. "I put up with a couple of months of their hospitality myself, but I've been back here for over three months now. Where you all trying to go?"

Logan smiled a little at the sarcasm. "Yeah, we've been walking down from Rock Island, Illinois. Been at it for over three months, but we're nearing the end. Some of us are from down around Orrville, and the others are going to stop there for a few days before they head on to west Georgia. That is, that's what we're going to do if my folks are still around and have anything to feed us. If James Logan's still alive, I'm betting they've got something if there's anything at all to eat in that part of Dallas County."

"I'm from up at Sardis, so I guess I don't know hardly anybody from down at Orrville."

"The other fellow with us from that part of the county is Hugh McLemore from River Bend Plantation. I guess you remember his father, Major McLemore? He's the old white-headed fellow who's the veteran of the Mexican War."

"Oh, yeah, everyone has at least heard of Major McLemore. My folks tell me that he's still around—getting old, though. He's going to be awful glad to find out that his boy's still alive."

"Yes, I'm sure he'll be plenty glad, and if things go anything like right, he's going to know before dinnertime tomorrow."

The foreman smiled and jerked his head down with a sly wink of approval. "You guys come on over here. We got some rice cooking over behind the sawmill, and I think we can share a little of it with you."

"Now, you know that you and your crew are on short rations as it is, so I absolutely refuse to take any of your dinner. Me and my people are going to be in Orrville tomorrow, and I'm guessing that there'll be plenty to eat down there." As he said this, Logan silently prayed that he could make good on such a bold statement. He could almost see his mother carrying a basket of sweet potatoes and a ham hock in from the smokehouse. The vision grew shadowy, but the picture strengthened his resolve so that he refused to share the crew's meager rations. However, he did allow the foreman to fix a tin can of rice "for the sick boy." Saying their good-byes to the work crew, they walked out of the settlement of Cahaba continuing to marvel at how the place appeared to have grown smaller since the early days of the war.

As they were leaving the built-up area, they passed an ancient black woman digging in a small garden plot near the road. Sergeant Jackson walked over and spoke to her. "Good day, Auntie. Are any of them prisoners that used to be in that stockade down by the river still around?"

"Lawd no, boss. Da was all gone in a couple of days after dat gate got opened up. I heard somebody say dat there wuz over a thousand of 'em in dare at the end, and da was all gone in a day or so's time. A lot of 'em got sent over to Vicksburg and get kilt in dat big steamboat wreck on the Mississip."

"What's that all about, Auntie? We never heard nothing about that. We just got back to this country a day or two ago."

The old woman leaned on her hoe, obviously delighted to have an audience for her story. "Yus, white folks, the Yankees took 'em from here to over at Vicksburg and put 'em on dat big steamboat, the Sultana, to take 'em back to the North. And you knows what, dat boat blowed up somewhere round Memphis, and jus 'bout kilt all of dem. And dats jus' after being here in dat jail for a bunch of months."

Jackson nodded to indicate that he was following the story and said, "Yeah, I've always thought that those steamboats was dangerous. If the Good Lord had meant for us to go up and down rivers like fish, he'd have given us a set of fins."

"Dat's right, white folks. I ain't never been on one of dem things, and after dis I gone to make shore I never get on none." The old crone leaned forward on her hoe handle and issued a high pitched peal of laughter.

The captain moved closer to the woman and asked, "Auntie, what place you from and how you been getting along since you were freed?" He smiled to encourage her to expand her answer.

"Sir, I's from Massa Perkins's Sunrise Plantation. That place lay from here over to the river. Might rich land, and it sho turns out de cotton. We even made a right smart crop last year. 'Course we had to grow a lot of corn and wheat to feed ourselves and the soldiers during the past two years. Thangs done gone pretty good since freedom. I don went to Selma to see my sister for two weeks. She wus cookin' for some white folks in town, so's we et right good. After dat I got home to Sunrise to be help wit de choppen. Gettin' freedom was like havin' two Christmases. Yes, sir."

"Two Christmases in a year, eh? Guess we can't beat that. I don't know your Massa Perkins, but how's he doing here after the war?"

"Boss, he doin' good. De plantation's lucky to have him. Dat what I think. Hopes we can keep 'em. He lot better than some."

Logan chuckled at this original analysis of a plantation owner. He guessed that this was slave psychology talking, but it was an interesting reply. "Have a good year, Auntie. Hope your garden grows off good."

The old woman gave them another round of laughter and went back to her hoe.

When the men reached the top of the low ridge overlooking the area, they stopped and looked back on what was left of the town of Cahaba. The sergeant said nothing, and Logan just stood thinking back over the town's history. It was hard to believe that this miserable village was once the capital of the state and still the county seat of Dallas County.

Most of the bigger houses arranged around the outer perimeter of the business and government buildings were obviously in bad repair and unoccupied now. Two or three appeared to have been partly burned out. The business district, huddled between the dwelling houses and the river, appeared to be only partially occupied. From this distance he saw only a few people moving around in the vicinity of the sawmill and a couple of wagons with their attendant drivers in front of the two active stores. And he could still see the old black woman in her garden. Otherwise, there were few signs of anything going on. Neither was there any sign of activity on the river nor on the tumbled-down dock. The most common characteristic of these towns of '65 was the near total lack of human activity.

With slumping shoulders, Logan turned to his companion and after a long sigh said, "Come on, Sergeant, let's go sleep for awhile and then get our people saddled up and go see what's left of Orrville."

CHAPTER VIII

HOME AT LAST

When the sun came up on 21 September 1865, the six men were still two or three miles from the Logan place. They had cut cross-country to save a little time and were not yet back to the Five Forks Road. As they struggled through the woods, the sergeant was leading the mare with Hood slumped down, barely conscious. Slaughter had wanted to tie the man in the saddle, but McLemore took the big man by the shoulder and growled out the message that they were not tying anybody to a horse as long as he was conscious, or even close to conscious. After this rebuff, Slaughter fell back and brought up the rear while evidently just waiting for Hood to fall off the mare. However, he was careful to stay well away from the lieutenant, who walked along at a bouncing pace while swinging his stick at the clumps of leaves that he could reach on either side of the trail. He had begun whistling "Lorena" again. Slaughter clearly considered McLemore to be some sort of madman, but in any event he stayed well to the rear and said nothing.

When they got back to the Five Forks Road, Logan sent Li'l Georgia off to the south with instructions to climb the next ridge and take a look at the town of Orrville. The other men sat down on the side of the trail to rest while the boy was off on his mission. After a half-hour Li'l Georgia came back with the information that the town appeared to be in pretty good shape. He thought that the settlement was probably about two miles away from the tall oak tree he had climbed. From that point Li'l Georgia could see that three or four buildings had been burned out and that a cotton gin appeared to have been partially destroyed. Otherwise the place seemed to be in fairly good shape.

"It looks like old Wilson's bummers thought that there just wasn't much worth burning here in the most beautiful village of the prairie, and I suspect that they were quite right. Anyway, I guess we got by light down in good old Orrville. I suspect that when they had burned out the store with the post office and the cotton gin that they thought they had just about taken care of this center of culture. Not even worth much burning. My, my." After giving his analysis of the situation, McLemore added his little mocking laugh and began pushing Hood back up on the mare.

"Maybe this means that they were feeling merciful the day they spent in this end of the county. Let's mount up and get over this last slope and just face the music. Whatever they've done to us, it is not going to go away just because we wait around," Logan said and went over to help McLemore get Hood settled in the saddle. He felt Hood's pulse and growled, "Hold on, fellow. I'm guessing that you're going to be in the care of Miss Earlene in about forty-five minutes. You'd better start praying to God that my guess is right. Let's move out."

About 1030 on the morning of 21 September 1865, the men topped the last ridge and looked down on Providence Church. The little white building was still standing, but about half of the gravestones had been broken or pushed out of the ground. As they passed by, they saw that the two front doors were off their hinges and that the grounds were cut up by the usual hundreds of wagon tracks and covered with horse signs. Three of the church benches were still outside and were now badly deteriorated from the summer's sun and rain. Everyone, even McLemore, looked away and walked on in complete silence.

They walked down the long slope from Providence Church toward the edge of the Logan place. The rest of the group slowed their pace, allowing the captain to walk out a little in front. It seemed that they wanted to avoid the moment when the house place would come into view. Finally Logan walked around the last little curve and into the cleared cotton field, now partially grown up in weeds, that stretched out to the trees and to the house itself. Logan blinked and rubbed his hand over his eyes. The house was still standing, and the crepe myrtles were still blooming.

He was still too far away to pick up many of the details of the house and yard, but the roof was still on and the chimneys were still up. A little of his dread of the moment began to recede, and he picked up his pace. The men behind him suddenly began to talk softly. After a moment he could make out the end of the front porch and saw that it was down and part of its roof was lying in the yard. The well house was partially smashed. No humans were to be seen anywhere. He hurried on.

As he moved nearer to the house, Logan could see that the front gate was gone but that the gateposts were still standing. The graveled avenue running from the main road to the house was badly washed out in several places but appeared to be still passable. The wisteria vine that had covered the south end of the porch for as long as he could remember now looked to be wild and overgrown. When he could see the front of the building clearly, he noticed that there were no chairs on the front porch. However, there was a wooden table with two adjoining goods boxes that were evidently serving as chairs behind the edge of the wisteria. Clearly someone was living in the house. He began to walk faster.

The captain led his group off the main road and up the drive of a couple of hundred yards leading to the house. All was still quiet around the building. Three cows grazing along the drive looked at them as though mildly curious about their passage then lowered their heads once more to the grass. Suddenly a door was opened into the dogtrot, and a half-grown black girl walked out and stood at the edge of the porch looking at the approaching men. Just as suddenly she began yelling excitedly as she turned and ran back into the house.

Moments later the door flew open and several women, black and white, came rushing through the dogtrot and onto the porch. A rather heavy woman, dressed in the usual dark clothing of the countryside, separated herself from the others and came running forward. McLemore held up a hand and stopped the men so that the captain could go forward to meet the oncoming woman by himself.

The woman threw herself on Logan and began to laugh a bit hysterically as tears rolled down her cheeks and fell on her bosom. She turned back to the women on the porch and yelled out in a broken voice, "It's Wes! It's Wes back from the wars! I just knew it had to be soon. I guess I knew it had to be today. I knew it! I knew it!" The women on the porch rushed together and hugged each other, talking excitedly.

"Well, Mama, it's you all right." Logan finally found his voice, and the idiotic statement that came tumbling out seemed to break open the floodgates as the group of women on the porch rushed forward. Two whites, whom he recognized as cousins, and several blacks suddenly began yelling to each other and dancing around Logan and his mother. Yet even in this moment of unrestrained excitement, one ancient old woman remained on the edge of the porch, leaning against the railing and smiling a tight little smile as she rolled her snuff brush back and forth in her mouth.

The mare had now stopped, and the emaciated men gathered around it holding on to some part of the saddle or bridle. The men, even McLemore, were looking with fascination at the "home from the wars" scene. Hood, who was too sick to understand, simply swayed in the saddle and dropped his head on the mare's neck.

As the first burst of excitement receded and the captain had hugged everyone in the circle of women, he moved up to the edge of the porch and reached out to take the hand of the ancient woman. "Grandma, I see you made it through the war with as big a smile as ever."

"Oh, pshaw, Sonny, don't be giving me a lot of jollies about smiling. You know I'd make it through somehow. I'm still here, and I'm still breathing. And I see you have a bunch of people with you, and all of 'em hungry and one of 'em sick. Guess we'll have to start getting the water boiling and start catching the frying chickens." She again rolled the snuff brush around in her mouth. He laughed with much affection as he gave her hand one more squeeze before turning back toward the group.

As he got back to the group of women, a heavyset, red-faced man came bounding around the end of the house, closely followed by two aging black men. Logan was again suddenly engulfed in handshakes and back slaps from both white and black.

After a moment the heavyset man waved his hand vaguely up toward Logan's mutilated ear and the facial scar. "Well, son, I see they liked to 'ave got you. I'm awful glad to see you still walking around, even if you look like you got a lot of eating to do to get back in working order." The two old blacks immediately pulled their eyes away from the scars, but not so quickly as to miss the two fingers gone from the left hand.

"Yes, sir, I suppose I have thirty or so pounds to put back on, but I've been telling my people that if we could just get back here alive that we'd make it. I'm hoping that you can back me up on that little buck-up story. We've been very, very lucky. Only one of the bunch is sick, and I think maybe he's got a chance now."

"My boy, we've got vittles. Not much change to it, but plenty of stick-to-you-ribs stuff like peas, cornbread, hominy and even a little meat. There's your mother investigating the sick boy. I guess you told him that he'd sho luck out if he got here still breathing."

"Ya sir, ya sir. Ya mighty right, he's in good hands now." The old blacks vigorously nodded their agreement.

"Yes, I've been telling him for a month now that he just had to hold on 'til we got to Dallas County. I think he's been too sick to understand much of anything for the last couple of weeks. But, God knows, he's lucky to be here and still alive. A couple of days ago a doctor up in Selma told us that he could see that our man was very sick from dysentery but that he saw no signs of any of the other intestinal horrors. He thought that he had a fairly good chance for recovery."

The mare was being held at the edge of the yard, and Earlene Logan was making a quick inspection of the semiconscious Hood. She then directed Li'l Georgia to lead the mare over to the porch, and in the next breath she issued instructions to McLemore to get the man off the horse and into the house. Next she told one of the girls to start cleaning on an area she called a shed room. Her voice had turned firm and driving. In a moment McLemore had Hood off the horse and into the house, closely followed by one of the older black women and her Missus Earl.

As the flurry of activity continued, Logan suddenly felt very weak, so he shuffled over to the porch and sat on the floor, propping up against one of its supporting posts. He was a bit surprised to see that even his father was entering into the activity. The two black men were trotting around the yard in a flurry of activity also. They had already built a fire under the wash pot and were now lugging in water from the spring. They looked to Big Massa for directions, of course, but this source of all authority was hard to talk to because he too was in an absolute frenzy of activity as he dodged about the yard. The smokehouse, the spring, the garden and the chicken coop all got a quick visit. One of the black children was running back and forth between these places and the house bearing eggs, okra and even a little piece of some sort of meat. They all finally ended up around the fire, which by now was blazing away under the wash pot. The blacks stood in amazement watching Big Massa chunk up the fire with his own hands. A few minutes later one of the older black women began dipping the boiling water into a tin washtub. Within moments a black girl came trotting out of the house and put an armful of worn-out shirts into the washtub.

"Missus already got that sick boy washed up and into de bed. Day's cutting all his hair off now, and Missus says she think he's gwin be all right, and I believes it too. But him still don know a thing in the world. Just layin' in there groanin'."

"Lord, gal, Big Missus sho got things jumping high, rat now. Jus' stay out of de way and stays ready to hop on whatever she say," the older woman said as she dipped more boiling water out of the wash pot and stirred the clothes around in the tub. "Jus' you look at dat. Da must be 'round a thousand dead lices floatin' up from dem old ragged clothes."

Logan and his four walking companions made little protest when they were directed to get down the hill to the spring and clean themselves up. When they had undressed, one of the little black boys gathered all their ragged underclothes in a cotton basket and disappeared up the hill to the boiling wash pot. Although McLemore kept insisting that his good duds really didn't need the boiling water and lye soap treatment, he knew it was really hopeless; so he surrendered his rather fancy outfit without too much protest.

An hour and a half later with their clothing still a bit damp, they made their way back up the hill and into the big kitchen that was separate from the main part of the house but attached by a covered passageway. The elder Mr. Logan stopped the captain to tell him that one of their hands had been sent over to River Bend Plantation to report to Major McLemore and his family the arrival of, as he put it, the refugees.

Inside the big kitchen the family eating table had been moved into the middle of the room. A long bench and four cane-bottomed chairs provided places for all to sit. As they moved to the table, Logan suddenly realized that most of them had not been seated for a meal in months. He noted that fresh sand had been spread all around the floor of the eating area. McLemore and Slaughter looked at the sand with some amazement, but the others accepted it without a second glance.

Cora the Cook appeared, starched head cloth and all, and immediately directed Logan to the head of the table and pointed McLemore to the chair at the other end. Well, thought Logan, some things just haven't changed; I guess I'd better mind my manners, or she'll crack my knuckles with her fly switch. Be that as it might be, she was all smiles just now, so he supposed that she must have something good to eat on the old "Southern Belle" and plenty of it.

The cook stood behind Logan's chair and reeled off the items of food to be served in the usual sing-song voice used for such occasions. "Sir, today we got hopping john, fried poke shoulder, fried okra, cornbread, butter and coffee. And that's real coffee, sir. We been saving up for this day for a long time, so y'all eat up now."

With a big smile lighting up her face, Miss Earlene came in to give her blessing to the procedure. As the cook was finishing her speech, the Missus walked to the stove and looked into the pots and then in the oven. Everything seemed to meet her standards, so she smiled broadly and patted the cook on the back as she went out. The cook's smile broadened to the point that her gold tooth almost twinkled.

McLemore suddenly clapped his hands together and shocked everyone into total silence by saying, "Let's give our thanks to the Powers Above for bringing us all back alive to Dallas County and to the safety of this place and this family." He then bowed his head and began to recite the Presbyterian blessing of the food before a meal. At the end of his formal recitation he added, "We give our special thanks for this family and their hospitality and for allowing us all to return to this area of our youth. We ask your guidance to our leaders as we try to put our shattered world back together. In your sacred name we pray. Amen."

Around the table there was a moment of hesitation as everyone stole a quick glance at McLemore, who was back smiling his little smile. Lightening did not strike.

Cora the Cook, who did not know McLemore except by reputation, overcame her shock quickly and continued addressing Logan. "Sir, I knows that y'all ain't had much to eat for a long time, and I can tell by looking that y'all sho lost a lot of fat. So please remember that ya can make yoself real sick in a big hurry. We's going to feed you good for two, three days. So jus' y'all take it a little easy today. By de way, we got a little sweet tater pie, when you had enough of this here hopping john and stuff. Young Massa McLemore, if you don't have hopping john down at River Bend, it's really jus' some field peas over some rice and with a little white meat, and we'uns even got a onion in dis pot."

McLemore tossed his hands into the air and laughed. "Cora, we know what hopping john is down at River Bend. We used to have it plenty of times, and I hope we still have a little white meat for ours."

The group ate for some time, but eventually even Slaughter began to slow his attack on the hopping john. Mr. James Logan came into the kitchen and stood near his son's chair. He chatted with the group, warning them again about overeating after their long hunger.

Captain Logan stood and said, "During the hustle and bustle of this morning, I guess some of you missed this, but this is my father, Mr. James Logan, who owns and runs this place. And yes, we've already been warned about eating too much by Cora."

After a few minutes of conversation about the cook and the food—with Cora smiling away in the background—Mr. Logan began to explain how they had managed to have their food stuff even after suffering through the Wilson raid. "I guess we really got off a little lucky. At least we didn't have it as bad as some of the people around here. I will say that the Yankees burned down only two dwelling houses in this area. When they run in here to our house, there was about ten of 'em, and they had a young corporal with 'em. I think that young feller saved us plenty.

"It looked like they were mostly interested in jewelry, silver and stuff like that. 'Course, like all soldiers, they were plenty interested in any kind of eating stuff. Not that we had very much of that either, back in April. Most of what we did have had been hidden in Big Muddy Swamp for at least three weeks before they showed up. Then too they didn't seem to know what some of the things like field peas was. So we ended up with plenty of seed peas and okra. They didn't seem too interested in sweet potatoes neither.

"One old dirty looking fellow was just itching to rip up everything around, and I'm sure if he'd been alone we'd have lost everything to include the house. He'd probably have killed somebody, or maybe all of us, like that family over in Safford that they shot all up. That slimy old bastard was the one who slashed your grandpa's picture with the saber."

"It sounds like our place came out pretty easy. Maybe the Feds were hard pushed for time."

"Yes, son, I reckon we did get by pretty light compared to what happened to some folks. One thing that the picture slasher did that let us all laugh—and right in the middle of his horrible visit—he tried to rob one of the bee hives, and I guess he didn't know much about bees 'cause he just walked up and pushed the bee gum over and started to pull at the honeycomb. 'Course about a thousand bees came roaring out and settled right on that dirty bastard and on the young kid that was with him. They came running back to their horses slapping bees and cussing a blue streak. Guess they got stung fifty or sixty times apiece. All the other Yankees thought it was about the funniest thing they'd ever seen and about rolled on the ground laughing. Even me and the servants laughed a little. The rest of the Yankees were still laughing away as they mounted up and rode off."

"Sir, you're awful lucky, really. They could have burned you out, just as an afterthought, and that by just jerking a piece of fire out of the stove and running around the house sticking it to everything in sight. And that's just what they did in plenty of places." The captain looked down in his plate and ran his hand over his eyes. "I know that stove had to have fire in it 'cause it ain't been out in ten years."

"Yeah, of course it did, but they just ignored it. And all the local folks are saying if you ain't got a picture or two with a saber cut across 'em, you must have been in cahoots somehow with those damn Yankee slimes. We still got Pa's picture on the wall, cut and all. Earlene says we mustn't ever have it patched, just leave it there forever with that cut, just like it is."

"I'm not so sure that that's the way to go. Somehow we just got to make our peace with the Yankees and begin to put our lives and our state back together again." The captain ran his hand over his face and fell into silence.

He could barely imagine anything as bad as the guerrilla warfare that continued opposition would almost certainly have brought on. Maybe slashed pictures displayed for years in southern homes would be acceptable, but that sort of thing would be going far enough. Maybe people like his parents needed to visit Winston County and get a better feel for what guerrilla warfare was all about. Women and children burned to death in locked cotton houses; men dragged to death by frightened horses; men butchered and left to die staked out in the blazing sun; and every worthwhile thing destroyed.

Yes, eventually one side would win and the guerrilla war would end, but what would be left from which to regenerate a worthwhile life? The South owed its escape from such a horror to Lee and the people around him—and yes, to Grant also. Maybe a modified guerrilla war would have been the route to take back in '61 or '62, but '65 was much too late for such an attempt—even if Southerners could stomach such a thing and if such warfare could be controlled so that it did not turn into a grotesque carnival of murder.

But the elder Logan had suddenly stopped talking about fighting to the death and produced a jug of scuppernong wine, from which he passed out a little drink to all hands. Logan noticed that everyone, including the juvenile Li'l Georgia, took his ration and drank it down. He also noticed that no one seemed to be interested in his father's tirade about the need for further opposition to the Yankees. It seemed that they had all been checked out on this approach to life and were pretty much ready to give up the fight. Logan looked at them and felt that he could see a lot of support for his own deep yearning that the federal government would see its way toward doing as little as possible to drive the wedge any deeper between the sections of the country. But maybe that was too much to hope for, particularly after the assassination of Lincoln.

After all the food, including the sweet potato pie, had been eaten, McLemore led the men back out to the porch.

There they sat leaning against the wall or one of the posts; and, of course, within two minutes they were all asleep.

As the cook cleaned the table, Logan and his father remained seated and continued talking about life in Dallas County during the war. Of course, the community had lost its share of men to combat and disease. This had started at First Bull Run and continued until the very end. One young man from the community who was really not old enough for Logan to remember had been killed only a week before Appomattox.

Strangely enough, by far the biggest impact could come not from the men who were killed but from the men who returned to their homes. Unfortunately or maybe fortunately, the men who were killed would be largely forgotten within a few years. However, some of those who returned home with scars, missing eyes or missing limbs would be around for sixty years to remind the people what had happened in 1861-1865. One man from the area had come home missing a hand and a leg below the knee. The elder Logan recalled that this individual was only sixteen years of age and might easily live until the 1930s.

Then his father suddenly gave the answer that he had dreaded hearing since his arrival. "I'm sorry to have to tell you this, but we don't know one thing more about your brother James than we knew in '62. He seems to have just disappeared from the face of the earth during the battle of Shiloh. Not a word since. Now even your mother seems to accept that he must be dead. Your kid brother Edward's all right. The British seized his ship and he's just been lying around Kingston in Jamaica ever since. Of course, he will eventually be released."

Commenting about his missing sons seemed to have left his father spent, but he finally calmed down a bit and turned his mind to more general subjects.

The tax situation was the cloud hanging over every landowner in the county. No one yet knew the details of this coming problem. Mr. Logan thought, however, that since very few county land holders were allowed to vote that the tax system could be used unchecked to run them out of business. These people were barely surviving without the burden of the tax bills that must be collected if the county government was to begin even to crawl forward.

Then if the Feds really intended to break the present economic system completely, all they had to do was run the tax up, break all present owners and sell their properties to the carpetbaggers already swarming around Selma. Mr. Logan was convinced that the final, complete destruction of their county would lie in the hands of these speculators, mostly from Ohio, Indiana and Illinois, who were becoming more numerous each week.

The poor blacks thought that somehow they would end up owning the farms and plantations. This outcome, of course, was totally unrealistic. None of them, or at least not over one or two in the county, could handle such a situation. And even if the Yankee government in Washington City should force such an unlikely event, within a year or so all the land would be back in the hands of the carpetbaggers and other speculators. The captain noticed that his father had not mentioned the scalawags, evidently refusing to recognize that native Southerners could be involved in such a scheme.

After several additional minutes discussing the terror generated by Wilson's passage through the county, Logan got up from the table and walked over to the big kitchen stove. "It looks like the old Southern Belle came through the invasion in one piece. And I see that most of the pots and pans that I remember still seem to be around. That's a bit of a break, I'd say."

"Yeah, that seemed to be the usual case in the houses around about here. I guess they weren't really interested in cooking gear, so if you'r house didn't get burned, you most likely still have all that stuff."

Looking around the kitchen, Logan recognized most of the things that were there before the war. There was an outline of a clock etched on the wall, and his father motioned that the clock itself had gone north. So the clock that had been hanging there since his earliest memory had been carried away to Ohio or New Jersey. Otherwise, things looked much the same as he remembered.

Logan noted details of the house as they walked back to the open dogtrot passage. The whitewash that had been used as a substitute for paint on the outside as well as the inside was now badly chipped and streaked, leaving the building a rather dirty white. The big chestnut logs forming the walls of the original two pens of the building were exposed in the passageway but boarded up on the entire outside. He remembered helping nail up the pine ceiling used throughout the house. In the passageway he looked up the narrow stairway leading to the two loft rooms where he and his brothers had slept while growing up. He could see that these attic rooms still were not ceiled but that whitewash had been used to make them considerable lighter than in his day.

He walked across the porch and into the yard—swept clean each and every day as he remembered and which evidently had been so brushed this morning. From the yard he could see that some of the boards on the roof were beginning to rot and that the top of one of the chimneys had been smashed and not repaired.

His father saw him looking at the wrecked chimney and began to explain with a scowl, "Yeah, there was a Yankee battery set up on that ridge behind Providence Church, and one day those worthless cutthroats just started shooting at our chimney. Hit after four or five rounds and then they just quit firing. Hope they got a big laugh out of that. Needless to say, that little deal just about scared us out of our wits. I guess the bastards in that battery are still laughing about scaring us bunch of Rebels about to death. I sure need to get it fixed before cold weather sets in; however, I haven't gotten around to it yet."

Logan smiled a little despite his father's reaction. "Yep, I've seen our artillery folks do that trick; I think they call it checking their firing figures. I guess soldiers do things like that now and then—sometimes even when they're in their own home states. Of course they always use solid shot for that kind of firing. The red collars all end up laughing and hollering when they finally hit. I will say that I never heard of anybody getting hurt during one of those parties, but it sure don't spread love for the army among the locals. Come to think about it, not much we did tended to do that. Maybe we were pretty popular when we let people eat our rations, but I tell you that didn't happen very often. And I reckon I should say that we were rather popular in the early days of the war when we still had decent looking uniforms and now and then had parades and band music. But I saw nothing like that for at least the last two years of the war. Corn mush, patched pants and lice don't tend to make you too popular with the natives."

The elder Logan looked at his son and said with a deep sigh, "My boy, I'm sure you know that during at least the last two years of the war we civilians tried pretty hard to stay away from all soldiers, no matter what color suit they had on. Most folks around here decided that there was no hope after Gettysburg and Vicksburg, so those that had any get-up-and-go tried hard to get in position to somehow live through what we knew we had to face.

"Of course there were those who appeared to be in some sort of a trance; they just chewed their tobacco, dipped their snuff and waited. And I don't mean just the poor whites acted like that. There was plenty of yeoman farmers and some small planters that went that route too. People like that have already lost their livestock and what little equipment they had, and most of these people are already losing their land. If the rest of us don't take care of 'em, they will surely go hungry; and I just can't see how the darkies can keep from starving.

"And the end is surely not in sight yet. Maybe it will be as bad as Ireland's potato famine. Of course, I don't think that it will ever come to that, but who knows. The British let it happen in Ireland only twelve to fifteen years ago."

Logan listened to his father with a gathering sense of depression. The old fellow was usually optimistic about life and its problems, but now he seemed close to saying that they should just sit back and wait for the poorhouse. Obviously this approach implied help from some governmental agency, and help appeared to be completely beyond the capabilities of the county or state. Further, it appeared absolutely unrealistic to expect any sort of help from the federal level; at least nothing whatsoever had been done up to this point.

He responded, "I think that we have to keep in mind that the really bad time will be from now until April. When the grass and flowers come back, the people who are still alive then are going to make it. We all know that. Make it for six months, and those Yankees who would like to destroy us completely have missed their chance. And I don't believe for a minute that the majority of the northern people really would like to destroy us."

"Don't know about that, but I think that it's already clear that the majority of the people north of the line have no intention of turning much of our country over to the blacks. I think that the danger of that was already past by the end of the summer. Now the carpetbaggers will probably grab everything through the use of the tax and credit system. I really believe that this outcome will be more difficult for our people than a true forty–acres-and-a-mule program with the mule and land taken out of our hide."

Logan's eyes began to get heavy as his father droned on about his southland and its coming fate. Three months of walking and starving were taking their toll. In addition, his arrival at the Logan place and the relief of finding things somewhat better than he had anticipated were leaving him a bit relaxed and almost ready to let things drift for a while. His last thoughts as he fell asleep presented a picture that wasn't quite as dark as he had been imagining for the past several months.

Logan awoke with a start and pulled himself to a stand as a one-horse buggy came clopping down the driveway from the main road. The horse was a dilapidated animal that appeared to be unable to pull the buggy any faster than a slow walk. The driver pulled up at the edge of the yard and climbed down. Logan noticed that the new arrival looked almost as dilapidated as the horse; however, the old fellow seemed to straighten a bit as his feet touched the ground and he walked to the porch. Logan then recognized the visitor as Major McLemore of the River Bend Plantation.

"Hello, sir. Come in. I' m John Wesley Logan. I guess you haven't seen me in four or five years, but maybe you remember me."

"Why, greetings, Captain. I do remember you, but it has been quite a long time since I've seen you. Guess you were about twenty when I last saw you. And I see you've seen plenty of the elephant since that time." The older man's eyes ran up to the scar on Logan's cheek and over to the mutilated ear.

"Yes, sir. But I got through it all and I'm still alive. I know that you must have already heard that your son's with us and that he's all right. Let me rustle him out here." Logan stepped up on the porch and went back into the dogtrot to awaken McLemore.

While the major waited, James Logan came bounding forward to greet the older man. "Come in, sir. We're honored to have you visit the Logan place. Haven't seen you in several weeks, but I can see that you're doing all right. I'm sure you know that your boy's here and that he's in good shape. Just about as good a shape as any trooper I've ever seen come back from the wars."

Major McLemore pulled off his battered straw hat and straightened his worn suit coat. "We're all doing fine, thank you. Naturally I'm very glad to know, finally and for sure, that our boy's getting by in his usual fashion. Admittedly, I was getting a little worried this time—it's been so long."

"Sir, I know you're awful glad. But here he comes. Don't he look just right out of the bandbox? Yes, sir!"

McLemore came over with little show of emotion other than his flashing broad smile. The father met the lieutenant with his own smile and an outstretched hand. As they clasped hands, the older man made an obvious inspection of his son's face and extremities.

"Now, sir, I know that they already told you that I'm all in one piece and that I've even gotten pretty well fattened up since they let me out of Rock Island."

The old man looked at his son's bulk and shook his head saying, "You know that nobody here knew where you were; nobody knew that you were in prison or even if you were alive, for that matter. And I can sho see that you just about got your weight back. How come you got so much better clothes than the other people? Have you turned scalawag?"

"No, not yet," he replied with an unrestrained peal of laughter. "However, I want you to know that if things start to get real rotten, I'm sure going to think about it. Anybody done that around here?"

"Well, no. Not that I know of, at least not yet. But I've heard that one of the politicians up in Selma may go that way."

"Ah, some will. Sho as shooting. They'll find it's a lot better than starving." McLemore finally looked down at himself and remembered that he owed an explanation of his presentable clothing. "I've been on a little side trip down into south Mississippi herding a few of our black folks off towards Mexico. Some harebrained scheme to move a whole bunch of ex-slaves to south Mexico to work some sort of plantation. I got some better clothing out of the deal, and I've got a fine young mare that we can use for a while. Not a plow horse, you understand, and I'll have to take it back to Nashville in a few weeks. That's when I go back to help push a couple of hundred more darkies down across the Rio Grande."

Old Major McLemore shook his head in disbelief at his son's capers, but after squeezing the boy's arm again he walked over to speak to the other released prisoners. The group left the porch and crowded around the old fellow, obviously pleased to get the attention of this important person.

* * *

A few days later old Mr. Logan talked his son into taking Major McLemore up on his invitation to visit River Bend. The mistress of the Logan place—referred to as Miss Earl even by the awesome major—had been invited, of course, but declined because she felt she couldn't leave the very sick Hood for the entire day. So on a beautiful day near the end of September, the Logan men dressed themselves in their clean but patched best and walked the three miles to the McLemore homeplace.

This plantation, which Logan remembered as the biggest and best kept in that part of the county, showed plenty of signs of wear and neglect. As soon as they reached the edge of the McLemore property, they could see that the operation had suffered severely from the passage of Wilson's cavalry and from other problems arising during the last months of the war. Fences were down in many places, a couple of cotton houses had been wrecked—probably for their logs and wood floors—and one big barn had been burned to the ground. The cotton fields near the road had not been cultivated during the past season.

Walking on down the dirt road with a little of its gravel still showing in widely scattered places, they had to avoid an occasional mud hole partially filled with water from the last rain. They walked through a grove of pecan trees, many of which were uprooted; several near the road had been cut and removed leaving only a pile of brush to mark their original positions. The trees had evidently been cut into logs that were now buried as a part of the roadbed. The Logans were wearing rawhide moccasins; although they were presentable as footwear, they transmitted the feel of each log and gravel up into the men's feet and legs.

As they approached the River Bend headquarters, the Logans first passed the commissary with its regularly spaced, small windows set high in the walls. The front of the building had the customary front porch extending around to the side to cover windows that opened into the store. Logan remembered these windows as the place used by the overseer and his assistants to issue selected food items and clothing to the heads of the slave families. The windows opened into a small office partitioned off in the front of the store. The heavy doors into the front of the building were secured by a rusty padlock, which did not appear, judging from the cobwebs and dust, to have been opened for its primary function for several months. However, the store must have been left open during the inspection of Wilson's cavalry or it would surely have been broken into and burned when it was discovered to be empty.

A number of barns and service buildings were visible behind the Big House; and a dirt road lined with slave cabins ran off into a grove of trees behind the buildings. All of these buildings were dilapidated, showing little sign of painting or other repairs having been done for several years.

At the rear of the main house a low tower with a tank was connected by a pipe to the roof of the house. At ground level a low building enclosed the legs of the tower. Logan had seen such tanks in Virginia but had never seen such a structure in this area. His father saw him staring at the building and offered the explanation that the structure was a bath house and what the McLemores called a water closet, a sort of indoor privy that could be washed out periodically into a cesspool that was down below the hill.

As for bathing, Logan's father added, the ladies' fashion books said that it was all right to take a bath, even as often as once a week, if you got it over with very quickly and if you did so in the morning. The elder Logan laughed at this whole idea and added that the regular privy and the tin tub on the kitchen floor seemed to work all right. However, the McLemores had always wanted to have the very latest thing, and this setup had certainly been the latest thing in Dallas County when it was put in a year or so before the war.

The Big House, which dominated the entire scene, was the usual white, two-story building with four square columns running up to the roof line. Logan recalled from his boyhood that the house had four rooms down and four up with central halls on each floor and a two-story wing elled off to the rear. Five chimneys were still sticking up over the roof line. Several of the green shutters were missing, and some of the window glass had been repaired with cardboard. As with the service buildings, no paint had been wasted on the wooden siding for some years.

At the McLemore house the landscape differed from the usual sparseness found around similar houses. Here were evergreens, azaleas and camellias in profusion although many were broken and dying and others badly in need of trimming.

The house's most unusual feature was the extension of the front porch floor all across the front of the house. The floor was uncovered except for the center section under the roof extension supported by the four columns. Thus a sort of patio on each side of the covered porch had been created. Logan recognized the house as the type called a Kentucky

House by the people of the Shenandoah Valley, and despite the disrepair it was clearly a most handsome building.

As they approached the Big House, the elder Logan talked about the McLemore plantation and what he thought they would have to do to survive the coming hard times. "Old Major McLemore has over three thousand acres in this place, and I believe he used to have over eighty blacks around to work it. I've heard that most of his labor left sometime during this past spring. 'Course, that's been the usual case on these big places. A lot of these people came home after a month or so; but even with that, these big planters got hit a lot harder than us little fellows."

Watching several of the returnees digging in a kitchen garden fenced off at the back of the house, the captain replied, "Well, I can see that at least some of 'em came back."

"Oh, yeah. They sort of had to come home when the Yankees up in Selma quit feeding 'em, back there in the early summer. I hear that about half of the major's people came back, but they showed up too late to do any good toward putting in a crop for this year. Little guys like me got just about all of our people back and most of 'em early enough to get the late stuff planted."

"Yeah, your handful of darkies are almost like part of the family. But you know that if you have eighty or more of these people working on your place, and with some of 'em hired out as carpenters in Selma or as stevedores down on the river, there just ain't any way you could have much of a family relationship with 'em."

"'Course not, son, but what I'm saying is that people like these big planters could've done a hell of a lot better. And they're paying for it now. I'm really thinking that the old major's going to have a hard time making it through the next three or four years."

"Well, sir, I'm afraid 'most everybody's going to be wallowing in that ditch. However, we should be thinking of some bright ideas, and maybe the McLemores can help on this score, as to how we can get through these tough, tough times." As he spoke, Logan noticed that several of the brick pavers of the verandah floor were missing. He pulled on the bell cord and waited.

Within moments a young black in a white jacket, now yellowed with age and patched but clean and pressed, opened the door and asked them in. As they stood in the hallway, Logan noticed immediately that the house was now rather sparsely furnished; however, the portraits on the wall seemed to be in excellent shape. As he was looking at the pictures, old Major McLemore suddenly appeared.

The major noticed his visitors' interest in the portraits, so he explained their excellent condition. "Those pictures are about all we have in the house that's still in the shape it used to be. We shipped 'em off to a cousin of mine down in Marengo County. Sent 'em out in '63 when I first began to suspect that our people couldn't win the war. Just got 'em back last week."

The elder Logan whistled softly. "A lot of luck connected to that, eh? The blue bellies could have gone there just the same as here."

"Sure they could have, but they didn't. We just guessed right. Our army took most of the livestock and the rolling equipment, but they didn't bother the houses or the furnishings—leastways, not often. And very few Yankees ever went down there to Marengo. Anyways, we got the pictures back, and if they had been here they would've been slashed to bits."

"I don't remember much about this house before the war, of course," the younger Logan put in, "but I suppose they grabbed up or ruined a lot of your furniture."

"Just smashed it up, mostly. Anything that looked like it was any good got slashed and busted up. That old square piano that we had in the drawing room was pulled outside, and some Yankee moron tried to play it. That was while the others danced around and sang. Finally they smashed it up with an axe."

"Big old party, eh? Low life sons of bitches. I'm sure your wife was sho disturbed about the piano," said the older visitor.

"Yeah, she was really crushed. I think she was more disturbed about the piano than she would have been if they'd burned down the house. She just stayed upstairs and cried in disbelief. I was in Mexico City back in '47, so I was prepared. Saw it all happen before; I reckon I even participated in a little of this type thing down there. I sure knew it was coming, but Mrs. McLemore just couldn't believe it. Just sobbed her heart out for hours."

"Yes, I understand," replied James Logan. "The waste of such a thing is nearly unbelievable. Thank the Lord we missed most of that type destruction."

"Well, let's think about more pleasant things for a while. Come on and let's join the ladies." Major McLemore led them into the parlor to meet his wife and daughters. Logan remembered the wife and noticed that she had come through this disastrous period without too much change in appearance. Her dress was very good, perhaps a little behind the latest Goody Book plates but somewhat better than anything he'd seen for three years. He remembered her as being stately in appearance, and after four hard, hard years there she stood—still stately.

Mrs. McLemore gestured to a gangly girl and said, "This is my younger daughter, Martha, who perhaps you men remember from her childhood."

After the introductions they all chatted for a moment until Major McLemore directed their attention to another girl just entering the room. "Neither of you gentlemen has seen my daughter Caroline for some years, so I have to warn you that she's all grown up now. Right, Caroline Jean?"

The girl smiled a quick little smile. "Ah, Papa, you know that being fifteen don't make you all that grown up. Mr. Logan, I remember you and your wife from the church. I haven't been there since the surrender, I'm afraid, but I understand that things are settling down some now and that maybe we can get ourselves a minister and all start going back again."

Mr. Logan started to answer, but the girl had already turned away to talk to his son. "Captain Logan, we're all so pleased to have you back home again. I'm afraid that I don't remember you from before the war, but my brother tells me all kind of fine things about you. That's from during the war and during that long, long walk home." Logan noticed that the girl had given absolutely no indication that she had seen his scars or his mutilated ear. He also noticed that she was indeed rather grown up, at least physically. She was a very pretty girl.

At this point the lady of the house dispatched her daughters on some errand into the rear of the house before serving the men tea. The younger girl appeared to be happy enough to escape the grownups, but the adolescent Caroline was visibly unhappy with being chased out of the presence of the famous Captain Logan. Mrs. McLemore turned to the Logans and with a little chuckle informed them, "Oh, she'll be back, don't worry. I find it nearly impossible to run her away from any visitor, and the chance to practice her charms on two new men is something I'm not prepared to deny for very long. You saw, of course, that my younger girl is quite content to go out to the kitchen house and spend her time talking to the cook. I hope it's a long time before she reaches her sister Caroline's state."

The major smiled in obvious approval of his elder daughter and said, "Now, now, she's a very clever bird who's just learning to fly. In a year or so she ought to be settling out on a straight course."

"I sure hope so, for the sake of all our sanity," Mrs. McLemore rolled her eyes and gave her head a bit of a toss before excusing herself to check on the dinner arrangements.

When the three men were alone in the parlor, the major took the opportunity to turn the conversation to those things that he clearly thought should be nearer to the heart and mind of the community than the status of his daughters. He began talking first about what must be done in his own business for the plantation to survive the next few years. Then he jumped right into a discussion of the thing that was first on everyone's mind—how to replace the slave labor system with some workable scheme of labor that would allow the plantation system to get back into operation by the start of the next crop year.

"I really hope we'll be able to get away with paying our labor off with a yearly lump sum, paid after the cotton is sold in the fall. The pay will have to be quite a small amount, if it's paid on top of their food and clothing. The part I can't figure out about this scheme is how to feed and clothe the labor until the fall of next year gets here."

"On our little two-horse place, we're still putting out as much food as we can get our hands on, but no clothing or shoes—'cause we can't buy any. So far we're getting about as much work out of 'em as we used to in the old slavery days. Or at least as much work as we can use now, which ain't so awful much," the elder Logan said. He looked to his son for some sign of agreement before continuing. "Now, I'm just hoping they stay around when the hard work starts at the end of March. When cotton chopping time comes in June, I just don't know how we'll hold 'em. That's when we're going to find out if this type system is going to work."

The younger Logan shook his head as he entered the conversation. "Major, my father and I have talked about this a lot during the last few days, and I'm convinced that the people in Washington City will never stand still for us continuing a system that is so near the old slavery setup. I think that these people are going to have to see a little money now and then. And not just at the end of the crop year. What do you think about that, sir?"

The old gentleman straightened himself a bit before replying, "You're probably right about us having to pay a little money now and then, but we simply can't do it right now. It seems to me that the boys up in Washington City ought to establish some kind of credit at the furnishing merchants' stores so that the black folks could charge at least enough for shoes and some work clothes. Then we planters would have to pay some part of this back when our cotton is sold in the fall."

The major's face seemed to brighten as though he had just thought of a brilliant solution to one of the South's immense problems. "'Course if the government would pick up a big hunk of this bill, maybe we could all, black and white, have a chance of making it through the next couple of years. I think that we—and I mean both races—simply must have access to some sort of credit system so we can come up with at least seed and equipment. But I know that even Mr. Rothschild himself might have trouble coming up with such a lash up."

"Sir, I think that some such scheme might work. However, I don't believe for a minute that the abolitionists will ever go along with anything that looks as soft on the plantation people as this does." Listening to his son, the father shook his head in disbelief that anyone could consider such an approach workable even if the Yankees would go along with it. However, his son continued, "Maybe the Feds will just round up most of these people and move them west to start a totally new life. Sorta like what Andrew Jackson did to the Indians back there in the thirties."

"Just sort of let 'em go in competition with the Indians for part of the desert. Is that what you mean?" the elder

Logan chuckled bitterly. "I can jes see our darkies, or me either for that matter, turned loose in the desert to compete with a bunch of Comanches. I'm guessing that every one of us, black and white, would be scalped inside a week."

"Yes, sir, I know you believe that you could do a whole lot better for your people than just turning 'em out in the wild to sink or swim, but I'm not sure there's any better way available. And I certainly don't think the plan that I understand General Grant's been pushing—just grab up our black people and send them to Santo Domingo or Cuba or Mexico—could ever work. Those places are overpopulated right now, and they certainly don't want our ex-slaves. At the very least it would take a little armed persuasion from us to get our neighbors to accept them."

Major McLemore replied, "I think we have to remember one more thing and that is that those mills up in Massachusetts have to have cotton, and soon. I'm guessing that a lot of the Yankees are going to come to their senses when there just ain't no cotton at all next year. Right now all of us know that there jes can't be much cotton until we get the black folks back in the cotton fields."

"Major, there's lots of people in the upland country of Alabama and Tennessee who don't agree with you. They think they can turn out a lot of cotton if they don't have to compete with our black labor. Many of these people are convinced that slavery was a grossly inefficient system." The younger Logan drained the last of his sassafras tea and set his empty cup on the mantel.

The elderly man shook his head and said, "I don't doubt that the uplanders can do better than they did before the war, but surely we would all agree that there's little hope that our white people can turn out enough cotton for all those mills in Massachusetts. There's just not enough white people around. I think that a big bunch of the eastern population thinks that if they could just get rid of the planter class down here that everything would be all right. So they'll just use the tax system to break our landowners and everything becomes just fine."

"I'm scared to death about that one." The older Logan drained his cup and set it beside his son's on the mantel. "I hear from Cahaba that the plan is for the carpetbaggers to increase land taxes until we all go broke, and then they jump in and buy up all the worthwhile farmland in the county."

"Yep, I'm just scared to death that's exactly what's planned." The major rolled his eyes heavenward. "They'll come up with some ridiculous tax rate, which nobody can pay, and then they foreclose on everybody. They'll claim that some of this land, maybe even the famous forty acres, will be assigned to each black family. Of course the Yankee bastards that cooked up this scheme already know they'll have all of it back in their hands within a couple of years."

The parlor door swung open suddenly as Caroline Jean came bouncing in carrying another tray of cups. The butler came behind the girl, showing just the tiniest suggestion of a smile on his shiny face and carrying another jug of steaming tea. Logan noticed that the jug had a large chip out of the lip.

When the tea had been passed around, Wes Logan found himself talking to the older McLemore girl. She was indeed, as her mother had warned, busy practicing her charms on anyone who would listen. She chatted about Richmond and how she was supposed to have gone there to attend school this fall; but now that Richmond's world had collapsed, she just wasn't going anywhere.

The major broke into her chattering to remark that it was most fortunate that she didn't want to go anywhere because since the surrender it didn't make any difference to the McLemores what happened to Richmond or Charleston or even Mobile—nobody from that family could afford to go to school in any of those places. They couldn't even travel anywhere past Selma.

After they drank their sassafras tea and ate a few more of the toasted pecans, the lady of the house came back to announce that dinner was ready. They moved into the dining room, which Logan noticed was also sparsely furnished except for the portraits of McLemore ancestors, who looked out from their very well kept frames and appeared to be in perfect order. The chairs at the narrow table, which obviously had been substituted for a much bigger table, were mismatched and the tablecloth was discolored. Much of the china was chipped, and at least three patterns had been used to make out the required settings.

Mrs. McLemore did not apologize for the furnishings but acted as though all was in readiness for a visit from the governor himself. However, the major explained, "You see that the only part of the tableware that we got past Wilson's raiders was the silver. I buried it down in Big Muddy Swamp and made sure that there was no witness to the act. Otherwise I suppose we'd be eating with our fingers 'cause the bummers took all the pewter and even the old iron spoons and forks. So right now we've still got all the silver, but I guess we'll soon have to start selling it off a few pieces at the time just to keep eating." At this remark the wife flung back her hair and shook her head in disagreement as she rolled her eyes heavenward.

After everyone had been seated, the door flew open suddenly, and Hugh McLemore came gliding in and seated himself on a stool across from the guests. The major scowled at his son for his tardiness but said nothing, so the lieutenant evidently thought that it was safe to enter the conversation. "Mr. Logan, has the good captain settled down into Dallas County life yet? I suppose Miss Earl's got him partly strengthened up with that good cooking of hers."

"Well, she's working hard on it. I think she and the cook have blown most of our winter rations on getting him and his friends back into running order. But I guess it's necessary. In addition to feeding 'em, we've spent a lot of time trying to convince 'em how hard it was on us here trying to keep the home fires burning. I think I've got Li'l Georgia about convinced, but I haven't made much progress with the others." Mr. Logan rolled back and forth with laughter.

Captain Logan smiled broadly at his father's remarks and said, "You can bet that after the first day, that little snake-in-the-grass had all the women feeding him extra and patting him on his stupid head while they begged him to eat more."

Mr. Logan responded, "Sure, that's exactly what happened. I think he's got all his weight back already. I just don't think that women are capable of resisting those rosy, smooth cheeks. I think even the cook, who, God knows, is hard to fool, was completely taken in."

Mrs. McLemore tapped her glass with some impatience. "All right, let's leave this poor boy alone. It sounds a bit like you people are just jealous of this nice young man. Major McLemore, let's bless the food, and we'll all think about how lucky we are to have all that we do have." Their hostess gave the lieutenant and his two sisters a bit of a scowl. The two girls immediately dropped their smiles, but her son seemed to smile a bit broader.

The butler in his off-white coat, followed by a young black woman who was also in dingy white, came in bearing the food. The main dish, as announced by the butler, was a rabbit pie. Then a corn pudding, a dish of squash and onions and some fried sweet potatoes were all added to the table with a bit of a flourish. The drink was hard cider for everyone except the girls, who got buttermilk.

As they ate, James Logan rattled on endlessly about how good everything was. Mrs. McLemore acknowledged each compliment with a trace of a smile and a slight nod of her head. The elder Logan accepted this acknowledgement as encouragement and so continued the compliments at each break in the conversation.

Major McLemore steered the conversation away from food and into areas that he considered of more intellectual value. He addressed both of the Logans, but he obviously expected the younger man to supply most of the answers. After all, the elder Logan was using up his conversational powers in his endless compliments on the food.

The major started by throwing a question to the table as to just how the people of Dallas County were going to start toward recovery from the disastrous war. His opinion was that there was little hope for any sort of recovery for at least ten years. So the pressing question was just what should they be doing now to prepare for survival for the next several years. Those who survived through that period could then think about real recovery—maybe ten or twelve years down the road.

Logan listened to the older gentleman as he laid out some of the rudiments of his political philosophy for his county at the present time. Admittedly, Logan had little idea of what his own political philosophy was under '65 circumstances, but he was willing to accept almost anyone's philosophy as long as he could grasp its basic tenets and it promised some hope of recovery in the future.

Major McLemore had commenced a long monologue dealing with how the South's present dilemma related to Ireland's almost ageless fight to establish some sort of independence from Great Britain. The elder McLemore was droning on about the terrible storm that the Irish must weather before they could hope for enough stability to support a viable separatist movement.

Logan could barely follow some of the older man's reasoning as he talked about Machiavelli and Jefferson, admittedly way over a simple cavalryman's head. However, he realized that such a subject should not have been so foreign to him, and it troubled him a bit. A quick look around the table made it obvious that he was the only one who was perturbed by or even attentive to what the major was saying. Mrs. McLemore was sympathetic enough to her husband to quiet her daughters, who had begun chattering about some adolescent concern. Her son and the older Mr. Logan were rolling their eyes at each other in total boredom, obviously not understanding much about the subject.

The major ended by saying that it was now time that the South decided whether to start a long-range fight for a separate or semi-separate existence or just to relax and wait for complete integration into Yankeedom. He dropped his head into his hands and rolled it back and forth. He then sighed and declared that he was just too tired to continue the fight, so personally he was ready for integration into Yankeeland. "Let Boston, Providence and Washington City run the whole show. Evidently we can't do a satisfactory job, as the past four years sort of established. Now, for you young people, I'm not at all sure that I'd go that route. You're going to be around for a long time yet, and maybe you can break the cords that tie us to New England. And I say New England advisedly because if Illinois, Indiana and Iowa had been running the show this disaster would never have happened."

Logan responded to the major, "No, it wouldn't have happened. I've thought this for a long time. Those damn Puritans up in New England just seized control of everything and ruined us. One of the things connected to this Puritan thing that really hurt us was when our idiots began to talk about themselves as Cavaliers. That's all we needed, a bunch of cotton farmers acting like Sir Walter Raleigh." Logan could feel himself on firmer ice here, as opposed to all that skating around on Machiavelli. "Another thing I think is that a whole lot more effort should have been spent trying to hold Missouri and Kentucky in the fold rather than that total fixation on Washington City and Richmond."

"Yes, that turned out to be a bit of a disaster, or so it seemed to me. But looking back on things like that makes the solution appear so easy. I suppose we'd all have been tempted to let Bull Run and Mechanicsville call the tune if we'd been in charge. However, some basic changes in how we handed things on the upper Mississippi should have made a world of difference."

"Major, something that always worried me was all that loose talk about help from Europe. I never did have any confidence in getting anything worthwhile from England, and it turned out that's just what we got—nothing, just a lot of loose talk. And after we lost New Orleans way back early in the war, they could get quite a bit of cotton through that port. I did have some hope that the Italian Garibaldi might come over to help us, but it turned out that he was a flaming leftist and was not about to support any sort of revolutionary movement that even smelled of conservatism, even if we were fighting for freedom from an oppressive government. He was really all hot to support the free-labor Yankees. I suppose we should have guessed that from the red shirt he always wore."

Old Major McLemore smoothed back his mop of white hair, drained the last of his cider and fixed Captain Logan with his sharp brown eyes. "Yeah, I guess we kept thinking that somebody would come and pull our chestnuts out of the fire—sorta like the French did back there during the Revolution. It just never happened."

"Right, and I believe that such thinking was disastrous, because it encouraged us to go on and fight a conventional war until it was too late to turn ourselves into guerrillas. We used up all our chances for freedom by turning the whole thing into a set piece operation over Richmond and Washington City. If we had used the approach that the

Russians used against Napoleon and burned all the cotton and ginning equipment—I guess that's what a scorched earth policy would have meant to us—we would have had a chance to wear the blue bellies down and force them to quit. Of course, if we had managed to win like that, perhaps we would have been worse off than we are now in defeat. Who knows? I think, though, that if I had been sitting in Jefferson Davis's chair, I'd have tried it."

Suddenly the elder Logan spoke up. "I think that if we had let the thing fall off into such a horror that everything down at the Logan place would now be a pile of ashes and that at least half of the people living there now, white and black, would be dead and gone. I know that me and my people owe our very lives to Davis and Lee and the people who were there around them at the top. I, at least, shall never forget it."

"You're right, of course, but all those decisions were made long ago and we must now live with 'em. Captain Logan, you and the people of your age group must decide whether to pull back now and wait for another time or just give it up and try to fit yourselves to the Boston way."

"I must admit, sir, that I would like more time to think about that one." Logan shook his head, not willing to commit on such a critical question. "About as far as my poor brain will take me, here in September of '65, is to figure out what we should do to get past '66 and '67. Before we can start thinking about any sort of long-range plan, we must solve the short-range survival problem that is on us right now."

Major McLemore looked over at Logan with some surprise and considered the depth of the younger man's comments. "I agree, I agree. But please, Captain, I'm sure you would go along with me that this thinking in terms of short-term survival must be behind us in two or three years and that by, say, 1875 we will have started to recover. But in the short term, the occupiers—both those in uniform and their helpers, the damn carpetbaggers—are going to put out plenty of bread and circuses to keep the new freedmen quiet. And, yes, the poor whites will come in for plenty of those goodies too. But this kind of thing can't keep the dike from leaking forever, and in three or four years we must have our decisions made and have some sort of long-range plan in place."

Mrs. McLemore broke into the conversation. "All right, Mr. McLemore, enough of that philosophy. Let's let our neighbors rest a bit from all this heavy political conversation. We've got the first Lady Baltimore cake that's been in this house for these three years. Let's eat it and think some pleasant thoughts for a spell."

Mrs. McLemore rang her little bell, the door to the passageway to the kitchen flew open, and the butler entered bearing the cake, shining in all its sugary glory. When it had been sliced and served, it proved to be truly a superb cake.

The dessert course gave Mr. James Logan a chance to resume his praise of the hospitality of the McLemores. His hostess now smiled and thanked him with a bit more sincerity than she had previously used in reply to any of his first twenty attempts.

After dinner—the biggest celebration at River Bend for over a year according to Mrs. McLemore—the family and guests stood talking on the porch prior to the guests' departure. Caroline Jean once again practiced her charms on the guests. It had been so long since he had come in contact with such a flirtatious approach that Logan hardly knew how to react. He felt that he probably smiled too broadly and too quickly, but the girl seemed to accept his reaction very positively. In fact, her brother seemed a bit discomfited by her bold actions and scowled enough to drive her back under cover of her mother, who was standing in the front door. Mrs. McLemore laughed her silvery little laugh and guided her daughters back into the house. The elder Mr. Logan opened his mouth to add one last compliment, but his hostess was too quick for him and disappeared behind the closing door.

Major McLemore and his son walked down to the front gate with their guests. As they strolled along, their host began to tell about how he came to be in Dallas County. He explained how his life had unfolded since 1813 when he had arrived in Alabama from Tennessee with General Andrew Jackson's army as a fourteen-year-old militiaman excited about the prospect of gaining glory in the fight against the Redstick Creeks and maybe the British. As it turned out, he saw very little fighting; undoubtedly the rough and ready Tennesseeans had protected him because of his age, but he did get to go to both Horseshoe Bend and New Orleans. At least he got to see some of the results of that fighting.

He never went back to Tennessee but ended up in Dallas County and after four or five years an as overseer finally got started as a smalltime cotton planter. By the time of the Mexican War he had become a fair-sized landowner and was turning out a respectable crop each year. But he had been bitten by the soldiering bug, so in 1847 he followed Zachary Taylor off to Mexico. There he got to see all of the fighting that he ever wanted to see in this world—and in a big hurry. As a fifty-year-old major, he left the army at the end of the war and came back to Dallas County to settle down as a serious cotton planter. He was still at it when the Confederate War overtook him in 1861.

Mr. Logan responded to the major's reminiscing, "Yes, Major, I remember that we men here in Orrville had the very devil of a time convincing you not to get tangled up in this last war. I felt so cheesy about not going to the army myself, me not yet fifty and all, that I got wound up in that damn Home Guard when they were putting that thing together. Lord, what a mess that was!"

"Yes," said Major McLemore, "I suppose it was. I knew that if nobody wanted me in the Confederate Army that I certainly didn't want to get in some ragtag outfit like that. So for this last war, I would just let old Hugh here hold up the family banner." The old man put his hand on his son's shoulder.

"Major," said Mr. Logan, "you were well represented. Don't you fret. I heard it all from old Sergeant Jackson."

The lieutenant shrugged his shoulders and threw out his grin. Captain Logan nodded in silent approval.

"Mr. Logan, back there a while ago you mentioned keeping the home fires burning. Well, there was a lot of that kind of activity, and in my opinion it really helped us hold the Confederate effort together. Captain Logan, you were away fighting the war, so maybe you never heard much about some of these programs. Some things like the big drive to buy a gunboat, which got started up around Richmond, wasn't all that practical. It did bring on a lot of charity parties back in '61 and '62, and I think that the ladies really managed to buy some sort of boat for use up on the James River. But that was a bit beyond us here in Alabama."

Mr. Logan added, "Sir, I remember something about that drive, and I'm sorry to say that entering much into that sort of thing was just way beyond us two-team guys. Seems like I remember something about the big-time planters getting together and buying some rifles. Major McLemore, I suppose you were in on that?"

"Yes, several of us collected up a bunch of money and bought eighty Henry repeating rifles. This gun used a brass .44 caliber cartridge and could fire twelve rounds without reloading. It had a brass receiver and was truly beautiful. Some dealer in Nassau ordered them for us right out of Connecticut, up there in the heart of Yankeeland. We presented these weapons to our government at a ceremony over in Savannah. I sure hope our soldiers got some good out of those things."

Lieutenant McLemore spoke, rather excitedly for him, "Oh, yeah, one of Mosby's companies ended up with fifteen or twenty of those rifles. They were tremendous weapons. Of course, they were surrendered to the Feds at the breakup, and I'd guess they're now hanging over mantels all over Yankeeland. But you're sure right about those Henrys. If we could have armed every soldier in the Confederate Army with those things, we would have had a good chance of winning that war."

Captain Logan interjected, "'Course, if we could have done that, the Yankees would have done the same, and maybe we'd all just have gotten shot sooner."

"Yeah," put in the lieutenant, "as it all worked out, of course, we had a bunch of men in Hampton's Cav that were still carrying old .69 caliber smoothbores to the end of the war. I always thought that those things were pretty good at fifty yards or less, particularly when we could load them up with buck and ball."

"What's buck and ball, Lieutenant?" asked James Logan. "I guess that's a new one on us farmers."

"Sir, that's something that's been around a while. It's just a .69 caliber punkin ball with three buckshot loaded as part of the same round. Now, that would tear people up if you were at fifty yards or less. A lot of our guys just couldn't hit much farther out than that anyway."

"Those Henrys were beauties but, somewhat like the gunboat, probably a bit rich for our blood. I always thought that the effort that was most practical was the sewing of uniforms out of bulk cloth furnished to our womenfolk. Here at River Bend we got three sewing machines together and just set ourselves up a clothing factory. We kept those machines going nearly fulltime for over two years. Now, that was worth something."

The visit, a rarity between two-team folks and true cotton capitalists and probably never to be repeated, was coming to an end. A hush fell on the four men. After a moment the old major leaned rather wearily on the gatepost and looked back at the Big House and its surroundings. "You know, neighbors, I've always taken exception to that old saw that the Yankees are always throwing at us about how everything in the South looks like it's unfinished. I guess I've always been very sensitive about things that look poorly kept, most likely, but it's clear now that a lot of things down here do look, well, unfinished. After four years of war, those people really have us dead to rights. Everything is falling apart—shutters down, window glass replaced with cardboard, bricks missing from the porch floor and the paint almost gone. It'll be ten years before we can get this mess straightened up."

The elder Logan broke in. "Sir, I'm betting that you and the River Bend people will get this all straightened up in short order. You'll have everything back to normal inside of five years."

"Well, I hope you're right. About the only thing that's still working is the bath house and the water closet. Strangely enough, everything about that damn thing is still working like a charm. Now we've even got water piped into the kitchen house. I'll have to admit that I was opposed to building that contraption; I guess I remembered too much about digging all those sinks when I was a soldier in the Tennessee militia, and I kept thinking how they really did the job. But I got outvoted by my wife, and I'll have to say that this water closet setup is a whole lot better than the old way. I think that within a few years these things are going to be found all over the place."

"Now, Major, you know very well that within a couple of years that River Bend will be back up and sparkling." James Logan chuckled as he added, "Miss Catherine will just force you to get y'alls' place all straightened up, and this'll be in spite of the damn Yankees and their 'all unfinished' malarkey."

Then just at the end, Captain Logan pulled McLemore aside and slipped him a paper packet. "Here's your poker winnings, McLemore. I think there's almost thirty dollars in there. I just know you won't spend it recklessly." McLemore took the packet and with one fast motion pushed it inside his shirt.

With one final handshake the Logans were off down the dusty road for home. As he looked back at the house, the captain saw Caroline Jean McLemore waving away to them from an upstairs window.

CHAPTER IX

THE TEAM BREAKS UP

One early October morning Wes Logan went with his mother when she made her morning nursing visit to Thad Hood. The sick man was still bedridden but obviously greatly improved since his arrival at the Logan place ten days earlier. Even though he was still very weak, he was now sitting up in bed talking to everyone who came in the room. Some color was back in his face, and he clearly was once again taking an interest in what was going on around him. He had begun speaking with some enthusiasm about getting up and walking to Georgia and then, as he volunteered to Logan, walking on to his countryside home about five miles past the town of Columbus.

Logan encouraged the man in his ambitions; however, both his mother and Maggie Sharp, wife of the senior black on the place, who had assisted in the nursing of Hood throughout the time of his illness, were not confident that he would be able to travel within two or three weeks. Logan's mother discussed in detail how she and Maggie planned to get him up and, as she put it, start toughening him up for the walk to Georgia. Hood listened to the plan and agreed, rather tiredly, that this toughening-up was necessary. For the first time, Logan felt confident that the youngster would indeed make it to Columbus and still be walking.

The captain congratulated the man on setting his home-by-Christmas goal but immediately pointed out difficulties that would arise if he attempted to start the trip before fully recovered, talking at length of the danger of relapse if an attempt was made too early. Miss Earl stood at the foot of the bed and nodded her agreement to the delay of Hood's departure for at least two or three weeks. She came close to saying that she simply could not allow such a departure until her patient was better.

After hearing the matter thoroughly discussed, Logan gave his decision. "I'm sorry, you can't go for at least three weeks. You've heard the person in charge of your recovery, and I'm telling you that you can't go until she's satisfied that you can make it. Your messmates did not drag you along for all those miles to just stand by and allow you to put yourself in grave danger here at the bitter end." Both Miss Earl and Maggie nodded their enthusiastic agreement.

Hood dropped his head for a moment; then he sat up, straightened his back and smiled. The smile was a bit weak, but he still smiled. "Well, I think I could make it, starting out with the others, but I know that me going with 'em might keep 'em from getting home afore Christmas."

"Yep, that's right, Hood." Logan closed the discussion by saying, "I'll promise you that I'll go with you, all the way to your home. That is, when you're well enough to travel. With a little luck, maybe we'll even make it before Christmas." At this statement, Hood's smile was almost broad.

Cora the Cook, who doubled as the housekeeper, came in to check on the cleaning of the sickroom and stayed to add some of her own brand of guidance for Hood. "Mr. Thad, you knows that you got to get strong enough 'fore you leave us so that you can look plenty fine down there in Georgia. And beyond looking like you is getting well, yo folks down there got to know that we watched yo talking and yo manners real good while we had charge of yo. I knows that they would appreciate it." She picked up her dustpan and moved toward the door as she added, "And when yo gets up in a week or maybe less and starts moving about, we'll start talkin' 'bout how to walk again. Yo knows you'll be almost forgot how to do it right."

Logan followed Cora out into the hallway to talk about gathering together the rice and cooking the corn pone and bacon that would be necessary to get their other guests through the first few days of their trip.

"Ya, sir. About three corn dodgers, all hard and crusty, and a big helpin' of cooked bacon should get a man through at least a week. That is, if they can find a just a little dab of extra stuff to add to it." Cora patted her stomach as she spoke.

"I'm not much worried about them eating. They'll find food, and most likely plenty of it. Li'l Georgia is the best scrounger around; and Slaughter, who'll be by himself because he's going off west to Demopolis, will probably do all right in that department. We'll just give them enough to get them started."

"Maybe I can slip them a little of that beef jerky that our boy Samson stole from that Yankee supply wagon. That stuff should go good when it's boiled with some of that sock full of brown rice we're goin' to give each of 'em."

Logan watched the cook walk away, the shiny brass chain bobbing on her white turban, and thought that McLemore had hit upon a brilliant nickname for that character when he had started calling her The Duchess. She was both clever and tough, which of course she had to be if she was to pull her people through the next few years. His father had already told him that during the last year of the war he had sent her with her son and one other field hand down to Mobile Bay to boil sea water for salt. He had been plenty worried about the outcome of that safari; but after three weeks, up they drove in the wagon. Cora was leading the mule and her two assistants were wearing huge grins of triumph as they pointed to the three hundred-pound bags of salt in the bed of the wagon.

In early October the evenings became cool enough to allow the Logans to keep a low fire burning in the side yard. For several nights the two Logan men sat up long after the others had retired to their beds and discussed what would come to them in the first year of defeat. Wes Logan had been away from home for over four years, so he had forgotten some of his father's approaches to life. After a few hours of talk, however, he began to remember the concepts he had listened to back in the days of his youth.

James Logan was a very practical sort of man, so when he got around to talking about the political philosophy they had heard discussed during their visit to River Bend, the cotton farmer dismissed old Major McLemore and his political philosophizing as interesting but of little real-life value. His father's principal concern appeared to be how to make a living for the dozen or more people who were depending on him to make it through the winter by the use of the six hundred or so acres that he now controlled.

He quickly admitted that it was going to be most difficult. It would have been easy enough if things were like they had been before the war, but so many things had changed here in the fall of '65. For one thing, he was carrying a debt that would take eight to ten years to pay off, even if everything went well. And if the tax rate went up or he had a bad crop year, he could see little hope for his survival. In addition to debt and taxes, the land was in bad shape for cultivating during the coming year; the fences were down or had been burned by the Yankee marauders; he had no cotton seed; and only two mules were in shape for the '66 crop year.

As far as his work crew was concerned, it was in pretty good shape. Even Ole Sharp, who was now nearly seventy, was still in fair shape; and Sharp's wife, Maggie, was still plenty strong enough to turn in a good day with the hoe.

Their boy, Young Sharp, was a prime hand as were the other three blacks who were still around. Without counting the cook and the two children, there were six full hands who should be ready to work come springtime. All these people had gone to see the elephant back in April and May but were all now back and seemed to be ready to work. Even Cora had gone down to Safford to see her sister for three or four days back in July, but she appeared ready to go when she came back. As he often said, Mr. Logan was satisfied that his work crew was his operation's strongest element.

If push came to shove—evidently still one of his favorite expressions—he, his wife and Cora could all pitch in. Logan noticed that his father did not mention the Old Missus, his grandmother, as a possible worker. But he suspected that she could, and probably would, hoe in the garden. She had always done this even in the best of times, and there was no reason to believe that she would give this up in these desperate times.

Wes Logan watched his father's face in the light of the flickering fire as he discussed how the new freedmen could continue to live in the two double cabins they had been occupying for over ten years. After a while he suggested that maybe he could allow Cora and her son to move across the big road and build a new cabin on the off-forty. And then for the first time that Logan had ever heard it mentioned, his father mumbled that maybe they could work out some deal so that Cora could buy the forty and become the first black landowner in this area. His father added that he had thought about such a move ever since it became clear that the war—and with it the slave system—would be lost. He felt that the cook was the only one of his people who could safely take such a step at this time. Ole Sharp was probably too old for such a big change. Maybe others could follow Cora's lead in time, but this would be a difficult move for most of his people.

The master got up and stirred up the low fire before he continued. The fire blazed up and lighted his father's features as he reminded his son that the Old Missus, his mother, had been pushing hard for years for him to set Cora and her son up as independent farmers. If it was ever to be done, he felt that this was the time to get started. The captain smiled a bit at this statement because he had known for several years that his father leaned toward being soft with his labor. However, he realized that now was the time for softness, so perhaps this would work out all right.

According to the master, the people on the Logan place had an advantage that the ex-slaves from the big places like River Bend did not have. The gang labor system had never been used here, so his people were already familiar with working without the very close supervision normal in a gang system. Mr. Logan had never liked keeping a tight watch on his people and thought that his loose-rein approach even got more work done for the time and energy expended. Wes Logan remembered that his father had never tired of degrading the big plantations that, according to him, were just cotton factories that made grossly inefficient use of their labor—not to mention the fact that the workers hated the system.

After a couple of long discussions of the problems flowing from the loss of the very, very tight control of slaves, Logan felt secure enough to suggest to his father that the people of the upcountry had been using a sharecropping system to work the poor whites employed by the bigger landowners. For quite a long time some of these white people had been living on thirty-to-forty-acre plots on the bigger farms, working them for a share of the crop. If they had no farm animals or equipment, which was the usual case, they stayed on the place for the crop year and were paid with a place to live, such as it was, and one-half of the crop that they made on their part of the land. Some of these farms had operated with this sharecropper system for a number of years. The captain saw no reason why the black families couldn't be used in this same manner.

Mr. James Logan did not appear overjoyed to receive what sounded a bit like advice. The master's face clearly showed that he could get along without guidance from his son, even though he was a captain, CSA, trained to direct the activities of a bunch of soldiers and, as a cavalryman, given the additional responsibility of a horse for each of his soldiers. The captain saw the storm signals and dropped the subject, awaiting a time when it could be introduced with more care. His father changed the subject by talking about the desperate need for cottonseed prior to the coming of spring planting.

The next night Mr. Logan spent some three hours discussing the need for changing his farming system so that more time and effort would be spent on provision crops such as melons, garden products, corn for human consumption and field peas. He then added a long speech on planting enough sorghum cane to make syrup for all his people for the entire year. His father had talked about increasing syrup production ever since Wes could remember, but the farm had never turned out more than a month's supply in any year that he could recall.

After the sorghum lecture, Mr. Logan turned his comments to increasing pork production. This vision had a better foundation than most of the others because many of the farm's hogs had been saved from the Yankees by being driven into the swamps. Most of the raiders did not stay around much over a week and had left without killing many of these animals, so it really was possible for the farm to increase its pork production within a few months. Certainly this increase would be most worthwhile, but it would entail a great amount of detailed work, which his hands were probably not capable of doing. When the captain pointed this out, he was informed that several of the farm's people were capable of learning all about taking care of hogs.

Mr. Logan's next topic was increasing the number of cattle kept on the place. Admittedly this cow business would be much more difficult than the hog effort since the expansion of a cow herd took much longer and only two old cows had been saved from Wilson's raiders.

An hour into the talk about provision crop farming, the captain felt strong enough to slip in another reference to the sharecropping system he had heard about on his visit to the upcountry. This time Mr. Logan accepted his comments rather calmly and even asked some questions about how the system really worked. He might be interested in figuring out a work scheme for a family of poor whites who had been asking to come to the place as renters. Of course they had no rent money, farm animals, equipment or seed—nothing really except the labor of two adults and four little children. Some sharing system appeared to be the only way that these people could rent. There was an old shack on the lower end of the place that Ole Sharp thought could be made livable with two or three days' work. The master went so far as to say that if they could make some sort of share system work for these poor whites then he might let one of the blacks try it the following year.

Encouraged by this nibble from his father, Wes Logan became bold enough to suggest that perhaps some sort of cabin could be built on one of the outlying areas where one of the black families could be moved to sharecrop forty or fifty acres. Such a system would, of course, mean that the family would be farming on a semi-independent basis. Almost surely the selected family would be happy with this arrangement, as would any federal observer from the Freedmen's Bureau.

Mr. Logan reacted badly—swearing a bit, something which he seldom did—and declared that he didn't give a damn what the Feds thought about what he should do with his farm. Those damn people didn't know a cotton boll from the balls of a kangaroo. But after several such complaints, he finally admitted that he could see certain advantages of having his labor scattered over the farm rather than all living in a couple of cabins behind the Big House. Such a scheme might hold down some of the stealing that he felt was done by blacks who came over to his place from neighboring plantations and farms.

Wes Logan walked over to the fire, poked it up into a blaze and began agreeing with his father's comments about turning to more provision crops and cattle and hogs, adding chickens and eggs to the list of survival items that would be desperately needed for many years to come. He even suggested that the amount of acreage they had allotted to cotton in the pre-war days be cut down if the South was ever to recover from the disaster of '61-'65. His father went along with the basic idea, but he shook his head in disagreement with going very far in this direction. The older man reminded his son that cotton was still king.

The next day Mr. Logan took his son and Ole Sharp, the nearest thing he had to an overseer, to the creek to point out some timber and explain his idea for using it. "Now, I reckon that even you, good captain, would agree that some of these tall, straight oaks could be cut and turned into first-class roofing boards. There's sure a good market for roofing 'cause I know that you've noticed that half of the houses still standing need to be re-roofed."

"No doubt about that. However, how can we collect for roofing boards from people with no money? And that's no money whatsoever." The captain looked at his father and saw in the early sunlight that his face reflected great sadness. "And we have to remember that they probably will be penniless even five years from now. Maybe for life."

"Well, you are certainly a pleasant fellow. I suppose you feel that we must just sit down under our shade trees and wait for starvation. I know for sure that it's not going to be easy to get by, no matter what we do; but I feel that we must make a start doing something, and soon. You know that when Christmas time comes there ain't going to be any sugar plums or firecrackers unless those carpetbaggers down at the Freedmen's Bureau give them to us. And I figure that's not likely to happen."

Ole Sharp broke in, "Massa, you know that them Freedmen's folks ain't gon to give away nothing lessen they gets a whole lot back for hit. They wanted me to work in the boss Freedmen's garden for two weeks for a pair of old wore-out shoes."

Captain Logan laughed a bit at all the cynicism but then continued with his own line of thought. "I think that we'll have to do something for someone, and it has to be for someone who can pay. I believe that we'd be better off cutting crossties for the railroad. You know that the tracks are all owned by the Yankees now, and maybe we could get them to actually pay. God knows, they need plenty of ties and trestle timbers."

Again Ole Sharp responded, "Yes, sir, but they'll want 'em for jus' about free. You knows they's Yankees too."

"Yes, I'd thought about that, and I really hate to start dealing with those slimy bastards," Mr. Logan said as he spat on the ground.

"Yankees, bastards or not, are the folks that we have to deal with sooner or later. We'd better get started early before too many folks jump into the business. We got the timber and the labor, so I think that it would be smart to start cutting ties and floating 'em down the creek to that trestle that crosses the Big Muddy."

"We can do that, yes, sir. If the Massa will jus' give me the word, I can get three of us on that job, rat now." With this, Ole Sharp walked away and began counting and measuring oaks.

Mr. Logan nodded his approval of Sharp's reaction and turned back to his son. "Wes, you know that folks are saying that some of those big business people up around Prattville and Montgomery are coming down here to set up a cotton mill—you know, a spinning and weaving mill—right here in Selma or in Orrville. Maybe some of us around here could get a job at such a place. I can see us contracting to do some sort of job for these people, that is during the slack season. Now, what does the cavalier of the First South Carolina Cavalry think of that? As for me, I know that by next spring we common folks of Dallas County may be facing starvation, and working in a cotton mill looks a whole lot better than downright hunger."

The captain chuckled at his father's sarcasm and then slid in his own biting remarks. "Well, I guess you could set yourself up as an agent for some folks like Young Sharp and Samson. You could get them jobs on the railroad or in one of those pie-in-the-sky cotton factories. If you charge them about a quarter of their wages for arranging the job, it looks like you'd come out all right. Then you could board them here in the same quarters they've always lived in and keep right on feeding 'em. That ought to be worth about half of what they draw. They'd then end up with what's left over for themselves, and out of that they'd have to buy their own clothes. If you could arrange to get them hired for a dollar a day, which I doubt, then that would mean six bits for you to their two bits." Wes threw back his head and laughed again. "Of course, you know that within two weeks you'd have the Freedmen's guy out here waving his arms and threatening to arrest you."

"Good, Captain. I know you're just being a smart aleck, but just think about it. Seriously, how could you split the money up much of any other way? The only problem with what you're saying is that I couldn't hire out a prime hand for a wage of a dollar a day in the first place. A half-dollar a day would be more like it. That leaves the laborer getting about seventy-five cents for a six-day week. "'Course he'd get a place to sleep and his vittles above that. I've thought about this for weeks, and that's about as close as I can figure it. If everyone could accept this breakout on wages, I might be able to operate the place for the coming year.

"The fly in the ointment is that I couldn't get together the seventy-five cents that I'd have to pay the top hands each week. That's not to mention the little wage I'd have to pay the women and old folks that would be working around here. If you figure it out, it means that I'd have to pay out around two dollars a week. There just ain't no way I could come up with that much on top of my other expenses."

"Sir, in my opinion, we'd better stick mostly to farming and live or die by the results. But I do think that we'll have to move away from total dependence on cotton. That provision crop idea will probably be our ticket out of disaster, and I'd admit that we might get something out of hiring our people out now and then. But I think that's something that we'll just have to pray comes our way three or four times a month."

The elder Logan, his face looking tired and a little gray, said, "Son, I guess I'm closer to agreeing with you on most of these things than I'd like to admit. We—and by that I mean both the family and the black folks—are really just farmers or maybe just small time planters, so anything we do other than farm will have to come second to that. However, I think that we must try to get a little out of some of those other things we've talked about. If we could manage to get a few dollars out of the Yankee railroad or, yeah, those cotton mills over in Prattville, we'd have a lot better chance of making it through the next three or four years. And one of the things we simply must do is keep our working force here on the place and reasonably satisfied. If most of us are still here in '70 and able to smile now and then, I figure that we will have done all the Good Lord could expect of us."

* * *

As the fall came, Wes Logan and his men helped Ole Sharp and the farm hands pull the fodder. There really wasn't much to this, so after this job was completed they all went to the swamps to round up the stray hogs. They had better luck at this task. After a couple of days they had located twenty-two animals and had gotten them penned.

Captain Logan tried to get around to seeing Hood each day and usually managed ten minutes alone to talk with the sick man. During these visits he usually got to see Cora the Cook, who was normally around taking care of her housekeeping duties, and almost always visited with his mother and Maggie Sharp, the assistant nurse. Now that Hood was out of bed and sitting up for a good part of the day, Maggie was doing most of the actual nursing. She was also charged with the toughening-up program that Missus Earl had prescribed for the recuperating man. Maggie had him up and exercising several times a day—some simple calisthenics, a little walking about the house, some running in place. Finally Maggie got him outside and almost forced him to walk about. Logan was watching this routine one morning when he saw both his mother and Cora standing back in the shadows of the kitchen watching the process with smiling approval. Hood was almost well.

During one of these nursing visits Mr. Logan came in to tell his son that he had decided to let a white tenant, Pat O'Neal, move into the old shack on the lower end of the place and raise a crop, as he said, "on the halves." The master wouldn't even guess as to how this scheme would work out, but he was willing to give it a try. He added that if this worked, or even came close to working, then he might try letting Cora and her son Elias move out the following year and crop on the off-forty on their own. A cabin would have to be built, of course, and he would have to make arrangements for Cora to spend the necessary time at the Big House for her to do some of the cooking and housekeeping. Ole Missus, his mother, wanted to grant title to the off-forty, which she had held since her own mother's death, to Cora because the cook had been her pet girl ever since her birth. Mr. Logan added that he had talked to his wife about that possibility and had her enthusiastic agreement to the plan.

Later Wes talked to his mother at length about the plan to rent to the O'Neals and found that she was not really enthusiastic about getting involved with any white trash family but very eager to let Cora and her son have a chance to farm on their own. She admitted that she was prejudiced against dirt eaters, as she called white renters, who she was convinced were ignorant, shiftless, dishonest and usually too stupid to learn very much—honestly or otherwise. In her opinion, white people who had to crop on shares were almost universally worthless and nearly always thieves. Just about all they could do was have a bunch of children.

Logan was a bit taken aback by this outburst and reminded himself to discuss his mother's lack of enthusiasm for poor white renters with his father. Evidently the master had been less than convincing in his explanation of the sharecropping plan. But at least his mother was enthusiastic enough about backing his grandmother on renting to Cora and her son.

* * *

As the time for the departure of three of his team members approached, the captain began to worry about their morale as this very last deadline came closer. He thought it wise to introduce a few things that he hoped would help in this area. He arranged a visit to the town of Orrville so that they could familiarize themselves with the settlement they had heard so much about during their long walk south. After this trip, the men's growing strength—now near normal—encouraged him to let them cut a few oaks and hew them into railroad ties. This activity appeared to be therapeutic for the sergeant and Slaughter and even for Li'l Georgia, whose involvement in the operation consisted mostly of carrying limbs and brush. Also, their help was useful to Sharp and his crew, who were already busy turning out ties for sale to the railroad.

A couple of days prior to the departure date, Logan arranged a fishing trip down to where Big Muddy Creek emptied into the Alabama River. Since he was busy arranging some last minute details for the break-up of the team, the captain turned the expedition over to the sergeant. An hour before dawn on the appointed day the group gathered in the front yard, checked their rudimentary equipment consisting of hooks and line for a couple of trot lines and a fishing pole for each man. Elias, the cook's son, went along as a guide.

Since he was sure that they needed a little recreation, Logan was surprised when he looked out from the porch in the early afternoon and saw the group walking back to the house. Their faces clearly showed that something had not gone well on this junket. The rest of the group hung back a bit and allowed the sergeant to walk up to the porch alone, certainly not a good sign. The captain jumped down from the porch and walked toward the sergeant.

"Well, Jackson, what happened?"

"Sir, Li'l Georgia almost got drowned, and he sure would have except that Elias saved him at the last second."

"Okay, give me the details of this disaster." Logan ran his hand over his eyes as though to blot out the picture of another near catastrophe.

"It was a close-run thing for Li'l Georgia and Elias, but they made it somehow. The boy got too far out in the stream and almost got swept into the main current. At the last second, he got hold of a limb and managed to hold on. I thought any second that the branch would break and he would be gone." Sergeant Jackson shook his head in disbelief at how near disaster came.

"Great, just great! Come through the war and Rock Island, then managed to live through a walk across the whole country and finally almost losing it all in the Alabama River on a picnic. Sergeant, I'm charging you now with seeing that this childish fellow gets safely back into Georgia. You understand?"

"Yes, sir, Captain. I understand. He'll be under tight control on the way over. Let me get him up here now and let him tell the story as he saw it. Can we do that, sir?"

"Okay, get the clown up here." Logan shook his head in wonder that he had allowed such a situation to develop. He glowered at the young man as he approached, eyes down and feet shuffling. "All right, Georgia, tell us what happened."

"Sir, I got a little too far out in the river and got swept away. I was almost in the main current when I somehow got a hold of a limb that was hanging down in the water. I was just barely hanging on when Elias came swimming out, right through the edge of that current, and grabbed me and pulled me back into shallow water. Then Mr. Slaughter got a hold of both of us and pulled us into the bank."

"A pretty close call, I'd say." Logan shook his head again. "Elias, you come up here too. Georgia, go on with your story."

"Well, sir, they ain't much more to it. I was so weak that I had to lay there in the shallow water for quite a spell afore I could get up the bank. Even Elias had to rest a little while."

The sergeant added, "I don't think that I ever saw such a strong swimmer as that Elias turned out to be. Never in my life. Don't know how he did it."

"Cap'n, I knows that I never saw nobody swim like Elias. I knows that I owes my life to him." Li'l Georgia was still looking down at his feet.

"Well, I suppose you've told Elias what you owe him, and it wouldn't hurt to tell Mr. Slaughter too."

"Yes, sir, I knows. And, Elias, I just can't forget what I owe. And if I ever act like I might be forgetting, you just remind me, right then. And I'll tell Mr. Slaughter too."

"Okay, now get that done and then let's forget it. It's all over and we're all still here. Let's all get going on pulling out for Columbus in a day or two." The captain clapped his hands and pointed toward the kitchen. "Go ask Cora for something to eat."

* * *

On the morning of 10 October, a slim, swarthy man came riding in from the big road, dismounted from his mule and walked up to the front steps where Wes Logan was standing. The man removed his battered felt hat and let a mop of coarse, black hair fall down around his ears. Wes offered his hand and invited the man up on the porch. The stranger introduced himself as Johnnie South, a work companion and friend of Lieutenant McLemore. He explained that he came with a message for McLemore and a proposition for the captain. Logan acknowledged that he had heard McLemore speak of the man and introduced him to his mother, who was coming out on the dogtrot. Missus Logan sent a tiny black girl running to the woods to get Mr. Logan, who was helping the hands split stove wood.

Within twenty minutes the captain and his parents were seated at the big kitchen table looking at a map that South had spread out; over at the Southern Belle the cook was fanning the fire under the coffeepot. Go-Fetch, the Missus's tiny assistant, had been dispatched to River Bend Plantation to summons Lieutenant McLemore.

While they waited for McLemore, South used the map to talk his way through the trip he had just completed down to New Orleans. They had a chance to ask plenty of questions of the traveler while waiting. Mr. Logan was full of questions about the crops throughout the delta and along the lower part of the river. His wife, betraying her real interests, confined her questions to how the farm and plantation houses had come through the war. Of the three, the captain was the only one who displayed any interest in the mechanics of moving the group of laborers over the trail from Nashville down to the docks at New Orleans.

South answered their questions with what appeared to be all the details he could muster. Yes, crops looked fairly good, particularly down on the southern end of the trail, which had been occupied by the Federal army from '62. No, the farmsteads were largely in dire need of repair and maintenance. Most houses, however, with the exception of those around Vicksburg and Port Hudson, had come through the war with their roofs still in place. Finally, walking men could make some twenty miles a day if they were supported by supply and kitchen vehicles. And there was little danger other than that which arose at the rather numerous stream crossings. No, there was no sign of guerrilla warfare, but they did have a little trouble with their own people when they stopped near the taverns.

Lieutenant McLemore came riding up in the early afternoon with Go-Fetch sitting on a saddle blanket placed forward on the mare's neck. She was displaying a broad smile in recognition of this great adventure and her exalted position. McLemore dismounted and turned the animal over to the child to hold. As she led the mare away to graze, she did a little bow as she accepted the admiring glances of the older hands.

After the greetings were completed, McLemore sat at the table, gave his brightest smile to Mrs. Logan and then asked, "Well, South, have you got a batch of instructions for me from kindly old Mr. Ochs? I suppose he thought that I should have been back in Nashville about three weeks ago. That would have been ten whole days after I left Natchez."

"Nothing like that, sir. But he does want you back by the first of December. And he sure didn't forget to point out that you're to bring the mare and that fancy pistol with you."

"Oh, the mare and the LeMat, eh?" said McLemore. "Both of those jewels came in mighty handy during that little jaunt back from Natchez."

"Yes, he's expecting a little more trouble from the next batch of laborers, and he says that he needs you to keep 'em moving along." South smiled and nodded vigorously to add emphasis to the message.

"I bet he does. I'm guessing that he got a little trembly just thinking about the likes of Manasco as a leader and driver. Old Mr. Ochs must have been shaky as hell when that killer was in charge."

Mrs. Logan said, "It'll be almost necessary that you get started in a couple of weeks if you're going to keep to that assigned schedule." She looked at her husband and rolled her eyes as she continued, "I hear that some people try to cut down on the time to Nashville by taking the steamboat with their horse from Selma to Ashville up in St. Clair County before they have to get off and start cross-country by horseback."

Mr. Logan added, "Yeah, I understand that cuts down the time to Nashville by two or three days. And I hear that a boat makes the trip every week. I'd check into it."

"I sure will, I sure will," promised McLemore. "I need to do a couple of things around here; then I'll be ready to start pushing the mare toward Nashville. Short of some horror that's totally beyond my control, I'll be there on the first of December. A couple of weeks before Christmas will be a good time for me to visit the Maxwell again." McLemore rolled with laughter.

Then Captain Logan leaned forward on his elbows and asked, "Well, Mr. South, what's this lawyer got for me? It it's legal, I suppose I'd better at least listen."

"Sir, I suppose it's legal enough. Mr. Ochs told me about meeting you up in Tennessee, and he thinks that he needs you in his outfit. Now, remember that this business will be going on for a couple of years, and it should be something worthwhile for you to do while things are settling down from the war."

"It's true that I'm in need of some way to make a living, if that's what you mean. And, as you all know, the nearest thing I have to a profession looks like it was about closed out at Appomattox. A CSA cavalryman appears to be just about unemployable here in Dixieland in October of 1865. Some of our people have run off to Brazil on some harebrained scheme that seems to promise them that they can continue on as professional soldiers. Looks plenty shaky to me."

"Captain Logan, what we are doing does look something like soldiering. On this first trip, at least, we moved around a lot in all sorts of bad weather and slept in the woods. Also, down at my level nobody seemed to know a thing about what we were doing—or why." South ended with a disdainful smirk and a shrug.

Logan laughed a bit at South's witticism and announced, "I've already talked to Lieutenant McLemore quite a bit about this, and I've made up my mind that if I was asked I would give it a try. So after I finish up one job that I've already promised to do here, I'll come up to Nashville; then if he still wants me, I'm ready to sign on."

The elder Logans looked a bit shocked at the suddenness of this decision, but they did not seem displeased by the prospect. After all, they knew that something like this had to happen. Earlene Logan got a far away look in her eyes, but she made no comment.

McLemore and South followed Captain Logan out to the porch and sat down in the shade of the crepe myrtle to discuss in detail the adventure that Logan had just agreed to take part in. South, of course, reminded him several times that whatever he had to say about the matter could not be taken as the final word; however, such statements did not keep Logan from asking scores of questions about the trip to New Orleans that had just been completed. They discussed in detail what Mr. Ochs would anticipate happening on future trips. Their discussion went on until the cook banged on the plowshare hanging on the back porch to call them to supper.

As they pulled their chairs up to the table, McLemore suddenly said, "You know that I didn't get to go to New Orleans on that last trip. I left the team at Natchez and rode back to Alabama. It's true that I was down there once, but I was still a child at the time; and as I understand it, New Orleans is completely wasted on a child. If for no other reason, I would like to make another trip just to see if it's all that it's cracked up to be." Missus Logan and the cook were at the Southern Belle when McLemore made this statement. They looked at each other, shook their heads and rolled their eyes.

When everyone was seated at the table, Mrs. Logan and Cora began carrying in the food. Hot cornbread, butter, a ham hock and turnip greens were brought in and announced before Cora said that the other people, black and white, had already eaten. She then advised, "You'll just have to eat hearty." Mrs. Logan walked around the table and poured buttermilk for each person and then told them that she and Cora had some dried apple pies for dessert. South's black eyes got big as he looked at the food.

* * *

By 12 October the ex-prisoners had been guests of the Logans for some three weeks. Captain Logan decided that all of them, with the exception of Hood, were now in good enough shape to start on the last leg of their journey. On the afternoon before they were to start, Mr. James Logan called them up on the front porch and explained how he thought they should attack this last stage of their ordeal. He told them that he had been feeling around up in Selma and had discovered that the railroad from Montgomery over to West Point, Georgia, was back in operation. Further, he and old Major McLemore had gotten together and gathered up enough money to pay for two fares to Georgia. Major McLemore had even arranged for Slaughter to ride on a freight wagon going west from Selma to the village of Faunsdale, about twenty miles from his destination of Demopolis. Lieutenant McLemore had come over from River Bend prepared to walk with the sergeant and Li'l Georgia to Montgomery.

Hood immediately begged, for at least the twentieth time, for permission to start out for Columbus with the others. After listening to his pleading for several minutes, Captain Logan finally forbade the still very weak Hood to leave the house until he was considerably stronger. The semi-cripple finally said no more, probably realizing that he was in no condition to make the trip without the full cooperation of his companions.

The sun was sinking when Mr. James Logan finished his remarks, quieted the group and announced, "In celebration of your start for home tomorrow, we've scrounged around and got together some late season watermelons. I sent Sharp and his boy out yesterday to come up with anything that looked like a watermelon and to get 'em all cooled off in the spring. How did you come out on this job, Sharp?"

"Massa, sir, we found a bunch of 'em and a few cantaloupe besides. But afore y'all eat 'em, we got a little old shoat that Samson and Elias hunted down in Big Muddy Swamp, and him we done barbecued down there below the spring. All these fine things is ready to be et. My folks are bringin' this stuff up rite now."

Mr. Logan asked, "Have you got enough of these edibles for our visitors and all of us home folks too? You know that's nearly twenty people."

"Yes, sir, Massa. You knows that we got plenty for us all. Even for people like Go-Fetch and Elias, and you knows that if we got enough for people like dem, we got plenty—a lord's plenty." Ole Sharp pulled up on the piece of rope that held up his pants and flashed his broadest smile.

Hugh McLemore broke in saying, "You can see that I found out about the good vittles that Miss Earl and Cora were getting together, so I came over to get my part. I had to be here anyway to get started with y'all on the trip tomorrow. You'd better eat hearty 'cause we'll probably have to walk most of the way to Montgomery. I don't guess you guys have forgotten about that means of movement." McLemore laughed a bit as he continued, "We'll try to steal a ride on a steamboat, but I don't have much hope for that. As far as I can find out, there hadn't been one through here going up-river for about a week. So my guess is that we'll have to hoof it to Montgomery. I'm leaving the mare here for Mr. Logan to use while we're gone."

As the lieutenant was winding up his speech, Ole Sharp motioned his helpers forward. They walked in smiling triumphantly as they lugged in several watermelons and a whole barbecued pig. Cora brought up the rear carrying a bucket of boiled Irish potatoes and some knives. Last of all Go-Fetch came trotting in from the kitchen with a basket of brown biscuits. Cora arranged the knives on the table, and after a minute of furious activity turned to the master and said, "Sir, the barbecue is ready. You see we's goin' to have a real old Carolina pig picking."

"Sharp and Cora, thank you all and your helpers for this send-off spread. Now let's give our thanks to him who provides all." The master raised his arms and gave the Methodist prayer of thanksgiving, at the end of which he added in his own style a request for guidance and protection for the travelers on their coming journey. "Now, let's fall to with a will and show our appreciation by making all this disappear. Sharp, it's turning a little dark outside, so let's punch up the fire."

Li'l Georgia and Slaughter led the way to the food table, followed by the other whites and then the blacks. After all these were through the line, the captain and lieutenant went up to the food, followed by the mistress and, last of all, the master.

Under a canopy of subdued conversation, the food indeed quickly disappeared. When all had eaten, the master had everyone gather around the fire outside and sit on the grass. "Now, Sharp had promised us a little something extra before we break up. I don't know what this amounts to really; but, Sharp, go ahead and show us."

"Massa, fust we wants to have some of our folks do a little singing for our visiting peoples." Ole Sharp then did a sort of bow and motioned out Samson and his wife, Lila, who were joined a moment later by Go-Fetch. These three moved into the circle of firelight and prepared to sing. Wes Logan noticed that all three were dressed for the occasion. Samson had on a Federal naval officer's uniform coat over his homespun pants, topped off with a Yankee kepi. The two females had starched white aprons over their dark dresses and white turbans, complete with sparkling glass pins. The two older ones were wearing shoes, but Go-Fetch was innocent of footwear except for the red ribbons she had tied in a bow around her legs. Logan wondered where this fancy rigging had been hidden during the period of starvation. Back in May and June even the big time planters had been selling items of their clothing just to keep food on the table.

When a quiet had settled on the gathering, Samson and Lila threw up their hands and began singing "Go Down, Moses," which was followed by "Blow Your Trumpet, Gabriel." Go-Fetch quickly joined in the singing and danced around in time with the music. After another spiritual that Logan did not recognize, they suddenly launched into "Lorena" as though they recognized that such a change was necessary to mollify the whites in their audience.

When the singers began so-called white songs, Li'l Georgia got up and entered into the spirit of the occasion. He asked Samson to sing "Juanita," and to the whites' surprise the three singers moved immediately into this piece. Li'l Georgia began to sing along with the blacks and guided them off into "Annie Laurie" and "Listen to the Mockingbird." Samson went to the porch, picked up an ancient fiddle and began to saw out "Arkansas Traveler," which he followed by a lively rendition of "Hell Broke Loose in Georgia."

In the lull following the fiddling, Li'l Georgia stepped over to the captain and asked him to make a request. Logan, who was painfully ignorant of any form of music, had to name the only tunes he could think of on such short notice. The singers first attacked "Bonnie Blue Flag" and then went on to "Dixie"; this left Logan a bit surprised at the enthusiasm with which the blacks picked up the tune. To Logan, it was almost as though they did not understand that they were singing the beloved anthem of the white Southerner. If there was any sense of objection, it was totally covered by the joy of the blacks in the rhythm and lyrics of the song.

The fire was burning down by now, so the master got up, thanked the group for participating in the music and reminded everyone that the travelers must get up and be off early the next morning. "So let's end our evening by singing my two favorites, 'Rock of Ages' and then 'Amazing Grace.'"

When the sounds of the old Scottish hymn had died away, the group got up and went to their beds.

After breakfast the next morning, everyone who lived at the Logan place, including Johnnie South, walked out to the patch of oaks standing between the house and the big road.

Both Ole Missus Logan and Thad Hood found the walk rather difficult, but they managed to make it. The captain gave his last minute advice to the travelers and then stepped aside to allow the other people to crowd around and add anything that they considered important.

Ole Sharp walked over to Sergeant Jackson and reminded him that there was a covered bridge across the Chattahoochee that tied in with Dillingham Street over in Columbus. Sharp did not know how this bridge had come through the war, but he had seen it in 1863 and had thought at that time that it would be the best way to cross over into Georgia. He pointed out, "The bridge was built by Mr. Horace King, who was a freed slave and who is surely the best bridge builder in the whole world."

"All right, Sharp. I'll sure keep it in mind, and if the railroad train can't cross from Girard to the city of Columbus, I'll damn sure look for the Dillingham Street bridge."

"Yeah, Sergeant, just keep in mind that you're going to have to get off the train at Opelika Junction and catch a short ride on another track down into Girard—that's the last town in Alabama—and then across the river into Columbus. That is, if the bridge is still up and operating." As he talked, the captain took a stick and drew in the dirt a crude sketch of the rail connections into Columbus.

As the four travelers began to strap their bundles to their backs, Cora the Cook, closely followed by Go-Fetch, came striding up and passed out three hard corn pones—dodgers she called them—and a package of cooked bacon to each man. Next she gave each one a cotton stocking filled with brown rice. She then bowed low and wished them luck. McLemore returned the bow and said, "Why, thank you, Duchess."

When all the gear had been strapped down, Sergeant Jackson reached out and took Master Logan's hand and began, "Sir, we know what we owe you, and—"

"Never mind all that. You all just save your strength for the road. Now git going."

Then facing away from Mr. Logan, the sergeant smiled broadly, saluted Captain Logan, turned on his heels and moved his people off toward Georgia.

Wes Logan walked a little way out into the cotton field, now growing up in grass and weeds as a result of last season's neglect, and stood watching the four men move away toward the Selma road. When they were a couple of hundred yards out, they stopped and he could hear them laughing boisterously as Li'l Georgia pulled a piece of blue cloth out of his shirt and began to wave it wildly around his head.

"Folks," Logan said to the watching group, "that's the infantry company guidon that Li'l Georgia grabbed from a Yankee outpost up in Tennessee. When I found out about that little trick, I got a little disturbed about him doing such a dangerous thing, so I decided that it would be wise to leave the road and walk cross-country for a couple of days to escape any Yankees who might come riding after us. Naturally, the other men were plenty put out because they had to walk through the underbrush for two days.

"Sergeant Jackson made Georgia put the guidon down inside his pants and walk along with it for a couple of weeks. I thought, of course, that the boy had gotten rid of it, but I see that he held on to that prize. I suppose that blue banner will be handing in some Columbus home for years to come."

At the end of his explanation, the captain jumped on a stump and issued a short rebel yell and then shouted, "Okay, Georgia, make sure that Yankee rag gets all the way back to Columbus!"

They could hear the four men laughing uproariously as they picked up the pace and moved away with morale high.

Missus Earl considered the joy that seemed to be bubbling up from all the observers, gave her crinkly smile and said, "I guess we should just float on back to the house and begin our day's work. I feel somehow that all our travelers will be safely in the bosoms of their families within the next week, and I think that our good man here,"—she reached out and began guiding Hood back toward the house—"will follow within three weeks. I'm sure that the hot part of the war is finally over for us all."

Mr. James Logan and Ole Sharp sat down on a log and watched the four men walk away. Captain Logan also watched them go. The though came to him that, other than McLemore, he'd probably never again see these men who had shared such an important part of his life. With just a little luck, even Hood would be gone within three weeks; and South would be in Nashville with McLemore.

"They're finally off on the last leg of their trip home, and I'm betting that they'll be in Selma by tomorrow morning and into Montgomery within three more days." As he spoke, James Logan pulled his pipe out of his shirt pocket, loaded it with his homemade tobacco and fired it up.

"Massa James," said Ole Sharp, "you jus' know that them men are sho goin' to be there, and I'm bettin' that they'll be there way fore day—jus' to be shor. I don't expect that the lieutenant will have a bit of trouble keeping them movin'. They'll be jus' as eager as our field hands is when we're comin' up on Christmas week."

"Yeah, like Sergeant Jackson ain't been home in three or four years, so I wouldn't want to be the one that has to keep him from getting on that train." The master pulled on his pipe, wagged his head and snickered.

Wes Logan grinned as he said, "Yeah, that would probably be a mistake on some trainman's part," thinking also about the trouble Li'l Georgia would be in if he should somehow cause the others to miss the train. Logan was confident that the tough, almost violent Slaughter would somehow get to Demopolis in short order. If everything went as he visualized it, the whole four months' ordeal would be over in four or five days for those men; and Logan was almost certain that by his making the trip with him, Hood would be back to his home outside Columbus within another three weeks. And then the whole thing would be history.

Logan turned to his father and Ole Sharp and said, "I think that this whole four or five month episode of our lives is about to be closed, with all us old soldiers still alive. I'll admit that I often wonder just how, other than through blind luck. I can see little other sensible explanation, and back there when we were stumbling around through those swamps, there were a couple of times that I almost lost my faith. But here we are."

"Son, I suppose that it will be most unusual if you ever see people such as Sergeant Jackson again. You just know that people with big plantations to run or those with a couple of steamboats to keep going will snap up folks like that redhead just as soon as he hits Columbus. He'll be some kind of overseer or foreman before winter sets in."

"Yes, I certainly agree. We're awful lucky that people like that made it through the war in fair shape. There'll be plenty of places that he can fit in. And you're sure right; we'll probably never see people such as Sergeant Jackson again—unless we go looking for them. But even if I never see him again in this life, he'll be one of the first people I'll look up when I cross the river."

"Amen, good cap'n, amen," mumbled Ole Sharp.

"I'd be happy to tell anybody that luck was sure with me when I ended up in the same boxcar with the sergeant back there in Illinois. Sometimes I doubt that we could have made it without him."

Here the elder Logan said, "Now, let's not forget the other two people. They seem like good folks to me, and even poor Hood is beginning to look like he'll be able to make it on his own. Lord knows, there is going to be plenty of room for them all here in Old Dixie of "After the War."

"Yes, I suppose there'll be room for most of us in one role or another, even Slaughter. That old boy had clearly demonstrated that he's got the strength to keep on going when everything starts falling apart—and that's just where we are right now. However, I fear that if he gets out on his own with nobody to watch him or give him guidance, he may very well wander off the straight and narrow and get a little too tough for most of us good Southerners. I hope he can control himself. God knows, we need him and his kind." Logan looked over at Sharp in time to see him shaking his head as though his white folks were clearly misguided in this case and he and his people could stumble along without the assistance of people such as Slaughter.

The master got up and motioned for Sharp to come with him back to the house. Before they walked away, Mr. Logan said, "Son, don't forget Li'l Georgia and Hood while you're closing out this adventure. Neither of them is too well formed yet, but I see them both as worthwhile folks that'll probably be around for a long time yet. Either of them ought to do all right. Personally, I can see Georgia as a politician somewhere down the road. All that singing and talking fits right in. As for Hood, I guess he'll have to get back into school and then go into some church or take up teaching. I'd guess he could do either."

"Yes, sir, I agree. His only problem will be getting into some school and learning enough to get started. My mother has already got him reading a lot better than he could when he showed up here back in September." Logan dropped the conversation when he realized that his father and the overseer were already moving toward the house.

Captain Logan turned back and looked into the distance, where he could still pick up the moving men. He watched until the distant woods swallowed them up. With the exception of McLemore, all of these departing people had been discussed, and that exception was possibly because he would be coming back home.

Thinking of McLemore almost always brought on a smile. This time Logan even chuckled as he smiled. Lord, what a character! As the heir of conceivably the most important plantation family of the county, a family now faced with very hard times and possibly financial ruin, McLemore still seemed as carefree and reckless as he remembered him from '61. It would appear, at least on the surface, that this man was prepared to simply go back to Mr. Ochs, continue his adventurous existence, issue his crooked grin and roll along with the tide. After all, the lieutenant had most of his positions in life established from birth. Most likely he was fully aware that his family and himself were facing very hard times, yet he appeared to be totally disinterested in this whole state of affairs.

As for the rest of the grand family of Dallas County, old Major McLemore seemed to be retreating into a philosophical dreamland from which he probably would simply float away into the last chapter of his life, and the women of that group might very well be left holding the family banner.

But Master James Logan clearly was ready enough to attack the new era, even if he had to accept this newfangled sharecropping business. As long as he had Missus Earl and the work crew, he should be getting back on his feet in a couple of years. Everything was going to be all right—for all of them, black and white, who made their living on the Logan place.

The picture of his own future was not so clear. He had accepted Ochs's offer to assist in moving and organizing several hundred ex-slaves in some sort of farming operation in Mexico. Most likely this would not be cotton production, but surely it would be some form of plantation agriculture. That should take care of his time for a year or so. He couldn't visualize how this scheme could amount to very much, so he would have to look for another means of livelihood in a couple of years. Soldiering might be open to him, perhaps in the West or somewhere overseas. If he couldn't work that out, he would have to turn to cotton planting in the South or to some sort of ranching in the West. He had always wanted to go up into Indian Territory north of Texas. That ought to be interesting.

John Wesley Logan, Captain CSA, pulled himself together and began walking back toward the house. When he came to the edge of the woods, he could see down the slope to the house. Missus Earl and Cora the Cook—The Duchess according to McLemore—were out in the front of the dogtrot. Each had a broom and was sweeping the floor of the porch. The sun was shining.

THE END

Walter Adkins

About the Author

Walter Adkins spent thirty years as a professional soldier serving mostly in the Airborne Infantry. Upon retiring from the Army, he went back to school to qualify as an organizational theorist. He then spent several years as a consultant in this field, working in the wood products industry. He is now again retired and lives with his wife on a cattle farm in Alabama.